A HEART'S GIFT

A LOVE'S ROAD HOME NOVEL - BOOK 1

LENA NELSON DOOLEY

WILD HEART
BOOKS

ISBN-13: 978-1-942265-32-0

To our son-in-law, Eric Waldron, who married our single-mom daughter, Jennifer, and made her son Austin his own in every way that counted. You are a much-loved member of our family.

To my Savior Jesus, who created me to be a writer, then fills my head with story ideas. Thank You for all your special gifts. They are precious to me, just as You are.

And all my books are dedicated to the man who has loved me for over 56 years. When you first came into my life, I didn't know that God sent you, but that became evident very soon. Sharing our lives has been the best adventure I've ever been on. I'm looking forward to many more years, even at the ages we are now.

CHAPTER 1

"Why do I have to stay here alone?" Lorinda Sullivan hated to have to beg for what she wanted.

The whine in her voice grated on her own nerves. Never in her life had she been able to make her own decisions. She had trouble controlling her voice while she held back threatening tears, and she refused to let Mike see her cry...again. He took her tears as a sign that she was weak, when they actually came when she was angry or upset.

"Why won't you let me go with you?"

Her husband of over five years strode around the two-room log cabin, his heavy boots drumming an irregular staccato on the rough plank floor. "Lori, I don't want to leave our land unguarded." The censure in his tone cut as deep as any dagger. That tone was often part of their conversations. "You know how to use the rifle. That's why I taught you to shoot. To help me when I need it."

1

Everything was always about him, not her.

He pulled back the clothing she'd packed in the satchel for him earlier that morning. Among the garments, he started hiding small canvas bags filled with the nuggets and gold dust he'd dug from their mine up the hill. The mine where the vein had petered out. Those pokes held the last of their gold, but there were at least two dozen pokes, maybe even more. An absolute fortune.

Lorinda crossed her arms. If he thought calling her his pet name would change her mind, he was sorely mistaken.

She swallowed the thickness in her throat. "Since you're only going to be gone a couple of weeks, I'm sure everything will be safe that long." The last word came out as a squeak.

Mike straightened. His hazel-colored eyes took on a dark green tint when he glared at her. "Why do you always question me? I only want what's best for both of us." As if dismissing her desires, he returned to his task. "Our mine isn't the only one that's played out. And other men, roaming these hills, never hit pay dirt. Desperate miners could try to take over our land since the mine isn't our only asset. We have this snug house, and most of them have been living in tents for years. And we have plenty of provisions. Many a man will do desperate things when he's hungry and destitute." Now he sounded as if he were explaining things to a child.

I am not a child. Why couldn't he see that? She clutched her arms so tightly her fingers bit into the flesh. At least the long sleeves on her dress would hide the bruises when they came. And they always came to her fair skin. Why couldn't Mike understand that her ideas were just as good as his? Sometimes even better? He clung to the old-fashioned notion that women were mindless and should be thankful for whatever their men did for them. Pa'd been like that. A shudder raced through her as bleak memories almost overcame her.

After Lorinda had married Mike to get away from her

father, she discovered her husband shared Pa's views on that particular thing. At least, her husband never lifted his hand to her. Even though he made all the decisions, he treated her with a measure of affection and respect. Was that all a woman could expect from her man?

"Maybe I'd like to go to Denver, too. I haven't been in over a year." She gritted her teeth to stop the sobs threatening to breach the dam she'd placed around them. "I need to do some...personal shopping." She didn't like having to talk about those things even with her husband.

Mike turned and lifted the last poke back out of the satchel and tossed it toward her. "I'll leave this with you." He gave her the smile that first drew her to him. Once again, it went straight to her heart, and she caught the fat bag with both hands before it hit the floor. "The next time we go to Denver, you can spend all of it on anything you fancy." He emphasized the *you*. Maybe her earlier thoughts had been too harsh.

He came over and enfolded her in his warm embrace, pressing her head against his muscled chest. The strong beat of his heart gave her a sense of well-being and slowly erased her anger. She slid her arms around his waist and closed her eyes while she felt the thumping increase its tempo. The familiar scent of lye soap, sunshine, and Mike's unique masculine essence calmed her.

He gently rested his chin on top of her head. "I'm only trying to look out for our future. Even though the mine has played out, we have five hundred acres of timber. When the money from the gold is gone, we can start selling trees to the lumber company, if we have to."

She leaned closer into his embrace, trying to absorb his aura to remember during the next two weeks. When his heartbeats raced, hers matched them in intensity.

"We need to say goodbye a different way." The husky words sent a soft breeze through her hair. He released her, took her hand, and with that special gleam in his eyes led her toward their bedroom.

This man she married didn't fight fair. He knew how much she enjoyed their intimacy, and no one else had ever loved her before Mike came into her life. She would relish every moment. The memories would keep her warm until her husband returned.

～

A week later while cooking a solitary meal she didn't want to eat, Lorinda heard the clopping of a horse coming up the trail. *It can't be Mike. It's too soon.* But in all the years they'd lived there, no one else had ever ridden up that path. She set the skillet on an iron trivet waiting on the wooden table and peeked out between the curtains. A lone rider made his way around the boulders beside the trail. *A total stranger.* Mike had been right to leave her to protect their property. Quickly, she hurried to the coat rack he'd carved last winter and pulled on one of his older jackets. Then she picked up the rifle always ready above the rack and stepped through the door, slamming it behind her. In just the week since Mike left, cold injected a sharp sting into the mountain air. Winter wasn't far away.

Lorinda raised the rifle and settled the butt against her shoulder. She sighted down the barrel which she kept pointed toward the intruder. "Stop right where you are!"

She spoke with as much authority as she could muster. No need to let the man get the upper hand.

The stranger halted and peeked from under the brim of his hat. His eyes glittered like polished coal–hard, brilliant, and cold. When his gaze lit on the weapon she held, he raised his hands. "I'm looking for Mike Sullivan."

He only peered straight at her for another moment before

shifting his gaze. It didn't light on anything for very long. A prickle of concern skittered up her spine. If he was honest, he should be able to look her in the eyes for more than a few seconds. She'd seen enough men when she and Mike had gone to town to know that.

"He's not here. State your business." Her tone hardened to steel, and she shifted the barrel of the rifle to point straight at the man's heart.

"I need to talk to him. We have some unfinished business." He relaxed and leaned his hands on the saddle horn. "When will he be back?"

His gravelly tone sent chills up and down her whole body. Although he rode a good piece of horseflesh, his clothes weren't clean. Neither was his long blond hair or the scraggly beard that came to his chest. A thick, dark trail down one side of his clothing showed he'd been chewing tobacco and spitting. Lorinda had always found the practice distasteful. Another one of her father's many bad habits. She quickly shut the door to those memories.

Mike hadn't said anything about having unfinished business with anyone. Of course, he might not have mentioned it even if he did.

"He won't be back for a long time." Lorinda rested her fore-finger on the trigger. She hoped her fabrication would keep him from returning anytime soon, just in case.

His eyes followed the movement, and he squinted into a hard frown. Lorinda wouldn't want to meet him on a dark night, and she didn't want Mike to either.

"Mike taught me how to use this rifle." She stared hard at the man, centering her attention on the middle of his chest.

The man thrust his hands into the air again. "All right. I'll just mosey back down the mountain."

He lowered one hand to pick up his reins, which rested across the saddle. He kept the other hand raised while he clamped his knees against the horse and turned the animal around. He didn't drop his other hand before he was out of sight beyond the bend in the trail.

Even though she didn't welcome the intrusion, Lorinda felt bereft when the stranger was gone. She'd never been alone this long in her entire life. The mountain felt lonely without Mike. She didn't look forward to the next week of waiting for her husband to return. After taking a deep breath of the clear mountain air, she went into the cabin and finished fixing her solitary meal.

~

*C*lutching the fur coat Mike had made close around her, Lorinda stared out the front door for the hundredth time today. *Where can he be?* She'd asked herself that question a thousand other times in the last few weeks. Mike said he'd be back in about two weeks. Her one week of waiting after she ran the drifter off had stretched into three more.

She shut the wooden door against the cold, but a frigid wind pushed in through cracks she couldn't even see around the windows and door. When the air was still, the cabin was easy to heat, but an early snowfall covered the ground in a light blanket, lowering the already cold temperatures. Then the north wind started howling down from the snowy mountain peaks. She almost wished for the first blizzard which would dump enough snow to bank against the walls and help keep the cold out of the cabin.

Lorinda went over and warmed her hands, thankful Mike had purchased the cast iron, pot-bellied stove last winter. He had a hard time getting the heavy thing up the steep trail to the cabin, but the added warmth was worth all the effort. *Thank you, Mike.* How she wished he were here to hear the words.

She had to admit that Mike was a good husband, even

though he was opinionated. Before he planned the trip to Denver, he'd gone to Breckenridge and stocked up with enough supplies to last all winter. Not only were her cupboards full, so was the dugout behind the house. Plenty of smoked wild game hung from the rafters, too.

When she thought about Mike, their last time of lovemaking gave her heartbeat a strong rhythm, and heat suffused her face. *If only he'd get home.*

CHAPTER 2

*T*he faint sound of hoofbeats on the trail once again drew Lorinda to the door. Maybe Mike was finally home. But something pricked at her skin, raising the hairs on the back of her neck, and she scrunched her brows. Lorinda reached for the rifle. She held the weapon loosely in her arm as she opened the door. Two more strangers on horseback picked their way between the boulders that marked the trail. One of the men led a third horse with a large burden on its back. She only hoped the rifle would let the men know she meant business. She never wanted to have to use a gun on a human, and if she started shooting, she couldn't get both of the men before one would shoot her. The thought almost made her heart stop beating.

After taking a deep breath, Lorinda stepped into the stinging wind.

*F*ranklin Vine glanced up from the trail when he heard the door hinges on the cabin emit a loud squeal. A tiny woman with hair the color of sunshine stepped through the open doorway, then shut the portal against the cold air. The flinty expression on her face and the rifle on her arm showed she didn't welcome the intrusion.

He glanced toward the man on the other horse. "Did you know a woman lived up here?"

His foreman's gaze traveled from the woman to his boss. "I never seen her before, and I don't remember Mike ever saying anything about having a woman up here."

Franklin didn't look forward to sharing the news of Sullivan's death with this woman, whoever she was. All they'd planned to do was give the man a decent burial on his own property. This woman was a complication he didn't want...or need.

"Stop right where you are!" Harsh words rang across the frozen landscape. Surprisingly strong from such a small woman.

Now she held the rifle to her shoulder and had taken a bead on his chest. Evidently, she knew how to use the weapon. She held the rifle still, and her hands didn't quiver. He wasn't ready to find out how good her aim was.

He stopped his horse and raised his hands with the reins dangling from one of them. "We're not going to hurt you."

Still holding the lead to the pack animal, Thomas stopped his horse beside Franklin's.

"State your business and be quick about it." Her words pierced the icy air like bullets from a six-shooter, aiming straight at them.

"I'm Franklin Vine."

At his words, a flicker of something lit her eyes, but quickly disappeared, replaced by the former hard stare. "The rancher?"

He gave a slow nod. He didn't want to do anything to spook her. Not with her finger so close to the trigger.

"I've heard Mike mention you a time or two." She relaxed her stance a little but didn't lower the rifle. "I've already asked what you want." The words held more than a hint of steel.

Franklin slowly rested his hands on his saddle horn. "Might I ask who you are?"

"Who am I? Mike's wife." She must have noticed the puzzled expression on his face. "Didn't you know he was married?"

"We only talked about business." Franklin didn't want to rile her any more than she was already.

Her shoulders lifted and stiffened again. "So why are you here?"

Franklin gazed over the pristine whiteness toward the rocky peaks across the large valley then back toward the woman. "I promise I'm not going to hurt you, but I'm going to dismount now. Please don't shoot." He swung his leg over the back of the horse and started toward her, taking a few slow, deliberate steps while he surreptitiously watched her from under the brim of his Stetson.

Mrs. Sullivan kept her eyes on him, only giving a quick glance toward Thomas when he shifted and his saddle squeaked. As she looked back toward Franklin, he raised his hands again.

"I need to talk to you, Mrs. Sullivan." He handed the reins to his foreman and walked the rest of the way up toward the house, stopping a few feet in front of her.

While she studied him up and down, the woman had a weary look about her. Finally, she lowered the rifle, but kept holding it with both hands, probably so she could quickly raise it again if needed. "So, talk."

He rubbed the back of his neck which felt stiff from all the tension coiled inside. This wasn't going to be easy. "Mrs. Sullivan, this is my foreman, Thomas Walker." Franklin flipped his gloved hand toward Thomas. "He actually knew your husband better than I did."

For a moment her eyes widened, and he could read the fear in them.

"Thomas found Sullivan's..." Franklin stopped and cleared his throat. "... your husband's body at the edge of the Rocking V today. We brought him home to bury him on his own land."

As if punctuating his statement, the woman crumpled to the ground, and her rifle pitched into the snow, the barrel tunneling into the few inches of the white stuff.

While Thomas quickly dismounted, Franklin rushed to her side. He slipped his arms under Mrs. Sullivan and lifted her against his chest. "You get the rifle and come in. I'm going to find some place to lay her down. Shock must've been too much for her."

It had been a long time since he'd been close to a woman, and he'd never cradled one in his arms like this. Feelings he thought he'd killed long ago threatened to break free, but he stuffed them far down inside, closing and locking the door. Franklin didn't need this kind of complication in his ordered life. But the warmth of her body nestled against his chest made him feel off balance. After he entered the house, he glanced around the room.

The cabin was well-built and showed a woman's touch. Franklin's quick perusal soon revealed the absence of a bed in the first room, so he paced across the floor toward the other door. After placing the rifle on the table in the main room, Thomas came and opened the door for Franklin, who gently deposited the woman on the bed covered with a colorful quilt.

"See if you can find some water for her to drink." Mulling over what to do now, Franklin stared down at the woman.

Thomas returned and handed him the tin cup.

"Stay here with me. Can't have any impropriety attached to her name...or in her thoughts."

～

*L*orinda fluttered her eyelids, trying to decide where she was and what happened. Two strange men stood beside her bed. Reality crashed in on her. Mike wasn't coming home...ever. Tears spilled down her cheeks while she tried to sit up. She quickly swiped them away.

"Here, let me help you." The gentle voice came from the tall rancher who had pronounced the death knell outside. His arm slid behind her back and lifted her away from the bed until she could sit on the side.

He hunkered close beside her. "Mrs. Sullivan, we need to bury your husband. Where would you like us to dig his grave?"

His gently-spoken words took a moment to sink in. *Grave?* Lorinda had never thought about such a thing. She knew people died all the time, but not Mike. He was such a young man...so strong and virile.

She glanced at Mr. Vine, then away. "I don't know." Lorinda slowly rose to her feet, and he stood, too.

"If it's all right. with you, I'll let Thomas choose a place. Maybe under one of the trees." The rancher led the way into the main room of the cabin.

Lorinda followed almost in a daze. "That's fine with me."

Her legs still felt shaky. The news had hit her hard. She'd never fainted in her life. Not even when the pain from the beatings Pa gave her overwhelmed her. She settled into the rocking chair Mike made for her last birthday. The motion of the chair added to her feelings of unease, so she stopped it.

After his foreman left the room, Franklin Vine stood by one window and moved aside the gingham curtains to look out. Lorinda had chosen the red color to cheer up the cabin, but it wasn't helping today. The pall of her sorrow made the air in the room almost too heavy to breathe.

The man turned and strode back into the bedroom and

returned with the cup of water. *Mike's cup*. The thought caused a hitch in her heart and almost led to another sob.

"Here..." Mr. Vine thrust the cup toward her. "...drink this."

Obediently, she took the cold metal in her hands and lifted it to her lips. The water did taste good in her dry throat. While she drank, a thought hit her like a steam engine. *What if it wasn't Mike?*

"I haven't seen the body." She hesitated when the man frowned. "I have to be sure it's my husband."

His frown deepened until his strong brows dipped almost hiding his eyes. "He was pretty beaten up, and we didn't find him right away." He paused as if he were gathering his thoughts. "I think you'd rather remember him the way he was the last time you saw him." He shoved his hand into the front pocket of his denim trousers and quickly drew it out. "He had this on him." When he thrust his hand toward her, a gold pocket watch lay in his open palm.

Lorinda picked it up and flipped open the cover to read the inscription inside. *To Mike from Lorinda.* She closed the cover and clutched it in her right hand, remembering how proud she'd been when she gave it to her husband on their first anniversary. And Mike had been just as proud. *So this really is him.* Her moment of hope evaporated taking most of her fragile strength with it.

"How did he die?" She almost hesitated to ask. Did she really want to know what horror befell her husband?

"We're not sure..." He rubbed the back of his neck with one hand again. "No way to tell."

Numbness settled so deeply inside her that she didn't think she'd ever feel anything again.

"I've been thinking about what needs to happen now." Like a caged animal, the rancher walked toward the stove, then back while he talked. "I've decided the best thing would be for you to come back to the homestead. I have a housekeeper who would be glad to have you there. You don't need to stay here alone."

He has decided? Another man who wanted to tell her what to do. Just like Pa... Just like Mike. Well, *he* wouldn't get away with it. She didn't have to obey him. Lorinda stood and pulled herself to her full height before facing him. "*I* don't think it's a good idea."

His eyes widened. Obviously, he'd expected her to be compliant.

"Before Mike left, he bought plenty of supplies to last through the winter. I'll be just fine." She lifted her chin at the end of the last statement, hoping it would show her determination.

"You'll be snowed in before long. Besides, you'll need people around you while you grieve. Maybe you could go stay with your family. I'd be glad to make sure you have a way to get there." His eyes held sympathy as they bored into hers.

Lorinda turned away from his intense gaze. "I. Have. No. Family." She bit out the words one at a time, and they fell like stones against the hard floor.

Out of the corner of her eyes, she saw the man rub the bridge of his nose between two fingers of one hand. Lorinda looked him full in the face and was surprised that pain had drawn his eyes into a squint, and his mouth tightened before he relaxed. Perhaps he had a headache.

"Can you tell me anything about my husband's death?" She was glad she got all the words out without sobbing.

"Not really. We don't know exactly what day he was killed." When his foreman opened the front door and came in, Mr. Vine looked relieved.

"I've found a good spot." Thomas Walker took off his hat and held it in front of his waist. "If it's all right with you, Ma'am, we'll bury him under the large aspen tree to the west of the dugout. The one that stands off to itself."

Lorinda nodded. Any place was fine with her. At least she didn't need to think about choosing a spot anymore.

"If the ground's frozen too hard, we'll use some of your wood for a fire to soften it, if that's all right with you, Ma'am." The tall rancher didn't move until she nodded.

Burying her husband took far longer than Lorinda ever dreamed it would. While the two men dug in the ground they thawed, she sat in the rocking chair by the stove remembering all the good times with Mike. She didn't want to think about the hard times. The pain from her loss was too intense.

Memories assailed her—Mike when he came for her and carried her away from her father's house while he was passed out drunk on the bed. Tall, strong, and handsome, Mike had earned her trust. He took her to the next town where he had a preacher ready to marry them. After that, they'd ridden across country for over a week, camping at night until they reached the Rocky Mountains.

Lorinda had never seen anything so majestic. They'd spied the hazy purple peaks that reached to the cloudy sky for three days before they reached the foothills. The stop in Denver had only taken a couple of days while Mike bought all they needed to prospect for gold. As they climbed up the rugged roads, then the tiny trails, toward the gold mine Mike had discovered, she'd been happy, loving this man who'd brought sunshine into her meager existence.

Tears continued to stream down her face, and she dabbed them away with the damp handkerchief she pulled from her pocket.

Their first home had been the dugout, where all her provisions for winter now resided. They'd worked side by side felling trees, then building the cabin. Even though Mike was bossy, she'd loved him with all her heart, reveling in the freedom from the pain that had filled her life before.

By the time the rancher and his foreman returned to the

house, tears had soaked every thread of the handkerchief she twisted in her hands. She looked up as they came through the door.

"Ma'am, we're ready to say a few words over the grave. Would you like to join us?" Once again, Mr. Vine's voice sounded calm and soothing. No man in her life had ever spoken to her as he did.

Lorinda patted her eyes, but the sodden cotton couldn't hold another tear. Mr. Vine reached into his pocket and pulled out a bandanna that had been ironed into a neat compact square. He unfolded it and handed it to her.

~

Franklin stood behind the crude cross Thomas made out of a limb and a leather thong he had in his saddlebags. His foreman and Mrs. Sullivan were on opposite sides of the new mound of dirt. Both stared at the ground. Franklin cleared his throat.

"'Yea, though I walk through the valley of the shadow of death, I will fear no evil, for thou art with me.'" The words he'd often read poured from his mouth as if he had spent time memorizing them. *Thank you, Lord, for bringing them to mind.*

Mrs. Sullivan's quiet sob pierced his heart. How he wished he could somehow comfort the forlorn woman. If only she'd let them take her away from this lonely mountain.

"'Thy rod and thy staff, they comfort me.'" Franklin searched his memory for the next words, but nothing came. This woman needed all the comfort he could give her. "'And I shall dwell in the house of the Lord forever.'"

Thomas murmured a quiet "Amen," and another sob wrenched from Mrs. Sullivan. Slowly, she sank to her knees on the cold, wet ground and buried her face in her hands. Her shoulders shook, but no other sound escaped her.

A tiny crack slithered down the hard shell Franklin had built around his heart. If only things were different. If only...

He didn't like revisiting the hurt he'd sustained when his intended ran off with his best friend. Franklin hadn't trusted anyone since that pivotal time. And he never let himself feel any emotion. This broken woman demanded nothing of him, but something inside him wanted to take away her pain. If she wouldn't accept the help he offered, he needed to get away from her as quickly as possible.

~

*L*orinda felt the rancher's presence before he spoke a word. Probably hunkering beside her as he had in the bedroom after she fainted.

"Mrs. Sullivan, I'd feel a lot better if you'd come home with us. You wouldn't have to stay long, but I don't want to leave you here alone."

She lifted her head and turned to stare into eyes so dark, they were almost black. The intensity of his gaze pierced all the way to her soul. She reached one hand to the ground to steady herself as she started to stand.

Mr. Vine must have anticipated her move because he rose with the sleekness of the panthers that roamed these mountains. He gently pulled her to her feet, then stepped back.

Lorinda lowered her head and concentrated on his cowboy boots. "Thank you, Mr. Vine, but I'll be all right. I don't want to leave our land." She pointed toward the newly-turned dirt. "Or my husband."

Even though Lorinda meant every word she said, when she watched the two men head back down the trail, a feeling of desolation washed over her almost sweeping her away... A cumbersome loneliness settled in her heart like one of the many boulders lining the trail. She stood beside the mound that covered her husband's body until no more hoofbeats echoed off the rocks.

"Mike, why did you leave me behind?" A wealth of meaning accompanied the thundering words as she stalked back into the cabin, pulling the door closed behind her.

She looked at everything with new eyes. Her world had just been torn asunder. This was her home, not hers and Mike's. She touched his jacket that still hung on the peg beside the door, lifting the sleeve and breathing in his essence. One day, she'd pack his things away , but not right now. The need for her surroundings to stay the same engulfed her.

Mike had been her whole world. She'd stayed on the mountain whenever Mike went to Breckenridge. She didn't want to chance being seen by her father or uncle if they came this way looking for her. Mike always brought her whatever she asked for, and she was satisfied to work on their happy home.

She'd never felt this strong need to be around other people, and she was too stubborn to change her mind about going to the Rocking V even though her solitude made her soul ache.

"How will I ever make it through the winter?" She spoke the words out loud, because for that moment she needed to feel as if she were talking to someone.

Life should be more than just sustenance, but that's all she could see in her bleak, lonely future.

CHAPTER 3

MARCH, 1894

*F*ranklin Vine's attention was shanghaied from the book-work on the desk in front of him to that time right after the first snowfall when he took Sullivan's body up the mountain to his wife. Almost every day since, her tortured expression broke into his thoughts at some time or another. More than once, he'd even sent one of the hands up to check on her, but she always insisted she was fine. Then the heavy snows made the trail impassable.

Since he'd had the men cut enough wood to last her through the winter and then some, he knew he didn't have to worry about her. But that didn't stop his uneasy feeling. When he and Thomas had been up there, he'd even checked the dugout she'd mentioned. Plenty of supplies for a couple of people reached the earthen ceiling. Being alone in a cabin for so many months caused more than one man to go a little loco. What would it do to a grieving young widow? He'd never been able to understand what made women tick.

As Franklin turned back toward his desk, he glanced over

the wall of shelves lined with leather-bound volumes. If he knew he would spend the winter cut off in a cabin alone, he'd have made sure he had plenty of books to read. He couldn't remember seeing any in the Sullivan cabin, but he hadn't been looking for books. He hoped she had some packed away in a trunk. Or maybe, like many of the settlers, she couldn't read. If she couldn't, what would she do to while away the long hours...days...weeks in isolation?

Why did this widow weigh so heavily on him? She was really no concern of his, but maybe the Lord kept bringing her to mind because she didn't have a protector. Surely God didn't want him to step into the breach, but who else was there? She'd said she had no family, and something about the way she said it made him think that wasn't all that needed to be said about her past. But if she had family somewhere, why would she stay on the remote mountain alone?

Franklin forced his thoughts back to the lists and figures on the pages of the ledger. The ranch finances were in good shape, and he should feel satisfied. Instead, restlessness ate at him, making him want to jump up and pace. But pacing wouldn't balance the books. Neither would it provide any kind of assistance to Mrs. Sullivan.

He worked his way through three separate accounts before the sound of a horse's hooves thundered closer and closer to the house. Might as well see what was going on. He laid his pen beside the capped inkwell before he stood and stretched the kinks from his shoulder then headed toward the front door.

Thomas pulled his lathered horse to a stop beside the hitching post outside the picket fence. The one Mariam insisted on. Franklin shook his head. Why was he thinking about her now? For years he'd been able to keep her locked in the dark dungeon of his mind, but since holding the Sullivan woman in his arms, memories of Mariam often intruded as well. He should have the men pull up that blasted picket fence. Anything to purge her from his thoughts.

Franklin stood on the porch and frowned as he watched Thomas jump off his mount. Steam rose into the frigid air from the lathering sweat coating parts of the horse. His foreman must have ridden fast a long ways for the horse to be in that condition. Thomas loved good horseflesh, and Franklin had never seen his horse in this condition. Must really be some emergency.

"Boss, there's a fire!" Thomas stomped up the flagstone walkway and placed one booted foot on the bottom step. He stared straight into Franklin's face, waiting for his response.

The dreaded word made Franklin's heartbeat race. Uncontrolled fire was never good, especially on a large ranch, even if the spring thaw was just starting. Enough dry trees and brush stuck up out of the dwindling blanket of snow that a small fire could quickly turn into a blazing inferno.

"Where?" He glanced around, trying to see the smoke.

Thomas took a heaving breath. "Up the mountain, near where we buried Sullivan."

Once again, Mrs. Sullivan's face swam before him, tears tracking down her pale cheeks. "Do you think it could be the cabin?"

Thomas nodded. "Looks like it, but we can't tell for sure from here. Whatever it is, that woman'll need help."

"Hitch up the wagon and load it with barrels of rainwater, buckets, and blankets. Round up some of the hands on the way. Maybe we can keep the flames from spreading. Plenty of snow up there, too. We can throw that on the fire, if need be." Franklin pulled the front door of the ranch house closed before stepping off the porch.

"I'll get right on it." Thomas shot the words over his shoulder as he barreled toward the barn.

"I'm going on up the mountain." Franklin scurried after him.

~

*L*orinda awakened from another bad dream, a scream stuck in her throat. The dreams came far too often. But this one was different. It was filled with smoky air. She peered into the darkness, wondering how long it would be before dawn. She felt as if she'd been sleeping for hours. The smell of smoke gagged her, too strong to be a dream. She had banked the coals last night, and she'd need to add kindling and stir them up to get the stove going.

The air hung heavy and burned her lungs with every breath. She could hardly see the door through the denseness. This was not a dream.

Fear surged through her heart. Something was terribly wrong.

Reaching under her pillow, Lorinda grabbed the two small canvas bags of gold she'd hidden there. Mike had added the second one after their final time of lovemaking, and she always kept them near her. They were cold comfort and didn't ease the loneliness, but they were the last things Mike ever gave her. She shrugged into the warm woolen robe she'd made Mike for Christmas last year and shoved the pokes into her pockets before tying the belt around her. Even though this robe was larger than her own, now it barely met over her expanding belly.

Usually the cabin was much colder when she awakened. She felt toasty warm with her flannel night dress and Mike's extra union suit underneath. She crept toward the door and slowly eased it open far enough to see into the main room of the cabin.

Flames danced on the opposite side of the room from the cold black stove sitting on a slab of rock. The smoke didn't come from the pot-belly. *Flames?* Her heart jumped into her throat and thrashed like a bird caught in a snare. She stared, fascinated at the macabre dance before her. The fire leapt, eating its way through the log wall and wooden floor. Wavering tongues of light took a bite from her curtains then raced up the fabric, consuming everything in their way.

Panic rose like a specter in her mind. The fear stole her breath away. She had to get out of here. Lorinda took a deep breath and held it. She quickly turned around and thrust her feet into the men's boots beside her bed. Her breath swooshed out. She leaned over for a moment, light-headed. She'd never make it across the burning room if she couldn't hold her breath any longer than that.

Her agitation reached the baby, and it squirmed and thumped inside her. She grabbed a handkerchief from the top drawer of the chest and held it tight over her nose before plunging into the mounting inferno. She pulled her garments close, trying to keep the flames from grabbing them as well.

Lorinda lumbered across the dwindling floor to the front door. The door stuck. Panic screamed inside her. The metal handle was almost too hot to hold. Using the hem of the robe, she grasped it again. She put her whole weight into wrenching the heavy door open and stumbled away from the intense heat melting an ever-widening circle in the dwindling snow. Tongues of fire burst after her, and she was barely able to stay out of their reach.

When the flames no longer scorched her, Lorinda stopped and took several deep breaths, trying to cleanse her lungs from the choking smoke, but the hacking coughs continued. She felt woozy, swaying a moment before straightening her spine. She walked around the log cabin, watching the fire that consumed everything she owned. Her hands clutched the hard pokes in her pockets. *Everything, except the gold.*

She reached the side where the fire had started. Tracks in the snow worried her. Not from an animal. Someone had come up to the cabin. The pungent scent of kerosene mixed with the acrid smoke. This fire was no accident. Footprints came from the woods to the west of the cabin and returned the same way. She listened for a hint of unusual movement through the trees but heard nothing. The arsonist was probably long gone.

Just the word arsonist shocked her. Brought such horrible images. Lorinda had too much to deal with right now. How would she ever survive?

Who could hate her enough to kill her? Or maybe the person didn't know she was in the cabin. Helplessness joined the loneliness she'd experienced all winter. Tears pooled in her eyes, and she blinked, trying to see through the blur.

Weakness rushed over her, and Lorinda sidled over to the tree near Mike's grave. She leaned back against it and tucked her chin close to her chest. Reaching behind, she clasped the bark-covered trunk, the rough places biting into the tender skin on her palms. She stayed on her feet...barely.

Oh, Mike, why didn't you come home to me? I didn't know how hard it would be to go through a winter without another person to lean on.

Finally, she realized the morning sun had been sending its warming rays over the peaks for some time. Just then, the baby gave a big kick. It felt to Lorinda as if he or she tried to turn a complete somersault. Not enough room in there for that. With one hand, she rubbed her bulging belly and cooed nonsense to soothe the infant. At the sound of her voice, the child in her womb settled down, relieving the physical pain it caused.

If only there was something to soothe her worries as well. What was she going to do now? Of course, she still had plenty of food in the dugout. Mike had bought enough for two people, and some of the time she hadn't been very hungry. Maybe she'd just have to move in with the provisions. But what would she wear? And what if the arsonist had stolen the provisions? No, the footprints didn't lead to the doorway in front of the stash.

Questions continued tumbling in her head as tears erupted down her cheeks.

~

*S*now still covered most things as Franklin raced across his ranch land. When he reached the foot of the mountain, he slowed his stallion.

Now he could see the conflagration between some of the trees. The trail up to the cabin needed all his concentration. Franklin helped his horse pick its way through the difficult parts. On easier sections, he scanned the area above. No sign of the woman. His heart almost stopped beating at that thought. Surely she wasn't still inside. If so...

Franklin didn't want to finish that thought. Finally, he was close enough to catch a glimpse of the tree beside Sullivan's grave. Mrs. Sullivan sat huddled against the trunk. Her golden hair covered her shoulders and streamed down her back, the curls in wild disarray.

The horse turned where the trail jagged, and the woman slid from view. Evidently, she awakened to the fire. The robe she wore looked to be her husband's, since it almost swallowed her.

By the time he and his mount circled the last boulder and moved into the clearing with the burning cabin, Mrs. Sullivan had gotten up. She stood staring toward him with a faraway look in her eyes. Franklin wasn't sure she knew he was there.

But he became very aware of her and the evidence of her condition. The woman was going to have a baby, and she'd spent the last several months alone on this mountain. Why hadn't he followed his first instincts and forced her to come to the ranch house? He'd had a strong urging to. Probably, the Lord tried to tell him, and he hadn't realized how important that nudge was. How could he ever make it up to her?

Franklin dismounted and walked toward the woman, leading his horse behind him. He didn't want to approach her atop the animal. With the heat emanating from the fire, he unbuttoned his coat and let it hang open.

"Mrs...." He'd been clenching his teeth so hard, a lump had formed in his throat. He huffed to clear it. "Mrs. Sullivan, ma'am... I've come to help."

Evidently she didn't hear him because she never looked at him. Just continued to stare across the valley far below.

"Mrs. Sullivan." This time he spoke louder and stepped closer. "Ma'am, I'm here to help you."

Finally, her tear-filled eyes turned toward him, and she clutched her arms over her swollen body as if to protect it. "Mr. Vine?" Her tone carried a note of surprise. She looked down and bent over.

Franklin dropped the reins and lunged toward her, wanting to keep her from falling. He placed his arms loosely around her. "Do you need to sit down?" *What a crazy question.* He glanced around and saw nowhere for her to sit. "I can put you on my horse. The saddle would be better than sitting on the ground."

She gazed up at him for a moment before grabbing the front of his flannel shirt and burying her face in it. Wails split the air and arrowed straight through him. When he pulled her closer, she relaxed against him and sobbed as though her heart had shattered. He knew what that felt like even if he had kept the hurt inside instead of letting it out the way this woman did.

While she cried, Franklin rubbed her back and murmured softly to her. He didn't know where the words came from, or exactly what he said. He felt a thump near his belt. For a moment, he thought she had hit him, but both fists still clutched his shirt. Realization rushed over him. *The baby.* Something he'd never feel from his own wife and child. That thought brought a hitch to his heart. This was probably the one time he'd ever feel movement from a child in the womb. The wonder of it almost stole his breath.

Mrs. Sullivan shook with more than just the sobs. How long had the woman huddled in the snow? He pulled the edges of his jacket around her and continued holding her while she cried.

"Boss?" The sound of his foreman's voice wrenched Franklin's attention from the woman drawing warmth from him. "The trail is still pretty treacherous for a wagon. I came to see if there's any need to bring it up."

Franklin stared at Thomas, then glanced over toward the charred remains of the cabin. Pockets of flames still flared amongst the rubble. "Not much left." He felt Mrs. Sullivan raise her head. "We need to make sure all the fire is out."

Thomas dismounted and reached for a large roll behind his saddle. "I brought some of the blankets with me. We can fill them with snow and use them to smother the rest of the fire."

Two more of Franklin's ranch hands rounded the last boulder and rode across the clearing toward them.

"Get Charlie and Joseph to help you, but I need one of the blankets for Mrs. Sullivan."

When the woman tried to step away, he gently tugged her back, and she stiffened in his arms. "Don't want you to get sick from being too cold." He whispered against her silky hair.

"Okay." A hiccup followed her agreement.

Thomas untied the bundle and brought a well-worn horse blanket toward them. "This one's softer, and it's still warm."

Franklin stood beside Mrs. Sullivan, protecting her from the chilled wind while he wrapped her in the heavy piece of wool.

"Thank you." Her blue eyes held bewilderment and a hint of some deeply-buried hurt.

He touched the brim of his Stetson. "My pleasure, ma'am."

He couldn't help wondering what could have filled her with that pain. Surely more than this fire...or even losing her husband.

*L*orinda watched the four men work to put out the final glowing embers. Her thoughts tangled. Just having other people around eased the lonely part of her that had intensified throughout the winter. No matter that they weren't talking to her. They communicated with each other in monosyllables, understanding what the other man meant without wasting any extra words. Even though one was the boss, the rest employees, they worked as a unit. She'd never been a part of a group so completely in tune with each other.

What was going to happen to her now? As the question once more flitted through her mind, the baby became restless. This child was so sensitive to her moods.

"Mrs. Sullivan?" Mr. Vine's voice penetrated her thoughts, scattering them in all directions.

Lorinda had to look up at him. The man was much taller than Mike had been. Taller than her father and uncle. She'd felt the strength in his wide shoulders. Enough to ease her grief, at least a little.

"Yes, Mr. Vine?" She glanced down at her red, raw hands clutching the blanket close, wishing she could hide them.

"Some decisions need to be made." His commanding tone made her want to put up a shield.

Instead, she nodded. "I know. I've been trying to think." Why did all men treat women as if they couldn't think?

He widened his stance and crossed his arms. "I really wanted to take you off the mountain last fall. Now I wish I had."

She raised her head and stood as tall as she could with the baby weighing her down. "It was my choice, and I made it." She wasn't about to let him know how many times she had regretted it over the intervening months.

"What are you planning to do now?"

"I still have plenty of provisions in the dugout." She tilted her chin higher. Mustn't let him think he could decide for her.

He brushed one gloved hand across his mouth before speaking. "I didn't want to bring this up, but I'm sure the fire was intentionally set by someone."

"I know." She hoped he couldn't read the fear in her face. "I saw the footprints in the snow."

Just the thought of them once again brought agony to her heart. Her father had been a mean drunk, but he hadn't wanted to kill her. Knowing someone tried made her sick at her stomach. The baby jumped, and she began to rub her belly with one hand while the other held the blanket closed.

Concern puckered his brow. "Do you have any idea who it might have been?"

Lorinda shook her head. She didn't have any enemies, and she hadn't thought Mike did either. But someone did kill him. She wished she knew who.

"Ma'am, I can't leave you here again." Mr. Vine removed his hat and slapped it against his woolen trousers. "My conscience won't let me."

"Once again, it's not your decision." She couldn't let him start controlling her the way her husband and her father had. She'd have no more of that in her life...ever. "But I'd be much obliged if you'd let me come to the ranch, at least until the baby is born. I can't let this property go. It's my child's inheritance. Surely, you can understand that."

He nodded, then put his hat back on, pulling it low on his forehead. "That I can."

"If we bring the provisions from the dugout..." Lorinda saw his eyes take on that stubborn set she'd seen on both her husband and father, "...then I'll be paying my way. I won't be beholden to anyone."

He stared from under the brim of his hat. She felt as if he could see straight through to her soul.

After a long moment, he nodded. "All right. I'll have the men load the supplies in the wagon. We wouldn't want whoever burned the cabin to come back and steal them from you."

Lorinda hadn't thought of that, but the rancher was right. She didn't want the arsonist to take anything else of hers. "Mr. Vine, I'm worried about my land. What if squatters come and try to take it over?"

He glanced around, watching his men complete their tasks. "I'll have my men keep an eye on it like I did before the trail closed."

"Thank you."

He turned toward his foreman. "Thomas, when the three of you have made sure the fire is completely out, take Joseph and Charlie and follow those tracks. Maybe we can catch the varmint that started this fire."

While Mr. Vine gave further directions to his men, Lorinda took another long look at all she had lost. Her husband's grave, the blackened rubble that once was her home. She'd also lost her sense of safety on her own property. She would never be able to protect her child if the evil man returned and she was living in the dugout.

She reached into her pocket and gripped one of the bags of gold. At least she wasn't destitute, as her family'd often been back in Missouri. Going to the ranch was the only thing for her to do right now.

When Franklin returned from talking to his men, Lorinda stood staring across the valley, just as she did when he first arrived.

He laid his hand on her shoulder, and she turned toward him. "I'm going to take you down the mountain now. We'll ride my horse."

She glanced down at the blanket covering her body. "How is that going to work?"

"I'll lift you up onto the saddle sideways. Then I'll get on." His tone was gentle, assuring her there would be no danger.

After a moment, she gave a slow nod. He quickly lifted her into position before mounting behind her. He pulled her across his lap with her legs on the left side of the horse and settled into the saddle. He shifted a couple of times as if trying to get comfortable. While the horse took the first few tentative steps, she remained stiff.

"The ride will be much easier on you, if you'll relax. We have a wagon waiting at the bottom of this trail, so the ride won't be too long."

Finally, she leaned against him. He encircled her with his arms and signaled his stallion to start down the trail. For some reason, his arms felt comforting on the treacherous journey. But she couldn't let herself enjoy the feeling. She was never going to give any man a measure of control over her, no matter how safe he made her feel.

CHAPTER 4

*M*r. Vine was right. After Lorinda relaxed against his solid chest, the journey down the mountain trail wasn't as scary as she thought it would be riding sideways on the tall stallion. Even though the trail was steep and winding, the fortress formed by his strong arms rocked her as gently as a baby cradle. Almost falling asleep, she felt the muscles in the rancher's thighs tighten, then loosen as he communicated with his sure-footed horse. When they reached the bottom of the mountain, the trail leveled. Two more of Mr. Vine's ranch hands waited beside a wagon filled with wooden crates.

"How are things going up there, Boss?" A thin young man, with dark red hair peeking out from under his hat, cut his eyes toward the mountain behind them as he shoved his hands in the front pockets of his woolen trousers. "Is the fire out yet?"

She didn't detect even a hint of surprise from the cowboy when he saw her perched on the rancher's lap. But that couldn't keep embarrassment from flooding her cheeks with heat that chased away some of the cold. She didn't have anything to be ashamed of, but somehow she couldn't stop the feeling. She had never been this close to any man who wasn't her husband. Mr.

Vine must be used to doing things like this, or maybe he was able to ignore the fact that she was a woman carrying a child... And she was sitting in front of him. How long would she have to stay up here? She tried not to squirm too much.

"Rusty, you and Jake move things around in the back of the wagon so we can make a comfortable bed for Mrs. Sullivan." She felt as well as heard his masculine voice rumble in his chest.

The two men jumped up on the wooden bed. Jake shifted the barrels and crates toward the sideboards, leaving space down the middle, and Rusty grabbed several blankets from under the seat. He dropped a couple on top of the closed containers. The cowboy partially unfolded each of the others and stuffed them into the empty space.

Fascinated, Lorinda watched the way the ranch hands followed orders without question. Mr. Vine must be a powerful man for his men to obey like that so quickly. But then Lorinda hadn't had much experience with men besides her husband and her father, who she didn't want to think about.

Mr. Vine pulled one foot out of the stirrup and slid off the back of the saddle, all the while making sure she was secure in the seat. "Are you all right?" His words were only loud enough for her to hear.

She became aware that she missed his warmth surrounding her. "I'm fine." She refused to shiver in the icy wind.

He finished dismounting. "Now I'm going to help you down."

She leaned over and placed her hands on his shoulders, hoping he could get her down without a mishap. He put one arm under her knees and the other around her waist and gave a gentle tug. When she was free from the saddle, the rancher didn't set her on the ground as she expected. Instead, with long strides, he marched across the rocky ground and set her in the back of the waiting wagon. The things stacked along the sides of the wagon cut off some of the cold wind.

"I'll climb up and help you settle." His words, spoken in a rich baritone, sounded almost tender.

"No!" Lorinda hadn't meant to sound so harsh. "Thank you. I can move back just fine on my own."

After she settled into the welcoming nest, Mr. Vine climbed onto the wagon anyway. He took the waiting blankets from atop the barrels and covered her, tucking them both in all around, just leaving her face uncovered. Lorinda didn't remember anyone ever taking such tender care of her physical needs, not even her mother. And for sure, no man ever did.

Once more she whispered, "Thank you," before the rancher got down and turned toward his men.

"Jake, take my horse and go on back to the ranch house. Tell Mrs. Oleson to get a room ready for Mrs. Sullivan. Rusty can ride along as our guard on the way." Evidently Mr. Vine planned to drive the wagon.

Lorinda wondered why he didn't just have one of the cowboys take her to his ranch house. But soon those thoughts left her mind. Since she was so tired, she relaxed in the warm cocoon he'd created for her and closed her eyes. However, sleep eluded her, jumping just out of her reach, crowded out by the thoughts that invaded her mind.

She'd been so young when her mother died. Probably no more than five years old. But she remembered every detail as if it happened yesterday. Her mother's swollen belly...the moans when she'd gone into labor. Lorinda didn't even realize what was happening. She just knew how it scared her to hear her mother's anxious whimpers grow in intensity.

Pa couldn't go to fetch the doctor because of the terrible ice storm that surrounded their log cabin. Lorinda had heard about it many times through the intervening years when her father came staggering into her room so drunk he couldn't see straight. As she grew older, Pa ranted longer, revealing more about what happened. His graphic descriptions of his disappointment the night her mother died after giving birth to a still-born son always triggered the memories of his anger and her mother's horrific screams during the ordeal that echoed through the tunnels of her mind even now.

Those rants scared her spitless. For years, she'd planned to never let a man close enough to her to get her with child. But love for Mike drove those fears away. Her life with her husband was so different from the way she was raised that she'd been able to almost completely obliterate those memories.

Now Mike was gone, and she had spent six months alone snowed-in at their cabin. The larger her own body had grown, the larger her fears had become. She was afraid that when she went into labor, she would die on that mountain as her mother did trying to give birth to her little brother. Occasionally, she had reminded herself that her mother had survived one birth, but those thoughts didn't last long enough.

Mr. Vine and his cowboys rescued her from the work of an arsonist. Maybe she should feel better about everything. And she was glad to be down from the loneliness, but her fears still persisted, haunting her like ghosts from the past. Would she ever be able to outrun them? How would she face the birthing time that fast approached?

~

Franklin wanted to make sure Mrs. Sullivan and her baby weren't jostled too much. By driving the wagon, he could do that. And he wanted to make sure someone had a rifle ready in case the varmint that had set her cabin on fire tried to follow them. Disgust filled his thoughts. What kind of animal would torch a cabin with a woman inside? Maybe the man didn't know she was there, but surely he would've spied on the place for awhile before he did anything. Wouldn't he have just broken into the cabin if he thought it was empty? What reason would he have to burn it down? This event sounded like someone with a grudge against Sullivan. Or maybe he was trying for revenge against the dead man. Perhaps he didn't know Sullivan had died.

Franklin wished he had gotten to know the neighbor before he was killed. Somehow, he didn't think the same person who killed Mike Sullivan also started the fire, because it had been so long since the man was murdered. He also couldn't imagine why anyone would take a chance on burning a whole lot more than just a cabin. If the wind had been stronger today, the fire could have swept down the mountain and onto his ranch. And a lot of valuable timber in both places would've been destroyed. Maybe even some of his cattle...or the buildings. Or even people.

As soon as he could make sure Mrs. Sullivan was settled at the ranch house, he planned to alert the other ranchers to the presence of an arsonist in the area. Maybe they should band together and start patrolling their ranches and surrounding mountains to see if they could find the man. He assumed it was one man, since only one set of footprints led from the trees toward the house, then went back the same way. He hoped the man wasn't part of a gang roaming the area. So many of the mines were playing out, and some of the miners could be hanging around. Since Colorado was sparsely settled, other men could be running from the law and trying to hide in the expanses of wilderness. But this arsonist was far too close to Franklin's own ranch for comfort. And after what the scoundrel did today, he knew the fiend wasn't afraid to kill anyone in his way. A chilling thought.

All the way on the half-hour trip to the ranch house, Franklin studied the road so he could go around any holes or humps. In between each sweep of the ruts in front of the wagon, he also glanced at the trees and bushes that lined one side of the trail, looking for any sign of movement. He didn't want to be ambushed. He also glanced at Rusty and found that his trusted employee was keeping an eagle eye on the surroundings as well.

One thing he didn't do was look at the woman tucked up in the back of his wagon. He'd made sure she would be comfortable, but he didn't want his mind to dwell on what her presence meant.

Making his way down the treacherous trail showed him that he needed to help the woman and get her into a place where she could belong as soon as possible. The soft contours of her body rested against him in a way he'd never experienced before, even with Miriam. Though Mrs. Sullivan's body was swollen with her child, she was so tiny she didn't weigh much. But the impact of cradling her body close to his would be hard to erase from his mind. Visions of holding his own wife and child that way crashed through his mind before he finally captured them and thrust them away. He couldn't let himself dwell on such thought.

He. Would. Never. Marry. His heart couldn't take another breaking.

Mrs. Sullivan brought out his protective instincts. He needed to get her far away from the ranch, so he could shore up the wall he'd built around his heart after Miriam's defection. No matter how soft Mrs. Sullivan's skin was...no matter that even though the scent of smoke surrounded her, so did a faint, clean flowery scent. One that drew him one minute, then repelled him as soon as he realized he was softening toward her.

Since Miriam broke his heart, no other woman he'd seen had made any kind of impact on his senses. He spoke to them at church, but kept his distance. Holding this fragile creature caused a trembling inside him. And he didn't need to let it continue. No matter how much he wanted an heir. He would never give his heart freely to another woman. Maybe he'd just break up the ranch by willing portions of it to his most loyal ranch hands. Three or four of them had been with him a long time, pouring all their efforts into helping him create one of the most valuable ranches in this part of Colorado. He'd hate to break it up, but what other option did he have?

When he finally spied the roof of his house, he relaxed a bit. He didn't expect the outlaw to come this close to a thriving ranch with cowboys working all around. The man had to be a coward to slink through the night and set fire to a cabin with a helpless woman inside. He wouldn't want to face an honest fight.

As they drew closer, Franklin saw Jake and Mrs. Oleson, bundled in warm coats and waiting on the porch that spread across the front of the two story ranch house. They both watched his approach with eagerness shining on their faces. He had good people working for him. People he could trust and depend upon. Although he didn't know how to handle this new development, he knew he'd have plenty of help as they worked everything out. They'd make Mrs. Sullivan feel welcome.

And help him find a solution for her problem as soon as possible.

CHAPTER 5

*L*orinda could walk just fine, but Mr. Vine lifted her, blankets and all, from the bed of the wagon. She quickly wrapped her arms around his neck and held on while he headed toward the gate in the white picket fence. Strange to see one out here in frontier Colorado. She had seen plenty where she grew up, but they surrounded neat houses not run-down shacks like the one where she existed. She never learned what it meant to really live until she married Mike.

The red-haired cowboy had already jumped down from his horse and tied the reins to the railing of the fence. He opened the gate and held it wide for them.

"Thank you for all you did, Rusty. You can go on back to your chores now." The rancher's voice rumbled in her ear pressed against his muscular chest.

Since the wind had picked up during their ride, a shiver raced down her backbone. He pulled her even closer in his arms, and his warmth seeped into her. Restless movements by her baby kept her stomach from settling down. At least, she thought it was the baby that caused the uneasy feeling.

"Boss, you need some help?" Jack stepped lively down the front porch steps.

"Yes." Mr. Vine nodded toward the wagon. "Get all that unloaded, and let Terrell know to come up and help Mrs. Oleson. We'll all eat in the main house tonight, since so many of the hands have gone into town for their day off. No need to have two separate meals."

Lorinda tried to figure out what he meant by that. Was the ranch so big they had a cook for the bunkhouse? She hadn't realized how large Mr. Vine's holdings were. The piece of land she and Mike owned must look pretty paltry to him, even though it had seemed huge to her.

"Oh, you poor dear." A tall woman stood with both hands clasped under her ample bosom.

Lorinda figured the woman with a kind face must be his housekeeper or cook. If there was a Mrs. Vine, where was she? Shouldn't she be welcoming a guest into her home, even if the person arrived uninvited? She'd always heard that hospitality was part of the code of the west.

The older woman held the door open until Mr. Vine was completely inside. Then she shut it against the cold wind.

"I wasn't sure where you'd want to put Mrs. Sullivan, but since Jake told me about her condition, I thought maybe she wouldn't want to climb the stairs. I made up the room next to yours down here. Hope you don't mind."

Lorinda glanced up in time to catch a quick scowl on his face. *What is that all about?* "You can put me down now." She tried to pull away from the man.

His arms tightened and his gaze connected with hers. A sad smile flitted across his face. "I'll just take you in here."

While Mrs. Oleson held the door open, he stepped into a very feminine room decorated with pinks and blues and lots of flowers and ruffles. Lorinda knew wealthy people had nicer things than she ever did, but she'd never imagined a place filled with this much beauty. The flowers on the striped wallpaper matched those in the long curtains, the bedspread, and pillow covers, surrounding her with serenity. She'd never lived in a house with wallpaper, and the only curtains they'd had were those she'd made herself. When she was a girl, she covered the often-broken glass by tacking feed sacks over it. But she'd made the gingham curtains in the cabin she shared with Mike by just hemming them top and bottom. She'd never seen ruffles and lace used for decorations.

Actually, she'd never had ruffles and lace on any of her clothing either. And here she was in her flannel nightdress, Mike's union suit, his too-large robe, and wrapped in blankets. At that thought, she realized she didn't belong in this room...or even in this house. If only she had somewhere else to go. Anywhere but here.

Mr. Vine lowered her gently onto the bed with the turned-back covers. When he stood up straight, he focused on his housekeeper. "This is fine. It's high time we started using this room. I'll let you get Mrs. Sullivan settled. She had a rough night and early morning. She might want to rest awhile."

He spoke as though she wasn't in the room even though she was staring up at him. The man had been good to her, but his highhandedness galled her. She didn't dare express that opinion. At least, not until she knew what was going to happen to her and her child.

"Of course." Mrs. Oleson watched him exit, then turned back toward Lorinda. "I know it's cold out there. Would you like some good hot coffee or tea to warm you up? Maybe some toast or scrambled eggs? I'm sure you haven't eaten since last night. Right?"

Lorinda wondered if this was the way a mother would have treated her. She remembered so few things about her own. "Tea would be wonderful. And now that we're here, I do feel hungry."

"First, let's get you settled." The kind woman helped remove the scratchy blankets from around her.

When Lorinda relaxed on the sheet covering the soft mattress, Mrs. Oleson pulled the top sheet and two quilts up over her. Everything was made of finer material than any she had ever touched. Smoother...softer.

"Thank you." Lorinda's eyelids felt heavy, but she worked hard to keep them open.

"I'll be back in two shakes of a lamb's tail, as my mother used to say." With a smile, the woman hurried out the door and closed it gently behind her.

Now that she was alone, Lorinda decided to close her eyes for a little while to rest...just until Mrs. Oleson returned with her food. Instead, exhaustion quickly dragged her deep into slumber.

Flames leapt around her. The smell of acrid smoke filled her nostrils, almost choking away her breath. She had to get away, but no matter how hard she tried to move, some kind of force held her back. She called out to Mike to come help her, but no one answered. Over and over she called until her voice was about to give out, and the flames crept closer. When she'd about given up all hope, the click of the door opening aroused her from her terrible dream.

"Here, now." Carrying a tray, Mrs. Oleson bustled through the doorway.

Steam curled from the spout of a china teapot ringed with pink roses, and the smell of warm biscuits wafted toward Lorinda. Her stomach let out a loud growl signaling her hunger. She blushed, hoping Mrs. Oleson didn't hear the sound. If she did, the kind woman never mentioned it.

After setting the tray on a table beside the window, the older woman came to the bed. "Do you want to sit up and eat, or should I bring your food to you in bed? I can put more pillows behind you."

"I can get up. That chair by the table looks comfortable." Lorinda sat up and swung her legs over the side of the mattress.

Mike's boots rested on a rag rug nearby. She wished she had put on her own shoes before she escaped from the burning cabin. She didn't want to clomp around this house, sounding like a thundering herd of cattle.

Mrs. Oleson went to a chest that sat against the wall opposite the bed. She opened the top drawer and pulled out something knitted. "Here are some warm, woolen socks. You can wear them instead of the boots if you'd like. Those look far too large for your dainty feet."

Dainty? No one had ever called her that. "Thank you."

"Let me help you." The older woman knelt beside the bed, making Lorinda feel uncomfortable. "It'll be easier for me than for you to reach so far with the wonderful blessing you're carrying."

Was this baby a blessing? Lorinda hadn't even thought about anything like that. *Yes.* She would consider the child she and Mike had created to be a very special blessing.

If only the rest of her life weren't such a mess.

⁓

*F*ranklin paced across the great room of the ranch house. He'd told Mrs. Oleson he wanted to talk to her after she'd taken care of the Sullivan woman. Maybe his housekeeper would have an idea about some place they could take her.

Even though it had been over three hours since they arrived at the house, he still missed the feel of Mrs. Sullivan cradled in his arms. A feeling he couldn't afford to enjoy. Not if he was going to protect his heart. The sooner the woman was out of his house, the better. He'd get back to his settled lifestyle and forget her. At least, he hoped he could.

Footsteps approached from the hallway that led to the two bedrooms on this floor. *Finally.* Now he could get this taken care of and return to ranching. Running a spread the size of his took all his concentration.

"There you are, Franklin." His housekeeper stopped in the doorway. "I'm assuming you want to check on our guest."

"Of course." He waved her inside and dropped down on the long sofa covered in cowhide.

Mrs. Oleson sat in one of the two wingback chairs. "She has eaten a bit of breakfast, and she's fast asleep."

He nodded. "That's good." Maybe now he could forget she was here. And get some work done. "I've been trying to figure out the best way we can help the woman."

The more he said her name, the more she seemed like a good friend. So he'd see how long he could get by without calling her by name.

"I know that what we're doing right now is helping her a lot." Mrs. Oleson kept her eyes trained on his face.

He hoped he wouldn't give away his inner thoughts. But Mrs. Oleson had been with him long enough that she often discerned his thoughts before he spoke them. He got up and went toward the front window. Crossing his arms over his chest, he kept his attention on the great outdoors.

"I wish she had some family, but she indicated she didn't. I'd be glad to pay her way to wherever she wants to go." He heard Mrs. Oleson shift behind him. *Might as well get it all out in the open.* "She can't stay here."

The older woman cleared her throat.

He knew she was not going to agree with him, so he turned to face her. "Do you have something you want to say?" He hoped his question would remind her who ran this ranch.

She stood. "Maybe the good Lord had us rescue her for a reason. We mustn't be too hasty to send her away. Besides the poor dear just lost everything. I think we should help her face the difficulties."

"We have helped her...a lot." His statement sounded lame even to his own ears.

Her frown indicated she thought so, too. "I know she's thankful you saved her life, but this young woman will need a lot of tender care."

He wanted to say *it's not our problem*, but the glint in Mrs. Oleson's eyes alerted him that might not be a good idea. "I can talk to her and try to find out where we can send her."

The frown on his housekeeper's face deepened. "You're the boss, Mr. Vine, but there are other factors to consider."

When she called him boss and Mr. Vine, he knew how strongly she disagreed with him. "What factors?" He tried to smile to soften his words, but it felt more like a grimace.

"She's been through a lot in the last few months, and this latest thing is really affecting her." Mrs. Oleson walked over to stand in front of him. "When I took her breakfast tray in, I had heard her cry out for her husband before I got to her door. And she sounded terrified. I think the poor dear was having a nightmare."

That put a new face on their dilemma. He didn't have the heart to add to the young woman's bad fortune. But helping her more would place him in a troubling situation. He was strong, so he could guard his heart and help her a bit.

"If possible, we should offer her shelter for as long as she needs it." Mrs. Oleson tucked her chin against her chest and waited for him to comment.

She knew he liked to think things through, and evidently, she was giving him time without staring at him.

He turned back to the window. The mountains on the other side of the valley, where his ranch nestled, stood tall. Covered with snow that glistened in the mid-day sunlight, they looked like a fortress protecting his holdings from the rest of the world. How could he not offer protection for a helpless woman and child? The Bible said a lot about taking care of widows and orphans. He knew without a doubt that he needed to help Mrs. Sullivan and her child. But it would take all his strength to keep himself aloof from her. And that was essential to his peace of mind.

Lord, give me strength.

CHAPTER 6

*A*nticipating a visit to five other ranches spread over the valleys in Summit County, Franklin ate an early breakfast and was on his horse Major before first light seeped over the mountain peaks. He'd witnessed the foaling of his red chestnut stallion and had helped train him. He'd trusted his steed with his life on more than one occasion. Often, when he was currying the horse, he'd filled Major's ears with a problem he was dealing with. Too bad Major couldn't talk back and tell him what he should do about Mrs. Sullivan. The hard day of riding would give him plenty of time to think about the situation at home. He hoped to come up with some kind of solution before he returned to the Rocking V.

Yesterday, Mrs. Oleson hadn't been as helpful as he'd hoped she would. Instead of coming up with somewhere to send their unexpected guest, she'd convinced him she needed to coddle the woman. Even called her by her first name. *Lorinda.*

What kind of name is Lorinda? He'd never heard it before...and he couldn't get it out of his head. Without thinking, he let the word spill from between his lips. Somehow it sounded different when he actually said it.

By the time he and the four hands, left on the ranch this weekend, came in to eat last night, Lorinda was sitting in the kitchen with Mrs. Oleson, clad in one of the older woman's dresses that fit her like a tent. And her blond curls were tamed into a long braid that reached down her back. He'd kept his eyes averted from the woman as much as he could, but his gaze kept returning to her like steel balls to a magnet. And some flowery scent wafted through the air. He hadn't remembered that from the time he held her in his arms on his horse. Where had it come from?

At least today, he wouldn't be anywhere near Lorinda Sullivan. Maybe he could gain control over his thoughts on this ride. *Lord, what am I going to do about her? I need some answers.* He wished God would just speak out loud to him for once.

Reining in Major outside the gate to the RM ranch, he opened the latch and led his horse through. After closing the gate securely, he mounted up and headed toward the one-story ranch house at the end of the long drive. A number of outbuildings clustered close. Franklin hoped he would find Rand nearby, since it was barely dawn.

When Franklin almost reached the front of the house, he spied his friend exiting the barn, so he wheeled Major toward the large, weathered-red building.

"Hey, neighbor." Rand greeted him after he dismounted. "What has you out so early this Sunday morning?"

"Disturbing news."

Rand's brow furrowed. "Come on up to the house for a cup of coffee while you tell me about it."

They went in through the back door and wiped their boots in the mud room.

"I don't want to disturb Stella this early." Franklin followed his friend into the warm, welcoming kitchen.

"We've already had breakfast, and she's upstairs laying out the kids' clothes. She always wants them to look good when we go to town for church." Rand poured two steaming mugs from the coffeepot perched on the back of their kitchen stove. He handed one to Franklin and leaned back against the cabinet, with his ankles crossed while he sipped his drink.

Franklin pulled out a chair and turned it around to straddle it. "You remember that miner Thomas and I took up to bury late last year?"

"Sullivan, wasn't it?"

"Yeah. Well, yesterday his widow's log cabin burned to the ground. Thomas saw the flames when he was out on the range and came to tell me. We took four of the men with us and a wagonload of stuff to fight the fire, but the cabin was gone before we got there."

For a moment, the picture of Mrs. Sullivan when he first saw her yesterday flashed through his mind, and his heart stuttered. An unwelcome emotion rushed through him. He arose from the chair and stared out the window toward a peak flooded with sunshine that glinted off the snow like diamonds. He loved these mountains at any season of the year. He wished he could just forget his problem and go on a long ride through the passes.

"What about his widow?" Rand set his mug down and crossed his arms. "You did say he was married, didn't you?"

Franklin turned back toward his closest friend and nodded. "She'd gotten out of the cabin by herself."

"Who had?" A feminine voice invaded their conversation as Stella joined them. "What am I missing?"

Franklin liked Stella. She was just the kind of wife Rand needed. Daughter of a rancher and used to the isolation. But she was interested in everyone who lived in Summit county.

"I was just telling Rand the Sullivan house burned yesterday." She gasped.

"Mrs. Sullivan lost everything in the fire, except the provisions her husband had stored in the soddy they lived in before he built the log cabin."

"Oh my goodness. That's awful." Stella frowned. "We need to help her. I can find a few things to send to her. How big is she?"

That question was hard to answer, and it took his mind back to when he put her on his lap on the horse. He felt his face start to heat. If anyone noticed, he could blame it on being out in the cold and then coming into the warm kitchen.

"She's small. About an inch shorter than you are. But..." He really didn't want to keep talking about the woman. "...she is...large with child."

"She'll be needing a lot of things then. I'll go up and try to gather what we can do without before we leave to go to church. We can drop them by your house on our way." She headed toward the doorway.

"Thanks. I know she'll appreciate it." He knew no such thing.

She hadn't welcomed the help he offered, but she needed more than he and Mrs. Oleson could give her. And maybe Stella could come up with an answer to their dilemma.

Franklin turned back toward Rand. "That's not the worst part. Someone deliberately set the house on fire. I hate to think about an arsonist running around up here in the mountains. No telling where he might strike next."

Rand rubbed his chin while he considered that. "Do we know what he was looking for? Did he get it?"

"I can't imagine. Sullivan's widow was asleep in the cabin when he started the fire. She could've been killed." That thought sent a shot of fear through him, and sweat popped out on his forehead.

"Maybe the woman might have enemies. We don't know much about her." Rand pulled out another chair and dropped into it. "Tell me everything you know about it."

After Franklin told him, they agreed the ranchers should start their hands patrolling around all the properties. Maybe even form three or four groups to cover more ground and not leave gaps unprotected.

When Franklin was ready to leave, Rand got up and accompanied him out the door.

"I'm going to talk to Hogan, Burke, and Shelton before I head back to my ranch." Franklin mounted Major.

"You want me to take a couple of them so you can make it to church?" Rand's gaze slid across the landscape on this side of his ranch.

"It shouldn't take me too long. I might get there in time to hear Pastor Nelson deliver his message. I probably won't stop for coffee at each ranch." With a two-finger salute, he headed back toward the road.

Once again his thoughts strayed toward the frightened woman taking refuge in his home. With all the work it would take to organize the patrols, he should be able to push her out of his mind...at least most of the time.

$\sim$

*L*orinda had been ravenous at breakfast. Maybe because Franklin Vine wasn't sitting across the table from her. The hands had already eaten before she awakened, so it was just her and Mrs. Oleson. That woman made her feel welcome in a way she'd never experienced before. At supper last night, she'd felt out of place and wary.

Mrs. Oleson wouldn't hear of her helping wash the dishes this morning, so she walked around the lower floor of the house. Her body still felt some of the effects from the day before, so the walking helped work out some of the soreness in her muscles.

The house was exceptionally lovely, so much nicer than any place she'd ever been. The cabin Mike built her couldn't hold a candle to this place, and the house she grew up in was just a shack. She was afraid to touch anything, in case she should break something.

Polished hardwood floors were in almost all the rooms. However, the parlor had a large area rug in a pattern Lorinda had never seen before. The chairs were upholstered in sturdy fabric with subtle woven designs. Ties of matching fabric held the floor to ceiling curtains back, and lace panels between allowed in plenty of light.

Only the parlor was fancy. The rest of the rooms had a masculine feel to the heavier furniture, and the western decorations bespoke of the ranch owner. She assumed the man had never been married. The bedroom door beside the room where she had slept was closed tight, and she didn't feel like snooping in there. But she stood in the entrance hall at the foot of the stairs and peered up toward the second story. According to what Mrs. Oleson mentioned when she arrived, there had to be several bedrooms up there. Quite a large house for a single man.

The sound of an approaching buggy drew Lorinda toward one of the windows beside the front door. She hoped the lace panels covering them hid her from whoever stopped by the gate. A woman stepped down, leaving the others inside, and headed toward the front door. Lorinda hurried back into the kitchen.

"Some people just drove up in a buggy."

Mrs. Oleson dried her hands on her apron, then removed it and hung it on the back of one of the chairs at the table. "Let's go see who it is. We don't get many callers out here."

She followed the older woman into the entrance hall but stopped beside the doorway to the parlor. That way, she could duck inside if she needed to.

Mrs. Oleson opened the door as soon as the woman knocked. "Stella Morgan, come in."

Lorinda started to move into the room.

"Come in and meet our guest."

Both women smiled at her, and she stopped.

"So you're Mrs. Sullivan." The newcomer hurried toward her.

Lorinda wondered how the woman knew her name.

"If I'd have known you were living up on that mountain all alone, I would have come calling." Her friendliness was overwhelming.

Since she'd never had another woman as a friend, Lorinda didn't know what to say.

"How did you know she was here?" Mrs. Oleson led the way toward the sofa.

"Franklin stopped by to talk to Rand this morning, barely at sunrise. He must've started out very early." Stella stopped in the doorway. "When he told us of your plight, I knew I had to do whatever I could for you." She turned toward Mrs. Oleson. "I have some things in the buggy for your house guest."

Flabbergasted, all Lorinda could do was stare at her. No one had ever gone out of their way to help her, except for Mr. Vine and Mrs. Oleson. She didn't know how to react to such generosity.

"Let me help you bring them in." The housekeeper walked back to the front door with her.

"Thanks. I think the two of us can carry all of the things in one trip."

Mrs. Oleson turned toward Lorinda. "Just have a seat in the parlor, and we'll bring the things in there."

While they were gone, she watched them through the front windows. Each woman picked up a fairly large wooden crate and started toward the house. The things in there mustn't be too heavy, because the women didn't strain to pick them up. When they walked up the steps, Lorinda hurried to open the door for them.

"Why, thank you." Mrs. Oleson flashed her a bright smile. "I was just starting to set this down when the door opened." She headed into the parlor and put the crate beside the low table in front of the sofa.

Lorinda perched onto the front edge of one of the chairs on the other side of the table. She didn't know what to say...or do. So she clutched her hands together and tried to hold them still. She'd always heard her father rant about accepting charity, even though they needed it. Now she felt awkward about this, but since everything she owned had burned in the fire, she and her baby needed whatever the woman brought.

The visitor dropped onto the cushioned couch. "If some of the other women out here hadn't given me assistance when Rand and I married, I don't know what I would've done. So I do the same for whomever I can." Her brilliant smile beamed at Lorinda. "I hope you don't mind."

"Stella and Rand own the RM ranch, which is our closest neighbor." Mrs. Oleson sat beside the rancher's wife. "And this is Lorinda, who owns property up on the mountain on the opposite side of our ranch."

With twinkling eyes, Stella studied her. "May I call you Lorinda?" After she nodded, the other woman continued. "And you must call me Stella. I want us to become good friends."

Lorinda wasn't even sure she knew how to be friends with another woman. She felt overwhelmed by all of this, so she just sat and watched while Stella and Mrs. Oleson started unloading the crates.

"I think these clothes will fit you." The dress Stella pulled from the box was a beautiful shade of dark blue. It looked like a soft woolen fabric...and it had a lace collar with matching cuffs. Along the bottom, a ruffle was edged with the same lace. "I wore this when I was carrying both of my boys."

"I'm afraid something might happen to it." But Lorinda wanted to wear that dress, more than she had ever desired a garment. "What if you need it again?"

"I may or may not need it again." Stella held it out toward

her. "But you do need the dress right now. I want you to have it."

Finally, Lorinda took the garment and held the soft wool up to her cheek. "Thank you."

"And that's not all."

Stella kept pulling things from the boxes. Four more dresses, one fancy like this one and the others plain. Unmentionables, some of them Lorinda had never seen before. She didn't know how to wear them. A couple more nightdresses. Some thick stockings.

"I don't know if these shoes will fit you. When I asked Franklin if your feet were about the same size as mine, he told me you had been wearing men's heavy boots when he found you, so he couldn't tell." Stella held out a pair of dainty, button-up shoes. "See if they'll fit."

When Lorinda slipped her feet into the first one, the shoe fit as if it was made just for her. She held out her foot and turned it this way and that, trying to see how it looked.

A broad smile spread across Stella's face. "They're a perfect fit. How fortunate."

Lorinda couldn't do anything except return her smile.

By the time the boxes were empty, Lorinda had more clothing than she'd ever owned. And a pile of things for the baby spread around her. Tears filled her eyes. She tried to blink them away. No one in her family had ever let her cry about anything. But these were tears of joy, and she'd never experienced them before.

Stella got up and came to where she sat. "Out here in the west, we take care of each other."

The hug from Stella matched the ones she'd received from Mrs. Oleson. Her life was a mess, but for the first time in her adult life, she had two friends. She was pretty sure they couldn't have gone through all the terrible things she had.

She hoped she could keep her secrets hidden from them, so they would keep liking her.

CHAPTER 7

*F*ranklin was no closer to an answer to his problem than he was when he first clapped eyes on Lorinda Sullivan beside her burning cabin. He stood in his office staring into the evening duskiness, his hands clasped tight behind his back. A bright moon gave the snow a pearly sheen, and stars twinkled in the cloudless, inky sky.

His circuit of the nearby ranches hadn't given him even the glimmer of an idea about what to do with the woman. At each house, the rancher had agreed with him about the need to stay alert and try to find the arsonist. And the wives opened their hearts to Mrs. Sullivan's plight, gathering all kinds of things the woman needed. He almost had to bite his tongue to keep from blurting his desire to get her away from his house as quickly as possible. His emotions churned, feeling a tug toward the beautiful blonde, then erecting a barrier against those feelings.

He didn't dare trust another woman. A second betrayal might put him in the grave. The first one almost did.

Each visit took so long that Franklin hadn't made it back in time to attend church in Breckenridge. Probably a good thing. He wouldn't have been able to concentrate on Brian Nelson's sermon, even though the preacher usually kept his attention as he unfolded the truths of scripture.

Mrs. Oleson and their guest had already finished eating Sunday dinner before Franklin returned to the ranch. The housekeeper kept some food on the stove's warming shelf, so he hadn't gone hungry. At least Mrs. Sullivan was resting while he ate dinner. But although she was absent in person, she wasn't absent from his thoughts, no matter how hard he tried to shake her away. After the lonely meal, he kept himself busy in the barn, only coming in for supper.

His housekeeper had fixed sandwiches using the left-over roast from the noon meal. Even though he always liked roast beef sandwiches, for some reason today, his tasted like straw and almost stuck in his throat. Maybe it was because he had so much on his mind. He really couldn't remember taking a single bite, even though only bread crumbs remained on his plate when he left the table.

When he asked Mrs. Sullivan if he could talk with her in his office, she bristled, then agreed.

What is taking her so long?

As if in answer to his unspoken question, a tentative knock sounded on his door. He hurried over to jerk it open.

Franklin had tried to keep his eyes from straying toward the woman during the meal. Now she stood in front of him, in a dress that fit her far better than the one Mrs. Oleson had loaned her. The material brought out the rich blue of her eyes. He'd never seen her lovelier. For a moment, he couldn't tear his gaze away from her. With unwavering tenacity, she studied him as well. The thin mountain air was even harder to breathe until he finally escaped from the magnetic pull of her eyes that were bluer than the spring sky.

He stepped back. "Please... " He gestured toward the two upholstered chairs near the window. "Come in. Have a seat."

After she perched daintily upon one, he dropped into the

other. He cast around his mind, trying to decide how to start their conversation. A clear question settled in her eyes.

"How...are you feeling?" *Why couldn't I come up with a better question for her?*

She settled deeper into the chair. "I'm...fine."

Evidently, she felt as uncomfortable as he did. He'd never imagined having a conversation like this with any woman.

"Good...good." *I sound like an idiot.*

He was a successful rancher who was respected by many people living in the area. He could do this. "I thought we needed to discuss...things."

She nodded. "All right." The sound so tentative it was almost a whisper.

As he studied her, he wondered if she'd been taking good care of herself. Besides the burden she carried, she was far too thin. He didn't remember her arms being that skinny when they took her husband's body to bury it. She'd raised the heavy rifle with a show of strength almost equal to a man. Had she been eating right? With no one to encourage her during the long winter months, had she just barely managed to get along?

"I didn't check while we were up at your place. Did you run low on provisions?"

His question must have bothered her, because she winced.

"No." Her voice was soft. Musical. "You had the provisions brought down here."

He nodded. "I know, but I didn't check to see how much was left."

She gave him a tentative smile that didn't reach her eyes, and her neck stiffened. "Enough to help pay for my being here."

That comment sent a knife through his gut. Did she really think he wanted her to pay? Maybe his remaining aloof from her gave her that impression.

"You don't owe me anything." The words felt good to him.

"I don't want to be a burden on anyone." She rearranged her

skirt around her limbs and clasped her hands together so tight her knuckles matched the snow outside the window.

"You're not a burden." But wouldn't the things he wanted to say to her reinforce that thought in her mind?

"Then why did you want to talk to me?"

A simple question. He wished he had a simple answer.

"I just wanted to know what...you want to happen in your life." He stopped himself before he added *now that your husband's dead and your cabin's gone*. Why could he talk to his men and make perfect sense, and this little slip of a woman had him babbling like an idiot?

Tears trembled on her lower lashes. "I wish I knew." She sat there staring down at the floor before glancing up at him. "At least with all the things your neighbors brought me, I have clothing for me...and my child. But I don't have a home."

Although he didn't think it was a good idea, he had to ask, "Do you want my men and me to rebuild your cabin for you?"

That question must have surprised her. Her eyes cut toward him, a startled expression in them. "I'm not sure that's a good idea." Finally, she released her tight grip on her hands, and one waved toward the mountain behind him. "I must keep the land as an inheritance for my child, but after this last six months, I don't think staying on the mountain with a baby is the right thing for me to do."

He couldn't disagree with her assessment of the situation. This discussion was going nowhere fast. "We don't have to decide anything tonight." He stood and tried to give her a pleasant smile. "If you think of anything else you want to do, just let me know."

She quickly arose from the chair, then stood none too steadily. "I'll do that."

Without thought, he raised his hand to help her, then noticed her spine was straight as one of the aspen trees on her property. He figured she wouldn't welcome his touch, and that was fine with him.

As she exited the room, he couldn't help noticing the sway of her slim hips as she walked away carrying a vulnerability that beckoned his protective nature.

~

*O*nce again, Franklin arose long before dawn. Not because he had plans that necessitated the early morning, but because he was tired of losing the fight with his covers while tossing and turning most of the night. He went out to the stable and started mucking out the stalls. Anything to keep himself busy.

He wanted to help Mrs. Sullivan, and something about her tugged at his heart. But he didn't dare let her inside his wall of defense. He'd loved one woman and that didn't end well.

Miriam had professed her love for him right up until the day, two weeks before their wedding, when she ran off with his best friend Marvin Pratt. The three of them had grown up on ranches here in Summit County. Marvin was the son of Franklin's father's foreman. The three of them had been together for years before Franklin asked Miriam to be his wife.

He thought Marvin was happy for them. He laughed and agreed when asked to be the best man.

Miriam wanted a big wedding, so she and her mother sent away for special materials and other doodads while he waited anxiously to make her his wife. He'd shared his heart's deepest dreams with Marvin, and they'd had interesting conversations about them. Up until that cataclysmic day.

Marvin was the one who told him what was happening. How he'd always been jealous of all the things Franklin had. How he wanted them, too. How he'd wooed Franklin's bride right out from under his nose. Then they climbed into a new carriage and rode away, trampling Franklin's heart beneath the horse's hooves as he watched them stop to kiss passionately right before they were out of sight.

I'll never, ever trust a woman or have a man for a best friend again. Those words spoken aloud that day had become his litany, even after his parents were killed in the wreck of a runaway wagon, and he became sole owner of the ranch.

Rand Morgan was the closest friend he had now, but he'd never let Rand invade his heart as Marvin had. They helped each other and watched each other's backs, but didn't share the deep secrets of their hearts.

Remaining aloof from all the women who let him know they were interested in him was easy...until now. That's why he had to come up with a way to help Mrs. Sullivan find a new home that would be good for her and her child. It would be too easy for him to fall for a woman like her, despite his decision not to.

When he leaned the pitchfork against the wall and started pushing the last wheelbarrow full of the soiled hay toward the doorway, his stomach growled. He suddenly realized the cold was seeping inside his heavy coat and gloves. After dumping this load, he'd head to the house. Mrs. Oleson probably had breakfast ready by now. At least, she'd have hot coffee for him.

He ran his soles across the wrought iron boot scraper beside the back door before entering the mud room. When he hung up his coat and pulled off his gloves, he blew his warm breath on his fingers, then stepped into the toasty kitchen.

"I wondered where you were." Mrs. Oleson leaned over to remove cinnamon rolls from the oven.

The sweet, spicy smell made his stomach rumble even more. "You made my favorite."

"I thought you could use some encouragement." She set the hot pie tin on a trivet. "I heard you moving around a lot last night. Did you sleep at all?"

"Not much." He knew her room was right above his. Maybe

that hadn't been such a good idea, but she'd been in that room when his parents were alive, and he didn't want to make her move.

"Worrying about our guest?"

His housekeeper was much too astute.

"Maybe."

She lifted the speckled, graniteware coffeepot from the stove using a folded kitchen towel. "Have you found a solution to the situation?"

He sat down at the table while she poured the dark, steaming brew into a large mug. "Not yet."

Franklin really wished he would soon. He hated all the uncomfortable memories that had bombarded his mind.

She returned the pot to its warm perch, then brought a plate filled with crisp bacon strips to the table. "I have an idea that might work."

He helped himself to several pieces. "What idea?"

"Lorinda needs something to keep her busy. It'll make it easier for her to come to grips with all her troubles. She needs to feel useful." After pouring herself a cup of coffee, Mrs. Oleson joined him at the table.

He took a large bite from the last strip of bacon he'd put on his plate. Chewing it gave him time to mull over what she said. He couldn't think of anything Mrs. Sullivan could do to *feel useful*.

When he hadn't made any comment, his housekeeper leaned her arms on the table and curled her fingers around the warm cup. "You are always wanting to hire someone to help me."

"And you keep being insulted by my suggestions." He laughed.

"It's not that I can't do the work anymore, but you could offer her a smaller salary and room and board to go with it. Then she wouldn't feel as though she's a charity case."

The words touched a chord in his spirit. Not many people

around these parts wanted charity, but when they helped each other, everything was all right. "She's not physically able to do much. I was really surprised by how thin the woman has become. I don't think she ate as much as she should have during the winter."

A knowing glint flitted through his housekeeper's gaze and quickly vanished. He wondered what that meant.

"I'm not saying to work the woman to death, but I can find plenty for her to do to feel useful without taxing her too much." Mrs. Oleson took a sip of her coffee.

He appreciated her idea about helping the Sullivan woman this way. Maybe after a while, she would be able to stand on her own two feet. He couldn't help hoping that time would come sooner, rather than later. He'd seen the woman's stubborn streak of pride. She might see through their suggestion and not accept. But that wouldn't be a bad thing. Would it?

CHAPTER 8

*L*orinda sat beside the kitchen table, peeling potatoes for the stew Mrs. Oleson was preparing for tonight's supper. The last two weeks had rushed by while the wonderful woman stirring the pot on the stove helped keep Lorinda's mind off all her losses. Teaching her to knit, something she had always wanted to do. Helping her sew a few things for herself and for the baby. Giving her tasks that were easy for her to complete.

It had to have been Mrs. Oleson's idea to offer her a job with room and board as part of her pay. Franklin Vine never would've come up with that idea by himself. He kept himself aloof from Lorinda, not saying ten words a day to her. But she didn't really care, did she? She and her baby would have a home, and with her not needing to spend much of the money he paid her, she could save for their future. Someday, that money, along with the value of the two pokes of gold she had hidden in her room, would give the two of them a start somewhere else. Of course, she didn't want to settle too far from the property they owned, but maybe she could find a job and a place to stay in

Breckenridge, Dillon, or Frisco. Keystone or Silverthorne would be farther than she wanted to go.

Mrs. Oleson turned toward her. "How are you doing with those potatoes?"

"Almost finished." She picked up the last vegetable. "Only one more."

The housekeeper wiped her hands on her apron as she came toward the table. "You finished those quickly. I'll have to set them in water until it's time to add them to the stew. Potatoes don't take as long to cook as the carrots do."

After dropping the peeling, cut in one long curling ribbon, into the bucket for the pigs, Lorinda quickly quartered the potato. "All done." She stood and reached for the filled crockery bowl on the table.

"Here. Let me get that for you." Mrs. Oleson set the potatoes on the cabinet and poured water from a large pitcher into the bowl.

"Why do you do that?" Lorinda peeked around the other woman's shoulder. "Put them in water, I mean."

"So they'll stay crisp and don't turn dark."

"I never knew that. Mine always had black on them if I didn't use them right away."

So much Lorinda hadn't learned about keeping house and cooking. But Mrs. Oleson was patient, teaching her as they worked together. She wondered what the older woman would do if she were to give her a big hug. Her mother had died a long time ago, and she yearned for a motherly touch.

"I'm glad to see you looking better, dear." Mrs. Oleson smiled at her. "I worried about you when you first came. You hadn't been eating as much as you should have. I could tell."

Lorinda nodded. "Sometimes, it wasn't worth the effort when I wasn't feeling so good." She tried not to dwell on that awful time when she was alone for so long. "Of course, I did have good days when I cooked up a storm. I stored the leftovers in the snowbank, and they would last for days. But nothing tasted as good as what I've had here on the ranch."

She put her hands on the sides of her waist and stretched her tired back. The baby grew heavier every day. She patted her swollen belly, and the baby tapped the same place from the inside. Such a wonder to get used to.

"Let's make something special to go with this stew. I brought some dried apples up from the root cellar earlier this morning. They've been simmering with raisins while I worked. How would you like an apple and raisin pie?" Mrs. Oleson set a mixing bowl on the table and gave Lorinda a measuring cup. "We need two cups of flour, full to the top."

After Lorinda followed the directions, the older woman sprinkled a pinch of salt into the flour.

"I love apple pies, but we hardly ever had them. We didn't get much fruit in the winter." Lorinda went to the stove and lifted the lid to take a sniff. "Besides, no one ever taught me how to make crust, so I just stirred up some biscuit dough, added sugar, and plopped it on the top of the apples in the pan. I never cooked them ahead of time either. And I never thought about adding raisins. Of course, we didn't have those very often."

She hoped Mrs. Oleson didn't pity her because of her upbringing. At least, the older woman didn't know the worst of it, and she never would.

"Here's the best way to make a flaky crust." While she demonstrated, Lorinda watched everything the woman did, trying to commit it to memory. Besides the flour and salt, Mrs. Oleson added lard, cutting it into the mixture using two table knives, the same way Lorinda did for the biscuits. And she sprinkled in the cold water, a little at a time, while stirring the dough.

"Why didn't your mother teach you?"

That question caught Lorinda by surprise. She had never told anyone much about her early life, not even Mike. Should she trust this woman with some of the information? Maybe she could let down her walls a little, because Mrs. Oleson had been nothing but kind to her.

"Ma died when I was young. I barely remember her. After that, Pa and me just muddled along the best we could. Most times, we didn't do a very good job."

She knew that was vague, but she didn't want to tell her the whole truth. The shame she carried most of her life. At least, Mike hadn't probed too deeply, so he loved her instead of pitying her.

"Then you had no way of learning what you needed to know. That's not your fault."

Mrs. Oleson's words poured over her like warm honey, filling the cracks in her defenses. Lorinda nodded.

"You've really picked up on the things I've been showing you. I imagine you could probably write down a receipt for the pie crust since you were listening so intently." Mrs. Oleson sprinkled flour over one end of the table, then turned the dough out of the bowl and patted it down until it was about an inch thick. Then she used her well-worn, wooden rolling pin to start flattening it even more. "You don't want to work the dough too much, or it'll become tough. Would you like some paper so you can write down the instructions?"

Lorinda would, but paper was a luxury item to her.

"Did you go to school?" That must have been an afterthought for the older woman.

"Not much. But after we were married, Mike taught me to read and write. I can even cipher numbers. Maybe not really big ones, but some."

Mrs. Oleson wiped her hands on her apron and left the room, returning with a sheet of the nicest paper Lorinda had ever seen and a sharpened pencil. "Go ahead and write it down. When you're finished, sprinkle cinnamon and sugar over the apples and raisins then mix it all together."

While they finished creating the pie, their conversation flowed like an ebbing river. Lorinda lost herself in the rhythm of the words. Having a woman discuss things with her was heavenly. Pa had hardly spoken to her unless he was drunk, and the things he said then felt more like rocks hitting her heart. Mike had talked to her, but he didn't really listen to what she wanted. His way was the only way to do things. At least, his lovemaking made up for all the rest...almost.

"So you can read. What kinds of books do you like?"

"The only book I've ever had was my mother's Bible. But Mike and I read it together a lot." She watched how Mrs. Oleson folded the crust to transfer it to the greased pie tin. That looked easy enough.

"I like to read on a long winter evening after all the chores are done, so I have quite a few books. I'd be glad for you to borrow some of them."

Lorinda thought this must be what heaven was like. Being treated with such honest caring, having plenty to eat, and even books she could explore.

If only she didn't feel like an interloper here.

∾

Today, while he worked with the hands on the ranch, Franklin also checked for signs the arsonist might still be in the area. None of the patrols his men had been on could find a trace of him beyond the footprints he left at the Sullivan claim, and they only led to where a horse had trampled the snow. After the man had mounted his horse, he made his way to the road across the mountain, so there was no way to follow him beyond where his hoofprints intermingled with so many others. Maybe it was time to relax and quit worrying about the blackguard. He was probably long gone.

Every time his thoughts turned toward the miscreant, they

then meandered in the direction of Lorinda. No matter how hard he tried to keep his mind on his business, his thoughts had a will of their own.

When he'd been at the house these last couple of weeks, he'd done his best to stay away from the woman. Mainly just seeing her at mealtime. That suited him just fine. Of course, Mrs. Oleson kept him apprized of the events at the house, and the woman had been settling in quite nicely. Even if that wasn't what he wanted. And the two women got along really well.

After arriving back at the stable behind the ranch house, he took care of Major before heading in to supper. An enticing smell greeted him at the door, a mingling of hearty stew and his favorite pie. Apple raisin. His stomach gave an appreciative growl, and hunger overtook him. He quickly cleaned up in the mud room and entered the warm, brightly-lit kitchen.

"Mrs. Oleson, something smells delicious."

Lorinda glanced up from where she was setting the table, her blue eyes reminding him of a warm summer day, instead of the lingering cold of spring. She quickly averted her gaze.

The woman looked much healthier than she had when he'd found her beside her burned-out cabin. Staying at his ranch must be good for her. Until now, he hadn't noticed how much her size had changed the last two weeks. Her impending motherhood had progressed, and her arms and face looked like they had filled out. All that did was increase her beauty. He took a deep breath and looked away.

He would have been married by now, probably with a child or two, if Miriam and Marvin hadn't broken his heart. No matter how much he wanted a son to inherit his vast holdings, it wasn't going to happen ... ever.

Spears of jealousy lanced his gut. How could he be envious of a dead man? It hardly seemed fair that a corpse's wife was nearing her delivery time, and Franklin had no hope of a family. No way would he ever trust his heart to another woman, even if she was beautiful, with curls the color of summer sunshine. Why would a loving God let such a thing happen to him?

"Did you want to eat now or after you read the mail Terrell brought from town when he went in for supplies?" His housekeeper stood beside the stove, stirring the pot of stew.

Needing to rein in his emotions, he headed toward the doorway to the hall. "I'll just check what arrived. I should be back to eat in about fifteen minutes."

"Dinner will be on the table by then." He heard Mrs. Oleson put the cover on the simmering stew pot.

He didn't look back as he hurried toward his office. After reaching the desk, he shuffled through the envelopes, reading the return addresses. Nothing looked to be pressing, so he walked over to the front windows. He crossed his arms over his chest and stared out at the mountain peaks in the distance.

He loved this land. When he was younger he'd had dreams of being like his father and passing it on, but all that was futile now. Why was he working so hard to preserve the ranch? Probably because he didn't know what else to do. Maybe when he died, the ranch could be divided between his most loyal employees.

He huffed out a deep breath. Why was he worrying about that? He was a young man with plenty of time to decide what to do. *Mike Sullivan didn't expect to die when he did either. He was younger than you are.* The sudden thought blind-sided him. Well, he didn't need to dwell on that. Good food awaited him.

On the way back down the hallway to the kitchen, he identified the pleasing aroma of baking biscuits intermingling with the other scents. Once more, his stomach let him know he was way past hungry. With all the work today, he'd developed an enormous appetite.

Mrs. Oleson looked up when he stopped in the doorway. "You're right on time, Franklin. Lorinda and I just put out the last of the food." She tucked the tea towel around the golden biscuits to keep them hot.

He took his place at the head of the table with a woman on either side of him, facing each other. At least, his newest employee wasn't across from him where he'd see every move she made.

After they were all seated, he bowed his head. "Father God, thank you for the food and the hands that prepared it. In Jesus' name. Amen."

Before he started eating, he turned his gaze toward Mrs. Oleson. "Everything looks delicious."

"I made the stew for the most part. Lorinda peeled the potatoes."

He nodded his thanks toward the younger woman. When his housekeeper passed the basket of biscuits to him, he took two and put them on the saucer beside his bowl of steaming stew.

While he reached for the butter, Mrs. Oleson added, "Lorinda made these biscuits and helped me with the pie. She's a good cook."

He glanced once more toward the younger woman and found her sitting with her hands in her lap and her face turned down as if she were still praying. A becoming blush stained her cheeks. Maybe she wasn't used to compliments, but surely her husband had told her he liked her cooking...and how lovely she was. If not, the man was an ingrate.

After a moment, she picked up her spoon and tasted the stew.

Why hadn't he paid any attention to the woman? His callous treatment may have contributed to her reticence. Perhaps he should make her feel welcome as long as she was here in his home anyway. He wouldn't have treated any of his other employees the way he'd been treating her.

He sank his teeth into the biscuit dripping with melted butter, the perfect accompaniment to the steaming beef stew.

"These biscuits are every bit as good as Mrs. Oleson's. Thank you, Mrs. Sullivan."

A slow smile spread across her face, finally reaching her eyes. "Th...thank you, Mr. Vine."

That broke the ice, and the conversation flowed freely throughout supper.

When they had finished eating the main part of the meal, Mrs. Oleson cut the pie. Franklin noticed Lorinda didn't take a taste until after he did.

"Ladies, this is wonderful. It's still warm." He shoved another bite into his mouth, and that shy smile once again crept over her features.

After Mrs. Oleson set down with her dessert, she smiled at the younger woman. "Lorinda dear, I have a cedar chest I'm not using anymore. I'll have one of the hands move it into your room. You can put all your new things for the baby in it."

Lorinda's eyes widened, then tears glistened on her lashes. "Thank you."

"That's a good idea." Franklin got up and patted his stomach. "I'm as full as a tick on a hound dog."

Both women laughed.

"I can move the cedar chest for you." Franklin welcomed his housekeeper's thoughtfulness. From now on, he would try to be more kind to the young widow.

After all, she wouldn't be here very long.

CHAPTER 9

On a cold evening in late March, Franklin leaned back in the rocking chair on the front porch and crossed his feet on the railing. Lacing the fingers of both hands behind his head, he watched the fading colors of the sunset slip behind the mountain peaks, revealing a clear, starry sky. Everything was calm on the ranch. Just the way he liked it. With the number of calves his cattle had produced, he'd be able to thin the herd and sell a goodly number to the mining companies. Even ship beeves to the Denver market.

Things had settled down on the home front as well. He'd gotten used to Lorinda being a part of his household, and she was more relaxed around him. If he were honest with himself, he welcomed her presence.

Mrs. Oleson often told him how much she was enjoying all the help Lorinda gave her. She'd been missing having a woman to talk to and hadn't realized how much until Lorinda came. Maybe he'd offer the widow a permanent place on his staff. The long winter ahead would be more comfortable with his housekeeper having another woman around the place. They did work well together.

The front door squeaked open behind him. He'd need to have Rusty oil the hinges tomorrow.

"Franklin." Mrs. Oleson's voice sounded agitated.

His feet dropped to the floor with a thud, and he rose to face her. "Do you need my help?" When he caught a glimpse of her face, he knew it wasn't something simple. "What happened?"

Wringing her hands, she was more frantic than he'd ever seen her. "Lorinda has gone into labor, and it's progressing right along. We need the doctor to come as soon as possible. Could you send one of the men to get him?"

Franklin stared at her for a moment while he figured the best thing to do. "Major is the fastest horse in the stable. I'll ride into Breckenridge myself." He had to do something to help the two women under his care.

He quickly entered the house and grabbed his hat, coat, and holster. Running toward the barn, he buckled the gun belt around his waist. After he saddled his stallion, he rode out of the building while Rusty waited to close the door. He gave a quick wave to Mrs. Oleson as he sped past. A strong feeling of unease held him fast in its grip. He hoped Doc was available. Lorinda needed the man, and he'd make sure she had his help.

Major enjoyed a good run. Since the moon shone bright in the night sky, Franklin could let him have his head. While they thundered down the road, he whispered a quick prayer for Mrs. Oleson and Lorinda. But soon he ran out of the right words. He'd heard other men at church say that having a first child could be dangerous. Too many women died in childbirth. Thinking about the possibility of that happening to Lorinda punched him in the gut. He couldn't let that happen, no matter what he had to do to prevent it. The sooner he got the doctor and they returned to the ranch, the better.

Franklin made good time reaching the edge of Breckenridge. He expected the town to be quiet, except for the area where the saloons were located, but that wasn't the case. Hordes of people were out and about, scurrying here and there. All the conversations sounded ominous, even though he couldn't distinguish the words.

The windows on the parsonage were well-lit, but not at the doctor's house. Still he knocked on the door, trying to raise the medical man. After he waited a couple of minutes, he pounded even harder. No one came, so he headed toward the parsonage.

Just before his knuckles reached the door, it opened, and he almost rapped the pastor in the face. The man quickly raised his hand to catch Franklin's fist.

"Sorry, Pastor. I wasn't trying to slug you."

The man of God smiled. "I know. I didn't mean to startle you."

Both men chuckled.

"So what can—"

"So where were—"

After they spoke at the same time, Franklin stepped back. "Go ahead, Pastor." He hoped the man wouldn't be long-winded with his answer as he sometimes was on Sunday.

"I was asking what I could do for you." Reverend Nelson thrust his hands into the front pockets of his slacks. "But you were asking me a question as well."

"I've got to find Dr. Winston. No one answered the door at his house. We need him at the ranch right now." It took all Franklin's determination to keep himself from hurrying away. He would have if he'd had any idea where to find Doc.

"Mrs. Winston has gone to Denver to visit their daughter, and Doc is at Farncomb Hill. There's been a mine cave-in. They're digging out the men who were trapped. Some of them are pretty banged up. I was there earlier, but I came home for supper. I'm heading back over to see if I can help."

"I'll tag along. Mrs. Sullivan is in labor, and Mrs. Oleson sent me for the doctor. I sure hope he can go back with me." What would he do if Doc couldn't? *God, please let him go.*

"It's her first baby, isn't it? She hasn't brought a child to church with her, but she could have lost a child before." The minister swiftly headed toward the livery where he kept his horse stabled.

"Yes, it is. I'm sure she would have mentioned losing a child ... at least to Mrs. Oleson." Franklin led Major as he walked beside the pastor. He didn't want to let on how worried he was about Lorinda. That could raise all kind of questions in Brian Nelson's mind, and he didn't need that right now. "How many men are trapped?"

"They've rescued most of them, but five were still inside when I left."

Brian saddled his horse, and they headed east from town. Once more the bright moon lit the way. They rode so fast conversation wasn't possible, which was fine with Franklin. His thoughts kept returning to the women at the ranch, and his stomach roiled. He wished he hadn't eaten such a large supper. The way he was feeling right now, some of it might erupt at any time.

When they wound around the last mountain, the area of the mine was lit up, and men scurried all over the place like ants on an anthill. As the two men reined in at the front of the main building, the area of the mine was well-lit with a multitude of candles in the building, and lanterns swung from poles and trees. Searchers also carried lanterns with them.

After tying their horses to the hitching rail, they entered the large room that looked like a makeshift hospital.

When they opened the door, Dr. Winston raised his head from hovering over a patient.

"How's it going, Doc?" Brian headed toward him. "Have they brought out any more men?"

"Not yet. But there's plenty for me to do here." Worry creased his brow as he glanced down at the man lying on the improvised bed on the floor, then walked over to meet them out of earshot of the injured men. "I'm not sure whether everyone here is going to make it."

"I'll go and start praying for them individually." The minister stepped away.

Dr. Winston turned eyes, bloodshot with fatigue, toward Franklin. "Did you come to help?"

"No. Mrs. Sullivan has gone into labor, and Mrs. Oleson sent me to bring you back to the ranch." He held his hat so tight, he crushed the brim.

The doctor dropped his head against his chest. Franklin waited, but the man didn't say anything for quite awhile. This made Franklin more anxious. What could he do if the doctor wouldn't come?

Finally the man raised his head. "I just can't leave these men right now."

Franklin knew the doctor needed to be here to try to keep as many men from dying as he could, but Lorinda needed him too. Despair fell over him like a smothering quilt.

"What do I tell Mrs. Oleson?" He couldn't keep his worry from shouting through his words.

"That I can't leave these men." His tone emphatic, the doctor put his hand on Franklin's shoulder. "And everyone around here is helping with the cave-in. Women have had babies since the world began, son. I'm sure Mrs. Oleson will do just fine helping Mrs. Sullivan. Maybe you can ask the pastor to pray for them while he's praying for the injured miners."

Before he left, he did talk to Pastor Nelson. Then he headed out to mount Major. He'd been gone from the ranch much longer than he'd thought he would be. He was sure Mrs. Oleson was wondering where he was.

As he headed toward the ranch, he decided to take the doctor's suggestion to heart. All the way, he prayed for the two women, and this time he didn't run out of words. He'd never prayed for any woman the way he did for Lorinda. The widow'd had enough sorrows in her life, so he prayed for her labor and for the birth to be easy. He prayed for the baby to be healthy, and he prayed for Mrs. Oleson to know exactly what to do. He reached the edge of his property before he realized where he was. He'd trusted Major to get him home safely.

He reined in at the front gate, then jumped down, tying the reins to the hitching rail outside the fence. Rusty came down the steps from the porch and met him by the gate.

"I stayed close, Boss, in case the women needed me."

"You're a good man." Franklin clapped him on the shoulder. "Everything go all right?"

"Think so. Haven't heard much from inside." The ranch hand glanced down the drive. "Is the doctor far behind you?"

"He's not coming. There was a mine cave-in, and he's busy with the injured." Franklin started up the walkway to the porch.

"I'll take care of Major for you. You won't have to worry about him."

"Thanks." Franklin hurried up the steps.

Just before he opened the door, he heard a mewling cry that quickly changed into a squall. He rushed inside and followed the sound toward the bedroom where the women were. He knocked on the door.

It opened, and Mrs. Oleson thrust the newborn, swaddled in a flannel blanket, into his arms. "It's a boy."

Then she firmly closed the door between them. He stared down at the tiny, red face with the infant's mouth wide open. The baby continued bawling like a newborn calf, his tiny tongue vibrating with the noise. What was he supposed to do now? He'd never held a newborn infant before. What if he did something wrong?

Trying to forget his nervousness, he pulled the baby close to his chest and started gently rocking his torso, the way he'd seen other new fathers do at church. He hummed a nameless tune, the kind he often crooned to settle down the cows for the night on cattle drives. Within a couple of minutes, the little scrap of humanity settled his head close to Franklin's heart. Soon it felt as if the infant's breathing matched Franklin's heartbeat, and some kind of unexplainable connection slammed into him almost taking his breath away.

He walked into the parlor, staring at the tiny child the whole time. He couldn't get enough of looking at the baby. He'd always thought newborn babies were ugly, but this little guy leaned toward cuteness. A fluff of blond hair surrounded his head, and his mouth sucked on his own fist, even though his eyes were closed.

Something deep inside Franklin wished this child were his. The child he would never have. Longings he'd suppressed held him in a firm grip. He imagined the tiny boy taking his first steps, growing and learning about manly things under his own tutelage. He could see riding the range with the young boy in the saddle in front of him.

This baby needed a father to teach him and love him. And holding him so close to his own heart, Franklin knew he could love this child. Maybe the strange connection he felt was the beginning of that love.

The baby stretched his neck and opened his eyes. Franklin had heard women say newborns couldn't see clearly, but this baby's eyes locked on his and drew Franklin into his heart as well. The connection was complete.

Why can't I be the boy's father? He didn't have to open his heart to the woman, just because he did to the child. Maybe this was the answer to his desire to have an heir. People got married all the time and had successful marriages with less than a child to keep them together. He could offer marriage to Lorinda. He would protect her, give her a home forever, and they could share this child. She wouldn't want anything deeper, because of loving and losing her husband. He didn't want anything else, because he couldn't allow his heart to be trampled again. The more he thought about it, the more sense it made to him.

Finally, a way he could have a son.

CHAPTER 10

"*S*orry, Franklin." Mrs. Oleson came into the parlor and startled him.

He was concentrating on the baby and his plans so much, he hadn't heard the sound of her approaching. "Sorry for what?"

"I didn't mean to leave the boy with you so long. I just had to take care of Lorinda and needed you to hold him for me." She came over and peeked at the infant sound asleep in his arms. A slow smile spread across her face. "He's a really cute sprite, isn't he?"

"Yes, he is. And you don't need to apologize. We got along just fine." He could hardly pry his eyes from the treasure he held. A tiny baby had changed his perspective completely. "How is Mrs. Sullivan?"

"She's resting." Mrs. Oleson ran a finger lightly across the downy cheek of the sleeping baby. "He's so soft." She turned her attention toward Franklin. "Don't you think you should be on a first name basis with her after all this time?"

His housekeeper had a point. He'd been thinking about her as Lorinda for a while now, trying to be careful not to call her that out loud. "I don't want to make her feel uncomfortable."

"When we're alone, she calls me Ingrid, instead of Mrs. Oleson. I don't think it will make her uncomfortable at all."

That settled it in his mind. He was relieved to stop trying to remember not to call her by her first name. From now on, she would be just Lorinda.

A pretty name for a beautiful lady. He was glad he hadn't blurted that thought aloud, but why was he noticing things like that about her? He didn't want another pretty woman to get past the wall he'd carefully built around his heart.

His housekeeper put her hands on her hips. "Why didn't the doctor come out here?"

"Mine cave-in at Farncomb Hill." The baby wiggled in his arms, and Franklin's eyes were drawn to his tiny face again. "I went out there to talk to him, but he had patients he couldn't leave. I prayed all the way home for you and Lorinda." He settled onto a chair, gently cradling the boy. "Have a seat. You look tired."

She complied and heaved a relieved sigh. "I'm glad you were praying, Franklin. The birth was a little scary for both of us. But God was present, and everything worked out all right. Of course, if the doctor had come with you, he would have been too late for the birth anyway."

They sat in silence for a few minutes while Franklin tried to formulate the words he wanted to say. "You've known me all my life, and I've really depended on you since I lost my parents."

She nodded, interest sparking in her eyes.

"While I've been holding this baby, I've been mulling over an idea, and I'd like your opinion about it." That sounded so stilted. He'd never had a problem talking to her before.

She perked up and smiled. "What kind of idea? I'm all ears."

He wondered how to say this without giving away too many of his thoughts. "I've always wanted children, especially a son. Someone to inherit this ranch. It's been in my family for two generations."

82

"Of course, you have."

He felt silly for mentioning that, because she already knew it. He'd told her before that he wanted an heir. But she didn't know he'd promised himself not to ever let a woman past his defenses again. He couldn't face the consequences if it didn't work out. Just thinking about it tied his stomach in knots.

"You know how hard it's been for me to trust anyone since Miriam and Marvin...disappointed me." The words were hard to force through his throat. On the way, each one tore a bloody path through his heart.

"I don't know what could have gotten into their heads to treat you so badly." She frowned, tsked, and shook her head.

"That's neither here nor there, but they're both out of my life. And I'm glad." He glanced down at the sleeping baby—so trusting, depending on him. "Since that time, I've shied away from any woman who set her cap for me... Also from mothers looking for husbands for their daughters."

"I noticed that." She laughed. "I think everyone has. And plenty of them have flocked around you at church and socials anyway."

"That's why I try to spend most of my time at those things talking to other men."

This was harder to put into words than he thought it would be. He just wanted to clutch the baby in his arms and hush, but he had to get it all said before he chickened out. Thank goodness no one else was within hearing distance.

She quirked one eyebrow accompanied by a chuckle. "That you do."

"I look at this boy who lost his father even before he was born. Maybe we were made for each other." He stopped and his gaze wove over the tiny features. "Do you think Lorinda would ever consider marrying me if I asked her?"

Surprise raised her eyebrows before she answered. "I know she has settled comfortably here. And I don't think she's in a hurry to leave." A smile spread across Mrs. Oleson's face. "I think it's a great idea. I've mentioned plenty of times to you that I don't like you being alone."

"Yes, you have."

The baby opened his eyes and started to fuss.

"Here, let me take him to his mother." She gently lifted him from Franklin's arms.

They felt so empty and cold with the child gone. Reluctant to let him go, he thrust his hands into his front pockets.

She headed toward the doorway, but stopped and turned back. "I think you should wait a while before you say anything to her. She needs to recover from childbirth without having serious things to think about. She'll want to spend most of the next few days alone with her son."

Too bad Lorinda didn't have a husband to share all of this with. He was sure that's what every woman wanted when she had her children. Things would've been different if Mike Sullivan had lived.

Mrs. Oleson hesitated. "Maybe you should go with me. You can hold the baby outside in the hallway while I check on her."

Once more, he held the tiny boy against his chest. The pain of his own loss speared through him. Maybe he and Lorinda could settle on a way to help each other, with neither of them getting hurt again.

He certainly hoped so.

～

*L*orinda awoke from a dreamy state where so many things mingled together without making any sense. Pain, loss, a baby's cry, then silence, Ingrid's soothing voice. She realized she was sore all over her body from the birth of her son.

Silence?

Why was everything so quiet? She definitely remembered her son's first tiny cry, then the loud wailing that caused her mother-heart to leap within her. But at that time, everything connected with the birth wasn't over, and now the house was so still. Nothing but the cool breeze ruffling the curtains.

Lorinda remembered Ingrid cooing to her son to comfort him, then thrusting him out the door to someone before she came back to finish looking after her own needs. Where was her son, and why didn't she hear him crying? *Please, God, don't let anything happen to my baby. He's all I have now.*

What if she lost him as well as his father? *I don't think I'd ever recover from another loss so soon.* Was she destined to lose everyone she loved? Mother...Mike...her unnamed son. She wouldn't want to go on living if he was gone, too.

The door to her bed chamber opened, letting in a sliver of light from the hallway. She didn't even know what time of the day or night it was. She had gone into labor in the evening. Was it still nighttime?

Ingrid peeked around the door and smiled. "You're awake. How do you feel?"

Her sweet tone brought a semblance of comfort to Lorinda. Would Ingrid sound calm if something had gone wrong?

"My throat's dry...and I'm sore." She tried to lean up on her elbows, but quickly settled back against the comfortable bed.

"Of course, you are." When the housekeeper opened the door all the way, she carried in a pitcher and clean glass. "I thought you might be wanting this."

She poured some of the fresh water into the glass before setting the pitcher on the washstand on the other side of the room. Swiftly, she crossed to the bed and slid her arm beneath Lorinda's shoulders. Carefully tipping the glass, Ingrid helped her sip the cool liquid. After a few swallows, Lorinda pulled back.

"Do you want to see your son?"

"Yes, I do." The words rushed out of her.

Ingrid went to the door again. "Franklin, you can bring him in."

Immediately, Lorinda touched her hair. It must look like a rat's nest. The baby wouldn't mind, and she shouldn't care what Mr. Vine thought about how she looked...but she did.

The tall, muscular man stepped into the room, filling more than his share of the space. Something about his strength made her feel so weak and inadequate. And he cradled her son in his arms. An arresting sight. It almost took her breath away. For a moment, she wondered if Mike would have been as tender with him.

Her baby would never have a father to hold him, but if he did, she would hope he was a man like Franklin Vine. In the short time she had been here, she'd discovered him to be a good, upstanding man who could be trusted. Something that had been sadly lacking from most of her life...until Mike came into it.

"You have a fine son, Lorinda."

The way her name rolled off his tongue caused a catch in her throat. She wondered why the man had started calling her by her first name.

"Thank you...Franklin." Hearing his name come from her own mouth was even more strange. It would take her a while to get used to saying it.

When he gently laid her baby into her arms, his hands brushed against her. The first time they'd touched since he'd helped her down from Major and carried her into his house. Today, his touch felt different somehow.

He straightened up and looked back down at her, but his gaze didn't land on her face, or the hair she had worried about. He studied her son. "Get some rest. I'll be seeing you later."

After uttering those words, he exited the room, relieving some of the pressure from the space. She could breathe easier.

Ingrid bustled around, taking care of her and her son.

86

Finally, she stopped and stared down at the baby. "Do you have a name picked out for him, Lorinda?"

"Not really." She studied her son. Everything about him looked perfect. His fluffy almost-white hair, his tiny lips, the dark blue eyes. "Maybe I should name him after his daddy. Mike's name was really Michael, but he always went by Mike. I'd like to name him Michael and call him that as well." Calling him Mike would hurt too much.

Ingrid leaned down to kiss his soft cheek before heading out the door. "Just holler if you need anything. I'll be close-by."

Lorinda's son opened his eyes and looked straight into her face. "Michael Sullivan, your mother loves you with all her heart."

Tears came with the words, and she let them roll unchecked down her cheeks. For some reason, her emotions seemed to be going crazy. She wondered if that was usual after having a baby. So many things she didn't know. With Ingrid's help, she had learned a lot since she'd lived on the Rocking V Ranch, but she was always finding other things she had never heard about. She got tired of constantly asking questions that other women evidently already knew.

Lorinda liked it here, and she wondered what would happen to her and her son when she was able to be up and about again. She realized Mrs. Oleson had been making busy work for her. Yes, she'd learned how to do a lot of things she hadn't known before she came, but the housekeeper had been taking care of this ranch house by herself for a long time before Lorinda got here. The older woman would do just fine when she and her son left. A pain sliced through her heart at that thought, probably because she didn't want to leave Ingrid.

How soon would she have to leave? And what could she do? She knew how to keep a house...and sew, but who would pay her to do that? Perhaps she could open a dressmaking business, but where would she get the money to start such a thing? Yes, she had the gold Mike gave her, but she didn't want to use any of that if she could keep from it. She and baby Michael might need the money later.

She had saved all of the salary Franklin had paid her, too, but that money wouldn't carry them far. The future lay in front of her like an unknown road, completely hidden in shadows. Dare she try to follow where it led her?

Right now she didn't want to think about going anywhere else. This place felt so much like home.

CHAPTER 11

One month old. Michael was thriving, and he was Lorinda's whole life.

After nursing him, she held him against her shoulder to help him expel air from his tummy before cradling him in her arms. As she looked down at his precious face, his gaze found hers and stayed there. She loved these times when they connected and stared at each other. Their kinship was so strong, the strongest one she'd ever known. Even more so than the one she and his father had shared. With her son, she could be herself completely. He totally accepted everything about her. The feeling empowered her somehow. Too bad that feeling went away when she was around other people.

"You are so precious." She leaned to plant a kiss on his soft cheek.

His mouth worked around a little, and he uttered a soft coo. His eyes widened as if he were as surprised as she was at the new sound. Lorinda smiled as she reveled in the music from her son's heart.

"Nothing is sweeter than that." Ingrid's soft voice invaded Lorinda's thoughts. "He's really growing, isn't he?"

She hadn't noticed her friend come into the parlor. Ingrid bustled around the room straightening things that looked just fine to Lorinda. It must have been wonderful living in places that were always clean and neat. She forced the memories that started to creep into her thoughts back into the trunk deep in her mind. She mentally turned the key to lock them away. Maybe someday, the uncomfortable memories would disappear altogether.

"I can put him in his bassinet. I think he'd like to watch what we are doing. I'm sure it's time to start fixing supper." Lorinda stood, being careful not to jostle her son.

She really didn't want him to spit up on her. She didn't have enough clothes to change several times a day, and she didn't like the sour smell it left on her.

"Spending time with your baby is important, too." Ingrid picked up the newspaper Franklin had been reading the night before and folded it. "I'll just drop this off in his office."

Lorinda took Michael into the kitchen and laid him in the basket-like bed they had set close to where the women did the cooking. He spent the nights in the cradle in her bedroom, but most of the time in the kitchen, he was awake. She loved watching him kick and look all around while she helped prepare the meals. Mrs. Oleson had tied some colorfully painted wooden rings to the handle of the basket with yarn just long enough that his fingers could bat at them. The swinging movement captured his attention.

"I thought we could have fried chicken tonight. It's one of Franklin's favorites. I put the dressed one Stella brought by this morning in the spring house." Ingrid donned an apron that covered much of the front of her dress. "I'll let you make the mashed potatoes, and I'll take care of the chicken."

Lorinda leaned over and placed another kiss on Michael's cheek. "Want me to get a jar of green beans from the cellar?"

"Bring two, and I'll make the biscuits." Ingrid reached for the canister that contained flour.

Lorinda glanced out the window. Today was such a beautiful day. A few cottony clouds floated overhead, and three hawks whirled around gracefully as if they were playing chase. They looked so carefree. She wished she were. Flying away on the wind sounded wonderful, but so many things tied her to this place ... not just her son.

She really didn't feel she was doing her share of the work. Having her and her son in the household added more to the busy schedule, and the things she'd been doing couldn't make up for the extra stress. If something didn't change, she might have to leave and find another place to work. To relieve the burden on Mrs. Oleson, if for no other reason. But deep in her heart, she didn't really want to go. The ranch had been a sanctuary for her when she needed it most. Here she was creating happy memories that could someday force out all the dark ones. Humming a snatch of a hymn they had sung at church on Sunday, she felt carefree and alive for those few minutes. More than she had since losing Mike.

When she arrived back in the kitchen, Ingrid had picked up Michael and held him close to her heart. Lorinda enjoyed the sight. The older woman looked like a grandmother. The only grandmother her son would ever know. One more reason she didn't want to leave, but she couldn't add to this wonderful woman's workload.

"He really likes you, Ingrid." Lorinda had no memory of a grandmother in her own life. Could she deny her son the presence of one?

Her friend grinned. "And I really like him, too. I love his clean baby smell." She buried her nose against his neck and sniffed, then pressed a soft kiss there.

After opening the beans, Lorinda dumped them in a pot and

set it on the stove. "I'm glad to see you taking some time to relax." She glanced toward Ingrid.

"Oh, I relax quite often. More now than I ever did before." Ingrid slipped into another chair at the table and gently rocked Michael. Slowly his eyes drifted closed. "I think he's going to nap. I'll put him down and start supper."

Both women worked a few minutes in silence. Finally, Lorinda had the beans seasoned just right. "You know, sometimes I feel I'm not really doing my share of the work. You've been going too easy on me."

Ingrid turned toward her. "What are you talking about?"

"I'm not helping enough around here. I'm just adding to your already heavy workload." Lorinda stirred the beans again. "If I'm not doing my part, I might need to find somewhere else to stay...and a new job."

A frown snatched the twinkle from the housekeeper's eyes, and deep wrinkles grooved her forehead. "I would hate to see you go. Just having you here has made a big difference in my life. And both Franklin and I enjoy having this baby around." She nodded toward the bassinet. "If you want me to give you more to do, I'll find other jobs for you. I'd hate to face the long winter without you here, and I'd be worried about you and the baby if you left."

Lorinda hadn't even considered that possibility. "All right. I'd like to stay if I'm really a help."

Why had she brought this up? Yes, she felt as if she wasn't being productive enough, but she hadn't wanted to upset Ingrid. The other woman was right about the long winter. Visions of the solitude she experienced for six months in the mountain cabin circled like vultures in her mind. The deep ache of the remembered loneliness almost took her breath away. Of course, Ingrid wasn't truly as alone as she had been in that log house.

"Having a woman to talk to and work on projects with will

make the winter so much easier." Ingrid's smile dismissed Lorinda's idea to move on.

All she could do was nod. Relief rose within her. She knew she'd probably eat better if she stayed here, and her son needed her for his nourishment. If only she could settle her mind about the future.

The back door to the mudroom opened with a squeak. Lorinda glanced at the kitchen clock. "It's a little early for Franklin to be finished with his work, isn't it?"

Releasing an enticing aroma, Ingrid turned the piece of chicken she had picked up with her fork and replaced it in the pan of bubbling grease. "He has been coming in a little earlier each day this week."

Lorinda heard one of his boots drop to the floor with a thud. He was the first man she'd ever known who took off his boots in a mudroom at the end of a work day. That sure made keeping a clean house easier.

"Do I smell my favorite meal?" Franklin walked straight to the bassinet, and Lorinda realized he'd done that a lot lately. Even before he checked out what was on the stove.

Lorinda couldn't help watching him as he looked at her son with a gleam of love in his eyes. The warmth that brought to her heart crept up to her cheeks. She hoped neither he nor Ingrid would notice. Maybe they'd just think her face was flushed from the heat of cooking.

Ingrid laughed. "Yes, fried chicken, mashed potatoes and gravy, green beans, and hot biscuits. And I think I saw a dried peach pie around here somewhere."

Lorinda smiled. She loved the way laughter was such an integral part of the lives of those living in this house.

"How's the little guy doing today?" Franklin leaned closer to the basket and stared intently at her son. "I believe he's waking up."

Lorinda's gaze followed his, and sure enough, Michael stirred. Maybe he'd heard the masculine tone. Those words brought a pleasant rumble to the room.

Franklin glanced at her. "I'll pick him up, since you and Mrs. Oleson are busy with dinner."

She nodded, and his large hands grasped her son with care. Tears threatened in her eyes. She'd never seen a man so gentle with a baby. She wondered if Mike would've been like that. Mike had shown no interest in any child they encountered, infant or older.

"Hey, there." Franklin held Michael level with his face while supporting his neck and holding his head up. "Did you have a good day, little guy?"

Once again, Michael emitted the soft coo.

The smile that spread across Franklin's often-solemn face lit the room like sunshine coming over the mountain pass. He pulled the infant close and settled him in the crook of his arm before glancing at each of the women. "Did you hear that?"

Mrs. Oleson wiped her hands on her apron. "That's the second time today. It's so sweet."

"Yes, it is." Once again, Franklin turned his attention toward her son.

All Lorinda could do was stare at the two of them. Her heart was so full of emotions she really didn't understand. She knew she loved her son, but something else resided there as well. She shook her head and turned back toward the beans, while her thoughts wandered far afield.

~

*T*onight's the night.

After the wonderful meal, Franklin had retired to his office to go over the accounts, but he hadn't been able to concentrate. He needed to talk to Lorinda. If he didn't, he'd never get anything done.

Having an heir was important, but now he didn't want just any child. He wanted this particular baby. He had fallen in love with little Michael, and he couldn't imagine losing him. He couldn't love him more if he'd been his own flesh and blood.

When Michael was born, he loved him from the first moment he saw that little face. He didn't realize it at the time, but he did now. And he was going to do whatever it took to keep the child here.

What about Lorinda? The nagging question wouldn't let him go. She came in the package deal, and he almost wished she didn't. But that was unrealistic. He had to find a way to convince her to marry him. Since she'd loved her husband, she probably wouldn't be ready to love another man, and that was just fine with Franklin. Love could not be a part of the equation, now or ever.

He knew marriages of convenience often worked out well. He'd heard stories from several of the ranchers that lived close-by. He wanted no emotional ties to any woman who had the ability to rip his heart out and stomp on it. But he could pour all his love on their son. Surely that would keep her happy.

"Did you want to talk to me, Franklin?" As if she stepped right out of his thoughts, Lorinda came through his open office doorway.

"Where's Michael?" When he voiced his question, a strange expression flitted across her face. Maybe he'd been too abrupt.

"Mrs. Oleson wanted to play with him, so I thought this would be a good time to come see what you wanted. She said it wasn't anything urgent." Lorinda continued to stand close to the door, as if ready to take flight.

Franklin got up from behind his desk and escorted her to the leather-covered couch near the fireplace. "Let's sit down."

She sat at one end of the sofa, and he took the far end,

leaving plenty of space between them. He didn't want to crowd her. She might think he was trying to force his will on her.

He glanced at her face. She kept her eyes trained on her lap where her hands moved about, picking at possible lint on her dark skirt. Not that he could see anything wrong with it. Maybe she was nervous. He should set her mind at ease.

"Do you enjoy working here, Lorinda?" He kept his tone gentle, but restrained himself from allowing any emotional undertones to his question. He didn't want her to jump to the wrong conclusion.

Finally, she raised her head and looked at him. "I really like the ranch and being with Mrs. Oleson. She's helped me learn a lot."

Good. She must not want to go away. That gave him hope. "I enjoy having Michael around."

Now hope lit her eyes. "I was afraid adding a baby to your household might have been a bother."

"Quite the contrary. He brightens my day, and I think the little guy likes me as well." He couldn't keep his lips from forming a smile at that thought.

"I'm sure he does. He reacts to the sound of your voice."

He wasn't sure what was the best way to approach the subject. He'd always been direct, so maybe that would work best here as well.

He leaned forward with his forearms on his thighs, clasping his hands between his knees. "I want to tell you something about me."

"All right." Finally, her fingers stilled, but a wary expression still lingered in her eyes.

"Because of circumstances that happened at a critical time in my life, I never planned to marry. But I have a large ranch that has been in my family for a long time." Somehow, he couldn't look at her face while he poured out as much of his heart as he dared. "I really need an heir."

He lifted his eyes toward her face and saw her grimace. She raised her hand as if she wanted to interrupt.

"Please...let me finish before you say anything."

She nodded, dropped her hands into her lap, and stared at him while he continued.

"You need a new start, and it'll be hard trying to build a life and make a living with a baby to care for. I think I have a solution to both our problems."

She sat straight, lifted an eyebrow, and looked doubtful, but she still didn't comment.

"You and I could marry." The words sounded so stark and bare, even to his own ears. He hid his cringe.

"N–"

"Let me finish before you say no. This would be almost a business arrangement, but so much more. I'm not looking for love, or even a...physical relationship."

She sank back against the cushions and waited, her gaze skimming around him but never lighting on his face.

He couldn't sit still, so he arose and started pacing. "You would be my wife in every other way. You wouldn't have to worry about the future. You'd be respected as my wife and protected by me. And your son would become ours...and my heir."

She sat there so long he decided she wasn't going to comment at all. He stopped and glanced at her. The waiting was excruciating. The expression on her face a bland mask. Perhaps he'd bungled any chance he might've had to get her to agree.

"Mr....uh, Franklin, I really don't know what to say... Before I make a decision, I'll need to consider all aspects of the situation. Can you give me that time?"

"Of course, I can. How long do you think it will take?" He hated the hint of desperation in his tone.

"I'm not sure, but I'll let you know when I've come to a decision." She arose and regally walked out the door without even glancing back.

She carried the best chance for his future with her, and he wasn't a patient man. But what could he do but await her answer? He didn't want this opportunity to slip through his fingers.

He might never have another.

or the first time since Michael was born, Lorinda couldn't keep her attention on her son while she nursed him and got him ready for bed. The startling conversation she'd had with Franklin wouldn't let her thoughts settle. His idea had a lot of merit, and she wanted to know her future would be secure without constantly worrying about the unknown.

After that thought took hold of her mind, her heart lurched within her. How could she even consider such a thing? She didn't know if she'd ever be ready for another man to take Mike's place in her life. Not being under male domination had freed her to begin to learn just who she was. Ingrid was teaching her so much she needed to know to become completely independent. That was a heady thought. *Completely independent.* Would it ever really happen?

More than that, why had Franklin been so vague about the reasons he didn't want to marry? A handsome man like him, who wasn't afraid to express his love to her son, wouldn't be satisfied in a marriage relationship without love. What if she agreed with him and they went through with the wedding, then a woman he could love came into his life? Both of them would be trapped in a prison of their own making. Then what would happen to her sense of security?

Although Lorinda hadn't ever thought about marrying again, somewhere in the back of her mind, she knew she would want more of a family...at some time. A man could come into her life as well and fill that need inside her.

Besides, what was wrong with her that Franklin wouldn't even consider her worthy of his love? His rejecting the idea of a physical relationship in any marriage they would enter hurt her...but not as much as her father's continued abuse had. This pain was on a totally different level. In her marriage with Mike, she had moved beyond the feeling of being useless instilled in her by her father. But the internal scars remained.

Franklin was kindness itself, offering her a home and protection when these were just what she lacked. Could she really turn her back on what might be her only chance to have both? What if no other man ever came into her life who would accept her need to be somewhat independent?

As she rocked Michael, his eyelids drooped and finally settled shut. Maybe she'd have to pour all her love into her son and forget about a man ever wanting to love her. She'd spent plenty of her life without comfort and security, and she never wanted to go back to that dark, scary place. Her son must never know the kind of life she'd endured at her father's hand.

Marriage to Franklin, even this kind of sham marriage, would be better than living a lonely existence the rest of her life. Maybe in time, they could establish a mutually beneficial relationship within his boundaries...and maybe, pigs really could fly.

She laid Michael in his cradle. When he started to stir, she gently patted his back until he settled back to sleep.

After dressing in her dimity night dress and plaiting her hair into a loose braid, Lorinda blew out the lamp and got into bed.

She turned onto her side and closed her eyes. Thoughts marched through her head, their pounding keeping her from slumber.

She flipped over to her other side and scrunched the pillow up under her neck and head. Swooshing out a deep breath, she willed her body to relax. In only a few moments, every muscle tensed once again. No matter what she tried, sleep eluded her.

Finally, she arose and paced across the moonbeams bathing the room with soft, silvery light. She stopped to gaze at Michael sleeping peacefully. Oh, to be able to forget everything like an infant and just sink into rest.

Maybe she was going about all this the wrong way. She lit the lamp, picked up her Bible, and sat in the wooden rocking chair with the padded seat.

"Father God, you've brought me to this house of safety." She whispered the words so she wouldn't wake her son, but she liked talking to God as if he were in the room with her. She'd formed that habit during those lonely months in the cabin. "I don't know what to do. Please show me something in Your word that will lead me. I know Your word is a lamp to my feet and a light to my path, and I need a lot of light right now."

Lorinda opened the book and read a few passages. She poured out her heart to God, telling Him what she wanted and that she would listen to anything He revealed to her spirit. Her supplication must have taken quite a while because when she finished, the path of the moonlight had moved most of the way to the other side of the bed chamber.

She sat in wakeful silence for another period of time that stretched until the first blush of dawn barely touched the eastern sky outlining the mountain peaks in gold. Peace drifted on her like gentle snowflakes, but warming her inside instead of bringing the cold. She folded her hands on the open pages of her Bible and just basked in the peace.

Finally, she knew what she was supposed to do. She didn't

understand why God wanted her to accept Franklin's strange proposal, but she wanted to be obedient to God the way the women she'd read about in the Bible were. She wasn't sure how she would find the courage to step out in faith, but she knew she soon needed to let Franklin know.

~

*A*fter a long day out on the range, Franklin stood beside the washstand in his bedroom, circling his shaving brush in the cup with soap to work up enough lather. He'd started removing his whiskers in the evening so he could come to the table clean and well-shaven. He hoped Lorinda would notice the care he was taking with his appearance while in the house. Maybe it would help her make a decision in his favor.

Two whole days. Franklin wondered how much longer he'd have to wait for her to give him an answer. At least, he'd been busy enough during the daytime to take his mind off his proposal, if he could call it that. He and Thomas had ridden out to each of his pasturing areas to check on the divided herd and the cowboys wrangling them. Thank the good Lord, he would be able to send several railcars full of cattle to market in Chicago. He wanted them to feed on the tall mountain grasses for at least another month, maybe two, before they would drive them to Frisco in the next valley.

Both days, he'd come home near suppertime. After he left his boots in the mudroom, he'd gone through the kitchen on the way to clean up. He took time to talk to the infant he hoped to claim as his son and surreptitiously watched the boy's mother.

Lorinda smiled often, and she looked a little different. Kind of peaceful. But she never said a word about his idea.

He was not a patient man. If she didn't talk to him soon, he might have to do a circuit of the line shacks to make sure they were in good shape before winter. Never knew when someone might need to shelter during a storm. Sometimes, it was one of his hands. Sometimes, a stranger. That was part of the code of the west. To provide and help those in need. Give him something to do until she made up her mind. To keep himself from going crazy. Maybe if he weren't here for a day or two, Lorinda would miss his presence enough to come up with an affirmative answer.

He finished scraping the last of the shaving soap off his neck and glanced in the mirror. Lifting the small towel from the warm water in his wash bowl, he squeezed out the excess water before he patted his face, then wiped the last vestiges of lather from his cheeks and neck. He opened his bottle of Bay Rum Oil and poured a little in the palm of his hand, then gently rubbed this lotion on his face to heal any nicks. The fragrance of the product was light and pleasant, making him feel even fresher. He hoped someday Lorinda would get close enough to catch a whiff and enjoy it.

What am I thinking? He didn't need any emotional entanglements, but smelling nice would be a good thing even in a marriage of convenience. He'd decided he'd never marry, especially not a marriage of convenience. When had the idea ceased to be abhorrent? He glanced in the looking glass attached to the wall above his washstand. The face that stared back at him almost a stranger. He shook his head and went into the hallway.

When he stepped into the kitchen again, Lorinda was helping Mrs. Oleson get the food on the table. She was doing everything one-handed. Michael squirmed in her other arm.

"Here, let me help." As he reached for the baby, Lorinda glanced at him, a smile barely tilting the corners of her lips.

"Thank you, Franklin." She turned back toward the cupboard and lifted down the plates. Almost as if she couldn't get away from him fast enough. Or was she ignoring him?

While he played with the boy, the women quickly finished loading the table with a bounty of food. He loved this child.

Although he would never try to keep Michael from knowing about the man who sired him, he wanted to fill the role of father in the boy's life.

"I'm going to have to take Michael and change him. And he's probably hungry." Lorinda took her son back from him. "The two of you can go ahead and eat. I'll be back as soon as I can."

He watched her walk into the hallway, and he immediately missed her. He glanced toward his housekeeper. "Something smells wonderful."

"Lorinda cooked the pot roast today." She sat down in her usual chair. "I've been enjoying the aroma for several hours. It's nice to have something to eat I didn't cook."

Franklin sat in the opposite chair. "You like having her here, don't you?"

"I've told you that before." Mrs. Oleson put some roast on her plate and added potatoes and carrots beside it. "I'd hate to think of her leaving us."

"Me, too." He quickly took the dish she passed his way and heaped the delicious food onto his plate, hoping Mrs. Oleson didn't notice the flush heating his face.

The door to the hall was on his left. While he and Mrs. Oleson ate and carried on a sporadic conversation, his eyes kept drifting toward the open doorway. He couldn't remember it taking Lorinda so long to change and feed her baby. Maybe she was dawdling over the whole process because she didn't want to face him yet. Was she going to tell him she wasn't interested in his idea? A shaft of uneasiness pierced his heart. *The best-laid plans...*

Being the owner of the ranch and the boss to many people who worked for him, if he wanted anything, all he had to do was tell them, and it was the same as done. No questions. Now a little slip of a woman had him tied in knots. Was he selfish to want his way in this situation? He didn't think so. Both of them, actually all three of them, would benefit from an agreement from her. Why couldn't she see that? What was holding her back?

Halfway through the food on his plate, his throat almost closed. He might not be able to swallow another bite. He laid his fork on the edge of his plate.

"Is something the matter, Franklin?" Concern shouted through Mrs. Oleson's tone.

"Of course not. I'm just taking a breather." That sounded stupid even to his own ears.

His housekeeper arose from her chair. "Do you need more coffee?" She headed toward the coffeepot sitting on the back of the stove.

"Sure." He moved his earthenware mug closer to her.

"Good. I wanted some, too." She filled both cups.

"I hope you saved some supper for me." Lorinda's voice drifted toward them from behind Mrs. Oleson.

Without thinking, Franklin let out a deep breath. Both women stared at him.

"Are you sure you're all right?" Mrs. Oleson set the pot back on the stove.

He nodded, then got up to pull out Lorinda's chair for her. Scooting her close to the table, he noticed how her presence completed the circle. He sat down again. His hunger returned, and he reached for a biscuit, taking the time to smear softened butter on it. "Just wanting another of these delicious biscuits."

"You'll have to thank Lorinda for them. She cooked all of supper."

"Everything is delicious. Thank you." He glanced at Lorinda just as a rosy glow made its way up across her cheeks.

He smiled at her. Maybe she wasn't used to receiving compliments.

For the rest of the meal, he enjoyed the light conversation. In his mind, they felt like a family already.

When she finished eating her serving of peach cobbler with

thick cream poured over it, Lorinda stood and started removing the empty dishes from the table. While she put the first load of dishes in the dry sink, she stood with her back to the two of them. "Franklin, I'd like to talk to you after I finish cleaning up the kitchen."

Maybe she was shy about what she had to say, since she never looked at him when she said it.

"I'll be in the parlor, reading *Rocky Mountain News* that came in the mail from Denver today." He pushed back from the table.

"Oh, go on, you two." Mrs. Oleson gathered more of the dirty dishes.

Lorinda turned and opened her mouth as if to disagree.

"I'll clean up the kitchen, since you cooked everything."

Lorinda stared at his housekeeper for a moment before she gave a quick nod. He wished he could tell what she was thinking. Would she agree with his proposal? He wasn't really sure which thing he wanted more. He was afraid she would agree to stay. Actually, he was afraid she wouldn't, and if she left, not only would she take the boy, but he would miss having her here...to help Mrs. Oleson.

She headed out the door, and Franklin followed. His heart leapt. She didn't look upset or angry. Maybe...just maybe, she would agree with his plan.

She stood by the front window when he got to the parlor. After staring outside for a moment, she took a deep breath and turned toward him.

Clasping her hands, she let her gaze rove over the room where she'd spent so much of the time since she'd been in his home. But she never looked straight at him.

The dancing flames of the lamps and lighted candles shot glimmers of gold through her upswept hair. A few stray wisps lay gently against her neck. He wondered if they were as soft as they looked.

He needed to change his focus. His gaze roved the room

trying to find something to concentrate on but was drawn back to Lorinda.

"Your proposal surprised me, Franklin. I had never considered such a thing before." Finally, she looked straight at him. "Are you sure this is what you want to do?"

He stuffed his hands in his back trouser pockets. "I am."

"What if circumstances change?" She seemed to be holding her breath.

"I won't enter into marriage lightly. When I make a vow, I stand by it." He hoped that was what she needed to hear.

Lorinda wrung her hands, braiding the fingers together. "I can think of all kinds of things that could affect this relationship."

"When a man and a woman enter a marriage filled with love for each other, they have no real guarantees either, except their vows to remain faithful." He tried to read the depths of her eyes, but couldn't. "We'll be no different from any of them."

She took a step toward him. "I want my son to be raised in a happy home."

"That's exactly what I want for him, too." He pulled his hands free and crossed his arms over his chest.

Lorinda stood for a moment, not saying another word. Without taking her eyes from his, she finally whispered, "If you're really sure, I'm willing to follow through with this." She dropped onto the sofa as if her legs couldn't hold her a moment longer.

What should he do now? A momentary feeling of missing something essential rushed through him.

Franklin sat beside her, but not close enough to crowd her. He felt as if his throat was stuffed with cotton, and a lump rested in his chest.

After a discreet cough, he cleared his throat. "I'd rather no one else know the true nature of our relationship. I don't want any questions about our intentions. And I believe everyone will respect you more as my wife if they don't know the circumstances. It's enough they know we're getting married. And they need to see us as a family of three."

Franklin didn't know what to do now. If it had been any other kind of proposal, he'd be kissing her rosy lips, but he couldn't let himself think about that. "How...how soon can we have the wedding?"

Her eyebrows rose, and she turned her questioning gaze toward him. "I don't know."

"Our friends at church will want to be a part...of the celebration." He rubbed his sweaty palms down his denim trousers. "This is mid-May. I'll need to round up the cattle in September. How about October? That way you can plan whatever kind of wedding you want."

He felt as if he were babbling, and he was usually a man of few words.

All she did was nod.

Joy filled him because soon he would have a son and heir. *And even a wife.*

Suddenly, everything felt off kilter.

CHAPTER 13

*L*orinda didn't know what to expect after her announcement, but somehow everything felt off kilter.

Franklin just stood there after he suggested the time for the wedding. At first, a slight smile barely tilted the sides of his mouth. She took a deep breath and slowly let it out. He really wasn't looking at her, but something must be making him happy.

Then like a curtain falling across the window blocking out the sunlight, a confused expression descended over his face. She glanced around, wondering what she should do now. Leave the room? Or stay? She clasped her hands in front of her waist and realized she still wore the thin gold band Mike had placed on her finger at their wedding. As unobtrusively as possible, she slipped it off and slid it into the pocket sewn into the side seam of her skirt. When she got back to her bedchamber, she'd find a safe place to put it. For a moment, she felt as if she had torn her heart from its moorings inside her chest. The ache was real as it took her breath away. Michael would still keep her tied to her first husband, but soon her second husband would become his father...and her a wife in name only.

She sensed, rather than saw, Franklin turn toward her.

He clasped her free hand. "Let's go share our good news with Mrs. Oleson."

Lorinda almost missed the words. Franklin had never touched her since she'd recovered from having her son, except for inadvertent brushing of fingers when they passed Michael from one to the other. The newness of the strong connection of his touch raised all kinds of questions inside her. Questions she didn't want to consider. But she couldn't prevent the shiver that skittered up her stiff spine. She felt as if her body were betraying her husband's memory. But that would soon change. She'd have a new husband...and yet not really. A sigh escaped, and she trembled even more.

"Are you too cool in here?" More than friendly concern accompanied his words, but she didn't know what.

"No...I'm fine." She barely forced the words through her tense lips.

He accompanied her out the door and down the short hallway. Mrs. Oleson, who was busy working on cleaning up the kitchen, turned to glance at them. Then her gaze dropped to their clasped hands. A question quirked one eyebrow.

Lorinda peeked up at the tall rancher just as he gazed down at her. A broad smile lit his face like a lantern and twinkled in his eyes. She'd never seen him smile like that before. The sight stole her voice.

Mrs. Oleson rested her closed hands on her hips. "Is everything all right?"

Franklin escorted Lorinda into the warmly-lit kitchen. "Yes...we have something to tell you."

The older woman pulled out a chair and sighed as she dropped into it. "I hope it's good news."

At her comment, Lorinda realized she was probably frowning while Franklin smiled.

He looked down at her once again. "I think so, don't you, Lorinda?"

She nodded with as warm a smile as she could manage. She expected him to go ahead and tell Mrs. Oleson what had happened, but after the silence lengthened uncomfortably, Lorinda cleared her throat and blurted, "Franklin asked me...to become his wife."

"That's wonderful!" Mrs. Oleson jumped up with amazing energy for a woman her age. "I'm so glad you'll..." She paused and gave Lorinda an intense stare. "Did you accept his proposal?"

Lorinda nodded, and the smile returned to her older friend's face.

"I didn't want you to leave. And we've all come to love your little one. Now we'll all be a happy family."

Mrs. Oleson didn't seem to expect an answer, and Lorinda was glad. She wasn't so sure about the "happy" part. Franklin would be, and Mrs. Oleson. Probably even Michael. But Lorinda wasn't expecting a happy life. Security for herself and her son, yes...also, protection. Wasn't that more important than her own happiness?

"Well now, we need to celebrate. Sit down and have another cup of coffee and some of that chocolate cake from yesterday." Mrs. Oleson bustled about getting the food on the table while she plied them with questions.

When Lorinda hesitated, Franklin started answering them. She followed bits and pieces of the conversation. "September...wedding...dress..." other details she didn't catch.

Was she being a fraud, because she wasn't looking forward to a real marriage? Was what they were doing lying? Wasn't lying a sin?

The only book Lorinda had during the long winter alone in the cabin was her mother's Bible. She'd always kept it near her, because it was the only possession she owned that belonged to her mother. She longed for the peace Jesus brought to the lives of other people in the book. So she'd knelt beside the bed she and Mike had shared and told Jesus she wanted Him in her life. Somehow she knew a peace and assurance that things would be all right. She still had a relationship with the Lord, but she doubted that everything would be completely right for her ever again.

Never having been around other church people until coming here to live, she wasn't exactly sure what all would be considered a sin. She knew that bearing false witness was lying and a sin. But could living the way Franklin wanted be considered lying? She was going to have to spend a lot of time with the Lord until He could help her understand. He'd given her a peace about accepting Franklin's proposal. Surely, He could help her find the answers to this dilemma.

"Isn't that right, Lorinda?"

She blinked, wondering what Franklin was asking her. "I'm sorry. I was distracted."

"I was just telling Mrs. Oleson we know that our friends at church would want to be a part of our wedding celebration." He shot an indulgent smile her way.

Where was that coming from? He almost looked as if he actually cared for her. Too bad it wasn't true.

"Yes, I know they will. After all, they've been so helpful to me ever since I came to live with you." But would they want to if they knew it was just a sham marriage? Her heart lurched within her chest, fearing she would never know love again. She hoped her son's love would be enough to last a lifetime.

"Franklin... " Mrs. Oleson's brows drew together as if she were entertaining deep thoughts. "I'm not sure why you're waiting until September to get married. It's not unusual for a man or woman who has been widowed to marry quickly. Besides, it's been plenty long since Mike's death. Why wait?"

Deep red seeped up from Franklin's collar, almost reaching

his strong chin. Lorinda wondered why. Did he feel as flustered as she did?

He rubbed the back of his neck. "I thought...women needed time to plan...all those things a woman does for her wedding. Miriam did—" He stopped speaking, and his Adam's apple bobbed convulsively.

Who is Miriam? Lorinda had never heard anyone mention her before. She didn't know if she should ask or not. The air in the room filled with tension, and she didn't know why.

Mrs. Oleson shook her head, surprise gleaming from her eyes. "This is a totally different situation."

Franklin shoved his hands into the back pockets of his denim trousers. "You're right. We don't really have to wait. Maybe getting married soon would be much better."

"What do you think, Lorinda?" Mrs. Oleson rose and stood beside her. "We could put together a nice wedding in a week or two."

A week or two? Suddenly, that was far too soon. The muscles in her stomach tightened, and the meal she had eaten began to jump around as if it might try to escape. She crossed her arms over her abdomen, trying to settle everything. Lorinda could not disagree without having to tell her friend why.

"We could get married in July." She didn't know where that idea came from. "I would like to do that." This time her voice sounded more forceful.

Franklin glanced toward the calendar on the wall. Lorinda wondered if he was looking at the portrait of the pretty woman at the top or at the months below. *What a silly thing to think about when my life is hanging in the balance.*

"You should have the ceremony after the church service on a Sunday. That way anyone who wants to can stay for the festivities, and they wouldn't need to make another trip into town for the wedding." Mrs. Oleson gave a satisfied smile. "People are very busy in the summer...with their cattle and crops and all."

Franklin tapped his finger on the months lined up below the picture, stopping on July. "There are five Sundays in July. Should we have the wedding on the 8th or 15th?"

Lorinda shrugged. Everything was moving too fast. Even the 22nd seemed far too soon. But if the wedding was going to happen, they might as well go ahead and have it as soon as possible. The dreading, or the anticipation, would then be over, and life could return to normal...or as normal as it would ever be again. Whatever that would look like after the wedding.

"Let's do it on the 15th. That's plenty of time to put together a really nice wedding." Mrs. Oleson started gathering the dishes from the table. "Who knows. Maybe you'll have a little brother or sister for Michael before long."

Red rushed up under Franklin's tan all the way to his hairline. At the same time, Lorinda felt the heat build in her own cheeks. A little brother or sister? *Not even a possibility.*

❧

Franklin was amazed at the way Mrs. Oleson gathered all the women together and started planning the wedding. Every time he came home, someone else was in the parlor with Lorinda and Mrs. Oleson. Today was no exception.

"We really need to decide on what you will wear, Dear." His housekeeper patted his intended bride on her knee.

Lorinda hadn't seemed like herself since Tuesday when she finally agreed to become his wife. He could tell something was wrong. He wished he knew what. Like any man, he'd do anything he could to make her comfortable and happy. He wasn't used to this feeling of helplessness that consumed him whenever he entered his own home.

"Can you tell us what your favorite color is, Lorinda?" Pastor Nelson's wife, Mary, smiled at his intended.

He knew he was an intruder, sitting there on the porch listening to the conversation inside, glad he had a good line of sight to what was happening. He wanted to see if he could find out what was affecting Lorinda. Maybe in the conversation between the women, she'd let a hint slip out. He just didn't know how to go about it any other way.

"I like lots of colors." Lorinda's voice didn't carry quite as well as the others. He had to strain to hear her. "Maybe I should wear blue."

He could picture her in a soft blue dress that would match the color of her eyes, with her blonde curls shining in the sunlight. She was a real beauty. At first after she came to stay with them, she kept that hidden. But as she felt more comfortable, she relaxed and revealed her inner and her outer beauty.

"I'm so glad the Fuller sisters came to town last year to open their side-by-side businesses. Millie is such a good seamstress." Mary Nelson took a handkerchief from her handbag and dabbed at the moisture on her forehead. July was really hot this year. "I heard she received a new shipment of watered silk last week. Perhaps we should take you into town, Lorinda, so you could pick out what fabric you like from her stock."

"Oh, I couldn't do that."

Mrs. Oleson nodded emphatically. "Of course, you can."

Maybe that's what was bothering Lorinda. She didn't have enough money to pay for her trousseau. Franklin stood and ambled toward the front door, making plenty of noise so the women would know he was coming.

The voices stilled as he opened the front screen door and let it fall shut behind him.

He stopped in the doorway to the parlor. "Mrs. Oleson, could I have a word with you in my study?"

"Of course." She quickly arose and followed him.

The two women left in the parlor started talking softly, but he couldn't understand a word they said.

"What can I do for you, Franklin?" His housekeeper waited for him to speak.

"I have to make a confession. I was on the porch and heard some of your conversation."

Her eyebrows rose before she gave a slight nod.

"I want to give you enough money to pay for Lorinda's dress...and maybe one of those hats the women like to wear. But I'm not sure I want my bride in one as elaborate as some of the women wear to church."

She chuckled. "I'm sure you don't. I know Flora could make a very becoming bonnet that won't overpower Lorinda's beauty."

He joined her laughter. "Wouldn't want that. Now how much do you think you need? And be generous about it."

"I don't want you to do this."

Mrs. Oleson had never countermanded any of the things he asked before.

"Why not? Lorinda deserves a lovely wedding day."

"Of course, she does." His longtime friend rubbed her hands down her skirt, as if her palms were perspiring.

He'd never seen her do that before. Something must be bothering her as well.

"Lorinda feels like the daughter I never had, Franklin. I want to buy her dress and hat. It will give me great pleasure to make her lovely for your wedding." A smile spread across her face, lighting up the room.

"I can understand that. I'll give you that privilege." He put his arm around her shoulders. "We'll want you to fill a void in Michael's life...as his grandmother."

Tears glistened in her eyes. "I will love that. He already feels like my grandchild."

Franklin watched her walk back toward the parlor, and an idea slipped into his mind. Mrs. Oleson was going to outfit Lorinda for the wedding, but he wanted to have a part in the wedding, too. Tomorrow, he would go into town and visit all three jewelry stores. He wanted something special to give her, . besides his mother's pearls.

Excitement and anticipation filled him. More than anything had since Miriam had broken his heart. Funny how he could think about his old fiancée's name now without the deep hurt crashing through him.

When had his pain started to ease?

CHAPTER 14

July 15, 1894

*L*orinda lay in bed waiting for her infant son to awaken. She loved watching everything he did, even sleep. The way his long eyelashes fanned across his cheeks. His tiny hands were a marvel to her, every detail etched by the hand of God. His mouth worked as if he were nursing, but still he slept. His every breath felt like the beat of her heart, because he was now the love of her life. Her son needed a father, someone to teach him how to be a man. If Mike had come home, he would do that, and he would love her at the same time.

Now Franklin would be the man, but she would not be included in the love between her son and the man she would wed today. At least, she and Michael would have their own loving connection. Her stomach twisted and turned with that thought, but her future was already planned, whether she wanted it or not.

Today is my wedding day.

When Mike rescued her from her abusive father in the dark of the night and whisked her to the home of the preacher in the next small town in Missouri, she didn't really know what a wedding was. She knew most of the people in their small town were married, but she'd never been to, or even heard of, a wedding.

Mike told her he wanted to marry her before they spent their first night together. They caught the preacher just before he was going to bed. He quickly read words from a small black book and asked the required questions. "To have and to hold...to love and to cherish..." She didn't know what that meant. Her mother had loved her until she died, but since then... Lorinda didn't even want to think about the horrible things her father and uncle did to her.

Lorinda wasn't even sure what all the preacher had said. But when he pronounced them "man and wife," Mike had kissed her in a deeper way than ever before, and her body and lips responded to him. For the first time, she had a glimpse of love she'd never known. Later that night, he "made her a woman," as he said. She hadn't known what to expect, and though in the beginning she felt pain, the ending was wonderful.

Now she was finally having a normal wedding. This time, with all the correct pageantry she'd never heard about in that preacher's small parlor with only one candle burning and his wife as witness in her nightgown and robe. But the new marriage would be a farce. Emptiness gnawed at her stomach and her heart at the bleak prospect.

The last two weeks, Ingrid, Stella Morgan, and Mary Nelson had helped gather and create clothing they called her *trousseau*— even silky and lacy unmentionables—chemises, drawers, night dresses, a robe, and a corset. She had never seen anything like them, and no one would ever know she wore them, so why bother? Of course, the women didn't know the circumstances of the relationship.

One of the books Mrs. Oleson had shared with her was *The Scarlet Letter.* She wanted to blurt out that they should embroider a scarlet letter on the unmentionables, because she would be living a lie. But she held her tongue to protect Franklin from gossip. Her feelings, and his lack of them, really couldn't matter.

After her first wedding, Mike had kept her warm, inside and out. She knew these new clothes and the sturdy roof over her head Franklin had offered would protect her from the Colorado cold, but they wouldn't do anything for her heart. Tears slowly trickled down her cheeks before she swiped them away.

~

*W*hile Franklin mucked out the stalls, his thoughts drifted to the day ahead. He had chosen to go along with the wedding hoping to make Lorinda happy, but over the last two weeks, she had become more and more distant. When he asked her what was wrong, she always answered, "Nothing."

He should have learned from the mess with Miriam that he did not understand women at all. He couldn't imagine any woman not being excited about all the clothes and doodads Mrs. Oleson and the other women created for her.

Lorinda was a very beautiful woman who didn't need doodads. For all the time he'd known her, he hadn't let himself think about that. Even though he wasn't going to allow himself to become emotionally involved with her, his body reacted to the picture in his mind. His sweaty palms almost slid off the pitchfork.

The barn door opened.

"Hey, Boss." Rusty stalked across the dirt floor. "What're you doin' out here on your wedding day?"

"Mrs. Oleson doesn't want me to come into the house before they leave for town."

"Why ever not?" His ranch hand took off his hat and scratched his scalp before settling it on his head once again.

"Something about it being bad luck to see the bride before the wedding or some such female nonsense." He heaved the last pitchfork of sodden hay into the wheelbarrow.

"Won't we be sittin' together in church?" Rusty stuck his thumbs into his front trouser pockets. "Everyone on the ranch always does."

Franklin hung the pitchfork on the hook by the other tools. "I believe Mrs. Su—Lorinda and Mrs. Oleson will be in one of the adjoining Sunday School rooms, listening to the service from there."

Rusty huffed out a deep breath. "That's some crazy idea."

"You know women. It's best to go along with their plans." Franklin chuckled. "At least, I'm going to in this instance."

"So I guess they're taking the buggy, and we'll ride in later?"

Apprehension twisted Franklin's gut. *Bad idea.* "I really don't like the idea of them driving to town without an escort. We haven't caught that arsonist...or Mike Sullivan's murderer. Maybe you and a couple of the other hands can ride with them. Pick out whoever you want to ride with you."

"Whatever you say, Boss."

That was twice Rusty had called him Boss without him saying anything, but he had too much on his mind to make a fuss about it. "Would you please go up to the house and ask Mrs. Oleson if I could come to the back door and talk to her?"

"Sure." Rusty headed out and returned before Franklin had a chance to start a new chore. "She says it's safe if you'll come right now."

Franklin headed to the mudroom and quickly used the iron boot scraper to remove the gunk from the bottom of his boots. He stepped into the kitchen and found Mrs. Oleson slicing bread while she hummed a happy tune.

She turned toward him. "What can I do for you?"

"I've been thinking about something." He took off his Stetson and hung it on the back of one of the kitchen chairs. "Would it be bad to give Lorinda something that I had planned to give Miriam?"

She stared at him a moment. "What?"

"Well, I have my mother's pearl necklace and eardrops. My dad gave them to her on their wedding day."

A grin spread across her face. "That would be wonderful. Since you never really gave them to Miriam, and you wanted your wife to have them, it would be most appropriate."

"They're in my bedroom. Will it be all right for me to go get them? You can give them to her to wear in the wedding." He had never felt so awkward in his whole adult life. Like a little boy that didn't know what was expected of him... Maybe because he didn't.

"Go right ahead. Lorinda won't be coming out of her room for quite a while."

He headed down the hallway wondering how she could know that. Before he reached his room, he heard soft splashing and humming, and an enticing flowery fragrance teased his nostrils. *Lorinda is taking a bath!* His stomach quivered, and he took a deep breath, trying to settle his nerves. Try as he might, he couldn't keep pictures that hinted at what she might look like in the copper bathtub from flitting across his thoughts. This was not supposed to happen. All he wanted was an heir, not a woman invading his mind. After grabbing the velvet box that held the pearls, he hurried to the kitchen as if the hounds of hell were nipping at his heels.

"Here they are." With a thunk, he dropped the case on the table without looking at Mrs. Oleson.

Just before he went through the door, he turned back. "I'm leaving a couple of the hands to ride along with the buggy into town."

He was out the door and halfway across the back yard before

he slowed down. He needed to stay in the barn and pray until the women left. Maybe then he could control his base instincts. Why hadn't he even considered this kind of repercussion? He could not let his thoughts of Lorinda get out of hand. He would never, *ever* give his heart to another woman.

~

*D*ressed in a dark blue summer frock with tiny white flowers scattered across it, Lorinda sat beside Mrs. Oleson in the buggy. Rusty was in the driver's seat, and he kept his face forward, giving them privacy. He had tied his horse to the back of the buggy and two of the other ranch hands rode on either side of his steed. For some reason, this added to Lorinda's feeling of being protected since she'd been taken into Franklin's home. If only she could convince her stomach everything was all right. She had barely forced down a few bites of scrambled eggs and biscuits before they left the ranch house.

A whole flock of flying barn swallows were building themselves a home in her innards, creating a feeling she'd never experienced before. Although the sun shone with a cheery brightness, and a soft breeze caressed her face, all she could do was think about what was to come. Could she really go through with the ceremony? Of course, she knew she wouldn't embarrass Franklin by backing out. Her doom was sealed, and it would be wrapped up in fancy, colorful clothing that should make any woman happy. But she felt as out of place in the sham marriage as she did in the fancy unmentionables.

Rusty stopped the buggy outside the parsonage, then helped both her and Mrs. Oleson down to the boardwalk that led from the front door to the church on the next lot.

Glad they had made it to town without encountering any kind of trouble, Mrs. Oleson smiled up at the tall, red-headed cowboy. "Thank you so much, Rusty." She even reached up and patted his cheek, which took on a hue similar to his hair.

Lorinda knew she should thank him, too, her relief at making it safely to church was dammed behind anxiety about what would happen after she left the church as Franklin's wife. She nodded and gave him a tight smile. He doffed his hat toward them then headed to the livery with the buggy. The other cowboys ambled up the street. She wondered where they were going, but since it was early for the service, she figured they had some way to kill the time.

Mary Nelson welcomed them into her parlor. "Brian is already at the church. He spends a couple of hours on Sunday mornings going over his sermon notes one more time. So we have the house to ourselves."

Stella sat in a rocking chair with Michael asleep on her shoulder. "He's been a dear since we picked him up at the Rocking V this morning. We're getting along just fine."

Her youngest child had pulled up on the table beside her chair and was trying to reach the books stacked near the back.

Lorinda walked over to peek at her son, then looked down at Stella's daughter. "I haven't seen her stand by herself. When did she start that?"

"Just last night. Now she'll be getting into everything." She didn't sound the least bit upset about that. Of course, she had several older children.

"Are you sure you want to take care of Michael today? You'll have your hands full with the two of them."

A tender smile lit Stella's face. "I love babies, and I can take care of more than one of them. If Michael awakens and is hungry, I can nurse him, so your day will be just for you and Franklin."

Words wanted to burst through, but Lorinda worked hard to keep them inside. This wedding was just a formality, something to protect her and her son's future. That thought made her feel like a fraud. Her heart ached. Had she made a deal with the devil for her own gain, and would she lose her soul in the long run?

While Mrs. Oleson helped Lorinda into her wedding suit and all the underthings, complete with a corset, which she'd never worn before, Mrs. Nelson packed all her other new clothing into a small traveling trunk. Although Lorinda thanked the women, she didn't know when she'd ever need a traveling trunk. Her future would be spent on the Rocking V ranch.

Before she gave Lorinda the jacket or hat, Mrs. Oleson took Michael from Stella's arms without waking him. "Stella's going to dress your hair so the hat will fit just right."

Using a curling iron, heated on the kitchen stove, Stella curled and arranged Lorinda's hair, then took her to the cheval glass in the bedroom.

Lorinda wouldn't have recognized the woman staring back at her if she hadn't known what had gone on before. She had always felt plain, even ugly sometimes. But this woman was pretty...like a picture in *Harper's Bazar* magazine.

"Do you like this style?" Stella stood beside her and cocked her head to the side as she studied Lorinda in the looking glass.

"I'm almost speechless. I never dreamed I could look like those women in the magazines."

A white silk blouse with a short lace ruffle around the sweetheart neckline was just the thing to set off her new hairstyle, pinned up in a mass of curls on the back of her head, with one long, fat curl hanging on the right side of her face and across the front of her shoulder. The hair gleamed as if it were the gold Mike had dug from their mine. She could imagine him coming up behind her and twirling her hair around his finger as he promised her enough gold to fill her every desire. *Why am I thinking about Mike on my wedding day to Franklin? I need to tuck those memories away, burying them so deep they can't resurface.*

"Oh, you're so lovely." Mrs. Oleson came up behind the two women. She held a blue velvet case in her hand. "In all the excitement, I almost forgot Franklin wanted me to give this to you to wear for the wedding." She thrust the blue velvet case toward Lorinda.

When she opened it, she gasped. A pearl necklace and eardrops, nestled on a bed of blue satin. Her gaze flew toward her dear friend. "He bought these for me?"

"Oh my, no. These are the pearls his father gave his mother at their wedding."

"I can't...take these." Lorinda raised one hand to hover over the exposed skin above the neckline of her blouse.

"Of course, you can. He's been saving these for his wife."

The wide smile that beamed from Mrs. Oleson shot straight to Lorinda's heart. *His wife.* That's what she'd be after the cere-mony today. At least legally.

Her dear friend stepped behind her and clasped the neck-lace. The perfectly matched pearls encircled her neck and nestled right below her throat. The sunlight filtering through the lace curtains gave each bead a luster that warmed her heart.

"Let me help you with the eardrops." Mrs. Oleson reached for Lorinda's lobes. "Your ears aren't pierced, are they?"

"No, ma'am. I've never had any jewelry before." She glanced down at the empty third finger of her left hand. "Except the wedding band Mike gave me." *Now I'm talking about my dead husband. What must these women think of me?*

"I remember taking off the gold band my dear departed husband gave me and tucking it in my jewelry box. It signaled the time I needed to move on." Mrs. Oleson gave her shoulder a comforting pat.

Stella picked up the hat from the round hatbox on the chest of drawers. "Let's get this settled on her. The veil that covers her face will probably cover her ears."

The small blue hat perfectly matched the watered silk of her suit, and the veil made of an open netting was as white as the silk blouse. It had been attached at the front of the narrow brim of the hat and caught up under a cluster of lace at the back of the brim.

"Wait." Mrs. Oleson lifted the jacket from the bed. "Let me put this on her first, then the hat."

Feeling almost like a doll that two little girls were dressing, Lorinda held her arms toward her back, then turned one way and the other as the women told her to. A dim memory, from before her mother died, flashed across her mind She'd had a blond china doll with a blue velvet skirt and jacket, and her mother helped her put them back on the doll after Lorinda had removed them. She never knew where that doll went. It disappeared soon after her mother was buried. She hadn't remembered that for a long time. Her heart squeezed, wishing her mother could see her on her wedding day. For a moment, she even wished that her father had died and her mother lived. Her life would have been so different.

When she once again stood in front of the full-length cheval glass, she felt like a different person...and for the first time in her life, she felt like a beautiful china doll. But whose doll would she be? The veil that fit snug under her chin did cover her ears.

Mrs. Oleson clasped her hands across her bosom and sighed. "I can hardly wait until the first time Franklin sees you like this."

It would make no difference. She was just the woman who had what he wanted. That's the only reason he was marrying her.

Why does that thought hurt so much?

CHAPTER 15

*T*he July heat in the small room off the sanctuary of the church, where the women waited, forced Lorinda to remove her jacket. Mrs. Oleson opened both windows, then the door a small crack so they could hear every word. She broke out a folded fan and used it to stir the air around Lorinda.

Waiting was never easy, and today, the pastor seemed more long-winded than ever. She had no idea what he said. All she could think about was what would come after the service. Even with all the heat, her stomach felt as if a large lump of ice had crystallized there, chilling her insides while a drop of sweat made its slow way down her spine. She hoped the beautiful clothes wouldn't be ruined.

"Amen." The last word of the preacher's prayer penetrated Lorinda's attention.

"Oh, my goodness." She turned toward Mrs. Oleson. "I've got to put on my jacket."

The other woman helped her slip her arms into the sleeves and then worked the pearl buttons through the tight buttonholes.

"I have a special announcement." Pastor Nelson's smile

shone through his tone. "You are all invited to stay and witness the marriage between our good friend Franklin Vine and his beautiful bride Lorinda Sullivan."

A few surprised gasps could be heard. But most of the people already knew about this wedding. They had even helped prepare the reception to be held in the school building. Lorinda figured those who were surprised must live the farthest from Breckenridge.

"After the ceremony," the pastor continued. "We will have a wedding luncheon in the schoolhouse. Many of you brought food to share, but if you didn't, you're still invited. With our church-wide meals, there's always enough for extra people. Help us celebrate with this well-loved couple."

Lorinda didn't feel "well-loved." Many of these people had never met her.

"If any of you need to leave now, I'm sure everyone will understand."

After the final words from the preacher, Lorinda listened for footsteps on the wooden floor, but none came. Evidently, everyone chose to stay for the festivities.

"Let's go out in the narthex." Mrs. Oleson waited for her. "The sanctuary doors are closed. Mary will start playing the 'Wedding March.' It's become popular with brides for the walk down the aisle."

Lorinda had never heard about that or any of the other various and sundry things about weddings, and she wasn't sure she would be able to walk down that aisle alone.

"I'm going to stand in for your father and accompany you." Tears glistened in her dear friend's eyes. "You feel like the daughter I never had." Mrs. Oleson leaned over and pressed a soft kiss to her cheek.

Lorinda took a deep breath and slowly released it.

At least someone besides her son loved her.

~

Franklin stood at the front of the church, his gaze trained on the double doors at the back of the sanctuary. Rusty stood beside him, to be his best man. He surely was a better man than the traitor who was supposed to serve the post in his wedding to Miriam. He tried to shake that horrible memory out of his head.

That was the past. This was for the future.

Mary Nelson took her place at the piano. Everything was quiet and the people sat still, except for most of the ladies battling the heat with their fans.

He took a deep breath and slowly let it out.

The first notes of music brought his attention back to the double doors. Two of the men slowly opened them, revealing a sight that took his breath away.

Lorinda was more beautiful than any woman he'd ever known in his life. Dressed in blue and white that enhanced all her physical charms, she looked as nervous as he felt.

When Mary played a section of the music louder, Mrs. Oleson walked down the aisle holding Lorinda's arm. His bride carried a bouquet of mountain wildflowers. He'd always loved the summer blossoms, but her loveliness outshone them.

His throat felt dry, but his palms weren't. He wanted to wipe them on his trousers, but he refrained. He couldn't take his eyes from the vision of loveliness approaching him. How in the world would he keep his promise to her to not want a husband's physical rights?

Her outward appearance wasn't the only thing that drew him to her. Over the time she'd spent in his home, he knew she had a tender heart. She was a good mother, and her presence brightened every room she entered. Her love for the Lord was contagious.

As the two women reached the front of the church, Franklin

let out a breath he hadn't realized he was holding. He still couldn't take his eyes off her.

His pastor and friend went through all the formalities of the ceremony. He asked who was giving the bride, and Franklin's dear housekeeper placed Lorinda's hand in his before settling on the front pew. Both of them answered the questions when Brian asked them. After speaking about the sanctity of marriage, the pastor asked if there were rings.

Rusty dropped the ring Franklin had bought for Lorinda into his hand, and Mrs. Oleson placed a golden circle beside it. He wondered where that came from. He'd have to ask her later. Right now, she was slipping Lorinda's left glove from her hand.

Lorinda glanced up at him as he eased the ring on her trembling finger and repeated the words the pastor led him through. Then her gaze dropped to the jewels that adorned her hand.

When her time came to put the ring on his finger, she shook so hard, she couldn't get it past his knuckle. He grasped her fingers with his other hand and helped her move it into place. A strange tingle shot up his arm.

Finally, the minister pronounced them husband and wife.

"What God has brought together, let no man put asunder." Brian smiled at each of them. "You may now kiss your bride."

Without a pause, Franklin reached for the bottom of the veil that stretched across her face. Gently, he peeled it back far enough to uncover her ripe cherry lips. He planned to barely touch them. As if they had a mind of their own, his lips settled against her soft mouth. Heat rushed through his body like a wildfire. He thrust his fingers into the silky curls to hold her even closer.

A kiss had never touched him with the depth that this one did. He wanted it to go on forever.

~

*W*hen Pastor Nelson uttered the last words, Lorinda expected Franklin to maybe drop a kiss on her forehead or cheek. She wasn't prepared for the touch of his lips on hers. Never had she felt the strong emotions that rushed through her.

His fingers caressed her head, and her arms, of their own accord, slid around his waist. She barely noticed the tinkling sound of hairpins hitting the wooden floor. The racing thrum of her heartbeat almost obliterated it. Rock-hard muscles flexed under her fingertips. She lost herself in the amazement that flooded her. A new awakening shook her deep inside. She never wanted the kiss to end, but it must. *If he doesn't want our marriage to be real, why is he kissing me like this?* Her whole body flooded with fire.

When she slowly moved back from her new husband, he let her go, and she felt bereft. Finally, she realized they were standing in front of the whole congregation. No one had moved, and every eye was on the two of them.

Since some of her curls now lay against her neck, she figured her hat must be askew as well. The heat of a blush raced up her neck and across her cheeks. How would she ever face everyone again after that intimate display?

Then some woman clapped her gloved hands. Soon everyone joined the applause, and some of the cowboys hooted and stomped their feet. Someone even whistled.

Mary Nelson started playing a lively tune as Franklin led Lorinda back up the aisle. When they reached the narthex, he stopped.

He stared down at her. "I'm sorry if I embarrassed you."

"It's all right." She had to force the words out.

Nothing would ever be right again.

∿

*E*ven though the schoolhouse wasn't far from the church, a buggy with blue bows and streamers tied to it awaited them when they went out the door. Most of the congregation lined the road, and the clapping, hooting, and whistles accompanied them as Rusty drove them slowly toward the other building with its two storeys and tall bell tower.

Lorinda had read about parades with dignitaries and royalty. She felt like a princess as she saw each smiling face. She once again glanced at the ring her husband had slipped on her finger. A blue stone she assumed was a sapphire was set in gold with tiny diamonds surrounding it. She wondered if this had also belonged to Franklin's mother.

Most of the crowd made its way into the schoolhouse while Franklin helped her down from the buggy. His hands spanned her waist, burning an imprint of their presence. When she was steady on her own feet, he possessively placed his hand in the middle of her back as they walked toward the doorway. He was playing the part of an adoring husband too well.

"Congratulations." Rusty took off his hat and held it over his heart. "I'm mighty proud to know you, ma'am, and I know you'll make the boss happy."

She gave a quick nod toward the earnest cowboy. What would he think if he knew the truth?

An enormous amount of food covered the tables set up along one side of the room. Lorinda didn't feel hungry, but the wonderful fragrances of fresh-cooked vegetables, meats, and warm cakes and pies wafted through the warm air.

"This could be a long afternoon. We need to eat something first. I think they have several things in mind for the celebration." Franklin gave her a plate and picked up one for himself.

As they walked beside the table, he recommended his favorites to her. So many things to choose from—roast, fried chicken, ham. Various cooked vegetables were right beside sliced fresh tomatoes and salad. On a separate table, a tall layer cake was covered with some kind of white fluffy frosting.

"That's our wedding cake." Franklin's whispered words were accompanied by warm breath against her ear. She hadn't realized he was so close behind her.

She had often enjoyed viewing the turning patterns of the kaleidoscope that rested on a table in the parlor at the ranch. With all the colors and patterns moving around her, she felt as if she were in the middle of one right now. For a moment, dizziness gripped her and she swayed.

Franklin grabbed her plate before she dropped it. Leaving his sitting on the edge of the table, he led her to a chair beside a table near the wedding cake.

"Are you too warm?" Concern colored his tone.

He glanced around, looking for something. She didn't know what.

Mrs. Oleson noticed them and rushed to where they were. "Is something the matter, Franklin?"

"Lorinda needs more air and something cool to drink."

"I'll see about it." She gave them both a smile. "You just take care of your precious wife."

Precious wife? If only she were.

Mrs. Oleson went around the room opening the windows all the way. She also opened the door. Then she came back with several of the women wielding fans.

Franklin knelt beside her chair. "Let me help you slip off your jacket. You'll be more comfortable that way."

"I can do it." Knowing his fingers could accidentally brush against her, she didn't want him unbuttoning her jacket, so she quickly finished that task.

She did let him help pull it from her arms. Now she felt cooler, and the moving fans that almost surrounded her created quite a breeze.

Franklin left and soon returned with his full plate. He took the chair beside her, then turned toward the women around her. "Thank you so much for helping, but I think I can take care of her from here."

Mrs. Oleson returned with a tall glass of iced lemonade. "A shipment of lemons arrived on yesterday's train. Chris Kaiser over at the Market let us have the whole shipment for today's reception, and there's plenty of ice in the ice house."

"Thank you, I'm much better now." Lorinda did feel better– calmer and cooler.

If only her hair wasn't in such disarray. When she reached to feel how messed up it could be, not a hairpin remained, only the hatpin that held the hat atop her head.

"Here, let me." Franklin reached toward the hat before she could stop him.

He quickly removed it, and all her curls fell around her shoulders and down her back.

"I have an idea." He jumped up and hurried through the door.

He soon returned with a length of blue ribbon in his hand. He deftly pulled her hair back and tied it at the nape of her neck with the streamer. Memories of how rough her father had been when he combed and braided her hair after her mother died contrasted with Franklin's gentleness. She felt him tie a bow and wondered what it looked like. It didn't matter. With most of her hair up off of her neck, she was even cooler.

As they finished eating, people started bringing gifts to their table. Lorinda opened each one and thanked the giver. More embroidered sheets, pillowcases, and towels than she'd ever imagined owning. Some people brought baskets filled with their own specialties–jams, fruit breads, a handwritten book of family receipts so Lorinda had more choices of what to cook, cuttings from fruit trees, seeds for flowers, so many things she almost couldn't keep up with them.

Mrs. Oleson had arrived near the beginning and made notes

of who gave which gifts. Lorinda looked forward to expressing her thanks to the generous people with the thank you notes she'd been told about during the wedding preparations.

Soon the owner of the Arlington House hotel stood before them. "I've got a gift for your wedding night." He gave a smug smile. "I know you'll enjoy it."

Lorinda hoped so. So far every gift had been special to her.

"Franklin, remember when I turned two of the rooms into a special suite for those men from back East that were coming out here to see about buying the larger mines for their companies? I fixed it up real fancy for them."

"Yes, you showed me after you'd finished it. Looked real nice."

Lorinda wondered where this was leading.

"Well, you and your pretty wife—" He smiled straight at her. "—can spend your wedding night there, free of charge." He put his thumbs under his suspender straps and rocked up on his toes and down again.

Wedding night? That's what they got for not telling the truth about their marriage. *In a hotel alone with Franklin overnight? No...no...no...never!*

CHAPTER 16

*L*orinda waited for Franklin to give a good excuse for why they couldn't stay in town overnight.

"Thank you." Franklin stood and shook hands with the owner of the hotel. "We'll be pleased to accept your offer."

The man turned away with a smile and almost ran into Mrs. Oleson and Stella, who was carrying Michael. After apologizing, he went toward the table where the schoolteacher was serving the lemonade.

Lorinda tugged on Franklin's sleeve. "We can't stay at the hotel tonight." She tried to keep her voice low enough so no one else could hear her comment.

He stared at her. "I didn't want to offend him by refusing."

She didn't care if it would offend the man. She was not going to spend the night in that hotel room. Panic filled her like a flock of birds roused from the trees by a runaway wagon.

Stella reached her side. "This little boy is wanting his mother."

Lorinda pulled Michael into her arms and kissed his forehead. Why couldn't her new husband be more aware of her feelings on this matter? She knew the real reason. *Because he doesn't love me as Michael does.*

She turned toward Stella. "Did you have any trouble with him?"

"No. He's been very good." She glanced at Franklin, then leaned closer to Lorinda. "I fed him a while ago."

"That's probably why he's not fussing now." Lorinda knew she didn't want to wait much longer without nursing him.

What if she leaked and ruined her new clothes? Now that she was trapped in town for the night, what would she do for something to wear? Everything had been going along smoothly. Now their lie had created this situation that was about as comfortable as sitting on a cactus. Her heartbeat was as erratic as her breathing.

Mrs. Oleson stopped in front of Franklin. "What did Arnie Holcomb want?"

"His gift is for us to spend our wedding night in the luxury suite on the top floor of his hotel." Franklin glanced at her, his gaze lighting another blaze inside her.

Lorinda frowned. "We can't do it. I need to take care of Michael. That will be easier at home." Anything to get out of spending the night alone with a man who could stir her senses into a frenzy, but didn't love or want her.

"Nonsense," Stella insisted. "I can keep him. You only have one wedding night, and you don't need to be worrying about your son. We get along really well together."

Mrs. Oleson clasped her hands in front of her waist. "That's a perfect solution! Don't you think so, Franklin?"

"That's mighty nice of you, Stella." He glanced down at his new wife. "Don't you think so, Lorinda?"

I most certainly do not! She hoped he could read the sharp glance she shot his way, because she couldn't voice her fears in front of the two ladies. She tried to smile as she nodded but knew it didn't look sincere.

"Why don't I let you have some time with Michael before I take him home with me?" Stella must have understood. "We can stop by your ranch on the way and pick up more diapers and clothes for him. You know it's not out of our way."

Franklin's nod of agreement with Stella shot down Lorinda's way of escape from the night in the hotel.

"Thank you." Lorinda forced the words out through clenched teeth, while clutching her son closer. "Is there some place private I can go to be with him for a bit?" *And it better be soon.*

Mrs. Oleson nodded toward Mary Nelson. "Maybe you can go to the parsonage. Everyone is having a good time. Probably no one will notice you're gone. When you're finished, we can cut the cake."

Franklin headed toward where the men had congregated, a satisfied smile on his lips. Lorinda had never hit anyone in her life, but she wanted to slap it off his face.

Mrs. Oleson accompanied Lorinda to talk to Mary.

Soon she was sitting in a padded rocking chair nursing her son. The sound of the vows Franklin spoke to her never left her thoughts.

"To have and to hold." The words sounded so sincere. They sent shivers up and down her spine, and goose bumps raised on her arms. He had vowed before God, but except for that one kiss, he had never held her. Would he ever again?

"To love and to cherish." These words were equally sincere, but she doubted Franklin understood all that meant. If he had, he wouldn't have been able to promise her, in the eyes of God.

"Till death us do part." That part was true. She understood what that meant in a different way than Franklin did. He had never lost a wife, but she'd lost her husband. Although they were married for the rest of their lives, they weren't truly dedicated to each other. Would the lies never end?

I can't believe Franklin agreed to accept the hotel room for the night. Her life was getting more complicated by the minute. She knew this was a bad idea, but she couldn't do anything about it. They had taken vows before God. He knew what they were doing, but no one else did. She wasn't sure He was pleased with how things were going.

Why had she felt that God wanted her to accept Franklin's proposal? Surely He hadn't wanted her to tie herself into a sham marriage with a man who could make her forget everything around her with just one kiss. Well, maybe it was a bit more than one kiss...or a lot more.

She glanced down at the ring he'd placed on her finger. It was so much fancier than the slim gold band Mike had given her, but Mike's had meant something. This one was just for show.

Maybe she'd just made the biggest mistake of her life.

$\sim$

When Franklin joined the men, he received a lot of friendly ribbing about the wedding kiss. After that died down, the men started talking about ranching and the weather, as usual. The topic didn't hold his attention.

The kiss was bad enough, but why did he have to cut that ribbon off the buggy and use it to tie Lorinda's hair away from her face? The golden strands of curls felt like silk threads. They flowed around his finger like a shimmering waterfall while he completed his task. He wanted to bury his fingers in their mass as he had during the ceremony. The feel of her hair in his hands brought with it the absolute abandon of the kiss. He shook inside as he gave the bow a last tug to straighten it.

The chaste joining of his and Miriam's lips had never inflamed him as Lorinda's did. He had been about to gain control of himself when her arms slid around his waist and her fingers clung to his back, pulling a passion from him he didn't even realize he possessed. If Miriam hadn't left him for Marvin, he would have never known such a depth of emotion. His thoughts spun in circles, always returning to this one fact. It must never, *ever*, happen again.

"Hey, Franklin." He hadn't even noticed Arnie was close-by. "When will you and your pretty little bride be coming over to the hotel?" The man had one of those sly smiles men got when they were talking about relations between men and women.

He forced his attention from his inner angst toward the proprietor. "People are still celebrating. We haven't even cut the wedding cake. When everyone starts leaving, we'll come on over." *And do what?*

"Sounds good to me. I'll make sure everything's ready."

What did Arnie need to get ready?

Franklin tried to remember exactly what that suite of rooms looked like. It had a kind of parlor and a bedroom. With a door between. That could be their salvation. And a smaller dressing room and wash room with a copper tub. This memory ushered back the feelings he'd had when he heard Lorinda bathing before they came to town. *I won't go down that road again.*

Remember the door. They should be able to enjoy the night without a repeat of the mistake at the wedding. He'd promised Lorinda they wouldn't consummate the marriage, and he was a man of his word. He didn't want to scare her away. If he did, this wedding would have been for naught. He'd lose his son and heir.

Franklin kept glancing toward the doorway, hoping Lorinda and Michael would appear.

Rusty brought him a glass of lemonade. "You dry after all that talking?"

"Yeah, thanks." He swigged down the tart-sweet liquid all at once.

"Want some more?"

"Nah. Not right now. Thanks." He set the glass on an empty table nearby.

When he turned, Lorinda stood framed in the open doorway. Her...uh, their son lay contented in her arms. Something inside him relaxed. Had he thought she might skip out on him like Miriam did?

He had to stop thinking about his near miss with Miriam. If she hadn't eloped with Marvin, Franklin would've never met Lorinda, and marriage to Miriam could have been as tepid as lukewarm coffee on a cold cattle drive. Even if they weren't going to make this a real marriage, Lorinda's vibrancy was a welcome addition to his life. He'd just have to keep a safe distance from her.

～

*L*orinda shouldn't have given up the baby to Stella. If she had him with her in the hotel room, she'd need to take care of him. It would have given her an excuse to stay up all night. That chance had ridden away from the schoolhouse in Stella's arms. Lorinda needed to come up with another reason to stay away from Franklin. Sleeping in the same room with him was out of the question.

After the party, Rusty insisted on driving Lorinda and Franklin the few blocks to the hotel. She felt silly riding with all the ribbons and bows on the buggy and horses, but she didn't want to hurt the cowboy's feelings. He'd been so nice to her the whole time she'd been at the ranch.

When Franklin helped her down from the buggy, he did it by sliding one arm around her back and the other under her knees. And he didn't set her down. Amid more clapping, hoots, whistles, and stomping, he kept her in his arms as he entered the lobby and took the stairs to the second floor. Rusty followed him with her new traveling trunk hefted onto one shoulder and carrying in the other hand a smaller bag that had been in the back of the buggy.

The cowboys and maybe Mrs. Oleson must've known what Mr. Holcomb had planned. Although she knew she blushed when Franklin carried her, she felt even more heat fill her cheeks and neck. Did everyone at the wedding know? Wouldn't they be surprised if they knew the truth?

Franklin gently set her on her feet, then turned toward the opening to the suite.

Mr. Holcomb, who had accompanied them up the stairs as well, opened the door with a flourish. "Welcome, Mr. and Mrs. Vine."

He dropped the key in Lorinda's hand just before Franklin lifted her in his arms again, startling her.

"I'm going to carry you over the threshold." The husky murmur in her ear shook her.

Another of the many things the women told her always happened after a wedding. The heavenly smell of Bay Rum Oil and Franklin's distinct masculine essence overcame her senses. His warm breath caressed her cheek, and his ebony eyes smoldered as they gazed into hers. She forgot to breathe. Franklin didn't seem to be in a hurry to release her.

Rusty put both pieces of luggage down and doffed his hat. A wide grin split his face. "You have a good time tonight."

Oh, my goodness. Could she be any more embarrassed?

"Thanks, Rusty."

Wait a minute? She smiled at the cowboy. "Would you like to stay for a drink with us?" Maybe the men would get into a discussion of something at the ranch.

Franklin gave a slight shake of his head, and the cowboy exited. Franklin kicked the door closed. He started to put her down, but something happened and she almost tipped out of his arms too quickly. He grabbed her closer to him, and the front of her body slid down the whole length of his before her feet hit the floor. She felt the flexing of his muscles as he tried to keep her from falling. His physical strength overwhelmed her as his gentleness made her feel safe. But when her feet reached the floor, her knees almost buckled. She was thankful that Franklin still had his arms around her.

"It was a very good day, Mrs. Vine." His warm smile was almost her undoing.

She glanced down at his arms that still encircled her, and he pulled them away and stepped aside.

She walked over to a table where a bowl of oranges and apples sat beside a plate of cheese and crackers. Anything to stave off the shared night. Her hand shook as she picked up a cracker and took a nibble.

When Franklin didn't say anything, she turned to look at him. "How can we stay here together?" Her voice wobbled a little.

He took off his hat and tossed it onto the luggage and walked across to a closed door. "I'd seen this hotel suite before. Right after Arnie finished it. I knew it would be all right. There's a bedroom through here."

When he opened the door, Lorinda saw the beautiful bed with a carved headboard. Heavy draperies, which matched the bed covering, were tied back with large bows, so the outside light brightened the room. Everything was even more luxurious than the furnishings in the ranch house on the Rocking V. Lamps with crystals dripping from the bottom of the matched shades, even a lovely painting on the wall across from the bed. She didn't want to step foot inside the doorway.

"You will have the bedroom. I'll sleep on the divan in the parlor."

His gentle words were probably meant to encourage her, but Franklin stood well over six feet tall, and that divan would barely be long enough for her to sleep on.

"I can sleep in the parlor." She glanced up at him and caught the frown that flickered across his features. "You're much too tall to use the divan."

A smile curved his lips. "I've slept on the ground many a night with only a bedroll. I can use one of the pillows and some of the bedding and be happy on this plush carpet. It'll be much softer than the ground."

She started to object, but he raised a palm to stop her. "I insist."

He led her across the large bedroom to another door she hadn't noticed. "There's a wash room in here. It even has a water closet...and a bathtub." The last phrase was so low, she almost didn't catch it.

Lorinda glanced around the wash room, then walked inside to get a better look at the water closet, hidden inside a tiny, cupboard-like space. She'd never seen one up close. Would wonders never cease? *What will they think of next?* For a moment, she wished they had one at the ranch.

Franklin stood in the doorway, watching her. She turned toward him.

"Are we all right now? No one will ever know what we do in this hotel room...or what we don't do."

It seemed as if she went from one blush to another all day long. She hoped the embarrassing things would come to an end, but she knew they probably wouldn't.

She went through the doorway, trying not to touch Franklin anywhere. The fewer times they had physical contact, the better it would be for her. She couldn't face another day with so much to catch her off balance. She glanced back at her new husband and saw that he was also looking at her. She wondered what he was feeling. Did he sense her relief with the way the day ended?

Lorinda couldn't wait until they returned to the ranch, so things would get back to normal for them. She had no idea what normal might look like after today.

CHAPTER 17

*E*ven though he was comfortable on the floor, Franklin
didn't sleep a bit, not even a short snooze. He heard
every movement in the other room while Lorinda got ready for
bed and had to rein in his thoughts to keep from joining her
there and probably scaring her to death. After she went to bed,
he waited for her to settle down. When all was quiet, he shut his
eyes and tried to go to sleep, but the events of the day ran
through his head in a never-ending cycle. Most of the memories
were of Lorinda and the way she reacted to everything. Especially the kiss that shouldn't have ever happened. He could still
feel her cradled in his arms...the silky softness of her curls...the
nectar sweet kiss that spiraled into something more than he'd
ever imagined...how hard it had been to let her slip from his
arms. Since then, the emotional connection he'd felt never let
him go for even a moment.

From the time she walked down the aisle until she shut the
bedroom door, Lorinda had been with him...except for the short
time she went away with little Michael. When she returned she
had that satisfied maternal look on her face he'd come to enjoy.
He knew she had been nursing the baby.

Somehow, he felt excluded. He knew married men watched their wives nurse their children. Soon after Rand and Stella had their first baby, his best friend had mentioned how much it touched him to watch them together. How it strengthened the bond between them. Missing that made this marriage feel barren.

That's what he wanted, wasn't it? Holding Lorinda in high esteem, but untouchable. As though she was a statue on a pedestal. With a sinking feeling, he knew he'd made the biggest mistake of his life. He wanted a real wife in every way. Why had he given his word that he wouldn't want more from Lorinda than her son as his heir? Their life together could last a long time, decades even. Right now his future looked bleak.

He'd made the rash statement about not wanting a physical marriage because of what Miriam and Marvin had done to him. His heart longed to be a true husband to Lorinda. When would he stop making life-changing decisions that were mistakes?

Noticing the faint glow that preceded dawn, he got up and folded his bedding. After slipping on his boots, he strode to the window to watch the wonder of the sunrise over the mountain peaks. He always loved this time of the morning. First the glow intensified. Soon the first rays of the sun painted a thin golden rim on each mountain. It shone like the gold hidden under many of the peaks. The gold that brought hordes of men to the Rockies to seek their fortunes. It also drew swindlers and crooks like the arsonist who burned Lorinda's cabin, and the person who murdered her husband.

He should thank the Lord for that gold. Without it, he would've never met Lorinda. He couldn't go more than a few minutes without thinking about his lovely bride. He'd just spent his wedding night on the floor of a fancy hotel suite. *How pathetic is that?* No one could ever know.

At least Lorinda was comfortable.

Restlessness bubbled inside him. He had to get out of this

room before he erupted. He hoped no one would be outside this early. He'd have to think of a reason for being out, in case someone noticed him without his bride.

Breckenridge Bakery on Lincoln Street would be open this early. The establishment was only a few blocks away, but the walk would allow him to stretch his legs. Mrs. Oleson loved the cream puffs from that bakery. Perhaps Lorinda would, too. He liked their cinnamon rolls...huge, with lots of melted butter and cinnamon. They would make a good breakfast for them.

After tip-toeing across the carpeted floor, he eased open the door, praying it wouldn't squeak. He hadn't noticed it doing that yesterday, but he didn't want to awaken Lorinda. Let her sleep as long as she wanted. Give her a break from having to get up early to take care of Michael. Thoughts of Michael brought a smile to his face. He missed the little guy, too.

As he walked down the stairs, Arnie Holcomb came out of the small tavern attached to his hotel. "You're up early, Franklin."

"I decided to pick up some breakfast at the Breckenridge Bakery." He was glad he'd come up with that idea before meeting someone.

"Of all the six bakeries here, I like the food at that one best."

Franklin nodded in agreement with the hotel owner.

"We have plenty of coffee. I can have some sent up to your room when you get back."

"Thanks, Arnie. That would be right nice." Franklin wasn't too happy with the other man's smirk.

His boots sounded a drumbeat on the boardwalk along the closed businesses on his way. Soon all these other stores would be bustling with customers. He wanted to complete his mission before they opened. He'd hoped this walk would invigorate him, but his thoughts kept returning to the hotel room, wondering what Lorinda was doing. Wishing he were in bed beside her after having a satisfying wedding night. He was such an idiot to have come up with the idea of a marriage of convenience. Nothing inside him was satisfied. Probably never would be. He didn't like that grim reminder.

Enticing smells greeted him two blocks before he reached his destination. Cinnamon rolls hot from the oven made his mouth water. He hoped they also had those cream puffs this early.

If only this was the morning after a real wedding night. He'd be looking forward to feeding the cream puffs to his beautiful bride...one bite at a time.

He shook his head to dislodge that image.

$\sim$

*L*orinda slowly stretched as she awakened. Michael was still quiet. She opened her eyes and sat up, glancing around the room. *The hotel suite*. No wonder everything was so quiet.

She wondered if Franklin was awake. She didn't want to go into the parlor and find him asleep on the floor. How could she have agreed to that? What a callous woman she must be. What could she do until he got up? Maybe he'd be up by the time she finished her morning ablutions.

Heading for the wash room, she hoped to get freshened up before Franklin saw her. She splashed water on her face, then wiped it off. A polished mirror hung over the wash basin. She looked just like she did before she became Mrs. Franklin Vine. For some reason, she expected there to be some differences after yesterday. With nimble fingers, she quickly unwound the loose braid she slept in. Her hair fell into abundant, wavy curls that reached down her back. After brushing them out for several minutes, the air crackled around her, lifting strands and letting them go.

When she lived on the mountain, she often left her curls

hanging down or tied them back with a ribbon, much the way Franklin had done yesterday. But since she'd been living on the ranch, she pinned her hair up on her head in a soft style. That's what she'd do today if all her hairpins hadn't fallen to the floor at the end of the wedding. She wondered if anyone thought to pick them up. She hoped Mrs. Oleson did. If not, they'd need to buy some more.

She couldn't remember the wedding without reliving that amazing kiss. A kiss that gave much more than it took from her. And she'd given plenty in the long embrace. His tender caresses gently coaxed more from her, and she gladly allowed him to deepen the kiss. She'd felt protected and almost cherished. But that was only for show. So no one would know about their marriage.

No one but the two of them. She and her new husband shared a secret. She wished the secret was the lie and the kiss was real. She brushed her fingertips over her lips and the memory burned bright accompanied by tingling in her mouth. Heat pulsed deep within her...for only a moment. She wondered how often she would revisit the embrace and yearn for what was not to be. *How soon will my regret sour our relationship beyond repair?*

She donned a lovely, navy blue calico dress sprinkled with tiny white flowers that fit her figure like a glove, then tied her hair back with the blue ribbon Franklin had used.

A noise from the other room alerted her that someone had inserted a key into the lock on the door to their suite. *How dare someone invade our privacy like this?*

She opened the connecting door and found the bedding and pillow Franklin had used beside the doorway. She grabbed them and tossed them on the bed, then turned back. Her husband wasn't anywhere in the room. Had he left her already? Pain sliced through her. Just because Mike left and never came back didn't mean something had happened to Franklin.

He walked through the opened door, carrying a fairly large paper bag.

Mr. Holcomb followed him with a china coffee pot and two cups, saucers, and plates on a tray. "Here's your coffee. Have a nice breakfast. Take all the time you need before you leave for the ranch."

"Thanks, Arnie. We will." Franklin set the new-fangled flat-bottomed paper bag beside the tray on the table by the window.

After giving her a curious nod, the hotel proprietor left.

Franklin stood by the table, and she was rooted beside the bedroom door. They stared at each other for an extended moment. Once again, the connection between them made her breathless. She wished they hadn't lost the wonder of a real wedding night. Since Franklin was so thoughtful about her needs, she wondered about how marvelous their lovemaking would have been.

This has got to stop.

He glanced down at the sack. "I went to the bakery to get our breakfast. I didn't think we'd want to eat in the tavern."

He glanced up at her again, and his tenderness and thoughtfulness softened her heart.

Lorinda hurried toward the table to serve whatever was in the sack, but he was already placing a cinnamon roll on each plate. Standing beside him, she poured the coffee, his black and a lump of sugar and a dollop of cream in hers. She hadn't even noticed the sugar bowl and cream pitcher when Mr. Holcomb brought in the tray. Perhaps Franklin ordered them. Two large white napkins were under the plates. The warmth from his body enveloped her, and she glanced up at his face.

"Why don't you sit in that chair?" He shifted a step or two from her. "You can use the small table beside it to set your coffee." He picked up a plate and napkin.

Was she standing too close to him? Was that why he moved away?

She set her coffee on the indicated side table, then sank into the wingback chair. He followed her and handed her the fragrant pastry on the plate and dropped the napkin in a pile in her lap. She glanced down and started straightening it out.

"I'm sorry we don't have forks. I can go down and get a couple from Arnie." He headed toward the door.

"We can use our fingers." She picked up the roll and took a heavenly bite, relishing the taste of the sugary butter and cinnamon in the fluffy roll. When the bite was gone, she continued. "These napkins will work just fine. We can wet them when we're finished if we...need to get all the sticky off."

Franklin nodded. He ate standing up by the table near the window, his gaze fastened on the distant mountains.

One of the things she liked the most about him was his love of the Rockies. In her mind, the peaks held up the sky and surrounded them with protection. She loved living on the ranch nestled in the valley a few miles outside town. Remembering the small hills that scattered around her hometown in Missouri, she couldn't imagine ever leaving these majestic mountains to live in a place like that again.

Actually, Franklin's gaze roved over the room...everywhere except at her. Was he as nervous as she was?

He set his coffee cup in his saucer. "Would you like to do any shopping before we go back to the ranch? I've set up an account for you at the bank, so you have as much money as you need for anything you want."

"I'm not lacking anything I need." She smiled up at him. He had been paying her to work with Mrs. Oleson, and she'd hidden that money away with the two pokes of gold Mike gave her.

"I know." He set the cup and saucer down and shoved his hands into the pockets of his black suit pants. Once again, he stared out the window. "But now that you're my wife, you can look beyond needs to...wants you wouldn't ever spend money on before. Although some years are leaner than others..." He turned back toward her. "...I make a good living on the ranch, and it also belongs to you now."

She almost choked on the bite she'd just taken. Slowly, she chewed it up, trying to think about how to answer that statement. The twinkle of light that shot from the ring on her left hand caught her attention. "Franklin, did this ring belong to your mother like the pearls did?" She set the coffee cup down and fingered the glittering jewels.

His intense gaze brought a flush to her cheeks. She wished she didn't blush so easily around him. What did he see when he studied her so intently?

"No, Lorinda. I bought that for you...only you."

She was trying so hard to put emotional distance between them, then he would do something so tender and loving. She had to remind herself he didn't mean it that way. Perhaps his wife needed to own nice things so the neighbors would believe the marriage was real. Living with him was going to be so hard. Always wondering what he really meant by what he said and what he did.

They hurried to finish breakfast and pack. Having something to do took her mind off their problems.

Lorinda reentered the parlor. While she was in the bedroom gathering her things, the coffee, dishes, and tray disappeared. Franklin must have taken them downstairs.

Dragging her trunk behind her, she hadn't realized it would be so heavy.

"Let me help you with that." Franklin's fingers grazed hers as he slipped his hand in the handle. He stopped a moment before he hefted it up on his shoulder. Maybe he had felt the same spark she did when they touched. She rubbed at the tingles that shot from her hand and up her arm.

He opened the door, then lifted his bag with the other hand.

"I'll take these things downstairs, then go to the livery to rent a carriage to take you home."

Home. Yes, she finally had a home of her own again. A home she'd grown to love. A good place to raise her son. Their son.

"You can stay here in the room, or you can sit in the lobby until I get back."

Lorinda didn't want to be on display for whoever might come into the hotel. "I'll wait here."

Standing in the doorway, she watched her husband descend the stairs with their luggage. At least, no one was in the area of the lobby that she could see from her vantage point, looking through the stair railing.

When he reached the front door, a laugh burst from him, then he turned and looked toward her through the banister on the lobby side of the staircase. "Come on down, Lorinda. Rusty is waiting out front with *our* buggy."

CHAPTER 18

*W*hen Lorinda arrived on the board walk outside the hotel, Franklin and Rusty were loading the luggage into the buggy. "What a surprise to find you out here, Rusty."

For the first time, she saw the cowboy blush.

"Thought you and the boss would want to ride home in the buggy...Mrs. Vine."

The name, coming from one of the ranch hands, stopped Lorinda for a moment. She would have to get used to hearing people call her Mrs. Vine, instead of Lorinda or Mrs. Sullivan. With the deception attached to the wedding, the name didn't feel like it fit. *Lord, please help me.* Since they were lying about their marriage, would He listen to her?

"That was thoughtful of you." Lorinda tried to smile, but it felt tight.

"I brought Mrs. Oleson to town. She has several things to do today." He climbed up on the driver's seat. "I'm gonna drive you home, and I'll come back later to pick her up in the wagon. She's buying supplies, too."

Franklin leaned close to her ear. "That explains why we have a ride." The scent of cinnamon from their breakfast came with his breath.

He clasped her waist between his strong hands and lifted her to the buggy seat as if she were as light as a butterfly. Her stomach fluttered like the beautiful insect as well. Why did just the feel of his hands always cause some kind of unusual reaction in her person?

"Thank you, Franklin." She arranged her skirt without looking at him.

"My pleasure, *Mrs. Vine.*"

The emphasis he placed on the last two words intensified the feelings that unsettled her. She peeked at him, and his smoldering smile lit a fire in her heart. She knew he was only playing a part in front of the people who were out and about in town, but something deep inside wished it wasn't so.

Franklin climbed up and settled close beside her. "We're ready, Rusty."

As the buggy rolled out of town, many people turned to stare at them. Most wore smiles. A few had a kind of smirk that made her uncomfortable.

Lorinda felt she was on display, and she didn't like it. When they finally left the town behind, she relaxed. Even though the morning was heating up, the speed of the horses stirred a breeze that kept her cool.

For some reason, everything looked different today. The tall trees were greener. Wildflowers covered meadows with a myriad of colors, as if God had taken a paintbrush and splashed various hues across the fields. Birds sailed high in the sky against a cerulean backdrop for the few cottony clouds that floated lazily as if on a slow-moving river. Enjoying the fresh air, she took a deep breath and slowly exhaled.

Franklin leaned closer and put his arm across the back of the seat. "Are you all right?"

"Yes." The word whispered at the end of her exhale.

No, you're too close to me. Her gaze fell to her hands clasped in her lap. The faint aroma of the Bay Rum Oil he used yesterday still lingered, along with the unique masculine scent she'd become familiar with since she lived at the Rocking V. She wanted to turn away but didn't want him to notice.

"Are you sure?" The words blew against her ear.

When did he move that close? If she turned her head up toward him, their lips might almost touch...maybe they would. Maybe she wanted to see if that kiss yesterday was a fluke. But could her heart take it? The memory of the feelings she'd only experienced that one time flooded over her, bringing back the fire in her belly and capturing her breath.

How far are we from the ranch? She glanced around but couldn't tell for sure. Finally, she raised her eyes to peek at him. A frown wrinkled his brow and drew his lips down. He almost looked worried.

"Yes, I'm sure." She sat up as straight as she could...with his arm around her shoulders.

When had he put it there instead of on the back of the seat? Lorinda was more unsettled than at any time since she came to the ranch. Maybe she should have taken her money and gold and fled instead of agreeing to marry him.

They couldn't get home soon enough for her, so he'd move.

Home? Yes, she felt at home on the Rocking V, and Franklin had said the ranch belonged to her as much as to him.

At least her son would have an inheritance that was worth more than two small pokes of gold pebbles.

~

With his arm lightly touching Lorinda's shoulders, Franklin wanted more. Every spot on his arm where they touched tingled with the connection. Half of his heart wanted to cling to her until he could convince her to be his completely, the other half, to keep his distance. What a dichotomy! Yesterday and today must be an aberration. The sooner they got back to the ranch, the sooner things would settle down to what they'd been before the wedding...with a few modifications. Modifications that shouldn't affect the way he ran his ranch...or his family.

"Franklin, can we go to Stella's and pick up Michael?" Lorinda's quiet words penetrated his thought processes, bringing them to a halt. "I really miss him."

Why not? "Rusty, keep driving to the Morgan Ranch. That should still give you plenty of time to get us home and back to town before Mrs. Oleson is finished with...whatever she's doing."

"Sure, Boss."

Franklin didn't want to make a fuss in front of Lorinda about Rusty calling him that, so once again he let it slide. Was everything in his life changing, just because he made a business-like deal with...his wife?

Someone saw them driving up, because Stella came out on the front porch before they reached the house. She held Michael, and the baby's hands swatted through the air in a way that touched Franklin's heart. He was glad Lorinda wanted to come get her...their son. He'd missed seeing the little man. He wanted to get back to their rituals at mealtime when he played with Michael while the women got the food on the table.

He jumped down from the buggy, then reached back to help Lorinda. Her waist was tiny for a woman who'd had a baby less than four months ago. She practically ran toward the front porch.

Stella met her at the bottom of the steps and handed off Michael. "I was just about to feed him."

Lorinda turned toward Franklin. "Do we have time for me to feed him before we head to the ranch?"

He glanced at Rusty.

His ranch hand nodded. "I won't have to be back to town until mid-afternoon."

"Rand is out in the barn checking on a new colt." Stella held her hand up to shade her eyes from the sun.

"Let's go." Franklin nodded at Rusty, and the two men headed toward the large red building that housed the growing herd of Thoroughbred horses.

Rand's horses were known all over Colorado and even out of the state. He sold to the U.S. cavalry and other ranchers. His choice to change from cattle to raising the horses had carried him through the slowing economy so far. He didn't own as much land as Franklin did, so he hadn't been able to sustain as many cattle as were needed to keep a ranch afloat. Franklin was thankful his father and grandfather had the foresight to add so much land to the Rocking V. All the viable ranch land in the area was owned by someone, and people didn't decide to move away very often.

Now he had something else, besides his pretty new wife, to capture his thoughts...at least, he hoped so.

~

What bliss, sitting in a comfortable rocking chair, nursing my wonderful son. Lorinda didn't plan to spend another night away from him. Especially not a night and early morning that was as awkward as this last one had been.

"I've made us lemonade." Stella bustled in carrying a tray with a pitcher and two glasses. "We didn't use all the lemons at the wedding."

"Thank you. Today is already plenty hot." Lorinda cast another glance at her son, nestled in her arm, before she took the cold glass. "Where did you get the ice?"

Lorinda knew they had an ice house in town, but by the time

they would try to bring it to the ranch, the block would be melted.

"When Rand built the ranch house, he also turned a cave not far from the house into ice storage." Stella took a sip before continuing. "A cave is naturally cooler, and he layers sawdust to cover the blocks of ice the men cut from a small lake we own. We have ice all summer long."

"I wonder why Franklin doesn't have an ice house." She set her glass on the pie crust table beside her chair and snuggled Michael even closer.

Stella glanced out the window toward the barn. "I'm sure he'll make one for you if you ask him. From what we all saw yesterday, the man's completely crazy about you, as he should be."

Yes, he should be, but he isn't. "He's done a lot for Michael and me, so I don't want to be too demanding." That should end this conversation about ice...and heat.

A merry, lyrical laugh burst from Stella. "Honey, after the way that man kissed you yesterday, in front of God and everyone..."

Lorinda couldn't stop a blush from rushing heat to her cheeks. Probably part of the fire the man lit inside her.

"I'm sure last night was even hotter than usual." A wicked grin spread across her friend's face. "I'm glad Franklin has finally gotten over Miriam and what she did to him. The man deserves a loving wife like you."

Lorinda wished a hole would open up and swallow her. This kind of conversation is what she'd been dreading. Of course, having a friend like Stella might come in handy. Since she was speaking so openly about things that usually were kept quiet, maybe she could find out who Miriam was and what it was she did to him. She was tired of fighting the jealousy whenever someone mentioned that woman's name. *Now how should I approach the subject?*

She placed a diaper on her shoulder and held her son against it. With rhythmic patting on his back, he should soon release the air from his stomach.

"Stella, I shouldn't be asking you, but I want to know about something, and I don't want to upset Franklin or Mrs. Oleson by asking."

Stella set her glass of lemonade on the table beside her chair. "That's what friends are for, and you know I consider you a good friend. How can I help you?"

Here goes. She took a deep breath while she formulated the question. "No one has ever told me what happened with this Miriam. Her name has only been mentioned a time or two at the ranch and then skipped over. So what happened?"

Stella stared at her a moment. "You really should know. I don't know why Franklin didn't tell you. It might keep you from having trouble in your relationship."

"That's right." She didn't want the other woman to stop.

"Franklin, Miriam, and Marvin Pratt grew up together. Marvin was Franklin's best friend, or so he thought. I always thought something was kind of off with Marvin...that he wasn't sincere as he should be. And I guess I was right." She twisted her skirt with her fingertips. "Miriam and Franklin were to be married. Such a lot of plans were made. It was going to be the largest wedding ever in these parts. Franklin almost worshiped the ground she walked on."

Stella arose from her chair and went to the front door, where she stood studying something outside. Then she turned back. "Two weeks before the wedding, Marvin and Miriam eloped."

That wasn't what Lorinda expected. Poor Franklin. No wonder he had made that declaration to her. He didn't know if he could trust any woman. He must have built a wall around his heart. But why did he kiss her the way he did if he didn't want any kind of romantic or physical relationship with her?

Tears seeped from her eyes and down her cheeks as her son gave a loud burp. She nestled him at her other breast and began rocking him as he nursed.

"I didn't mean to upset you. Maybe I shouldn't have told you." Stella pulled a clean hanky from her sleeve and pressed it into Lorinda's hand.

"I'm crying for the hurt Franklin must have experienced." She patted the cotton square against her cheeks. "I'm glad you told me. I understand some things better now. And no one has to know that you told me."

❧

*R*usty delivered them to the ranch, and Lorinda handed Franklin her sleeping son. He stepped from the buggy, then reached his other hand to help her down.

After the ranch hand unloaded their luggage, he drove the vehicle toward the carriage house.

"Welcome home, Mrs. Vine." Her husband put the baby in her arms, then picked her up in his arms. With deliberate steps, he went up the stone walkway to the porch and carried her over the threshold. Evidently, what he did yesterday didn't count.

"I'll put Michael in his crib." She whisked into the bedroom she and her son shared.

After he settled into deep slumber, she went into the parlor and found Franklin waiting for her, leaning against the mantel above the stone-cold fireplace, his arms crossed over his chest. This was the first time she had been alone with him in the ranch house. Everything felt different...and awkward. What would happen now?

"How will we keep Mrs. Oleson from knowing the truth about our marriage, since she lives in the house with us?" She hated to ask the question, but she needed to know what he expected.

He pushed away from the mantel and crossed to stand before the chair where she sat. "You are now the woman of the house. You can choose what you want to do and tell her what you want her to do."

She stared up at him. "I don't want to upset her routine." He was so tall, her neck felt crimped.

"You can take complete control of our rooms–the cleaning, the laundry, and other things, so she won't know where anyone slept. There's a nice sized dressing room between your room and mine." He thrust his hands into the back pockets of his trousers. She had seen that pose many times when he talked to her about something serious.

She arose from the chair and moved far enough from him so she was comfortable looking at him without the crick in her neck.

"When she's in the room with us, we must make her think we're in love with each other." He turned away and glanced out the window.

That won't be hard for me. He'd awakened something in her heart that was drawn to him like metal to a magnet. She would have to silence the small voice that kept telling her she was living a lie.

"Let's get your things moved into the larger bedroom, where I sleep. It was the room my parents shared, as did my grandparents. That's what Mrs. Oleson will expect." He turned back toward her, his eyes searching hers. "Is that all right with you?"

"All right." She gave a tentative reply.

"I will actually sleep in the dressing room."

Lorinda let out the breath she hadn't realized she was holding. "That could work."

"The smaller bedroom you and Michael have shared can be turned into a nursery." Evidently, he had thought through all of this.

She was glad she wouldn't have to work it out.

"I'm even thinking of asking Mrs. Oleson if she'd like larger quarters for herself. There are two nice-sized rooms across the upstairs hallway from where her room is now. We can turn them into a parlor and bedroom for her, for when she wants privacy. She's not getting any younger, and I want her comfortable for the rest of her life here in our home."

Our home. The words were a balm to her heart.

"And then she wouldn't be sleeping in the room above our bedroom." A slow smile crossed his face.

Now Lorinda understood. Mrs. Oleson wouldn't be able to hear anything that happened in their bedroom...or anything that didn't happen.

CHAPTER 19

*U*nable to take his eyes off Lorinda holding their son on the front porch swing, Franklin walked from the barn to the house. "Michael really likes to be outdoors, doesn't he?"

Her smile was brighter than the evening sunlight filtering through the trees. "Yes, and it's cooler out here right now than it has been all day."

The empty space beside her drew him, but if he was going to keep his promise, he couldn't sit there. He ambled to the rocking chair on the other side of the front door. He pulled it out from near the wall until it was close enough for him to prop his feet on the railing.

Franklin had gone to the barn to work when they finished fixing the rooms they would share to put some distance between them. He made a conscious effort to concentrate on everything else besides this woman he'd married, and he'd been fairly successful. But with her sitting so near, an awareness that she was his wife teased his senses.

He cast a glance at her. "We got a lot done today, didn't we?"

"It helped that Mrs. Oleson left plenty of food for us in the spring house, so I didn't have to cook...and of course, those cream puffs you bought were especially good." She looked down at her son when he grasped one of her curls in his fist and pulled. "Michael is so much more aware of his surroundings now."

"Yes, he is." Franklin wished he was the one holding the silky strand of that golden curl in his hand. *How can I be jealous of a baby?* He'd dreamed about running his hands through her curls since he'd discovered she was a widow.

Lorinda met his gaze. "I'm glad we finished fixing up the rooms before Mrs. Oleson got back from town."

"And I'm glad it makes you happy." He shifted to get more comfortable in the hard wooden chair. *Ahhh.* He looked out across his property, thanking God for his blessings. "Listen, Lorinda. This is your home. If you want to change things around anywhere else in the house, you can. Maybe do different curtains, change the colors of the rooms, anything at all." The woman deserved it since he had no intention of giving in to his desires to make theirs a real marriage. Besides, she didn't want that kind of relationship, even if he was questioning his choice in the matter.

Surprise lifted her eyebrows as she stared at him. "Why, thank you, Franklin. I might do some of that...over time...but nothing right now."

"And if there's anything you want added to the house, just let me know." He watched her as she looked out across the property as he had only a few moments ago. For a while, a comfortable silence reigned between them.

"I was intrigued by the wash room and water closet at the hotel." She turned her attention back toward him. "Would it even be possible to have something like that in the house...out here so far from town?"

Well, he wanted her to feel a part of the ranch and house, and she took him up on his suggestion. He stared at the mountain peaks surrounding the ranch, making mental notes of just where the best springs were located. It would take some doing, but he figured it might be possible.

"I'll try to find out what all it'll take to do that." As he glanced back toward his new wife, he noticed a small cloud of dust on the road leading to the ranch house. "Looks like someone's coming. Maybe Rusty and Mrs. Oleson. 'Bout time they got here."

Lorinda stood and held Michael against her shoulder as she peeked around the vines growing on the trellis behind the swing. "I think she may have been giving us more private time."

"I wholeheartedly agree that we need private time." Had he really blurted out his feelings? He glanced at Lorinda, taking note of the blush coloring her cheeks at his words and what they indicated. He hadn't meant to embarrass his wife.

He got up and went down the steps. "It is them. I'll help Rusty unload the wagon."

He assisted their housekeeper down, then grabbed a heavy wooden box from the back and hefted it onto his shoulder before following her to the house.

After she climbed the steps up to the porch, Mrs. Oleson reached for Michael. Lorinda relinquished him to her and opened the front door. While the housekeeper cooed and talked to the baby, they started inside.

"Where do you want this box?" Franklin caught the door with the toe of his boot and waited until his wife preceded him. "Something smells really delicious."

"In here." Mrs. Oleson led them into the kitchen, and he set his burden on the table.

"The Ladies' Glee Club prepared our supper."

Lorinda reached for the baby. "How nice." She pulled him close and pressed a kiss to his cheek.

Franklin loved watching the two of them. His son would be well cared for by his loving mother. What more could he ask?

He wouldn't let himself go down that road, because he knew there were many things he would want to ask of her...but couldn't.

"I believe there's a pot of stew and cornbread still warm from the oven. Marjorie made her famous dried apricot fried pies for dessert." Mrs. Oleson started removing things from the box. "There's even a pot of butter and one of honey."

Franklin's stomach started rumbling like a thunderstorm. He was sure everyone in the room could hear.

Lorinda laughed. "How thoughtful of the ladies, especially since everyone did so much to make our wedding special." She glanced at him with an amused twinkle in her eye. "And we know Franklin's ready to eat."

"Isn't he always?" Mrs. Oleson winked at him and laughed.

With an atmosphere in the home like this, maybe they really could feel normal again...hopefully soon.

~

"That was delicious." Lorinda excused herself from the table, then carried her dishes to the dry sink. "If I keep eating like this, I'll be as big as the barn."

Franklin chuckled and the sound rumbled through her, almost causing her to drop her load. "I can't imagine that ever happening. Especially not if you work as hard as you did today."

An expression of confusion captured Mrs. Oleson's face. "Why did she work hard? The house was clean, and she didn't have to cook lunch."

He stood. "Mrs. Oleson, Lorinda and I want to discuss some things with you."

Lorinda studied their housekeeper, hoping she wouldn't find any hint of hurt or anxiety. "Yes, let's go into the parlor. We can wash the dishes later."

Mrs. Oleson took a seat on the settee, and Lorinda joined her. Franklin sat in the matching wingback chair.

"What's this all about?" The older woman's tone of voice sounded tentative.

He smiled at both of them. "We just wanted to talk about a few changes that will take place because we're married."

Mrs. Oleson nodded and clasped her hands in her lap.

Lorinda patted her on the shoulder. "Don't worry. You're very important to all three of us." She felt some of the tension drain out of the older woman.

Franklin leaned back in the chair. He looked comfortable and satisfied.

"You know that as my wife, Lorinda will now take a greater part in the running of the household."

"But I don't want you to feel that we don't need you." Lorinda nodded toward the hallway. "There'll be times when I have to take care of Michael...and other things. And you're not finished teaching me how to cook. We'll depend on you...a lot."

A slight smile lifted Mrs. Oleson's lips.

"And," Franklin boomed, "you're the only grandparent our son will ever know. That's very important."

The smile blossomed until it wreathed her entire face. "I'm blessed to fill that role. He is such a dear."

Franklin's ebony eyes sparkled, and that curl fell across his forehead. If they'd been alone in the room, Lorinda would have reached up and brushed it back. Once again, she wondered how it would feel to do that to her husband. Just the thought made her breathless.

"We rearranged the rooms we'll share, and I'll be the one to clean them." She watched her husband nod in agreement. "I'll probably take over more of the cleaning. We want you to enjoy being Michael's grandmother."

"Another thing I want to do..." Franklin garnered both women's attention. "...is turn two of the rooms across the hallway from your bedroom into your own private quarters. A larger bedroom and a parlor. You can have privacy when you want it, and you can take part in our family's life when you desire."

His words did make the change sound loving and kind. Lorinda hoped that would be the way the older woman heard it.

For a moment, no one spoke. Then Mrs. Oleson glanced from one to the other. "I knew this marriage would change some things. And I'm so glad Franklin finally found someone to love him...and someone he could love. But I never dreamed of these changes. A suite of rooms to myself. And I'll get to keep cooking and helping with the house. It's more than I imagined. Thank you."

Lorinda put her arm around the older woman's shoulders. "And my new life is more than I ever imagined it would be."

And also much less than I really desire it to be. She felt like such a fraud in so many ways. Hiding things from this dear woman. The truth about their marriage and the real reason they rearranged things so she wouldn't discover it. Guilt became a heavy burden for Lorinda to carry, and her spirit bent under the load.

❧

*A*s hoofbeats approached the house, Franklin glanced toward the window. Sounded like one rider, and he was coming fast. Who could it be so late in the evening?

"Ladies, please excuse me." He eased out of the chair. "I need to check it out."

He peeked between the lacy curtains, blowing in the cooling breeze. Thomas Walker was supposed to be with the other hands checking the herds scattered in several different pastures on the ranch. Franklin wanted an inventory of how many beeves they had, and which ones would be on the cattle drive to

Frisco to meet the train headed to a Chicago packing plant. Some needed moving to other grazing land. He wanted them fattened before the drive, even if it wasn't a long one.

A sharp knock on the front door drew him from the parlor. He opened the door. "Everything all right, Thomas?"

"We need to talk." The expression on his foreman's face was grim, and his tone ominous.

Franklin heard the women visiting quietly. He didn't want to upset them before he knew what was wrong. "You can come into my office, or we can talk outside."

"I'm too dirty to come into your house, and I've been in the saddle most of the day. How about if we just walk."

"Fine with me. Wait right here."

Franklin went back to the doorway to the parlor. "Thomas has returned from the pastures, and we're going to take a walk." He smiled at his bride. "It might take a while. Don't wait up for me, Lorinda." No need to alarm them unnecessarily.

He and his foreman ambled in the shade of the tall trees as the sun made its final descent behind the peaks.

"So what's happened? Is someone injured? Do we need to head out to help him?"

"No...no injuries." Thomas seemed to be taking plenty of time to choose the right words.

He'd been that way as long as Franklin had known him. But he also didn't raise an alarm, if there wasn't anything to worry about.

"You know we've been trying to find that man...or men... who might have murdered Mike Sullivan...and may be the arsonist. We thought whoever it was moved on."

That caught Franklin's attention. "Did you find someone?"

"Not really. But the numbers are lower than we expected. Some of our cattle are missing."

Not good. Franklin frowned. "Do we know how many?"

"Hard to tell." Thomas stopped and stared toward the mountains. "Seems to be a few from each part of the herd... You know, scattered out a lot. Maybe he hoped we wouldn't notice they're gone. But there are too many more missing than in other years."

Franklin needed the money from the beeves to carry them through the winter. They'd be able to make it all right, but he'd have to curtail extra spending if the herd was too small.

"So did you get all parts of the herd counted? Will we have enough for the drive?"

Thomas rubbed his hand across his stubbled chin. "I sent the men in teams of two or three to do the counts. Had 'em cut the cows with calves and then count all except the breeding bulls. Our numbers are down by about a fourth, but still plenty for the drive."

"That's a relief." Franklin huffed out a deep breath. He started walking again, and Thomas joined him. "When we were out at the RM Ranch today, picking up the baby, Rand mentioned things had gone missing around their place. Stella had baked two pies and set them on the windowsill to cool. When she came downstairs from taking care of their baby, one pie was missing, pie tin and all. Other things, too. Food missing from their spring house, which is farther from their house than ours is. Things like that."

Franklin stopped and sat on a stump, and Thomas rested one foot on a log that waited to be chopped into firewood. "That's the next thing I was going to tell you. All the supplies have disappeared from a couple of line shacks. Everything–furniture and pots and pans included."

"Looks as though we have a thief in our midst. I guess the person could be the same one that murdered Mike and burned his cabin." Franklin took out his pocketknife and started cleaning his fingernails. "But it could be someone else entirely. Were there tracks you could follow?"

"I sent a couple of guys to try to find some, but they soon returned when the trail led to an outcropping of rocks. Couldn't pick it up again at either place." Thomas took off his hat and twirled it in front of him. "I have most of the men following the fence lines to see if they can find a place where the cattle could have gotten out. They'll be fixin' any broken places and report their findings to me. I'll let you know."

Franklin got up and clapped his foreman on his shoulder. "I know I can depend on you. Why don't you go ahead and spend the night in the bunkhouse? And I'm sure the women can rustle up something for you to eat."

"I ate with the men at the chuck wagon before I came. But I would enjoy sleeping in my bunk. I'll head out early in the morning."

"Sounds good to me."

While his foreman headed toward the bunkhouse, Franklin hurried back to the house. He wasn't going to worry the women with this information. They should be safe here at the ranch house. He'd make sure at least one or two hands were close-by at all times.

He didn't want to risk losing his beautiful bride so soon after their wedding.

CHAPTER 20

*A*fter nursing him, Lorinda finished rocking Michael to sleep and placed him in his cradle. She had put him down before she, Franklin, and Mrs. Oleson had supper, but when Franklin left the house, the baby awoke and started fussing.

Even though her husband had told her not to wait up for him, she hoped he would come back in before she went to sleep. She wondered what had gone wrong. And she didn't intend to go to sleep until she knew he was in the house...and safe.

Besides, they'd only been married less than two days. Would this be the way their marriage went? Him going out to do things without telling her why or where he went. Not much different from her father or Mike. Once more, a man was controlling things in her life without her input.

Lorinda plaited her hair into a loose braid and tied the end with a thin strip of fabric. She donned the white dimity gown with all the colorful embroidered flowers across the top and around the cuffs. How silly dressing like this for bed when no one would see her, except maybe Michael when he awoke during the night.

Completely ready to lie down, she paced the room instead, her slippers not making any sound on the wooden floor. She didn't want Mrs. Oleson to know what she was doing. The sooner they got the woman's new quarters ready for her, the better. Then Lorinda wouldn't need to worry about what their housekeeper heard.

By the time she'd made more passes across the bedroom than she wanted to count, she heard the front door open, then close again with a click. *Franklin locked the door.* She didn't remember him doing that before. There had to be a reason. What might endanger them?

She jumped into the large bed in the room that had been his. Pulling up the covers, she lay as still as she could, closing her eyes in case he checked on her.

The door between the hallway and the room where Michael slept opened, and Lorinda was aware of her new husband tiptoeing toward the cradle. He stopped and stayed beside it for several minutes. Whispered words sounded in a loving tone, but she couldn't understand what he said. Her husband was pouring all his love into her...their son.

Tears slipped from under her closed eyelids and trickled toward her pillow. She needed love as much as Michael did. But her agreement with Franklin ensured she would never again experience physical love from a husband. She longed for the genuine love of a *true* husband. She gritted her teeth to keep from sobbing. It would never do for him to hear that.

When Franklin came through the open door of Michael's room into the dressing room, she felt his presence through her doorway. The aroma of heat, horse, Bay Rum Oil, and the unique masculine fragrance that was his alone circled around her, making her feel her barren life all the more. What a bleak future.

Desires for more than he was willing to give awakened deep in her belly. She was glad she lay in bed. If she'd been standing, her legs might just give out, the yearning was so strong and powerful.

He stepped into the room and stopped beside the bed. She was glad she faced the other direction. The tracks of her tears on her cheeks would surely give her away.

Franklin released a deep sigh, then returned to the dressing room. When he settled in the narrow bed, she was ashamed of herself for not insisting he let her sleep in there. This bed was more than wide enough and plenty long for the tall, strong man.

He quickly fell into a deep sleep. He didn't snore exactly, but the even rhythm of his breathing filled the silence with his presence.

Finally, she succumbed to slumber.

A dream captured her thoughts.

Strong arms embraced her, and she loved the safety of them clasping her close. Lips touched hers tentatively. She returned the kiss with abandon. Soon they were enmeshed in the rhythm of marital love, giving and receiving a love so strong and so sure. She relished it, soaking up the emotions like a sponge left out in the summer sun to dry.

They exchanged murmurs of love, their hands exploring the curves and planes of each other. Breathless, she glanced into Mike's face. Except, it wasn't Mike! Instead, Franklin's hooded gaze bored into her inner being.

She relaxed with his arms cradling her.

Her dream disappeared in a mist, and she rested in contentment.

✿

*A*wakening with a start, Lorinda wondered where she was. Glancing around the room, she noticed the sun was fairly high in the sky. *I overslept!*

Something felt off kilter. Why was she alone in this big bed?

Why hadn't Michael stirred? Had something happened to him? Finally recognizing the large bedroom that had been Franklin's before their wedding, she jumped up and ran into the room she and her son had always shared. Peering through the spindles along the side of the cradle, she found the covers disturbed...and no baby. Her heartbeat accelerated. Had he been kidnapped?

While she frantically threw on her clothes, she remembered Franklin locking the front door. If anyone had broken in, someone should have heard it. She stopped and took a deep breath, releasing it slowly as she buttoned the front of her dress. *God, please don't let anything be wrong with Michael.*

She didn't even take time to put on her shoes before she thrust open the door and rushed toward the kitchen. When she was three steps down the hallway, laughter rang out from that direction.

Franklin and Mrs. Oleson were there, and as the laughter slowed, she heard her son gurgling. Then he emitted a soft coo. Her heart melted.

As she stopped in the doorway, Franklin looked up at her. "Good morning, Sunshine." His smile went straight to her jittery heart. Her pulse throbbed erratically.

Why did he call her that? He'd always been more formal. *I think I like being called Sunshine.*

"I don't understand why Michael didn't wake up during the night." She wanted to reach for him, but he was happy resting in her husband's arms.

"Who said he didn't wake during the night?" A twinkle resided in Franklin's eyes.

"I didn't hear him."

"I don't think he was hungry." Her husband smiled down at Michael. "We had a good time last night, didn't we, Son?"

Confused, Lorinda shook her head.

Mrs. Oleson glanced at her. "I'm fixing your eggs right now."

"All right." She stared at Franklin. "What are you talking about?"

He lifted Michael onto his shoulder, and her son held his head high instead of resting it on the man. "I didn't see any sense in waking you if he wasn't hungry. So I got up and played with him. We even went outside and looked at the moon and stars."

This was almost too much for Lorinda to take in. Franklin had gotten up with Michael, played with him, and taken him outside?

"I didn't hear you unlock the front door."

He lifted one eyebrow and glanced at her. "I looked in on you, and you were sleeping so soundly, I didn't want to bother you." He kept his hand on her son's back while the baby wobbled in his arms. "If he'd have been hungry, I'd have awakened you."

What kind of crazy world had she walked into? She felt as if she had fallen down a rabbit hole and landed in Wonderland, like the Lewis Carroll book Mrs. Oleson had shared with her. Perhaps she was still asleep, dreaming all of this.

Dreaming? Suddenly, flashes of her night vision flitted in her head. Heat made its way up her body and into her cheeks. Why did she have to blush? She didn't want anyone to know about that dream. No telling what Franklin would think if he knew. Another secret to keep from the man.

∾

*F*ranklin had never seen Lorinda immediately after she awakened. Usually by the time he saw her, the rosiness of sleep had worn off, and the wrinkles from the linens had disappeared. And her hair was combed and styled. This messy braid with curls springing around her face hit the pit of his stomach. He'd always thought her pretty, but a new beauty shone through her today. He wished he had the right to tuck one long curl, that rested on her shoulder, behind her ears. If he hadn't been an idiot, he could exercise that right.

"Come sit down, Lorinda." Mrs. Oleson set a filled plate on the table.

"I need to feed Michael first." She glanced at the baby, but her gaze evaded Franklin's.

"He's happy right now." Franklin sat down in the chair across from her. "Your breakfast won't be as good after it sits a while."

Finally, her gaze met his. She looked as if she were trying to read something into what he said. Then she bowed her head for a moment. After she raised it, she concentrated on her food, only peeking sometimes at their son.

Franklin set him on his knee, being careful to hold him with fingers high enough to keep his head from wobbling. He lifted his heel from the floor just enough to gently rock the baby up and down. A soft laugh filled the silence in the room.

"Did you hear that?" Lorinda smiled at the boy. "I haven't heard him laugh before."

Franklin didn't want to upset her, so he didn't tell her Michael had laughed a little when they were outside during the night. Just letting her think this was his first time wouldn't hurt anything...would it?

"That was so sweet." Mrs. Oleson came over and bent over Franklin's shoulder so she could look the baby in the face. "You're such a happy boy, aren't you?"

Another laugh ended in a gurgle. Franklin took the folded diaper from his shoulder and wiped the drool from his son's face.

"He must be getting ready to cut a tooth." Mrs. Oleson straightened up and placed one hand on her arched back. "I'm getting too old to be leaning over like that."

Finally, Lorinda looked up from her half-eaten food. "You're not that old. Even I get aches and pains sometimes." She picked up her biscuit. "What kind of jelly is this? You made it before I came to live here."

"Plum. The thickets grow wild in some areas of the ranch." Mrs. Oleson dropped into the chair beside Franklin.

"It's delicious." Lorinda took a bite, and a drip of butter started down her chin. Quickly, her pink tongue flicked it away.

The memory of the kiss at the wedding rushed into his mind. That memory almost choked him, and he stopped bouncing the baby.

Lord, help me. Without being able to let her know how much he liked having her around, his life could turn into a misery. The only bright spot right now was this tiny boy who had captured him in all the right ways.

Franklin was responsible for so much. How could he take care of the worries he and Thomas discussed last night? What scared him most was his inability to guarantee the safety of the three people who shared the house with him.

The most important people in his world.

CHAPTER 21

$\mathcal{A}$s Lorinda forced down each bite and held back the tears, she watched Franklin play with her baby. He was a natural father. When he looked at Michael, his expression turned so tender, his eyes twinkled. The baby leaned against his chest showing how much he loved and trusted him. Often, their gazes connected and held so long she wished she were part of the connection. Too bad Michael was the only child he would ever have.

Franklin stood and lifted his son high above his head while the baby laughed and sent slobber down the front of his starched shirt.

Lorinda grabbed a napkin and started dabbing the mess. "Just look what he did."

He handed the baby to her, and their fingers intertwined on Michael. For a moment, she felt so connected with both of them. He stared into her eyes and the connection grew stronger. She backed away, pulling her son against her shoulder.

Franklin dropped his hands. "Not a problem. I'll just change before I go."

Go where? She couldn't bring herself to voice the question.

What rights did she have in this marriage? Not that she had very many in her first, but Mike did at least tell her where he was going and when to expect him back. What exactly was wrong to cause those worry lines on Franklin's face? Maybe he thought she wouldn't notice...or maybe he didn't look in the mirror this morning.

"All right." Her gaze followed him as he left the kitchen.

"You want me to hold him while you finish your breakfast?"

Lorinda had almost forgotten Mrs. Oleson was in the room. "Yes, thanks."

After passing off her son, she dropped back into her chair. She really wasn't hungry anymore, but she knew she had to eat to keep up her strength and provide her son the nourishment he needed. She took a fork full of eggs and slid them into her mouth. She chewed them even though they seemed tasteless to her. Tasteless...colorless. Everything in her life, except her son, had changed.

She listened and swallowed back the tears until Franklin went out the front door. She didn't want Mrs. Oleson to know how unhappy she was so soon after the wedding.

The housekeeper talked and played with Michael until Lorinda finished eating. "Just leave the dishes on the table. I'll clean them up."

Lorinda took her son and started nursing him. It felt so good holding him close and knowing that she was providing every-thing he needed. After dropping a kiss on his smooth forehead, she glanced up at Mrs. Oleson.

"Do you know where Franklin is going?"

With a shake of her head, the housekeeper responded, "No."

At least he hadn't told *her* while keeping the information from Lorinda.

"Well, what about last night? Do you know what was wrong?" She couldn't breathe as she awaited the answer.

Another negative response released a sigh from her. So she

wasn't the only person in the dark. "I hate to ask this...but is this usual in a marriage? Not telling the wife anything?"

Mrs. Oleson turned from washing the dishes and wiped her hands on her apron. "Not in my marriage. And not in Franklin's parents' marriage." She came to the table and sat in a chair across from Lorinda. "But it's been a while since they've been gone, and Franklin hasn't had anyone but himself to think about. A man can get set in his ways. He probably didn't even think about telling you."

"I've never liked having someone else decide everything about my life." She tried to keep the bitterness from her tone.

Michael stirred and stopped nursing for a moment. He always did that when something upset her while she was feeding him. She pulled him closer and murmured loving words into his ear.

After he settled down again, Lorinda raised her gaze. "When Mike and I were married, he made all the decisions, but at least he told me about it." She wondered if she should be comparing her husbands out loud to the housekeeper.

Tenderness filled Mrs. Oleson's eyes as she looked at her. "Give him time to get used to being married. It's a lot to take on all at once...a wife...a son. Maybe he'll tell us when he comes back later."

And maybe he won't.

❧

Franklin rode into the pasture where the chuck wagon was set up to feed the ranch hands while they were working out on the farther pastures of the ranch.

He dismounted at the edge of camp and walked Major toward the wagon to both cool his stallion down and keep from raising a dust cloud. "Terrell, has everyone finished breakfast?"

The rotund man did a quick glance toward the sun and his

gray handlebar mustache twitched. "Sure have. Gettin' closer to lunch time. Gettin' married musta slowed ya down."

Franklin expected to get some ribbing from his men, especially the ones that had been here the longest. "Maybe, for a while." He glanced around. "You know where Thomas is?"

"Sure thing, Boss." The cook grinned.

Just like Rusty. No matter how many times he'd tried to get Jerrel to stop. So Franklin just got used to it.

"Up at piney pasture. Found quite a bit of damaged fence." He didn't look any happier than Franklin felt about that development.

"Thanks. I'll find him."

He mounted Major and headed toward the highest pasture he owned. Before he arrived, the air had thinned enough that he felt almost dizzy. He must be getting soft from staying at the lower part of the ranch so long. At least, it didn't seem to bother the cattle. Maybe it wasn't just the thin air that caused him to feel different.

Across the pasture, Thomas and a couple of other hands worked on the barbwire fence for the upper boundary of the ranch. On the other side of the fence, the peaks poked through rocky outcrops and scrubby trees. If the cattle thieves tore down the fence here, they had a hard time controlling the cows they stole. No wonder his men couldn't find the trail.

He headed around the herd to get to where they were working.

Thomas met him far enough away from the other men that they could talk without being heard. "How can I help you, Franklin?"

He dismounted. "I've come up with a plan of action."

The older foreman nodded. "All right."

"We have to protect the homestead area of the ranch. I want to use a few of our best hands to do that. They're familiar with the layout, who should be coming to the ranch house, and who's up to no good."

"How many?"

"I tried to think how few we could get by with, maybe two or three." He walked closer to Thomas. "But I don't want to take a chance with my wife and my son. So it'll take six or eight to make me feel comfortable."

He wondered if he would ever feel safe until they caught the man or men who were cattle rustlers and the arsonist. Any of them could be the murderer. His family was far too valuable for him to take any chances with their safety. "I'll work with Rusty. He knows the men almost as well as you do. He can help me choose. We can scope out the best places for each to cover."

"Sure gonna make us shorthanded."

He expected his foreman to say that. "I know. So here's what we're going to do. You know which hands like to sign on for cattle drives and are the most dependable. Pick eight of them and offer them a job. They can cover for the ones we take back to the homestead."

"You want me ta do it?" Thomas scratched his head. "Thought you did all the hirin' and firin'."

"Usually." He stared out across the mountains wondering where the varmints could be hiding. Lots of wilderness area out there. "But I want to take the eight hands back to the ranch and get them started. And I'll keep the others working while you're gone. Don't want to be away from the ranch overnight."

Thomas settled his Stetson on his head. "Could take me more 'n one night."

"I realize that. Take all the time you need. We have to have the best men for the job." He mounted Major and looked down at Thomas. "Tell them we're hiring them from now through the drive."

"Sure thing...Boss." A smile split the foreman's face before he turned toward where the horses were ground tied under some shade trees.

Maybe Franklin should just let the men call him what they wanted. He was tired of trying to change them. He had more important things to keep up with now.

While he headed out to check on the other ranch hands and work things out with Rusty, he hoped the criminals stayed away from his home...and his family. Hopefully, they weren't aware that he and his men had discovered what they'd done.

~

*A*fter they finished cleaning house and preparing supper, Lorinda agreed to let Mrs. Oleson have grandmother time with little Michael. She sat on the porch swing enjoying the evening breeze and the happy sounds coming from the parlor. Now that he'd started cooing and laughing, he exercised his voice most of the time.

She pushed the swing with one foot while she gazed out into the changing colors of early evening. The sun slowly sank behind the distant peaks, leaving vibrant streaks of color across the sky, painting the few clouds various shades. She found it odd to see a pale lavender cloud beside a pink or orange one. Finally, her life contained all the color she wanted. No longer was it drab and uninteresting as her early years had been.

God, I know this life is a blessing, even though it's not what I long for.

Several cowboys rode across the paddock spread behind the barn. Her heart lifted when she identified the silhouette of her husband. He'd been gone all day, and she missed his presence at lunch.

Earlier in the day, his foreman had returned. He'd gone to the bunkhouse and packed his saddlebags. Then he came to the house to ask if they had any fixin's for sandwiches. Mrs. Oleson had prepared a fairly large burlap bag of food for him to take wherever he was going. He didn't say. Lorinda wondered where, but of course, she didn't ask. So many things that happened on the ranch were outside her knowledge, and she didn't want to be too nosy.

She didn't remember Franklin ever riding with so many ranch hands. Surely, something unusual was going on. If only she knew what it was. Maybe she and Mrs. Oleson would find out when he came to the house. At least, she hoped so.

The hired hands stopped near the bunkhouse, but Franklin continued on. He dismounted outside the gate to the picket fence and dropped the reins on the ground before coming up the flagstone path to the porch. Why did he do that? Wouldn't the horse wander off? So many things she knew nothing about. If she was going to be a good wife for him, she'd need to learn.

Franklin's boot thumped on the first step. "Are you enjoying the outdoors?" He stopped when he reached the porch.

"Yes. I'm taking a break after cleaning house." She smiled up at him.

He leaned against the railing and crossed his arms over his chest. That movement stretched the fabric tight over his muscles, in his arms as well as other places. She didn't want to notice his strength, but removing her gaze from his imposing figure wasn't easy.

Chuckling, he glanced at the open windows to the parlor. "I started to ask where our son is, but no need."

"They're having a good time." She dropped her gaze to the floor. "I've enjoyed listening to them as much as I've enjoyed the breeze and the colors of twilight."

He shifted, crossing his legs at the ankle. "You like it here, don't you, Lorinda?"

If she disagreed, he'd wonder why. But she did like it here. She just didn't know where she fit into the scheme of things.

She nodded. "It's peaceful."

He straightened. "Do I smell roast?"

"You do." She got up from the swing. "Mrs. Oleson cooked while I cleaned. Tomorrow, she'll teach me how to make meatloaf."

Holding the screen door open, he waited for her to precede him into the house. "Sounds good to me."

Mrs. Oleson was already in the foyer, holding little Michael. "I'm sure you want to see this guy." She grinned at him.

He pulled the leather gloves from his hands and lifted the boy to press a kiss to the curls on the top of his head. Then he handed the baby back.

"Give him to his mother. I want to clean up so I won't get him dirty." Franklin headed toward the rooms they shared.

Lorinda took Michael, propped him on her hip, and followed their housekeeper to the kitchen.

~

*W*hen Franklin arrived in the kitchen, he immediately reached for his son. Their boy was growing like a weed, as his mother used to say. His son laughed at him and patted him on the cheeks when he tried to give the boy a kiss. They played while the women got the food on the table.

"You want me to take him now?" Lorinda held her arms toward the baby.

"No. I can eat and hold him at the same time." He'd been gone from his son for hours. So he wanted to hold him as long as he could. Breathing the essence of the sweet baby, he sat in the chair he always used.

Mrs. Oleson set three filled plates of food at their usual places. "Eat up. We have plenty."

Franklin bowed his head and said a special word of thanks

to God, then raised his head. "You said there's plenty to eat. Enough for eight more men?"

The housekeeper nodded. "What do you have in mind?"

"I brought eight of the men back to the homestead with me. I'm going to have them work around here for now." He accepted a hot roll from the woman and set it on his plate to butter it one-handed. "Terrell is out with the chuck wagon. If we have enough food, I'd like to take it to them in the bunkhouse after we finish eating."

He wasn't sure he was ready to tell the women what was going on. He knew Mrs. Oleson wouldn't be a problem, but he didn't want to frighten Lorinda. If he didn't let them know, they might question having so many men stay near the ranch house all the time.

"What's going on, Franklin?"

Lorinda acted surprised by Mrs. Oleson's question. If she would look at him, he'd try to show her he wasn't upset by what was happening. But she concentrated on her food.

He laid his fork on his plate. "Criminals could be lurking out there. Until we know for sure, I want the home place protected."

Finally, his wife looked at him. "What kind of criminals, Franklin?"

He could tell she was trying to acting nonchalant about it, but she didn't quite come across that way. "Cattle rustlers. Too many from our herd are missing. There's always some that go missing, but not this many. We're not sure if this is one person or more...and one of them could also be the murderer or even the arsonist."

Lorinda gasped and placed one dainty hand on her chest. She was so ladylike. She reminded him of his mother when she was young. Why hadn't he noticed that before?

He reached over and clasped her other fingers. She looked startled, glancing down at their entwined fingers.

Warmth spread up his arm. "I don't want to upset you. I just want you to know to be careful. We'll post these men in strategic places, so every side of each building is visible to someone. I don't think you're in real danger. I just don't want to take a chance...with my family."

A soft blush spread across her cheeks, making his breath hitch. Franklin couldn't lose his heir so soon after obtaining him...and his wife became more precious to him every day.

He really was in a pickle. Not being able to let her know he'd changed his mind.

CHAPTER 22

*L*orinda held Michael close to nurse him. She enjoyed these special times with him, but she knew they were limited. Her son was growing much too fast. He wasn't satisfied to lie in her arms while she fed him. Instead, he was more sitting than lying down, and every few minutes, he stopped, raised his head, and glanced around as if he was going to miss something. She was pretty sure she knew what he didn't want to miss. About this time of day, Franklin usually returned to the house for the evening. She knew she listened for him to open the door.

During the last few weeks, her husband was true to his word, staying close-by and only riding out to check on the ranch hands occasionally. While he was gone, she didn't worry about being safe. Most of the time, she knew exactly where at least two or three of the men hid while guarding them, and she knew the others were close enough to see the road and the house at all times.

With Terrell back in the bunkhouse kitchen, she and Mrs. Oleson only had to cook for themselves and Franklin. Of course, Michael liked the mashed potatoes they ate with most meals. Mrs. Oleson fixed them more often since he was eating some of the table food.

Lorinda had learned to recognize the distinctive clip-clop of Major approaching the house. So had Michael. They both heard Franklin ride up outside. He would soon come through the front door. She could relax now, knowing he was so near, but her heartbeat grew stronger as she thought of her husband...even if he was in name only.

Their son wriggled and pulled away from her. His happy jabbering filled her heart even more with the love she felt for him. He sounded so earnest as if really telling her something important. She wondered what kind of thoughts babies had at this age. She wanted him to grow as he should, but since he would be her only child, she wished she could savor these times a little longer.

"Yes, your daddy will be here soon." She lifted him to her shoulder, and he strained to look toward the door. Her husband was the kind of daddy she wished hers had been. "Let's get you cleaned up before he comes into the house."

She loved every moment she spent with little Michael, and she knew when Franklin came through the door, their son would want his attention. Franklin gladly gave it to him.

After dawdling over washing Michael and dressing him in a clean, long white baby slip, she reached the front hallway just before Franklin entered. Michael's arms churned the air as he strained toward his father. She had to keep her hand on the baby's bottom to stop him from hitting the floor while diving toward Franklin.

Her husband plucked him from her arms and held him close, kissing and blowing on his neck and his tummy while the baby laughed and batted at his head. Lorinda enjoyed watching them. She wondered what kind of father Mike might've been. Since he hadn't been around babies and although he loved her and physically let her know, he wasn't very tender about other things. Perhaps Franklin *was* a better father than Mike would've ever been.

Her husband smiled at her, and her heart took a flip. "He smells so good. Did you just clean him up?"

"Yes. To get him ready for Daddy coming home." She glanced down at the tips of her shoes that peeked out from under her skirt.

She had called Franklin Daddy in her own mind and often to their son, but she had never uttered the word out loud to her husband. She peeked back up at him, and his gaze locked on her face.

"What did you say?" His voice sounded husky.

"I got him ready for you." Her answer came out tentative.

He clutched the wiggling baby in his arms, but his attention was trained on her. "That's not all you said."

She took a deep breath and let it out slowly. "I said you were his daddy."

A slow smile crossed his face until his eyes shone like the evening star. "I like that. I never called my father Daddy, but I want Michael to call me that. It sounds more approachable. And I want to be approachable...for both of you."

His gaze held hers in an almost physical grip, and her breathing became shallow. So far he hadn't made all the decisions as Mike had. She hoped that would continue through their marriage. "Thank you, Franklin."

What else could she say? *I want even more from you?* Never in a million years would she have the fortitude to utter those words. Things were going great right now. She wanted to keep everything the way it was. On an even keel. To change *anything* could cause a disaster.

～

"*J* cleaned up in the barn, because I knew Michael would be wanting me as soon as I walked through the door." Franklin gazed at his son, then looked up and sniffed. "Smells as if Mrs. Oleson has our supper ready. Good thing I already washed up."

"Well, both of us worked on supper while the baby took a nap." Lorinda's smile felt like a special gift just for him. "I think I've mastered meatloaf. You'll have to tell me if you like it."

He wanted to put an arm around her and hold his complete family close. *Wonder what she would do if I did.*

She entered the kitchen before him.

Mrs. Oleson looked up from mashing the potatoes. "There you are, Franklin. I hoped you'd get here before the food got cold."

"I didn't want to miss whatever it is I'm smelling. I didn't realize I was so hungry."

With one hand, he raised the table tray attached to the high chair he'd ordered from the Montgomery Ward catalog at the Mercantile in Breckenridge. The copy said the legs were wider spaced so the child couldn't tip it over and the tray would go over the child's head until he had grown much taller. After sitting Michael in the chair and moving the tray so it was in front of him, he grabbed the tea towel Mrs. Oleson held for him and twirled it into a thick rope. He didn't want the baby to slip out under the table, so he anchored him to the back of the high chair with the towel.

Michael laughed and beat his hands against the tray table, kicking his legs at the same time. *What a racket!* But Franklin enjoyed every minute of the noise. He loved having a happy baby.

Lorinda took a large spoonful of mashed potatoes and put them on a plate to cool. Then she and Mrs. Oleson set the rest of the food on the table. Enticing aromas of the meatloaf, mashed potatoes, gravy, and green beans made his mouth water.

Before she could sit down, Franklin pulled his chair close to Michael. "Can I feed him tonight?"

She stopped and stared at him a minute, her eyes widened. "If you want to. I'm not sure if he's very hungry."

He grasped the small spoon she handed him, their fingers brushing briefly. He should have been more careful. Every time he touched her, his body reacted. Heat spread up his arm, and he had to look away. He wasn't sure he could live years, even decades, like this. Whooshing out a deep breath, he dipped up a small amount of mashed potatoes and held them toward the baby. Like a little bird getting fed by its parent, Michael's mouth popped open, and Franklin slipped the potatoes inside. He watched the baby suck on the food and roll it around in his mouth until it was gone.

That little mouth popped open again. Franklin gave him another small bite.

When Lorinda fed the baby, she took bites of her own food in between. Franklin could do that. He forked some meatloaf in his mouth before Michael finished his.

He glanced at his wife. "This is very good. I believe you'll have to move on to learning to cook something else. You've mastered meatloaf."

The rosy tint he loved crept into her cheeks, and she glanced down at her own food. "Thank you, Franklin."

Michael banged on his table and opened his mouth. Franklin gave him another bite.

"Aren't you going to say grace tonight?" Lorinda's eyes twinkled as she glanced at him.

"Of course." Heat rushed into *his* cheeks. How could he have forgotten something so important?

He bowed his head and blessed the food and the hands that

prepared it. By the time he uttered those few words, his son was once again pounding his fists on the table tray. *How do women keep up with everything so well?*

Lorinda was quietly eating, but she looked up at him. He smiled at her and took another bite of the meatloaf.

Why had he waited so long to get married? Having a wife and child to come home to every night was wonderful.

$\sim$

*A*t first, Lorinda wasn't thrilled with Franklin feeding their child. Even Mrs. Oleson hadn't asked to do that. But the men of the house were having so much fun, she pushed down the flicker of jealousy. She glanced out the window and drank in the beauty of the mountains. That always settled her.

As Mrs. Oleson had told her, Franklin had gradually changed since the wedding. He became more talkative about the ranch, and Lorinda enjoyed hearing what was going on.

"So what were you doing today, Franklin?" She slowly turned her cup of tea in its saucer.

"We had to brand all the new calves. It's a dirty, smelly business." He slipped another bite into the baby's waiting mouth. "That's one reason I washed up in the barn. During branding, I always keep extra clothes out there so I won't bring the stink into the house."

She grinned. "I'm sure glad you do." She nodded toward Michael. "This little guy makes more than enough messes that don't smell very good."

Mrs. Oleson and Franklin joined her laughter. Lorinda enjoyed their banter. For too long, things had been uncomfortable in the household. Now they had settled into a pleasant relationship.

While Franklin fed the baby another bite, she took the

chance to really study her husband. Since the first time she laid eyes on him, she'd realized just how handsome he was. It used to make her uncomfortable. Now it bothered her in a whole different way, making her wish once again that she'd never agreed to their marriage deception.

A curly lock of hair fell across his forehead, drawing her attention. She clenched her hands together to keep from reaching across the table and brushing it back.

He grabbed another bite of his own dinner and chewed vigorously while watching Michael.

"Franklin, why don't you let me feed Michael, so you and Lorinda can visit while you eat?" Mrs. Oleson reached for the small spoon.

Lorinda didn't mind the housekeeper's interruption. Now maybe she could keep her husband's attention and learn more about what was happening on the ranch. Of course, she didn't want to raise the subject on everyone's mind. When would their mountain valley be safe from cattle thieves, murderers, and arsonists?

Franklin did turn toward her and smile, his dark eyes sparkling like the water in one of the springs scattered across the ranch. "I've contacted the buyer from the Swift Packing Plant in Chicago, and he'll arrive in Frisco on Monday. That's the same day the extra cattle cars will get here. So we'll spend tomorrow making sure all three hundred fifty head of cattle we're shipping are healthy."

Lorinda loved hearing about the ranch and what it took to keep it running. She hoped someday she would be able to work right along beside him as other wives in the valley did with their husbands.

Mrs. Oleson glanced toward him while the baby ate the last bite of potatoes. "When will the cattle drive start?"

Franklin laid his fork on the edge of his plate. "I don't want to push them too hard. Instead of heading toward the Brecken-ridge side of the mountains, we're going to herd them toward Ten-Mile Creek. We'll move them slow, letting them feed along the way. We'll bed down beside the creek, so they'll have plenty of water. When we get to the railcars, they won't have lost any weight."

Lorinda realized her husband really hadn't answered the housekeeper's question. "How long does it take to get there?"

"We'll take over four days." He picked up his fork and started eating again.

"Okay, today's Tuesday." She counted on her fingers in her lap. "Tomorrow, you get them ready...so you'll leave on Thursday?"

"Very early Thursday morning."

She had gotten used to seeing him every day. And she didn't go to sleep until he was settled in his bed. She wasn't looking forward to him being gone that long. But what if he had to travel to Chicago with the cattle? It could be so much longer.

"What happens when you get to Frisco?" Her tone was flirting with whining, and she didn't want to do that.

Since Michael had finished all his potatoes, he started fuss-ing. Mrs. Oleson picked him up. "If you don't mind, I'll just go change his diaper and clean him up."

Lorinda glanced at her. "Thank you."

Franklin enjoyed more of his supper during this interlude.

"The cowboys who help drive them will load the herd in the cattle cars, while I conduct my business with the buyer. Since I've sold to them for several years, I won't have to accompany the cattle to Chicago. A few of the cowhands will go to keep them fed and watered. The Swift buyer and I will conclude our business before the train leaves Frisco."

He reached across the table and clasped her hand, the warmth enveloping her and shooting a tingle up her arm. "I'm sorry I'll miss going to church with you, but I'll get home as soon as I can, either very late Monday or early Tuesday."

Relief rushed through Lorinda while a sigh slipped from between her lips. Franklin gave her hand a slight squeeze before he went back to eating. At least, he wouldn't be gone as long as she had feared.

CHAPTER 23

The baby awoke Lorinda before dawn. The bed in the dressing room where Franklin slept was empty, the covers haphazardly pulled up over the pillow. She knew he wanted an early start this morning, but not this early. Maybe he'd be home at the regular time tonight.

She carried her cleaned-up baby into the kitchen where Mrs. Oleson sat drinking a cup of coffee. The fragrance of bacon and biscuits permeated the room, adding to her hunger. Her stomach made a very unladylike growl. She hoped Mrs. Oleson wouldn't notice.

Before her breakfast, Lorinda sat down to nurse her son. "You're up early."

"I always get up this early to fix Franklin's breakfast when they're preparing for a cattle drive." She leaned forward and let Michael grasp her finger.

He let go of his mother and sat up straighter. He glanced around the room before his gaze returned to Lorinda's face. He looked puzzled.

Lorinda knew who he was looking for. She was disappointed she wouldn't see Franklin this morning, too.

"You are such a sweet boy," Mrs. Oleson crooned. She eased her finger from his fist and went to the stove. "I'll scramble some eggs really soft. Maybe our little guy would like some."

Lorinda coaxed her son back to his nursing. He was getting to be a real handful, the way he twisted and turned and kicked. Just a little bundle of energy. By the time Mrs. Oleson set a plate with the eggs, crisp bacon, and two buttered biscuits in front of Lorinda, he was finished.

She slipped him into his high chair and held him while their housekeeper tied the tea towel around him.

"I took out some of the eggs to cool for him." Mrs. Oleson brought a saucer to set on the table beside her chair. "I'll feed him while you enjoy your breakfast." She gave him a small bite. He wallowed it around in his mouth, and a bit of slobber leaked out the front. Mrs. Oleson wiped it away.

Lorinda's thoughts returned to Franklin. "Have you ever been on a cattle drive?"

"No, but my dearly departed husband was the bunkhouse cook when he was with us. He often manned the chuck wagon." A faraway smile played across her lips while she stared into the distance.

Michael pounded his fist on the tray table.

Mrs. Oleson fed him some more.

Lorinda poured honey on her biscuit and took a bite, the sweetness reminding her of Franklin's kiss at the wedding. Longing to feel another of those caresses tugged at her senses. She shook her head to get the thought from her mind.

"Have they ever had accidents on any of the drives?" Awaiting the answer, she held her breath.

Mrs. Oleson glanced at her before giving Michael another bit of egg. "A cattle drive can be dangerous. There are always scrapes and bruises, even blisters, but I can't remember anything major."

"That's good." Lorinda turned her attention back to her food.

Michael finished every bit of the egg, then started laughing while Mrs. Oleson cleaned his hands and face. She made a game of it, sneaking the cloth in while he was giggling.

"Since the railroads came to Frisco, the men don't have to drive the cattle very far." Mrs. Oleson spread a baby quilt on the floor on the side of the kitchen away from the stove.

She placed Michael on the blanket and put a few wooden blocks around him. He started reaching for one. As his grasping fingers stretched toward it, he flopped over, but the other arm was caught under his body.

"Look at that. He almost turned all the way over." Mrs. Oleson clapped her hands and laughed. "It won't be long until he can scoot across the floor. Before we know it, he'll be crawling."

Oh, my goodness. Lorinda didn't realize babies did things like that so early. For a moment, she felt overwhelmed with being a mother. What would she have done if nothing had happened to Mike? She didn't know what to do with a baby. Would her son have been neglected because of her inexperience? At least, Mrs. Oleson was helping her learn to be a mother the same way she taught her to cook and knit and sew. *Thank you, God, for putting me here in this family.*

After Lorinda cleaned up the dishes, she took Michael and put him down for a nap. As she went through all the house-cleaning she planned for the day, her mind was in a whirl.

Both she and her son anticipated the time Franklin would come to the house. When he arrived, his presence lit up every room. Michael wouldn't go to sleep at night until after his daddy played with him. She never fell asleep until he was in the dressing room and she could hear his breathing relax into the slower rhythm of sleep.

What would they do the four nights he'd be gone?

Fear grabbed her heart and squeezed it so tight she caught her breath. *What if he doesn't come home?* Even though nothing had happened the last few years, that didn't guarantee it wouldn't this year.

Mike hadn't thought anything would happen to him...or to her while he was gone. And look what happened. He was killed. Franklin and his men buried him on her property.

The thought of her new husband being carried to the ranch slung across the back of a horse made her stomach roil enough to cause her breakfast to try to come up. She swallowed and tears flooded her eyes. *Please God, don't let anything happen to Franklin, too.*

Yes, she wanted more from their marriage, but if it was the only way she could have him near, then this sham marriage would have to be enough. She couldn't face losing him altogether.

And neither could her son.

~

*T*he night before other cattle drives, Franklin had slept under the stars near the herd with the other cowboys. As he rode toward the homestead, the bright moonlight cast a pearly sheen over everything. All he could think about was seeing his son one last time before he left...and his wife, no matter how hard he had to fight himself to keep from sweeping her up in his arms.

Hope I'm not too late to see them both. As he approached the house, light poured from the kitchen windows. At least, someone was up. Was it Mrs. Oleson...or Lorinda? He went through the mudroom and peeked in the kitchen door. "Is Lorinda still up?"

His housekeeper looked up from where she sat at the table. "Yes. I know you said you'd try to get home tonight, but I really didn't think you would."

"I've still got to clean up. I'll be in as soon as I can."

As he walked Major to the barn, he whistled all the way. He would get to see his wife one more time before he left. That put a spring in his step. Now to get all this mess off him...and quickly.

When he returned to the kitchen, Mrs. Oleson held his son, all cleaned up and ready for bed. Franklin crossed the room and watched the baby's eyes light up. Mrs. Oleson released Michael into his arms.

"Are you glad to see Daddy?"

Sweet baby laughter followed his question, and the baby became a kicking, punching machine. The exuberance arrowed straight to his heart. His chest almost burst with all the love captured there.

"Daddy couldn't leave without seeing his boy one more time." He bestowed kisses along the baby's neck, and the laughing increased.

Mrs. Oleson stood near the hall doorway, smiling.

Tiny fists grasped the collar of his shirt. The little guy had quite a grip.

"Where's Lorinda?" He couldn't take his eyes off his son when he asked the housekeeper the question.

"She's getting ready for bed. I told her I'd watch the baby while she did."

That brought all kinds of thoughts to his head, almost taking his mind off his son...but not quite.

"So...do you want to take a ride?" He pulled the baby down toward his waist, then swung him as high as he could reach.

Peals of laughter trilled around the room. The next time he swung him up, he let him go just for a second, easily catching him with both hands. Michael loved it, so he tossed him a little higher...then even higher...and higher still.

"What are you doing to my son?"

The shrill shriek startled Franklin, but he never took his

eyes off the baby. Quickly, he grabbed him and held him close to his chest.

He turned toward Lorinda. "What were you trying to do? Scare me into dropping him?"

Her face was red, and she perched her fisted hands on her hips. "You were scaring him! You *could* have dropped him!"

Michael stopped laughing and his face puckered.

"See, he's about to cry."

He'd made the extra effort to come home, and here his wife was screaming like a banshee at him. He'd never heard a cross word from her before.

"Well, he didn't start crying until you started screaming."

Franklin stared at her, just now noticing she wore some kind of white, nearly transparent robe and gown, decorated with tiny colorful flowers. Good thing she had on both of them. Even with the two layers, he could see a hint of the luscious curves underneath. He'd never seen her in anything like that before, and his desire for her exploded into something he had a hard time controlling. After all, she was his wife. Heat throbbed through his body, making him sweat.

Sobs burst from her. "You...could have...dropped him."

He stalked across the kitchen floor and pulled her into the arm that wasn't holding their son. "Lorinda, I'd never...ever...put you or him in danger. Please believe me."

She shook as if she were out in the cold night air. "I just couldn't have faced losing him."

He leaned his chin on the top of her head. "Neither could I."

They stood like that for an extended moment, holding the wriggling baby between them. After dropping a quick kiss on her forehead, he handed the baby to her. She took Michael and hurried out of the kitchen. Her movements caused the robe and gown to cling close to the front of her body and puff out behind her. Thank goodness, he wasn't on that side of her.

Franklin glanced at Mrs. Oleson, who still sat at the table, holding a mug in her hands. "What was that all about?"

"Sit down, Franklin." She let go of the mug. "Look at it from her perspective."

He turned the chair across from her around and straddled it with his arms crossed along the back. "How so?"

"It's a very long time since she's been in a normal family, and I'm not sure that family was normal. I don't know exactly what all happened to her, but she has a hard time trusting people. I'm sure she has a good reason not to." She leaned toward him. "She's probably never seen a father play with his son the way you just did. It does look dangerous to a woman...even me, and I have total assurance you can catch the baby."

That hit him like a punch to his gut. All the air whooshed out of his lungs. He'd never realized those things about Lorinda. But then she hadn't shared very much about her former life with him. He must not be very discerning. At least, Mrs. Oleson was.

"I was out of line." He rubbed his forehead. An ache throbbed behind his eyes. "And I don't have time to make it up to her."

"Something else could be bothering her."

He must be really dense. "What else?"

Mrs. Oleson gave him her you're-such-a-man look. "Her first husband left for only a short time and never returned. You and Thomas took his body to her. She could be scared that something could happen to you."

"I hadn't thought of that." He got up and went to the water bucket and dipped up a drink.

"Thanks for telling me. I've got to get some shut-eye, or I won't be worth anything on the drive."

He entered the bedroom where his son slept. How quickly he'd fallen asleep. After pressing a gentle kiss on his cheek, he went to the door of his former bedroom. Lorinda lay in the bed, not moving a muscle, and her breathing sounded even. Hope-fully, she'd calmed down from their little scare.

Take him a while to forget what happened.

CHAPTER 24

*W*hen Franklin reached the herd the first morning of the cattle drive, he felt as lousy as a high-strung horse that had been ridden hard and put up wet. Sleep had been a long time coming last night, and early morning arrived much too soon. After he got over being angry with Lorinda, his mind was attacked by thoughts he should have considered before he made that stupid marriage bargain. They were as hard to straighten out as a stampede on a cattle drive.

Please, Lord, keep the herd from stampeding before we reach Frisco station.

All the time since Lorinda agreed to be his wife, he'd seen her only as a mother for his heir. He thought she should be thankful she didn't have to worry about how she would be able to take care of Michael. He would provide for them and protect both of them. The idea she might have other concerns never entered his mind...until Mrs. Oleson brought them up last night.

Today's job would take all his concentration, so he pushed these thoughts into a compartment in his mind and snapped the door closed. With plenty of cowboys to help, they got the herd moving the longer way to Frisco. They only had to keep them going at a gentle pace that allowed for some grazing, then they moved toward Miner's Creek. He wanted water close-by during the drive. They'd follow this stream until it connected to Ten Mile Creek and steer along this source of water until they were close to the railroad depot. The cattle cars should arrive by the time they did. He looked forward to dealing with Harley Smith. The buyer for Swift Packing Company in Chicago was a fair man that knew he could trust Franklin to deliver strong, healthy beeves.

Thomas had hired some of the best, most experienced cowboys that looked for work on the cattle drives, so they worked together like a well-greased wagon wheel. Even on the parts of the trail that were mountainous with scattered trees, they were able to keep the herd moving the same direction.

When they made camp the first night, Franklin's lack of sleep intensified his fatigue. He hoped to fall asleep as soon as he slid into his bedroll.

But that didn't happen. Satiated with Terrell's good cooking, he went to where his saddle and bedroll awaited him while many of the other cowboys still sat around the campfire. Their quiet talking didn't bother him, but as soon as he laid his head down, thoughts of the early morning burst forth from the box where he'd hidden them, like the Jack-in-the Box toy he'd had when he was small.

The things Mrs. Oleson told him ate on him like a passel of mosquitos, itching his mind just as much as the pesky bugs did his body. He'd become used to having Lorinda around and looked forward to coming home to her as much as he enjoyed seeing their son. Her sweet smile, the flowery fragrance that lingered in her hair, and the occasional soft touch when they passed the baby from one to the other had become important to him.

Last night when she screamed at him like the shrew in Shakespeare's play, he'd been blind-sided. Now he understood.

She'd been afraid of him hurting the baby. He couldn't believe she thought such a thing. Somehow, he had to make her understand he'd never endanger either her or their son.

The other things Mrs. Oleson said made him wonder just what had happened in Lorinda's past. If some man or men had mistreated her, he'd like to take his quirt to them. Although he never really used it on his horses, those men needed to feel the cuts from the leather thongs. Teach them a lesson, that real men didn't hurt women. They protected and cherished them. His own inability to erase whatever mistreatment his wife had suffered in the past, or might suffer in the future, daggered straight to his heart.

To love and to cherish. He'd vowed those words before God and a whole passel of witnesses. He'd had no plans to cherish Lorinda. Protect her, yes, but nothing else. *What kind of a man does that make me?* Not much better than any other man who'd hurt her. Wouldn't unfulfilled vows do as much damage as the other men had?

He took advantage of her vulnerability. Plain and simple. Offered her protection when he planned to withhold love and affection from her. She must feel unworthy, and he'd caused it.

Franklin turned over and tried to find a comfortable position. His own faults bruised his soul, like the sharp rocks he laid on bruised his back.

All the other cowboys now slept. A cacophony of various forms of snores, whistles, and snorts bounced around the clearing where they camped.

And here he lay castigating himself for his selfishness. How in the world would he be able to work tomorrow? Finally, his mind just shut down, and he slept.

∾

*L*orinda didn't sleep a wink the night before Franklin left for the cattle drive. Her heart ached, and she heard every time her husband twisted and turned in his solitary bed in the dressing room. Was he as miserable as she was about the quarrel they had? As far as she knew, he didn't care. She and Mike had never yelled at one another. They didn't always agree, but they were able to talk it out like civilized people. This shouting match brought up ghosts of her past, when her father came home drunk and took out his anger on her. The quarrel with Franklin bruised her heart as much as her father's beatings bruised her body and soul.

This wasn't what she'd agreed to. At least, Franklin wasn't in the dressing room sleeping, oblivious to the way she felt. She wanted to believe their quarrel was what kept him awake. She wished she had the right to go to him and talk it out, but she wasn't sure their agreement allowed that. Tears leaked from her eyes, dampening her pillow. When a sob tried to escape, she held the wet pillow over her face to keep from making any noise. She wouldn't let him hear her cry. She'd learned to muffle her crying when she was younger, because it infuriated her father even more.

Finally, Franklin got up from his bed. Lorinda heard every squeak, every rustle, as he dressed and left, taking the route through the baby's room. She didn't hear the drumbeat of his boot heels on the hardwood floor in the foyer. Evidently, he waited to put the boots on until he was outside. Maybe he was afraid that if he woke her, she would continue her tirade.

With him gone, she sobbed quietly, but it brought no relief. At last, sleep covered her with its dark veil, and she relaxed.

Far too soon, Michael awakened and needed her attention. She dragged herself out of bed, slipped on her robe, and tied the sash tight around her waist. Taking a deep breath, she headed into the baby's room. Then she wished she'd foregone the deep breath. No wonder her son was crying.

Leaning over the railing of his bed, she crooned to him as she lifted him out. "Mamma's here. I'll get you cleaned up right away. Then we can have breakfast."

When she walked into the kitchen, both she and her son were clean and dressed.

"There you are." Mrs. Oleson sat at the table with both hands hugging her mug of coffee.

The enticing fragrance sang a siren song to Lorinda, but she needed to take care of the baby first. After the two women got Michael situated in his high chair, Lorinda dropped into the chair beside his.

Mrs. Oleson studied Lorinda's face before she patted her hand. "You poor dear. You look as though you didn't sleep a wink last night."

Lorinda breathed out a heavy sigh, wishing her pain had escaped with it. Instead, the knot in her chest remained. "I did sleep...a little."

"I'm sorry last night was so painful." The other woman got up and went to the stove. "I was waiting for you to get up before scrambling the eggs."

Eggs? They didn't even sound good. "I'm not very hungry."

Mrs. Oleson cracked four eggs into the skillet and whisked them with a fork. "You have to eat to keep your strength up...and so you can produce the milk our little prince needs. Besides, I'm sure he's hungry."

Our little prince? Where had that title come from? Their housekeeper really took her grandmothering seriously.

"Oh, my goodness." A blush tinted Mrs. Oleson's cheeks as she brought the skillet to the table and served a portion for Lorinda, on a plate that already held a buttered biscuit and two slices of bacon, and a small amount in a bowl for Michael. "That just slipped out." She put the hot skillet in the dry sink before bringing a second cup of coffee and joining Lorinda at the table. "That's what I called Franklin when he was about this age. Michael doesn't look a bit like Franklin did, but they do love each other so much, just like Mr. Vine loved his son."

Lorinda took a sip of the hot beverage. Her husband had been raised in a family filled with love. She wished she knew what that felt like. At least, her son would know. One really special thing that came from the agreement. She would just have to get used to things as they were. She owed it to Michael. The knot in her chest tightened even more.

The first bite of eggs and bacon awakened Lorinda's hunger. While Mrs. Oleson fed the baby, she ate every bit of food on her plate, enjoying the coffee as well.

When everyone finished, Lorinda went to the sink to wet a corner of a tea towel. She used it to wash Michael's hands and face.

"I'll clean up the dishes." The housekeeper gathered the plates and put them in the dishpan.

"Thanks. I haven't nursed Michael yet."

Lorinda sat down and arranged her clothing so her son had easy access. He leaned back against her arm and *almost* let her cuddle him. These early morning times were so precious. Later in the day, he would be so much more independent.

Mrs. Oleson plunged her hands into the sudsy water. "You didn't have any younger brothers or sisters, did you?"

Lorinda glanced up at her. "No. My mother died trying to give birth to my brother. Neither one of them lived."

"I'm so sorry to hear that." The housekeeper continued to wash the plates, then dip them in the rinse water. "I guess you've never seen a father play with his son the way Franklin did last night."

"Never." Lorinda shook her head. "I'm really sorry I yelled at Franklin."

"It did surprise him. After you took the baby to get ready for bed, I told him I didn't think you understood it wasn't dangerous."

"Are you sure it's not? What if he'd dropped my baby?"

Mrs. Oleson turned around, drying her hands on the towel tucked into the waistband of her apron. "I've seen how much Franklin loves that baby...and he'd never do anything to hurt him. I promise. He was totally in control of his actions."

"I suppose so, since he caught Michael just fine." Lorinda leaned to press a kiss on the baby's hair. "I can see how much Franklin loves him. I'm sorry I overreacted."

Mrs. Oleson came back to sit in the chair across from her. "Things like this happen in a marriage...even the best of them. Just don't let it come between you and Franklin."

How could she keep it from coming between them? The distance they already kept would allow a runaway wagon to drive through.

Lorinda wanted to talk to Mrs. Oleson as if she really were her mother. Surely a mother could help her unravel this dilemma.

Perhaps she would have been able to be content with their arrangement...except for the kiss. Too many times each day, she felt the tender pressure that initiated the kiss, but it became so much more, touching all the way to the center of her heart and capturing it for all time. In the nighttime, she could still taste the intense sweetness, and it brought her body alive as never before, wanting so much more from the handsome man who was her husband...and yet he wasn't. When he was near, the aroma of Bay Rum Oil and his particular type of maleness always brought the memory of that one moment when they'd been so close and intimate.

Her emotions might not be able to take all the tugging this way and that.

Someday, part of her was going to break loose.

CHAPTER 25

*F*ranklin was riding ahead of the point man when the herd rounded the last mountain and headed toward Frisco's train station. The empty cattle cars waited on a side track beside a large fenced pen.

People were still stepping from the passenger cars of the westbound train. A tall man wearing a Stetson and carrying saddlebags over his shoulder caught Franklin's eye. The man made his way to the baggage car where he started talking to the conductor. Something about the man intrigued him, but he couldn't figure out what. Strangers often came to Summit County by train. Maybe it was the confidence he exhibited.

Harley Smith ambled out of the depot just as Franklin rode up and dismounted. "You're right on time, Franklin, as always."

The man thrust out his hand, and Franklin shook it. He liked a man with a strong grip and level eyes that stared him straight on, eye to eye.

"Good to see you again." Franklin nodded toward the herd. "We've got 350 head. I'm sure you'll want to inspect them."

Harley nodded, and the two men walked over to the wooden

fence and leaned their arms on the top, each with a booted foot resting on the bottom rail.

"I can get a good look at them as they enter the pen."

The cowboys had no trouble urging the cows through the gate, because feeding stations lined two sides of the enclosure. Franklin was proud of his men. All were real professionals that knew how to handle themselves and the beeves.

Harley stood up and walked along the fence, his gaze roving over each animal. The man really knew about quality in a herd.

"Looks like top-notch cattle again." Harley came back to where Franklin still stood. "They'll bring top dollar."

"Always glad to hear that."

Harley started toward the open door to the depot with Franklin by his side. "The station master has a pot of coffee on. We can take care of our business at a table in the corner while we enjoy a cup."

A nervous horse neighed as the stranger Franklin had noticed before led him down a wide plank from the baggage car. Franklin and Harley paused to watch.

"That's a fine horse he's got." Harley recognized good horse-flesh, too.

"Yup."

Before they went into the depot, they both watched as the man mounted and headed down the road toward Breckenridge. The westbound train pulled out of the station, going to the place where it would take the side rails, so the eastbound could come through.

By the time they finished with their business, Franklin held a bag of money, and the eastbound train had arrived. The cattle cars were already attached to the end of the train, and Franklin's cowhands had loaded most all the beeves into them.

When they finished, he called the men into a huddle over to the side of the train station, away from prying eyes. He paid each man, and the extra hands rode on into Frisco. Several of his own men were accompanying the cattle to Chicago. Everything was under control. Gave him a good feeling.

Too bad his family life wasn't.

He mounted Major and turned toward Breckenridge. First, he'd go to the bank, and he needed to talk to Brian before he returned to the ranch. Franklin wanted things to change, but he didn't have a clue how that could happen. He'd made such a mess of things. He wanted help, and the only person he felt free to talk to was his pastor, since he would keep everything Franklin told him in confidence.

On the way to Breckenridge, he gave Major his head. They'd had to keep pace with the cattle, and since Franklin didn't want to run any of the weight off before they were sold, the pace was slow. Major needed a good run, and Franklin enjoyed the dust-free air rushing around him. He slowed down when they reached the outskirts of town. The streets teemed with people. He picked his way through the crowds until he reached the bank. He tied Major's reins to the hitching rail in front and headed inside. On the ranch, Major was trained to a ground tie, but with all the busyness, he could get spooked.

After depositing most of his money in the bank, he went to the mercantile to pay off the balance his ranch owed. Since he'd been in the saddle so many days, he decided to leave Major tied to the rail by the water trough and walk the few blocks to the parsonage.

Brian answered his knock. "Franklin, to what do I owe the pleasure of a visit today?"

"I didn't know if I'd find you home, but I'm glad I did." He stuffed his hands in the front pockets of his denim trousers. "I wondered if you'd have time to visit with me a bit."

"Sure. Would you like to come in? Mary can get us a cup of coffee and a slice of cake."

Franklin glanced through the doorway, glad Mary wasn't in sight. "I've got a serious problem I'd like to discuss with you."

"All right. We can go over to the church and visit in the sanctuary, if you'd like."

"Sounds good to me."

Brian grabbed his hat, settled it on his head, and the two men went next door. When they stepped into the empty sanctuary, calmness settled over Franklin. Even though he had been wondering if this was the right thing to do, that peace gave him the answer. He needed help, and Brian was a good shepherd for his flock as well as a dynamic preacher.

The minister led the way to the front and took a seat on the first pew. As Franklin dropped down beside him, his eyes were drawn to the stained-glass window behind the pulpit. He'd always loved the depiction of Jesus as a shepherd. He felt as if he would have two people helping him today. He snatched his Stetson from his head and dropped it onto the pew on the side opposite the preacher. Franklin continued to study the window—the staff in one of Jesus's hands and the lamb cradled in his other arm. The eyes seemed to see right through him. But they were gentle, not condemning.

"Let's pray." Brian bowed his head and petitioned heaven for wisdom and guidance.

The words whisked away Franklin's lingering nervousness. He took a deep breath and slowly let it out. Time to be honest.

"What's going on, Franklin?"

Although he expected the question, he wasn't quite sure how to start telling his pastor. So he began at the point when he and Thomas took Mike Sullivan's body up the mountain and met his wife. As he continued the story, Brian watched him, taking in every word.

When he got to the part about him asking Lorinda to marry him, he had a hard time forcing the words out. He watched his pastor for his reaction to the agreement they made. At least the man's expression never condemned him.

"We actually had our first quarrel the evening before I left on the cattle drive. I didn't know how to make it better."

"It would be hard with your agreement holding you apart." Brian's wrinkled brow indicated how deep his thoughts were. "Go home. Have a private talk with her. Apologize to her for the quarrel. Tell her it was all your fault."

Franklin dropped his gaze to the floor, wishing he could sink through the boards and disappear. "But–"

"Sometimes, it's important for us men to take all the blame. It'll make her feel safe with you. Know that you really don't want to hurt her. Even show her that you'd lay your life down for her."

Is that what married men really do? "I didn't expect this."

"That's interesting." Brian looked him straight in the eyes. "I remember the wedding kiss. That didn't look as if it was forced. Actually, the temperature in the church went up about ten degrees." A chuckle accompanied the last statement.

Franklin felt heat creep up his neck and into his cheeks. Since he hadn't shaved after finishing the cattle drive, he hoped his few days growth made a dark enough beard to hide his embarrassment. "That kiss got away from me. I only meant to give a peck on her lips."

A laugh burst forth from Brian. "That was a mighty long, deep peck."

"Don't I know it. I can't get the kiss out of my thoughts. Every time I see Lorinda, I want to repeat it. But...we made this agreement..."

"Has Lorinda given any indication of how the kiss affected her?"

"Not really...sometimes, I do catch her staring at me with a bemused expression, but other than when we pass Michael from one to the other, we haven't touched again." That wasn't exactly the truth.

On their wedding night and the next day, there was some

touching, accidental or not. But he didn't want to explore the feelings those quick touches brought to him. If he did, he might just break down and grab Lorinda for another kiss. And scare her completely away.

"I haven't noticed anything about your relationship that would indicate what you've told me. Maybe Lorinda feels the same way you do. If so, what would you do about it?"

Franklin hadn't expected this question. What did he want to do? Make their marriage real in every sense of the word. Just thinking the thought sent heat rushing throughout his body. He needed to keep control over his emotions.

"I can tell from watching your face that you want the marriage to be real, don't you?"

All Franklin could do was nod.

"It's a good thing you don't play poker." Brian laughed. "You'd never win."

Franklin had to join him in his merriment. "What am I supposed to do?"

"Are you willing to risk your heart again? That's the only way. Open up to her. Nothing about your relationship has been normal. One thing you could do is try to woo your wife. Court her the way every woman wants to be courted."

That hadn't worked with Miriam. If it had, Marvin wouldn't have been able to snatch her right out from under Franklin's nose. But now, he realized she wasn't the woman for him..

"How?" Did he really ask that stupid question? He was in worse shape than he realized.

"Women glow, and grow, when they are loved. Compliment her. Take her a gift for no reason. Defer to her desires about things. The time will come when you can talk to her about how you feel. Can you wait for that?"

He'd waited this long. Of course, he could wait for her feelings for him to take hold. Just the thought of that coming to fruition made his heartbeat a few notches faster.

After Brian prayed with him again, asking God to reveal His plans to both Franklin and Lorinda, the men headed back toward the parsonage.

"Would you like to come in for coffee and cake now?" Brian's eyebrows lifted with the end of the question.

"Thanks, but I want to get back home as soon as I can."

Franklin thrust out his hand for their goodbye handshake. Then he headed toward the mercantile again. This time, he went to the part of the store where all kinds of doodads and things for women were displayed. He hadn't spent much time there before. The vast array surprised him. That department occupied several aisles.

He ambled along one of them waiting for something to catch his eye. Just before he headed toward another aisle, he noticed a music box shaped like a grand piano. With gilded trim, the ceramic top and sides had a pastoral scene painted on each panel. He picked it up and twisted the key. Tinkling notes trilled as the key turned. He looked closely at the label on the bottom. "Für Elise." He wondered if Lorinda would like this. He'd buy it anyway. If she didn't, he could always give it to Mrs. Oleson.

On the way to the counter to pay, he passed a case displaying jewelry. A pair of eardrops caught his attention. The blue stones in them would match the wedding ring he'd bought for Lorinda. They sparkled in the sunlight streaming through the front window of the store. He'd get them, too. That way, he'd have another gift for her before he had to come back to town for more.

Franklin whistled as he carefully placed the daintily wrapped items into his saddlebags. For the first time in days, he felt hopeful for the future of his marriage.

Now he must find a way to convince Lorinda to love and desire *him*.

CHAPTER 26

*L*orinda sat on the porch, one toe on the floor gently rocking the swing. Mrs. Oleson had Michael in his high chair banging a couple of spoons on the tray while she cooked supper. Lorinda wondered how the older woman could put up with all that noise. It was driving her crazy.

She stared across the large valley at the majestic mountaintops as the sun made its swift descent toward the horizon. Fluffy puffs of clouds rode the gentle breeze as the disappearing sun painted their sides in soft shades of pink, lavender, and peachy orange. The lower the light sank, the deeper the hues splashed across the clouds until dark red, deep purple, and wild orange streaked across the sky. This tranquil time of day was her favorite...except for today.

Where is Franklin?

After the first day he was gone, her anger turned into longing. She missed his presence that filled the house when he came in at the end of the day. The scent of heat, horse, and hard work that accompanied him had quickly become her favorite fragrance. Without him, the house felt cold and empty. And while she missed his presence, her memory returned to their wedding day and that...amazing...kiss. The taste...the feel of his lips, alive on hers...coaxing her to participate...the way it had—

With a shake of her head, she tried to shove the thoughts away, but she couldn't. Would she ever experience something as exquisite as that again? Not a chance. *How sad.*

Mrs. Oleson told her Franklin should arrive back from the cattle drive today. When some of the ranch hands rode in earlier, her heart leapt within her. Disappointment gripped her when she realized her husband wasn't with them. She didn't want to ask them where he was, because as his wife, she should know. Surely, one of them would tell her and Mrs. Oleson if anything bad had happened to him.

She hated knowing they hadn't parted on good terms. She needed to apologize for the way she treated him. The hurt in his eyes when she accused him of endangering Michael still lingered in her mind. Hurt that was almost as strong as the hurts she'd experienced growing up. She had never wanted to cause that kind of pain for anyone. Especially her husband.

The sun said goodbye to their valley, and it left a golden rim on each mountaintop. As her gaze followed the thin line of light, her ears detected the hoof beats of a lone rider approaching. In the familiar semidarkness of the gloaming, she strained to see if it was her husband. From the way the shadowy figure rode in the saddle and leaning slightly forward, his Stetson tilted just so, she knew. Franklin would be here in a few minutes. Tears of joy trailed down her cheeks.

She rushed inside the house and into her bedroom, swiping the moisture away. After lighting the lamp, she stared at her reflection in the looking glass. She brushed a few stray hairs back and quickly slid in a hairpin to hold them into place. Giving her cheeks a few soft pinches, she brought color to her face. After rolling her lips together several times, they glowed with life. So did her eyes.

Lorinda arrived back on the front porch right before

Franklin leapt from his saddle beside the gate. He dropped the reins to the ground, then looked toward the porch. Even in the low light, she saw his smile and his eyes light up as he continued to stare at her a moment before he opened the gate. Her heartbeat felt like a woodpecker pounding a rhythm on the trunk of a tree. Fireflies danced in her stomach.

～

*W*as Lorinda waiting just for him? He hoped so. *That would be a good sign.*

He turned back to take one of the packages from his saddlebag. He'd slip the other into the house later when she was busy. He loped up the walkway to the porch, drinking in the sight of her. Blonde curls piled on the top of her head, and her blue eyes matched the sky that had darkened before he could reach home.

He had to be especially blessed married to a woman like her. And he had done her wrong. Promising what he had no plans to fulfill. How long would it take him to undo the damage? Or could he ever?

"I was wondering if you would get home today." Her voice brought music to his heart.

"Were you worried about me?"

He went up all but the last step to the porch, ending with them face to face. He wondered if she would move back, since they were so close. But she didn't. The soft flowery scent of her surrounded him, and he breathed deeply of the fragrance.

Lorinda turned her gaze out across the ranch land. "Maybe a little...when the ranch hands came home and you weren't with them."

He took another step, so close his breath mingled with hers. "I'm sorry. I didn't think about you being worried."

Franklin wished he could close the short distance and taste her lips again, but he didn't dare. He would do nothing to scare her away. He tightened his stomach muscles and stepped up on the porch, but not crowding her.

She glanced up at him. "I need to apologize to you, too."

"What for?"

Clasping her hands close to her chest, she looked nervous. "I didn't understand what you were doing with Michael." She started wringing her hands. "Mrs. Oleson explained that fathers often played with their babies that way. I didn't know." Her last words were just a whisper.

A smile crept over his face. Maybe it wouldn't be as hard as he thought to woo her into becoming his wife in every way. "I promise you, Lorinda. I would never do anything that would put Michael, or you, in danger. Never."

Her hands slid down the front of her skirt, straightening imaginary wrinkles. "I believe you, Franklin."

Her words made him feel about ten feet tall. He glanced down at the package he held. "Let's go in where there's more light. I brought you a present."

"Why?" Her brow creased as if she was confused.

"No special reason." He opened the door then took her hand and pulled her along with him as they entered the house.

A warm glow came from the parlor. He hadn't noticed light coming from the windows when he rode up. Mrs. Oleson must have heard them and lit the three kerosene lamps that filled the room with a welcome radiance.

Lorinda stopped after he led her into the parlor. "I've never had a present for no reason."

His heart ached for what she must have gone through while she was growing up. Maybe someday she'd share it all with him, so he could help her make new memories and erase those bad ones. He didn't want to try to imagine what had happened to her. His free hand clenched into a fist. Not wanting to scare her, he flexed the fingers open.

"Sit down, Lorinda, so you can see what I brought you."

She looked like a child at a birthday party. Her wide smile brought a twinkle to her eyes. She started carefully untying the twine, but when she had a hard time, she slipped it around the corners and threw it on the floor. As she peeled back the white wrapping paper, a happy sound sighed between her lips.

Cradling the piano in her hands held close to her chest, she gazed up at him with a wonderful expression he'd never before seen on her face. "What is it, Franklin?"

How could she not know? "It's a music box shaped like a grand piano."

He reached for it and turned the key on the bottom before resting it back in her hands.

She closed her eyes and swayed to the beat of the music. He loved watching her like this. When the instrument stopped playing, she twisted the key herself.

While the music played again, she gazed into his eyes. "This is the most wonderful thing anyone has ever given me. Thank you, Franklin."

When the song ended, she set the instrument on the table beside the lamp and rose gracefully. Her arms crept around his waist, and she rested her head against his chest, right above his heart. He wondered if she could hear his heartbeat galloping. All he could do was fold his own arms around her and revel in the feeling of his wife in his arms again, glad he'd taken time in town to go to the bathhouse and barber to get a shave and change into clean clothes. She wouldn't have wanted to touch him if he was covered with the filth of trail dust, sweat, and a scraggly beard.

∾

hen Lorinda impulsively threw her arms around Franklin and leaned against his chest, she didn't expect him to put his arms around her, but she liked it. *Too much.*

She lingered as long as she dared, enjoying the warmth, the rock-hard muscles, and the familiar scent of fresh Bay Rum Oil. As she released her arms and slipped back away from him, he let her go. How she wished he would gather her once again into his embrace. A sigh slipped out between her lips.

"Are you all right?"

His tender tone brought tears to her eyes. She turned away to hide them. "Yes. I believe Mrs. Oleson should have our supper ready."

Franklin followed closely behind her as she led the way into the kitchen. She felt his every move.

"There's my boy." When the first word left Franklin's mouth, Michael dropped both spoons and lifted his arms toward him, jabbering away in his own baby language.

Lorinda smiled as her husband lifted her son from his high chair and cuddled him against his chest. Just where she'd placed her face minutes before. Michael stayed there only a moment before lifting his head and reaching to pat Franklin on his cheeks.

"Hey, buddy." Her husband's words rumbled through the room. "I missed you, too."

"Welcome back, Franklin." Mrs. Oleson dried her hands on the towel tucked into the waistband of her apron.

"Something sure smells good."

"Supper's not quite ready." The housekeeper took the lid off the large frying pan, then used a fork to start turning pieces of chicken. "Won't be long though."

Franklin turned to Lorinda. "How about I take this boy out to the barn while I put up Major?"

All Lorinda could do was nod and watch them head back up the hallway toward the front door. She knew what would happen. Franklin would hold Michael while he rode the horse into the barn. Those two really enjoyed spending time together.

Mrs. Oleson turned back toward the stove. She opened the oven to remove the biscuits that had risen tall and golden brown, filling the kitchen with another aroma to blend with the chicken. "I told you he'd be home today, but he was later than I thought he'd be." She bustled around putting the finishing touches on Franklin's favorite meal. "I'm surprised he already bathed, shaved, and changed clothes before he came home. He always comes straight from a cattle drive–dirty, smelly, and wrinkled. I guess being married has changed him in more ways than one."

Lorinda started setting the table, keeping her head turned. She didn't want the woman to see the blush making its way up her cheeks.

Yes, there were ways Franklin had changed, but they weren't due to her or their relationship, because there wasn't one. Could she really live this lie for the rest of her life? Everything within her rebelled at the thought.

Lorinda hurried from the kitchen before she could blurt out the truth. This had to stop.

Somehow.

CHAPTER 27

Since Franklin had been gone several days, he decided not to go out to work so early. He wanted to have breakfast with his family. Lorinda had already taken Michael into the kitchen by the time he finished dressing for the day.

Lorinda noticed him as he stepped into the doorway. "Here's your daddy." His wife's smile arrowed straight to his heart.

Wanting to gaze at her while he ate, he took the chair across the table and pulled it out before dropping into it.

Michael banged a spoon against the wooden tray of his high chair. "Da...da...da."

Franklin's head shot up, and his eyes zeroed in on the baby. "Did he just say daddy?"

Lorinda laughed. "Sounds like it to me. I was hoping he'd say momma first."

"He's started cooing and then babbling really early. And Franklin..." Mrs. Oleson brought a plate of bacon and eggs and set them in front of him. "...when you were an infant, you said daddy first. Your mother was so disappointed."

He looked up at her. "I didn't know that."

"You soon said momma." The housekeeper smiled at Lorinda. "I'm sure our little prince will call you momma any day now."

Our little prince? When had the baby become *our little prince?* He'd been missing too much of his family's life. That was going to change...right now.

The aroma of the food sitting in front of him made his stomach growl like an angry bear.

Lorinda fed a spoonful of scrambled eggs to Michael. "You must need your breakfast right now." She laughed.

He joined in her laughter. This homecoming was what he dreamed about the whole time out on the trail. The camaraderie lifted his spirits. But he wanted so much more from this marriage. Looking at his lovely wife's face, he yearned for the time when they could take the next step in their relationship...if it ever happened. He wanted to accelerate his effort to woo her but knew he couldn't rush her. It might push her away, and his heart couldn't take the chance of her turning away from him. But today was a new day, and he'd make the most of it.

The sound of cowboy boots and spurs on the front porch was followed by a sharp knock on the door.

"Do you want me to go? I'm already up." Mrs. Oleson dried her hands on the towel hanging from the waistband of her apron as she quickly stepped into the hallway. Soon the front door squeaked as she opened it. "Rusty, come on in. We're just now eating breakfast. Do you want to join us?"

"No, ma'am. I've eaten, but I need to speak to the boss."

"Can it wait until he's finished eating?"

Franklin could tell from the tone of his ranch hand's voice that something serious was happening. He quickly wiped his mouth with his napkin and dropped it beside his plate before he went to find out what.

Mrs. Oleson met him in the hallway. "I'll keep your food warm for you." She continued on to the kitchen.

Franklin hurried out the screen door, letting it slam behind him. Rusty stood on the porch, turning the hat he held in his hand. Worry wrinkled his brow.

"What's going on?"

"One of the men just came riding in real fast from where the lane meets the road. A rider is headed this way, and she's in pretty bad shape. I sent one of the men out with the wagon to check on her."

"She? Is it anyone we know?" Franklin glanced toward the lane and saw the dust cloud near the other end. "She's riding a horse, I see."

"Yeah, but according to Charlie, she looks like she might fall off any time. That's why I sent out the wagon." Rusty's gaze roved around the porch and out to the barn, even bounced toward the sky and trees.

Franklin wondered why he wouldn't look him in the eye.

"Thought you might want to go meet her."

"You didn't answer my question. Do we know her?"

"Yes, sir. It's Miriam."

For a moment, Franklin expected to feel pain. The name only gave him a momentary twinge. What he'd felt for the woman in the past was a distant memory. But why was she coming here now? She could really muddy the waters.

What would Lorinda think about his former fiancée showing up like this?

He went inside, stopping in the hallway. Grabbing his Stetson and jacket from the hall tree, he started to open the screen door. He stopped, turned around, and went to the kitchen. "I've got to check on something. I'm not sure when I'll be back."

Leaning down, he dropped a quick kiss on his son's blond curls.

Michael once again pounded his chair tray with a spoon. "Da...da...dada."

Even if they weren't really words, the sounds warmed his heart, causing it to expand in his chest.

"Wait." Lorinda grabbed a large biscuit. She broke it in two, piled it with scrambled eggs, then added broken pieces of bacon before putting the top back on. "Maybe this'll stave off your hunger till you get back." Her bright eyes as she handed it to him made him want to sit down and stay with her.

But he couldn't. "Thanks."

He took a large bite and headed out of the house, shutting both doors behind him. Rusty had Major saddled, waiting by the gate in the picket fence. He grabbed the reins and mounted.

"Want me to come with you?" Rusty sat atop his own horse.

"Yeah, I might need some help."

Franklin was able to finish his biscuit before they reached where the wagon had stopped beside the woman on the horse.

Charlie was trying to coax Miriam into letting him help her down, but she wasn't cooperating. Actually, she seemed to be in a daze.

Franklin dismounted and dropped Major's reins to the ground. It looked as if Miriam wasn't aware anyone else was around. That surprised him, because his horse and Rusty's made plenty of noise as they approached. Something serious had to be wrong with her.

As he neared the horse she was riding, he noticed she was heavy with child. Why was she here on the Rocking V, and where was Marvin Pratt? The dirty, low-down, sneaky cuss brought the taste of bile rising in his throat. He never wanted to even think about that skunk ever again. Was his former best friend the father of her baby? If so, why was she coming here alone?

This woman hanging onto the pommel of the saddle as if her life depended on it was the most pathetic looking female he'd ever seen. As if a gentle breeze might blow her off onto the ground. Her hair hung in a stringy mess, and most of her body looked emaciated, her clothes hanging off her as if she were dressing up in someone else's. And the palomino she rode didn't look in much better shape than she was.

He stopped beside her, but she never looked his direction. "Miriam?"

She slowly turned her head, and her eyes widened. "Franklin...I need...help." At the last word, her body tipped, and she lost her hold on the reins.

He moved quickly to keep her from hitting the ground. Clasping her in his arms, he was surprised at how light she was. Her bones stuck out with hardly any flesh between them and her skin that looked as thin as onion skin. He didn't want to hold her too tight, fearful he'd hurt her somehow.

Carefully, he made his way to the back of the wagon, glad to see a bed of soft blankets spread across the floor. He gently lowered her onto the pile and covered her with another of the covers.

Her eyes slid closed, and her body went slack. Had she fainted, or was she dead?

The thought startled him. He'd never wanted to see her again, but he didn't wish for her to die.

Leaning over the side of the wagon, Franklin held his fingers under her nostrils, trying to detect any air. She took a shallow breath, then a deeper one and let it out slowly, but she didn't open her eyes. Franklin grabbed the reins of the sick horse and tied them to the back of the wagon.

"Charlie, you ride Major into town and see if you can bring Doc Winston. I'll drive the wagon." He climbed up on the seat and picked up the reins. "I'll have to drive slowly, so I don't jostle her too much." He gave Rusty a pointed look. "Go back to the house and alert the women that I'm bringing in a patient. Miriam will need lots of help from them and from the doctor."

He had been making some progress on courting his wife, and he didn't want anything to come between them now.

Lord, please, don't let this interfere with my relationship with my wife.

~

*L*orinda had just finished nursing Michael when another knock sounded on the front door. She held out her son to Mrs. Oleson. "I'll answer the door this time."

Once again, Rusty stood on the front porch.

She opened the wooden door but stayed inside the screened one. "Where's Franklin?" Her heart beat double-time. Had something happened to her husband? If not, why was Rusty back and her husband wasn't?

"He sent me here with a message, Mrs. Vine."

Lorinda had never seen Rusty look so nervous. Something must have happened. "What message?"

"He's bringing a..." He cleared his throat. "...woman up to the house. She needs help, and he said for you...and Mrs. Oleson to get a room ready for her." He turned to go.

Lorinda opened the screen door and stopped on the porch beside him. "Why is he bringing her here?"

"She was about to fall off her horse. She looks really bad."

She shot her gaze toward the wagon slowly approaching the house. "Okay. I'll have a place for her when he gets here."

"Thank you, ma'am." Rusty settled his hat back on his head as he hurried down the steps.

If the woman was in a bad way, she might have trouble climbing the stairs. The only thing Lorinda could do was fix her a place to stay on the first floor. Without hesitating, she moved the baby's cradle and his other things into the bedroom where she slept. That would work for the time being. They could settle the patient in the room where Lorinda first lived when she came to the ranch. She closed and locked the door that connected it to the dressing room where her husband slept.

By the time she'd changed the sheets on the bed and fluffed the pillows, Franklin came through the front door carrying the woman. Lorinda had never seen her before, but the poor thing was almost skin and bones, except for the fact that she was breeding. Lorinda wondered how a body so frail could carry a baby this far along. She was glad she had a bed waiting so close to the front door. Where was the woman's husband? Was she a widow like Lorinda was when she came here?

Franklin pushed past her as he made his way into the room and deposited the woman on the bed. Lorinda pulled up the covers and tucked them under their visitor's chin. After her fingers touched some exposed skin, she went back to the linen closet to get a couple more quilts. Their guest felt almost as cold as a slab of marble. The poor woman needed care if she was going to be able to give birth. And according to the size of her belly, that event might not be far off.

Her husband ushered Lorinda out into the hallway. "I don't know what's happened, but this is...Miriam."

She couldn't keep her eyes from widening at that announce-ment. What was Franklin's former fiancée doing here? And where was the man she ran off with? Franklin must be hurting pretty badly because of the memories she'd aroused. *What in the world do I do now?*

Her husband led her into the kitchen. Mrs. Oleson held Michael sleeping on her shoulder.

"I took the baby's bed and his things into m—our bedroom. Here, let me have him. I'll put him down for his nap." Lorinda wanted to get out of the way before she came apart at the seams. Her hands shook as she transferred her son to her own shoulder.

When she returned to the kitchen, Franklin and Mrs. Oleson sat at the table drinking cups of coffee.

"Good..." Her husband looked straight into her eyes. "...I wanted to tell you both at the same time. Miriam is here, and she's in bad shape. I've sent for the doctor. She's sleeping right now, so I'll go put up the wagon."

"What happened to her?" Lorinda grabbed a heavy shawl from the hall tree and followed him outside.

He shook his head. "I don't know. She passed out before I could ask her anything."

She glanced toward the wagon and gasped.

Franklin stopped and turned around. "What's the matter, Lorinda?" He came back up the steps.

"Where did you get that palomino?" She could hardly get the words out past the lump in her throat.

"Miriam was riding it."

Lorinda couldn't hold back a shocked exclamation. "That's Golden Boy, Mike's horse! I'm almost sure it is. I've never seen him in such bad shape."

She accompanied Franklin out through the gate. Going to the back of the wagon, she reached her open hand, palm up toward the horse.

"Golden Boy, do you remember me?"

The horse blew warm air on her palm before nestling his muzzle on it.

"You do." Lorinda slid her hand up the horse's withers and into the tangled mane. "You're still a pretty boy, even if you haven't been taken care of." She turned toward Franklin. "We need to make sure he gets plenty to eat and is groomed."

Franklin stopped beside her and placed his arm around her back. "We sure will. Look, I don't know what's been going on, but we'll find out when Miriam feels well enough to tell us."

Leading her horse, Lorinda followed the wagon to the barn. She stopped by the water trough to let the horse get a drink, making sure he didn't drink too much.

When she led him into the barn, Franklin met her with a

feedbag. "Here's some oats for your horse." He hung the bag on the horse's head, so he could start eating.

While Franklin unharnessed the other horse from the wagon, she went to the tack room and got a brush and a mane comb. While Golden Boy munched on the feed, she started a rhythmic brushing of his sides and back. His muscles quivered under her ministrations. She wondered how long it had been since he'd been groomed. He'd always enjoyed the brushing.

Franklin picked up the mane comb from where she'd laid it on a bench nearby. He began to work the tangles out of the almost-white-blond mane and tail. "Someone needs to be horsewhipped for letting such a valuable animal get into this shape."

She smiled at this man she'd married. His heart for animals touched her. "Thank you for helping me."

"I'm not leaving you out here to finish this." His return smile shot straight to her softened heart.

"I wonder where sh...Miriam got our horse. I was disappointed when you brought Mike's body to me, but you didn't have his horse. I guess I figured someone had stolen him. Maybe even his killer. But maybe not." As she kept moving the brush over the horse's coat, removing loose hair and debris, the horse's hide began to take on a healthier glow, but his bones were still too near the surface of his coat.

When she glanced at Franklin, his face took on the expression she recognized as one he had when he was pondering something. Funny how she'd learned to read so many of his moods. Other times, she had no idea what he was thinking or feeling.

"If she obtained him in a legal way, I'll buy him back for you. If not, I'll make sure you get to keep him." He moved around to face Golden Boy's head.

Since the feedbag was now empty, Franklin removed it and started on the horse's forelock.

Lorinda enjoyed this time alone with her husband, but she was fearful of what changes Miriam might bring to their household. Why had that woman come here? Her heart quaked within her. She didn't want to lose her husband. Not when things were getting better between them.

CHAPTER 28

*L*orinda peered out the front window for what felt like the thousandth time today. An equal number of times, she'd opened the door to the bedroom where Miriam rested in the bed that had been Lorinda's before her marriage. Each time, the woman still slept, but her breathing was more even and less labored that it had been earlier in the day. That gave Lorinda a bit of faith to cling to.

Franklin had left her and Mrs. Oleson to watch over the frail woman while he went out to work, but often when she looked out, she noticed him working close enough so they could call to him if they needed his help. Of course, he would be worried about anyone under his roof that was in as bad a shape as Miriam, but Lorinda hoped that was all of his interest in their guest. For a moment, a stab of jealousy entered her heart, but she pushed it away. Franklin was her husband now.

When Charlie returned with the message that the doctor would come as soon as he could, Lorinda hoped it would be sooner rather than later. Now most of the day had passed, and the sun moved ever closer to the western horizon.

All this waiting reminded her of the day her son was born.

The doctor couldn't come because of the mine cave-in. She'd been terrified, and the fear rose up inside her again, as it did that day. She hoped nothing would prevent him from coming now. Mrs. Oleson had been able to help her while she was in labor and after Michael was born. But she doubted she could do much to help Miriam. Even Mrs. Oleson didn't know exactly what to do with someone this bad off.

What if Miriam died before the doctor arrived? What would they do next? She turned away from that line of thinking. It would only make her more unsure of herself.

Mrs. Oleson had started boiling beef bones early in the day. She told Lorinda she wanted some of the rich broth when Miriam woke up. And she kept the teakettle on the stove, ready to brew weak tea for their patient or Dr. Winston.

Miriam hadn't moved since Franklin laid her in the bed. Occasionally, Lorinda went close enough to her to make sure she was breathing. When she saw the faint lifting of her chest, she turned away. Once she even placed her hand on the woman's brow to see if she was still cold. Thank goodness, her skin had warmed once out of the chilly wind.

On her next trip to the front window, she noticed a buggy coming down the lane. A buggy just like the one Dr. Winston drove. Lorinda heaved a sigh of relief. Their patient was still alive, and help was on the way. She hurried to the kitchen.

"Dr. Winston is almost here."

"Praise the Lord." Mrs. Oleson threw her hands up before she moved the teakettle closer to the middle of the range, so it would heat even more. "The doctor may need some really hot water while he's taking care of Miriam."

Lorinda headed back to the bedroom. She tiptoed across the room and leaned close to the patient's face to check her breathing again.

Miriam's eyes slowly opened. She had a blank stare, and

Lorinda didn't want to move and startle her. After a moment, she focused on Lorinda's face.

"Who...who are you?" The words rasped between her dried and cracking lips.

Lorinda quickly straightened, clasping her hands in front of her to keep them from shaking. "I'm Lorinda Vine. Franklin's wife."

The hint of a smile flitted across Miriam's face as her eyelids slowly slid closed. "I'm...so glad...Franklin found someone...to love him."

The words that had seemed so hard for the woman to say brought an ache to Lorinda's heart. Yes, she loved her husband, but he didn't love her. And he had no idea that she loved him. Her life had never been so complicated. Now Miriam brought another unknown complication into her uncomfortable existence.

A knock sounded on the front door. Lorinda hurried from the bedroom to answer the summons. "We're so glad you're here, Doctor. Our patient is not doing very well."

"I'm sorry to have taken so long. We almost lost Mrs. Philpot. I just couldn't leave her until I'd done everything I could. I hope you understand." He handed her his hat, and she hung it on the hall tree.

Lorinda led the doctor down the hallway. "Does this mean Mrs. Philpot will be all right.?"

"I believe so." As they entered the bedroom, he swiftly approached his patient. "Miriam has been gone from this area for quite a while. What seems to be the problem?"

"We don't know." Lorinda wrung her hands as she talked. "She's very weak, and she is...with child. Mrs. Oleson made beef broth in case she needs some, but the woman has slept almost all the time since Franklin brought her into the house."

Dr. Winston pulled the only chair in the room up beside the bed. He took his stethoscope out of his bag and held the metal bell in his hand for a couple of minutes. When he reached over to place it on Miriam's chest, she tried to pull away, then settled back down, never opening her eyes.

"Sorry this didn't warm up more." His voice sounded soothing.

Lorinda wondered if he used that tone for all his patients and if Miriam could even hear his words.

After moving the bell of the stethoscope around on Miriam's chest, he turned his attention to the baby in her womb. "Both her heartbeat and the baby's are strong, so whatever is wrong with her hasn't affected the little one...yet."

Lorinda gave a sigh of relief, but she still worried about the woman being able to give birth. She remembered how hard it had been for her, and she was much stronger than Miriam.

"Mrs. Oleson was wise to plan for when Miriam awakened." The doctor folded up the instrument and stowed it again in his bag. "I believe she's dehydrated. We need to encourage her to take the broth and as much water and weak tea as we can get down her. Has she had a fever since she arrived?"

Lorinda shook her head. "She was almost freezing when she got here. It took her a while to get warm. Do you have any idea when her baby is due?" Lorinda hoped it would give them time to build up the mother's strength.

"From the looks of her, I'd say it won't be very long." He frowned.

"Do you think she'll have any trouble giving birth?" Lorinda's voice trembled. What would they do if he said yes? Would he stay with them until the impending birth, or would he go back to town?

"I'm not sure. We really need to start building up her strength. In addition to the liquids, I'm leaving you a box of Carter's Little Liver Pills, a bottle of Hensel's Tonic, and a bottle of Manola Tonic. These should help strengthen her." He dug in his bag and pulled out a small rectangular box and two corked bottles sealed with wax. He held out the box to her. "Give her one of these in the morning and one at night."

Lorinda took the box and laid it on the table beside the bed. "Let me get paper and a pencil, so I can write down your instructions."

Within a minute, she returned. She listed the pills and dosages on the paper.

Dr. Winston next gave her the Hensel's Tonic. "Mix one teaspoon of this into a quart of water. Have her drink a glass twice a day."

While Lorinda wrote those instructions, she kept glancing at Miriam to see if there was any change. When she finished, Miriam opened her eyes.

"Hello, Miriam." The doctor leaned close to her. "Do you remember me?"

She gave a slight nod.

"Are you thirsty?" He continued to study her.

"Yes." The whispered answer was so soft that Lorinda almost thought she'd imagined it.

"Good." Dr. Winston turned toward her. "Please have Mrs. Oleson bring some broth and water."

As she left the room, the doctor leaned closer to Miriam. "Do you know when your baby's due?"

Lorinda didn't hear the answer.

She and Mrs. Oleson rushed to the bedroom with the requested items. The doctor lifted Miriam's head and held the glass of water to her mouth. The patient tried to gulp the cooling liquid.

He pulled it back after the first mouthful. "You need to take it easy. It's been quite a while since you had water, so you must sip it at first. Then I'm going to let Mrs. Oleson spoon-feed you the broth."

After a few sips, he continued to hold up her head while the housekeeper added another pillow under her. Then she started dribbling the broth between Miriam's lips.

Even though some color had returned to Miriam's cheeks, she was still much too pale. Her gauntness made her look so frail she might fall over if a person blew a small puff of air toward her. Lorinda wasn't used to being around anyone so ill.

Dr. Winston turned back to Lorinda. "Here's one more liquid medicine I want you to give her. She should have one tablespoon of this Manola Tonic before each meal and at bedtime. I've had good results with it, so you need to follow my instructions exactly."

"Thank you. I will." Lorinda watched him pack up his bag and get ready to leave. "I'm not sure where Franklin is. He stayed close to the house much of the day, but I haven't seen him recently."

"That's fine. He can pay me next time he's in town. I trust him." He went out into the hallway, took his hat, and left through the front door.

She glanced out the window to watch the doctor leave. Franklin met him at his buggy. The men started a conversation. The expression on Franklin's face showed great concern.

Pain shot through Lorinda's heart. Was her husband sorry he'd married her? Was he wishing he'd waited for Miriam to return? And his former fiancée carried a child who could be his heir as easily as Michael could. *Does he realize that?*

Lorinda wondered if she would get to the place where she truly trusted Franklin.

She wouldn't give up hope.

But...

CHAPTER 29

*F*ranklin went to the house to see if Lorinda and Mrs. Oleson needed his help taking care of Miriam. They assured him they didn't. He studied Lorinda while he was talking to them. He tried to see if she was upset with Miriam being in their house. He sure hoped not. Lorinda was his wife. The woman he loved more than anyone else. But he'd never told her that. She couldn't tell what he felt. She was concerned about Miriam's weakness and her condition, but was she concerned about anything else?

The rest of the day, he couldn't keep his thoughts from drifting toward the three women, wondering what was happening. When he finally finished making sure all the horses had plenty of hay, he left the rest of the chores to his cowhands. He made sure all those standing watch were fed in the chow hall, and a new set would take over for the night shift. The cattle rustlers could still be nearby, and he wanted his women protected from the scoundrels. At least he had been able to get the herd he wanted to sell all the way to Frisco without the drive being attacked. If only they knew who was stealing the cattle.

When he thought about the women in his house, he couldn't help being concerned with his ex-fiancée. What had happened to her? He was glad the Lord had removed her from his life before he made the mistake of marrying the wrong woman. But why had the Lord brought her back into his household at this time? Just when he was falling so deeply in love with the woman he felt God had planned for him all along. Miriam was helpless, and he had the means to help her, but he didn't want her presence in their house to affect the way Lorinda felt about him. Somehow, he had to make sure his wife knew he loved her...and only her.

When he went into the house after work, Lorinda was sitting at Miriam's bedside, and their patient slept peacefully.

"How is she doing?" His voice must have startled Lorinda, because she jumped a little, then looked at him, her eyes hiding her feelings from him.

"She's resting. That's good."

He hoped she'd say more to him, but she turned back toward her patient and ignored him. They had been having comfortable conversations when he came to the house after work. He wanted that to continue. *Lord, please don't let Miriam come between Lorinda and me.*

He heard Michael and Mrs. Oleson laughing in the kitchen, and he headed down the hallway toward them.

Mrs. Oleson had supper ready for Franklin. While he played with his son, he ate the delicious beef stew and hot biscuits, sneaking Michael pinches of the bread and bits of the soft potatoes from the rich broth. When he finished, he gave the baby back to Mrs. Oleson. He couldn't let things stand like they were this evening. He had to let Lorinda know he didn't want anyone but her for his wife, but he wasn't sure how to do that.

"I'm going to check on Lorinda." With a nod to Mrs. Oleson, he headed toward the baby's room.

His wife sat with her back to the door, reading a book by the light of the oil lamp on the table by the bed. He stared at her, his heart beating double-time as it often did when he saw her. Her blonde curls were caught up and pinned at the top of her head, looking like a golden crown. His gaze slid toward her exposed neck above the top edge of her dress.

He had the strongest urge to tiptoe over and kiss the tender milk-white skin. In his imagination, she turned and welcomed his caresses. Her arms went around his neck, she pressed her soft body against his, and every curve fit at just the right place. Desire rose in him, and his palms began to sweat. He brushed them against his shirt.

"Franklin?" Her soft word brought his eyes to her again. Lorinda must have heard him, and she studied him intensely. "Is something wrong?"

"No." *Liar.* Everything was wrong, and it was all his fault. "I wanted to check on Miriam...and you."

She put a ribbon in the book and placed it on the table.

As Lorinda arose, he tried to discipline his features so she wouldn't know what he had been thinking. She came over beside him and leaned close. Her feminine fragrance almost made him lose control. He wondered what she would do if he clasped her against his chest as he had imagined.

"Mrs. Oleson and I were able to clean up Miriam and dress her in one of Mrs. Oleson's warm flannel night shifts. After giving her broth and the medicines the doctor left, she settled down and went right to sleep. I think she's completely exhausted."

He could stare into her blue eyes for just one more minute. "How are you holding up?"

"We've taken turns caring for Michael and staying with Miriam, so I'm fine." She glanced toward the book on the table. "I've even started a new book that's quite interesting."

"I'm glad." Not that she was reading the book, but that she was fine.

Franklin could never have imagined something happening like the events of today. He hoped Miriam would get better quickly, so they could find out why she was riding Mike Sullivan's horse, where Marvin was, why he wasn't with her, and even if he was the father of the baby. If he wasn't, that could open another Pandora's box, and the ramifications could be far-reaching. He hoped Lorinda wouldn't get hurt by having Miriam in their household. He needed to treat his wife with great respect and special tenderness until they were out of this situation.

As he dressed for bed, he heard Lorinda and Mrs. Oleson as they awakened Miriam and gave her more medicine. The two women left the bedroom before he was ready to lie down. He heard the housekeeper start up the stairs before Lorinda quietly entered her bedroom. She didn't notice him standing in the doorway to the dressing room, so he cleared his throat.

She glanced toward him, then over at the sleeping baby. "You startled me, Franklin."

Her soft whisper warmed his heart. He loved the way she pronounced his name. "I wanted to see if you were all right before I went to bed."

"Yes, I am." She crossed her arms over her chest.

"You look tired."

She nodded. "I am, a little. But Mrs. Oleson and I agreed that since Miriam was sleeping normally now, we could spend the night in our own beds."

"I'm glad." Reluctantly, he turned away before he made her more uncomfortable.

As he closed the door, her whispered, "Thank you," followed him.

Three different times during the night, he heard Lorinda tiptoe into the hallway to check on Miriam. After a few minutes, she would return to her room. His wife shouldn't have to be taking care of his former fiancée, but if he tried to take her place, she might misunderstand.

He hoped Miriam would quickly recover, so she could be on her way.

~

*L*orinda took care of Miriam for the next full day and night. By then, the woman had been asleep for almost two days and nights. Because she was sleeping so much, Lorinda had plenty of time to take care of Michael and clean the house. Mrs. Oleson cooked the meals.

When Lorinda went into the bedroom with the morning medicine on the third day, Miriam's eyes were open, and she was much more alert.

"Good morning, Mrs. Vine." Even the woman's voice sounded cheery.

"And a good morning to you, Miriam." Lorinda set the tray on the bedside table and sat in the chair. "Are you hungry?"

"Yes, for the first time in days." She flashed a sweet smile toward Lorinda. "Thank you so much for taking care of me."

"I've had plenty of help. I'm just glad you're better." Lorinda picked up one of the medicine bottles. "Let's get this all taken care of, then I'll go get you something to eat."

Miriam sniffed at the air. "Something smells really good."

While she measured and administered the medicines, Lorinda continued to question her patient. "We have biscuits and scrambled eggs. Do you think you can eat them now?"

"I know I'm hungry enough, and I've been taking broth and lots of water. Surely the biscuits and eggs are mild enough for my stomach." A loud rumbling sound from her direction confirmed just how hungry she was.

Before Lorinda left the room, she helped Miriam sit up in bed and added a couple of pillows behind her patient. Even though she was still very thin, Miriam didn't look as weak as when she arrived.

When Lorinda carried in the food tray, Miriam smiled at her. "I hope I haven't been too much of a bother for you."

"Not at all." Lorinda set the tray on the table and went to get another pillow to help balance it. "I'm sure you're tired of people feeding you." She moved the tray to the pillow she had laid across the patient's lap.

"That's right." After Miriam took a bite of the egg, she put the fork down and took her time chewing. Her eyes closed as if she wanted to remember every sensation. "This is so delicious. It seems like forever since I've had enough to eat."

Questions bounced around in Lorinda's head, but she didn't ask them out loud. Why was it so long since she'd had enough food? Surely, there was someone near her who could've helped. But probably not, since she rode to the ranch to get help from the man she had treated so badly. She must have been desperate.

Lorinda knew what it was like to be in an impossible situation. Much of her growing up years were like that. There hadn't been anyone to help her either. She'd been bothered by the arrival of Miriam, but now she felt sympathy for her.

After a few bites of both the egg and the biscuit with butter and honey, Miriam leaned her head back on the pillows. "I really need to talk to Franklin. Do you think that would be possible today?"

"I'm sure it would." Maybe now they could find out just what happened to this woman. "I'll tell him when he comes in for dinner."

"Thank you." Miriam raised her head again and went back to taking small bites of the food and slowly chewing them. She seemed to relish every single morsel.

Lorinda met Franklin at the front door when he came to the house for the noon meal. His smile melted her heart even more than before. She was as addicted to him as her father and uncle were to liquor, but this addiction didn't hurt anyone...except herself.

"I have something to ask you." She smiled up at him.

He took off his Stetson and coat and hung them up in the front hallway. "What do you need?"

His gentle tone felt almost like a caress. He would probably think she was silly if he knew what she was thinking.

"It's not so much what I need, but Miriam wants. She asked if she could talk to you as soon as possible."

"I think that can be arranged. Tell her I'll talk with her as soon as we finish our meal. I want you to be with me if that's all right with you." His dark eyes bored into hers, filling her with a deep longing.

While he washed his hands, Lorinda went into the room where Miriam was. "Franklin said he would come and talk to you as soon as he's finished eating."

Miriam heaved a sigh. "I'm so relieved. I really need to get everything out in the open. I won't be able to rest easy until I do." Her fingers fidgeted with the colorful patchwork quilt covering her.

When Franklin put his napkin on the table beside his plate, he leaned over and placed a soft kiss on Michael's head. Then he took Lorinda's hand and led her to where Miriam was.

"I brought my wife with me."

"Okay."

Lorinda moved to stand out of the way, hoping she could be unobtrusive. She just wanted to know what was going on, not get into the middle of the conversation.

Miriam scooted up in the bed and rearranged the pillows behind her shoulders. She kept her head down, almost as if she were praying. Lorinda wondered if that was what she was doing. She assumed Miriam had gone to the same church as Franklin.

"So much has happened...it's hard to say it out loud."

Franklin sat in the bedside chair and leaned back, crossing one booted foot over the other knee. He didn't push her...he just waited. Lorinda held her breath until Miriam finally spoke.

"I'm so sorry for the way Marvin and I treated you, Franklin." She stopped and took a deep breath, keeping her eyes averted.

"That's water under the bridge." He didn't move from his relaxed position.

"I don't think Marvin ever loved me as he said he did. He was just so jealous of you. He wanted everything you had, even me." She paused and blinked her eyes, a lone tear making its way down each cheek. "I was in love with the idea of marriage and starting my own family. His lies led me astray, because I wasn't really committed to you."

Franklin nodded. Lorinda couldn't see the expression on his face, but she didn't want to move and call attention to herself.

"If I *had* been, his words wouldn't have enticed me."

Maybe her words were meant to ease Franklin, but Lorinda didn't think they did. She saw the way the muscles in his lean jaw compressed and released, over and over. That was no surprise. She had often wondered if he was still in love with his first fiancée.

"Go on." He gave Miriam a nod.

"He promised we would be married as soon as we reached a place he had picked out for the wedding. He never told me where it was. We must not have ever reached it, because he never said we had arrived." She turned her face away and stared off into the distance. "He convinced me we were as good as married, and I held him off for a long time. But eventually, I succumbed to his expressed desires. After that, he never mentioned marriage again."

Lorinda realized that must have really hurt the woman. But she did make the wrong choices herself. Lorinda was pulled between feeling sorry for her and thinking she got what she deserved.

Miriam turned her eyes back toward them, the pain in her glance making them glacial. "We stayed together until after I told him I was...with child. Soon after, he left me with the horse and a small bag of gold coins. I haven't seen him since."

Lorinda couldn't keep quiet any longer. "How did he get Mike's horse?"

Miriam turned toward her. "He knew Mike had quite a bit of gold on him when he left for Denver."

"How could he know that?" Lorinda realized her question sounded harsh, but she didn't care.

"I don't know how he found out things. He just did." Miriam twisted her fingers together and held them close to her chest. "I'm so sorry." Tears poured down her cheeks now. "He came home very angry. I had to stay out of his way for a few days. He ranted about Mike not having the gold he planned to steal. In his anger, he killed the man. He took the horse, so he would at least get something for all his trouble."

Her shoulders shook with sobs, and she seemed to wilt with what little strength she'd gained melting right out of her.

Lorinda stepped forward. "I think we've done enough talking for today."

She helped Miriam scoot back down in the bed and pulled the covers up to her chin. Miriam's eyes slid shut. Lorinda took a hanky and wiped the tears from her cheeks.

Franklin stood and waited for her to finish. Then he ushered her from the room with his hand on her lower back. She leaned into that touch. She needed it right now. In the foyer, he pulled her into his arms. She rested her head against his chest, and he pressed a kiss atop her curls. Had she imagined that? *Surely not.* The gentle touch reminded her of what she was missing in their marriage.

"I'm so sorry, Lorinda. I know that was hard to hear."

Yes, it was. Very hard, but she couldn't stop herself from feeling sorry for Miriam. The woman made her own decisions, but she had been influenced by a very bad man...like the two Lorinda had grown up with. Raising her head from his chest, Lorinda gazed at his handsome face.

"It was hard for you, too, Franklin, wasn't it?"

Miriam's words had to add to the pain and betrayal he already felt.

"But we're far better off than she is. We can thank the Lord for that." His comforting words reached her heart.

Was the Lord still listening to them since they were living the lie? She hoped He was.

CHAPTER 30

*L*orinda followed Dr. Winston to the front door. "Thank you for coming to check on Miriam."

He settled his hat on his head and picked up his medical bag. "You're doing a good job, Mrs. Vine, helping her to regain some of her strength. But she's not out of the woods yet."

"She's been sitting up for over half an hour now." Lorinda hoped it was an indication Miriam was getting stronger.

"I'll be back out here in a couple of days...unless the baby comes sooner." He headed outside.

Lorinda closed the door behind him, then leaned against it. Memories of when Lorinda's own son was born were still fresh in her mind. It was hard. It hurt so much, and she'd been much stronger than Miriam was. *Dear Lord, please help Miriam regain her strength before the baby decides to make an appearance.* If she didn't, Lorinda wondered how Miriam would be able to push the baby out.

When she went back into the bedroom where Miriam sat in the rocking chair, the woman raised her head and glanced at her. "Mrs. Vine, I really need to talk to you and Fr—Mr. Vine this evening."

"Okay." Lorinda wondered what she might want to talk about. Her voice sounded so serious. Hopefully, she just wanted to ask for their help. Surely, she didn't want to rekindle her romance with Franklin now that he was married to someone else.

Lorinda went to where clean sheets were stacked on the bureau. "I'm going to change your bed and help you get cleaned up and in a fresh gown if you're not too tired."

"That would be nice." Miriam's hands clutched the arms of the rocker so hard, her knuckles paled in the sunlight streaming through the window.

While Lorinda changed the linens on the bed, she kept up a cheerful conversation despite the doubts whirling in her mind. The other woman only nodded or uttered a word or two. Lorinda often glanced at her. Even though she seemed to be wilting in the sunlight like flowers that hadn't had enough water, she was still beautiful. Lorinda could understand why Franklin had been drawn to a woman with dark hair that still had waves in it even though she was not very healthy right now. Those ice blue eyes were unusual for someone with midnight black hair. Quite a contrast to Lorinda's blonde hair and pale skin. Maybe Franklin preferred brunettes.

Lorinda hurried as fast as she could. After she fluffed the last pillow and folded the covers back, she set the pitcher of warm water and the empty bowl on the floor beside the rocker. She grabbed a washcloth and a towel from the bureau, then knelt beside their guest and gently washed her face and hands.

"Let's slip that gown off, so I can finish cleaning you up."

Miriam leaned forward and allowed Lorinda to do what she said, but she didn't help in any way. Her patient's strength and awareness faded. Alarm filled Lorinda. She had to get the woman back in bed as soon as possible.

After Lorinda finished, she held her crooked elbow out to their guest, and Miriam had a hard time rising from the cush-

ions of the rocker. She grasped Lorinda's arm with her fingernails and desperation and the grip was so hard it made her
wince, but Lorinda didn't let on it was hurting. Slowly, they
made their way across the room. After Miriam sat on the side of
the bed, Lorinda helped hoist her legs under the covers.

Their patient settled into the softness with a sigh and closed
her eyes. She immediately fell into a deep sleep. Lorinda's heart
ached for the woman who had been through so much. Yes, she
made wrong decisions, but she'd suffered almost as much
heartache as Lorinda had while she still lived with her father
and uncle.

She pulled the rocking chair beside the bed and dropped
into it. While watching their patient, she lifted prayers for the
woman and the baby she carried. As she opened her eyes, she
noticed the movement of the baby under the covers. At least, the
wee one was still all right...for now.

～

Franklin carefully opened and closed the door when
he came in for the noon meal. He hung up his hat
and coat and tiptoed down the hallway to the room where
Miriam was staying. Through the open doorway, he saw his
wife sitting beside the bed with her head bowed and her eyes
closed. She had to be praying for his former fiancée. Lorinda
was such a special woman. Who else would take in the former
woman in her husband's life and care for her so deeply? He
wished there was some way he could let her know just how
much he admired her. *Maybe soon.*

He went on down the hallway to the kitchen where Mrs.
Oleson was talking to Michael.

"Here you are, you sweet thing." She gave him a pinch from
the rolls she was putting in a basket for their meal.

His son grabbed it with his fist and was hard at work, trying to get it all in his mouth.

"Are you spoiling my son?"

She looked up with a smile. "It's hard to spoil a child before he's a year old. Or at least, that's what I've heard."

"I thought I saw Dr. Winston drive away. What did he say about Miriam?" He leaned against the doorpost and crossed his ankles, trying to look nonchalant.

"I'm not sure." Mrs. Oleson wiped her hands on the towel stuck into the waistband of her apron. "I worked on lunch and took care of our little prince while he was here. Lorinda will be able to tell you what you want to know."

He stood up and stuffed his hands into the front pockets of his trousers. "I saw her as I came by. She was praying for Miriam. I didn't want to disturb her."

"Your Lorinda is a good woman, Franklin. You made the right choice." Mrs. Oleson lifted the lid from one of the pans on the stove and stirred something that smelled very good. "I hope you're hungry."

"I know. It's just that I can't tell her..."

"Tell me what?" Lorinda came through the door and smiled at him.

For a moment, all he could do was study her. Her beauty overwhelmed him, even more so since he saw her praying for Miriam.

Finally, he realized she'd asked him a question. "What did the doctor say about our guest?"

He dropped into the chair on one side of Michael while Mrs. Oleson bustled about setting the food on the table.

Lorinda sat on the other side of their son. Worry creased her forehead. He'd seen that expression on her face before, and it didn't bode well.

"He actually got her up to sit in the rocker while he examined her."

"That's good, isn't it?" The heavy burden for Miriam lifted from Franklin's mind.

"Yes...and no."

Lorinda picked up the saucer with mashed potatoes Mrs. Oleson had fixed for Michael and held a small spoonful in front of the baby. He laughed and slapped his little hands on the table tray, then opened his mouth wide.

Franklin would never get tired of watching the two of them. His family. The family he never expected to have. God had truly blessed him.

"Why no?" The report up to this point had sounded good.

"She's gaining some strength, but she's not out of the woods by any means." Lorinda gave the baby another bite. "When I went back into the room after the doctor left, Miriam didn't look all that strong. I hurried to change the sheets, clean her up, and put her in a fresh gown. But by the time I finished, she could hardly get up even with my help. Now she's sleeping again."

"I saw you praying for her." His soft words were for her ears alone.

She turned troubled eyes toward him. "I'm worried about her and about the baby. I did see it moving around under the covers, but having a baby is very hard work. I'm not sure she's up to it right now. I hope she builds more strength before her time to deliver arrives."

"I hadn't thought of that." Franklin felt helpless. How did other men face the thought of possibly losing their wives during childbirth all the time?

Lorinda laid her hand over one of his on the table. "She wants to talk to us again this evening. I'm not sure why."

He thought Miriam had told them everything they needed to know. Maybe there was more to what had happened to her. For a moment, he wished Marvin Pratt was close-by. He'd like to give the man a strong dose of *what for*. Selfish scum. He'd ruined a very special woman when he lured her away. Franklin had been able to get over what he'd done to him, but Miriam might never get over it. And, even though she made her own decisions, she really didn't know what she was getting into. A man should protect a woman, not use her and discard her.

But isn't that what I'm doing with Lorinda? Using her?

He was trying to remedy that, and he'd never, *ever* discard her.

～

Lorinda checked on Miriam several times during the afternoon, and their patient slept the rest of the day. At least, this allowed Lorinda to catch up on cleaning and spend fun time with Michael.

Not long before suppertime, Mrs. Oleson found Miriam awake and took her food and gave her the medicine. So she was ready when Lorinda and Franklin finished eating supper.

With his hand resting on the small of her back, Franklin escorted her into the room where Miriam was sitting up in bed with pillows behind her.

Lorinda had a hard time keeping her mind on their patient. Franklin didn't often touch her in that possessive way. She wondered if he realized what he was doing, or was it just instinct? She was very aware of the presence of his warm palm touching her gently. So much heat spread through her she had a hard time catching her breath. Oh, how she wanted to tell him what he was doing to her. That marriage promise felt like a ball and chain hampering her every step. She wished she had the magic key to open the lock. She finally took a deep breath and slowly let it out.

"Are you all right?" Franklin's words, whispered into her ear, caused her to stiffen.

She nodded, then moved closer to Miriam. "How do you feel

now? Are you rested?" She dropped into the rocking chair, and Franklin stood close beside her.

"I am." Miriam smiled at both of them. "This morning must have tired me out more than I thought. I slept almost all day."

Lorinda patted her on her clasped hands. "I know. I checked on you several times."

"You're so good to me...I don't know that I would be if our roles were reversed."

That idea hadn't even entered Lorinda's mind. Thank goodness, they weren't.

Franklin cleared his throat. "You did say you wanted to talk to us again, didn't you?"

Miriam gazed toward the window, and a faraway look came into her eyes. "I've had a lot of time to think." She turned toward both of them. "I want you to promise me something."

Franklin frowned, and Lorinda leaned toward the other woman. "What?" She knew she couldn't make a promise unless she knew what it was.

"If anything happens to me, please promise you'll keep my baby."

Why would she even ask such a thing? Then another thought crept into Lorinda's head. It could be a way for her to be a mother to more than one child and have someone else who could love her unconditionally as Michael did.

"Nothing's going to happen to you." She sounded as serious as she could. "We're here, and the doctor will keep checking on you."

Miriam started wringing her hands. "You don't understand. I know I'm not going to make it, but I want a secure future for my baby. And I don't want Marvin to have the child."

"Why not?" Franklin sounded almost angry.

Lorinda glanced up at him. Something was really bothering him.

"Marvin never wanted me to have a baby. That's why he

deserted me when I told him. I'm afraid he'll finally figure out where I've come for help. If he does, he'll want the baby just to spite you, Franklin." A single tear slid down one cheek. "I don't want to even imagine how he would treat the baby. Please promise me. I would feel that my baby would be safe if you'll do that."

Lorinda's heart went out to the woman. Maybe she was right. She didn't seem strong enough to birth a child. Maybe it's a girl, and she and Franklin would have one of each to raise.

Franklin hunkered down beside the bed. "Miriam, there are legalities to consider. We can't just say the mother gave us the baby. We'll need some kind of documentation. Would you like me to get a lawyer out here?"

A look of horror passed over Miriam's face. "No. Marvin might find out sooner if you do that. Can't I just write out my wishes, and you can have two trusted employees sign it as witnesses? Wouldn't that work?"

Franklin stood back up and pondered her question. Miriam and Lorinda waited in silence. He paced to the other side of the room and back.

"I've known of wills being done that way. I don't know why it wouldn't work with this situation."

"Thank you." Miriam wilted deeper into the bed. "Let's do it right now."

Franklin left to get paper and the new Waterman fountain pen from his office. When he returned, Lorinda watched as he and Miriam worked out the wording for the document. Miriam wrote it out in her own handwriting, then signed it.

"I don't want Lorinda and me to be the witnesses, because it might look as if we coerced you to write and sign this paper. I'll go get Rusty and Mrs. Oleson to witness your signature. Both of them know when to keep a confidence." He left the room.

Lorinda knelt beside the bed and took Miriam's hands in her own. "Are you sure you want to do this?"

Another tear made its way down Miriam's cheek. She released one of Lorinda's hands and brushed it away. "I have to. I can't rest easy until I know my baby is safe from Marvin. That man is vile and unscrupulous." Her voice broke on the last word. "Oh, I wish I'd never met him."

Lorinda wished Miriam hadn't either. But if all of that hadn't happened, she might never have met Franklin.

Hopefully, all they had just done wouldn't be needed. At least, she could pray for Miriam to be able to have her child *and* take care of him or her.

CHAPTER 31

$\mathcal{A}$n unfamiliar sound startled Lorinda awake before dawn's light seeped between the curtains on her window. *What is that?* A foreign sound. Where had it come from? Another strange moan reached her ears.

Miriam! Lorinda pulled on her dressing gown, crossing one side over the other. She cinched the belt tight and slipped out into the hallway. Was their patient in distress?

A strangled cry sounded through the door. Lorinda rushed into the bedroom. Miriam must've been restless, because her bed linens were a rumpled pile with her in the middle of it. She twisted again, and a louder moan filled the room. Lorinda dropped into the rocking chair beside the bed and felt Miriam's forehead. She didn't have a fever.

Miriam slowly opened her eyes and blinked several times. Then her gaze connected with Lorinda's.

She leaned closer to Miriam. "Are you all right?"

For a moment, Lorinda didn't think she was going to answer because Miriam continued her blank stare.

Then she murmured, "Pain...I'm having pains."

"Where?"

At least, now the woman was alert enough to answer.

"Am I having my baby?" The words rushed from Miriam's mouth. "Is it time?" Fear shot from her eyes.

Lorinda smoothed Miriam's hair back off her face. "It'll be all right. How long have you known you were expecting a baby?"

Miriam closed her eyes and looked as if she were in deep thought. "Since about a month before Marvin left me."

That didn't help any. "And how long has he been gone?" Lorinda figured Miriam's time had arrived.

"At least six or seven months, maybe even eight." Miriam turned away and wiped tears from her cheeks. "It's hard to remember for sure. I didn't have a calendar...and I thought he'd come back any day...and he didn't." A sob broke free from her, and she placed the fingers of one hand against her lips.

Lorinda's instincts were right. Birth was about to begin.

Without hesitation, Lorinda gathered Miriam into her arms and held her close. "We're here to help you."

Miriam relaxed against her, and a sigh escaped through her lips. "Thank you."

Lorinda had to strain to hear the soft words. "You're welcome."

Before she could ask how close the pains were, Miriam gave a convulsive movement and clutched her swollen belly. She gulped, then stopped breathing.

"It'll hurt less if you'll breathe out slowly during the pain." She continued to hold the woman until she relaxed. "I need to go get some help. I'll be back before the next pain arrives."

Lorinda didn't like leaving her alone, but she knew she'd need to have help delivering the baby. She checked on Michael. He still slept, so Lorinda hurried up the stairs and knocked on Mrs. Oleson's door.

Their housekeeper must've heard the moans and cries,

because when the door opened, she was fully dressed. "Has Miriam's time arrived?"

"I believe so." Lorinda started down the stairs. "We must send someone to get the doctor. She may need more help than we can give her."

"I agree." Mrs. Oleson headed toward the open doorway to the room where Miriam was waiting.

Lorinda went through her bedroom and into the dressing room. She'd never been in there when her husband was sleeping. She felt strange...as if she were going somewhere she didn't belong. She never felt that way when she put his clean clothes in his bureau. It had to be because he was lying in the bed. The sound of his even breathing wove its way around her, and his very presence heated the room. With him in bed, a strong desire for everything marriage should mean clutched at her heart. Her body ached in places it hadn't for over a year.

She didn't know what she should do to wake him up. Evidently, the noise Miriam had made didn't affect his sleep. Finally, she reached out and touched his shoulder, shaking him gently.

"Franklin...please wake up. We need you."

He leapt from the bed and stood staring at her, his hair mussed and the shadow of dark whiskers on his cheeks and chin, his union suit clinging to his body. "What's wrong?" His voice was extra husky.

Here she stood in her nightshift and just a thin dressing gown. She felt almost naked in front of him. While she wanted to cover her private parts, heat rushed to her cheeks. She was sure they must be flaming red.

Oh, my goodness. The man was a handsome specimen when fully clothed, but standing here in his unmentionables? Every muscle and sinew outlined and defined in a way she'd never seen. No words came from her mouth. Her hand tingled from where she touched him, and the rest of her body burst alive in a new way she didn't have time to explore. What was she going to do? She didn't have room to breathe.

A loud cry sliced through the silence. *Miriam!*

"You need to go to town and get the doctor. We're going to need him soon. I'm so afraid Miriam isn't strong enough to deliver this baby." Tears streamed down her cheeks. She didn't know if she could stand to watch the woman or the baby die...or both.

He reached toward the clothes he'd hung on the back of the straight chair beside his bureau, and she rushed out of the room. She was careful not to make any noise as she went through the bedroom where the baby still slept soundly.

Mrs. Oleson sat in the rocking chair where Lorinda had been only a few minutes before. Miriam's pain must have been over, because she lay still.

"I sent Franklin to get the doctor." Lorinda trembled from head to toe. Too much had happened in such a short time. "If it's all right with you, I'll go get dressed."

The long night stretched into an eternity. Miriam's labor continued, gradually increasing in frequency and intensity. With each new pain, Miriam looked as if more and more of her strength leached from her. Lorinda sat beside her, holding her hand. After a while, her fingers were numb from the pressure, but she wasn't about to complain. Miriam needed her, so here she'd stay.

Mrs. Oleson took care of Miriam in other ways. Bathing her face with a cool wet washcloth, giving her sips of water, and trying to keep the bed linens fresh. At one lull in the pains, the housekeeper went to the kitchen to put pots of water on the stove to heat.

Between pains, Lorinda bowed her head and prayed for their patient. Why hadn't Miriam come to them before she was so weak? If that scoundrel, Marvin Pratt, was here, Lorinda would be tempted to scratch his eyes out. What a sorry piece of humanity!

~

 ranklin was thankful the doctor was home. The man dressed with amazing speed, and they headed out into the cold night. With the bright moon casting a silver sheen over the countryside, they made good time getting back to the ranch.

"You go on in. You know where she is." Franklin held the reins from the doctor's carriage. "I'll take care of the horses and put them in the barn out of the cold."

When he finished that task and headed inside, his wife sat in the parlor in front of a blazing fire.

"Lorinda, are you okay?" He moved to stand beside one end of the hearth, soaking up part of the heat.

Her gaze lifted from the flames to his face. "I'm so afraid for Miriam."

He hunkered down beside her. "Why?"

"She's not strong enough to deliver the baby." She rubbed her knuckles while she talked. "She's getting weaker all the time."

He glanced at her hands. They didn't look right. He took one into his palm. Bruises were beginning to form. "What happened?"

Her eyes met his. "You've never seen what a woman goes through having a baby. It hurts...a lot. I've been holding her hand while she's going through her labor pains."

Franklin lifted her fingers to his lips and gently kissed them. "I never wanted my past to hurt you, Lorinda."

Tears trickled down her cheeks as she pulled her hand back. "It's not your fault, Franklin. I wanted to be a comfort to her if I could."

He stood. "You're amazing. I don't know why God gave you to me."

Before she could think of anything to say to him, the loudest scream yet rent the air. Soon after, Michael's whimpers could be heard.

"You stay here, Lorinda. I'll take care of Michael. The doctor might need your help again."

As he left the room, his thoughts turned to the situation he and Lorinda were in. How he wanted her to be his wife in every sense of the word, but he wouldn't force her into anything. He wanted her to come to him of her own free will, because she loved him. *What a dreamer I am.*

~

Soon the soft cries of a newborn filled the house. Mrs. Oleson rushed into the parlor and thrust a flannel baby blanket at Lorinda. "Here. Warm this by the fire, then bring it back to me. We have another little boy." With those words, she immediately returned to the new mother's room.

Lorinda held the blanket as close to the fire as she could without scorching it, so it didn't take much time to have the whole thing warm. She folded it and held it close to her chest to keep it from cooling off.

When Lorinda opened the bedroom door, Mrs. Oleson was just finishing cleaning up the baby and pinning the diaper on him, while Dr. Winston continued taking care of his mother. Lorinda unfolded the blanket, and Mrs. Oleson gently laid the baby in it. Lorinda swaddled the little boy and cuddled him close.

He was so tiny. Michael was so big now that it was hard to remember him being this small. He probably wasn't quite this little. And her son was becoming independent. He didn't want to be cuddled anymore. Automatically, Lorinda began to sway in the age-old method of quieting a baby. The boy's eyes slid closed, and his breathing evened out.

When the doctor finished with all the cleanup work on Miriam, he turned to Lorinda. "Let's introduce Miriam to her son."

The new mother barely opened her eyes when Lorinda placed the precious bundle into her arms. "You have a little boy." She forced excitement into her tone, hoping to gain the woman's attention.

After a moment, the new mother looked down at the baby.

"I think he looks a lot like you." Lorinda tried to engage her in what was happening.

Mrs. Oleson stopped on the other side of the bed, where the baby's head was nestled in the crook of his mother's arms. "We need to put the wee one to the breast, Miriam. It will be good for both you and him."

She gently loosened the swaddling a little and helped hold his little mouth against his mother. It took a few times of encouraging him before he latched onto her. With the first tug, Miriam once again looked at the baby, and her arms settled him closer.

Lorinda almost rejoiced out loud. *This is a good thing*...but was it? Miriam continued to fade more and more.

Dr. Winston returned from cleaning up. He rolled his shirt sleeves down as he watched his patients. A frown quickly spread across his features, puckering his forehead. He motioned for Lorinda to accompany him into the hallway.

"Mrs. Vine, Miriam is not recovering the way she should. I'll stay the night by her bedside. Is there somewhere that you can take the baby to sleep?"

"We have a large basket I can place near the fireplace. We can make a bed for him in that." She left to get the container.

When she returned with the basket, a pillow, and some baby blankets, the doctor stood beside the fireplace holding the little boy. After Lorinda finished making the soft bed, he handed the precious bundle to her and went back to the bedroom with Miriam.

When the doctor reached Miriam's bedside, Mrs. Oleson left and came into the parlor. She sat beside Lorinda, clasping her hands in her lap.

"I have a bad feeling about Miriam's chances of survival. Will you be able to nurse our new little baby?"

Lorinda stared at him and smiled. "Of course." Whatever happened, this little one needed to be loved and cared for. She had plenty of love in her heart for another child.

CHAPTER 32

Franklin stood beside the gaping maw of the open grave. Even in his sheepskin and suede coat, he was chilled to the bone...by more than just the icy wind. As he gazed down at the closed pine box that contained the remains of his former fiancée, he grieved more for what had happened to her than for what she'd done to him. He knew he hadn't loved her enough, and he was sorry she'd made such poor choices. She shouldn't have ended up in this cemetery at such an early age. And her son would never know his mother.

"Let's pray." Pastor Nelson bowed his head, pulling Franklin from his thoughts, and everyone around them followed suit.

When had he moved from pain to forgiveness? *When Lorinda became my wife.* His thoughts turned toward her. She'd wanted to come to the graveside service, but both of the babies needed her. He wished he could've stayed home with her, but he wanted to make sure Miriam's body received the care she deserved. And he wanted to make sure that no one besides their pastor knew the circumstances of her last few years. He owed her that much.

Yesterday after he'd made arrangements with the undertaker and Pastor Brian, he'd had a talk with his lawyer. The man confirmed that the paper Miriam had written was legal enough to stand up in court. So he and Lorinda now had two sons, a surprise since he'd figured they'd only have the one.

Lorinda had seemed all right with what happened the night Miriam asked the question and wrote her desires about her son. But he wondered if she really was okay with the results. Had she believed the newborn would become theirs so soon?

At the end of the service, he quickly excused himself and set out toward the ranch, riding Major as fast as he could under the darkening clouds, heavy with snow. How should he approach Lorinda? He already felt he'd taken advantage of her in a way he never imagined. Brian had helped him see the error of his ways, and he'd started trying to court his wife. But was that even right? Would she feel beholden to him and only stay for that reason? He wanted more. For her to love him.

He'd come to love her so much that he wanted to clasp her even closer to him and not let her go. Both of them reveling in their love. Since his father had taught him to respect women, he'd never experienced the intimacy that should be saved until after the wedding. He knew the mechanics of it, but could only imagine the emotional depth of the actual event.

He'd been so unfair to Lorinda. Asking her to accept a marriage in name only had been a selfish mistake. One he'd regret to his dying day.

She'd been all right with it at first, but was that still her feeling? Especially now that she would have to help him raise not only her son, but Miriam's as well. How could he find out without pushing her...maybe even away from him. Franklin shook his head. He didn't want that to happen.

When he'd gotten home from Breckenridge yesterday, Lorinda had been nursing the new baby boy. She looked happy and satisfied. But was she really? Maybe she'd had time to think about the consequences of what had transpired. Had she considered what their future would be now? He didn't have the right words to ask her. Why could he talk to everyone else, but not to his wife about what mattered?

As he rode toward the house, he gave a small salute to the men standing guard, and each one gave an answering wave. Everything must've been quiet while he was away. He was thankful to have men he could trust working for him.

But he'd trusted Marvin for a long time. Hopefully, he'd matured enough to really recognize a man of integrity when he saw one. When he arrived at the barn, he took care of his horse, then headed toward the house.

After taking off his coat, he stuffed his gloves in the pockets and hung it up along with his Stetson. Franklin found Lorinda once again in the parlor near the fireplace. Even after wearing the lined leather gloves, his fingers felt like icicles. He leaned against the mantel, close enough to the fire to warm him up, but not in a place where he'd keep the warmth from reaching his wife and children. Children? That had a nice ring to it.

"You're back sooner than I thought you'd be." Her blue eyes looked as warm and welcoming as a summer sky.

He glanced toward the basket beside her where the new baby slept. Michael sat on the rug nearby playing with the wooden blocks Franklin had carved for him. He didn't seem to be affected by the new guy in the house. Almost as if Franklin had called his name, Michael's gaze shot toward him.

"Da, da, da, da."

Drool dripped from his chin, and Lorinda took her hanky and swiped it away. He picked up a block in each hand and started banging them together. Franklin figured all the noise would disturb the new baby, but it didn't.

"I didn't linger, because I wanted to get home to my family." His smile encompassed all of them.

"Now that everything with Miriam has been taken care of, there's something we must discuss." Lorinda sounded so earnest. "She didn't have time to tell us what she wanted to name her son."

"*Our* son." Franklin was thankful she didn't have anything more serious to discuss.

"Yes...that's what I meant." She heaved a sigh. "I don't know how to handle something like this."

"We didn't get a lot of time to talk yesterday, since it was so busy." He dropped into the wingback chair opposite the one where his wife sat. "I talked to the lawyer. The paper Miriam wrote and signed will stand up in court, so we can legally adopt him when we want to. Until then, he's ours anyway."

"So we need to decide what to name *our* son." Lorinda reached down and lifted him into her arms without disturbing his slumber, cuddling him close to her heart. "Do you have any ideas?"

"We can't name him after his real father. I don't think she wants him to even know who that man is." A slight throbbing took up residence in his head, right behind his eyes.

"Since he's to be your son, we could name him Franklin. Michael is named for his birth father." She began to rock back and forth in the chair as she held the baby closer.

The throbbing accelerated a little. "I don't think that's a good idea. We need a different name for him."

"All right." She seemed flustered. "Can you think of another name you would want to use?"

"How about your father?"

The words had barely left his mouth when a look of horror covered her face. "No!"

He'd never heard such a strong exclamation from her. What had she endured at the hands of that man to bring such a response? Anger welled up in him against the man he'd never met. He thought he remembered her saying she didn't have any more relatives when Mike was killed. Must mean her father was dead as well. What had the man done to her? Was he the reason she had a hard time trusting men?

Franklin wished Lorinda felt safe enough to share her pain with him. She knew all about his situation with Marvin and Miriam. *Please Lord, let her tell me soon.*

Lorinda laid the baby back in the basket and tucked the blankets close around him as he slept. "How about your father's name?"

When she looked back up at him, her face wore a serene mask, but he could tell she was fighting to keep it that way. He wanted to take her in his arms and tell her everything would be all right. His heart ached for her. Franklin wanted to make things better for her, but how could he when she wouldn't share with him about what had happened? Frustration gripped him.

"What was your father's name, Franklin?"

He drew his thoughts back to their conversation. "Andrew...Andrew Vine."

A smile lit her face, even reaching her eyes. "Andrew is a good, strong name. He'll need a name like that."

He wondered what she meant, but he didn't ask. Of course, every man needed a strong name, especially out here in the mountains.

"Since Mrs. Oleson planned to stay in Breckenridge to help with the funeral meal at the schoolhouse, I put on a pot of elk stew. It should be ready soon." Lorinda headed toward the kitchen.

Franklin was surprised that all the things on his mind had kept him from noticing the pleasing aroma of the stew. But then, the house usually smelled good when he came in near a mealtime.

Rusty had gone hunting last week and brought the large bull elk down. After they slaughtered it, the meat had hung in the cold smokehouse. Franklin was particularly fond of elk meat, so his mouth watered. He hadn't felt like eating when he was in town, but the stew Lorinda made emanated a delicious aroma throughout the house. As Franklin watched the two baby boys, hunger pangs assailed him. He could hardly wait for the meal to be ready. Soon after Lorinda left, the fragrance of cooking biscuits joined the other delicious smells.

Franklin picked up Michael and hugged him tight before also grabbing the handle of the basket that held Andrew. He took both boys to the kitchen, setting the basket not too far from the black cook stove and putting Michael in his highchair.

"Can I do anything to help?"

~

*L*orinda had never seen Franklin help with anything in the kitchen besides taking care of the fire in the stove. "Everything's ready. I'll just set the table, then serve the food."

"Okay. I'll watch the boys." His words sounded so normal, even though having more than one son was new to them.

He pulled up a chair beside the highchair and whispered secrets into Michael's ears. The baby's attention was focused completely on his daddy.

She gathered the silverware and napkins and began to place them on the table. When she glanced up, her husband's attention wasn't focused on Michael, even though he continued to play with him. His gaze followed her every move. A soft smile spread across his face. What was that man thinking? Did a wife ever know her husband's thoughts? She never had mastered that, even when she was married to Mike. He was always a mystery.

Franklin had never really tried to control her the way her father and Mike had, but she still couldn't figure him out. Would her life always be filled with unknowns? Or someday, would she be able to understand her husband?

Lorinda returned to the stove and slid the pot of stew off onto hot mats on the cabinet by the dry sink. She felt his eyes boring into her back. Was he deliberately trying to make her feel uncomfortable? She shook the thought from her mind when she turned around to carry the bowls of stew to the table. After removing the biscuits from the oven, she placed them in a tea towel-lined bread basket and pulled the edges up over the biscuits to keep them warm. She removed the crock of butter from the ice cold closet and brought both things to the table, all the time feeling awkward.

"Everything smells delicious, Lorinda."

The way he said her name made her feel cared for. Too bad he didn't.

CHAPTER 33

*N*ovember dawned cold and fair. Franklin had been out in the barn doing chores before breakfast. As he returned to the house, he studied the snow-capped mountains surrounding his ranch. Not much of the snow had made it all the way to the valley. As cold as the air was now, the next snowstorm could bury them in the white stuff.

Inside the warm, cozy ranch house, he shed his winter outerwear and left them near the front door. Laughter in the kitchen drew him the way the Pied Piper had drawn the children out of the German city of Hamelin. When he'd heard the tale as a boy, he'd often wondered how just a sound could draw a person so strongly. Now he knew. The women discussing the coming day, Michael jabbering and banging his hands on the tray of the highchair, and the softer sounds coming from little Andrew drew him like bees to honey.

He stood in the doorway for a moment before anyone saw him. The room, a kaleidoscope of color and action. Michael was the first to notice him.

"Da, da, da." A smile that melted Franklin's heart lit Michael's face as he pounded the tray between each syllable.

Lorinda turned and their eyes met. Did he detect delight in hers?

"How is everyone this morning?" He hunkered beside the basket near the stove and the tiny boy opened his eyes...wider than ever before.

Franklin picked him up and laid the baby close to his heart before taking a seat in his usual chair at the table. He should be able to handle eating while holding Andrew. The baby didn't move around much yet, and all Franklin needed was one hand to partake of his meal.

"Wonderful." Lorinda got up to help Mrs. Oleson put the food on the table.

His heart felt full with their expanded family. The week-old baby had settled in just fine, and his wife had a special glow about her. She was meant to be a mother to more than one child. He hoped the day would come when he could give her his own child to love and care for.

Mrs. Oleson set a cup of hot coffee in front of him. "Is it getting even colder outside?"

"Yup. It's way past nippy out there." He took a sip of the steaming brew, then cradled the cup with his hand until his fingers became toasty.

Lorinda brought a platter of scrambled eggs and ham in one hand and a basket of piping hot biscuits in the other. She set them on the table and sat beside him. After putting a large spoonful of eggs on a saucer to cool for Michael, she served Franklin a heaping helping of them, along with a thick slice of ham.

"You want me to butter some biscuits for you?" Her smile warmed him clean through.

"That would be right nice." He watched as she deftly split two biscuits open and slathered them with the fresh-churned spread. His mouth watered watching her drizzle honey on top.

Evidently, Andrew had fallen asleep. By the time they finished eating, he started squirming.

"Is this little guy hungry?"

A becoming blush poured into Lorinda's cheeks. She hadn't been shy about nursing Michael, even though she went into the other room to do it. When Andrew needed her, she was a bit more flustered. In a cute way.

"He probably needs changing, too." Lorinda eased the baby into her arms and hurried toward the bedroom that once again belonged to Michael plus the new baby.

After she closed the door, Franklin followed into the hallway. He could hear her sweet voice talking to Andrew as if the tiny infant could understand every word she said.

Franklin had given her plenty of privacy when Michael was this young. That's why he hadn't heard her talk to him at this age.

The sound of hoofbeats caught his attention. He went into his office that was opposite the parlor and watched a stranger approach the house. When the man got close enough, Franklin recognized him as the person who'd caught his attention when he exited the train while Franklin was finishing his business with Harley Smith, the cattle buyer. He'd know that horse anywhere. The gunmetal gray turned almost silver in the bright winter sunlight. *Wonder what he wants.*

Franklin waited until the man knocked on the door before he went into the front hallway to answer it. At first, he planned to step out on the porch to talk to him, but the wind had stiffened. So he invited the man into the entranceway, but no farther until he knew more about him.

"Dave Jefferson." The man held out his hand, the other holding saddlebags slung across his other shoulder.

He shook it, but still didn't move deeper into the house. "I saw you when you came in on the train."

Dave's eyes widened. "You're the rancher who had a herd you were sending back East."

"That's me. I'm not surprised you didn't recognize me. We were a little rough and dirty by the time we got there."

The men shared a laugh that broke the ice.

"What can I do for you?" Franklin slid his hands into the back pockets of his trousers and relaxed.

The other man cleared his throat. "I understand you're married to Mike Sullivan's widow."

Franklin stiffened. What did he want with Lorinda? "Yes." He didn't offer any more information.

"Could we sit down somewhere while I tell you my story?"

Did Franklin want to invite the stranger into the parlor? Not really, but something told him to do it anyway.

"Take off your coat and hang it up." He gestured toward an empty hook on the hall tree. "You can warm yourself by the fireplace."

After leading the way into the formal room, Franklin sank into one of the wingback chairs, the one farthest from the hearth.

Dave, still holding the saddlebags, took the one opposite and leaned even closer to the flames. "It's really cold out there."

"Yup, that time of year." Franklin propped one foot on the opposite knee and leaned back. "So what's this you mentioned needing to tell me."

Dave stared into the flames as if mesmerized. "It's not really a pretty tale, but it has a happy ending."

Franklin wondered what this man's story had to do with his family. "Go on."

"I used to be a scoundrel. Oh, I didn't murder anyone or commit a robbery or anything like that. But I did play poker, and I always won, because I was a slick cheater. No one ever caught me." A grimace accompanied that last sentence. "Real ornery."

Franklin wanted to get to the bottom line, but evidently Dave needed to confess. Brian had told him confession was good for the soul. He just hoped it wouldn't take too long.

"How does this affect me or my family?"

"I met Mike Sullivan before he made it to Denver to have his gold assayed." Dave wouldn't look at him.

Franklin dropped his foot to the floor and leaned forward with his hands clasped between his knees. "And you swindled him out of his gold?"

Finally, the man's eyes met Franklin's. "Yes, sir, I did. Won every bulging poke from him. Was really proud of that, too. I'd never made so much in a single game."

Where was this man going with the story? Franklin stared straight into his eyes and didn't blink. He could out-stare him, if he needed to.

Evidently the saddlebags were filled with something fairly heavy, because Dave dropped them beside his feet and pulled them as close as possible.

"I'd made a good bit of money that night from the other men, so I took the gold to Denver and, after having it assayed, turned it into cash, which I deposited into a new account at Capital Bank of Denver. While I was in town, I met a rancher from western Oklahoma. He was looking for cowboys. I made a split-second decision to go with him and try out ranching. Too many people in Colorado were unhappy with me. I got out while the getting was good. Best decision I ever made."

This was some tale. "How so?"

"I really enjoyed ranching. The hard work was good for me, and I felt better about myself because I was making my way honestly. Both the rancher and his foreman really took to me. We became good friends. That old rancher gave me the best gift I'd ever received. He told me about Jesus, and I chose to give my life to Him. The rancher and his foreman and I had Bible study together every evening. Those two men helped me begin to grow toward the man I want to be for the rest of my life."

Franklin relaxed again. "That's good news. I'm a Christian myself."

"Then you will understand why I want to see your wife." Dave took a deep breath and stood up. "I'm on a pilgrimage to make restitution to every person I can find that I had wronged." He picked up the saddlebags. "All the money I got for the gold I won from Mike Sullivan is in these. $254,000."

Franklin quickly arose. "In *cash?*"

"Every bit of it." Dave smiled. "I haven't let these saddlebags out of my sight since I withdrew the funds from the bank and headed this way."

A whistle burst forth from Franklin. "That's quite a story."

"It's all true."

"Why didn't you just come out here the day you arrived?" He really wanted to know where he'd been all this time.

"I was looking for Mike Sullivan. Since I met him at a poker table in a saloon, figured that's where I'd find him. I stayed in the background, watching and listening. I didn't want to make a big deal about it, since I was carrying so much cash." He glanced down at the saddlebags. "After visiting a different saloon each night, I made discreet inquiries and found out about him being murdered and you later marrying his widow."

Franklin had watched every expression and gesture the man made. He couldn't detect any indication the man was lying. Dave had kept eye contact through the whole recitation. No reason not to trust him.

"I'll introduce you to my wife, and we'll need to get that into the bank as soon as possible."

The story almost knocked him off kilter...and the money for Lorinda. Although most men would take control of their wives' money when they married, he had no plans to. It belonged to Lorinda and Michael, fair and square.

This brought him face to face with what a disservice he had done to her. She had a real need, and he'd talked her into this marriage of convenience. What would she do now that she didn't need his money...or protection?

If he didn't give her the option to stay with him or go, his treatment of her bordered on abuse of power. He used his money and power to talk her into marrying him for protection and a way to give her son a good life. He felt like less of a man because of it. And he was beginning to believe God wasn't pleased with him as well.

Last night when he was reading his Bible, he found verses in the seventh chapter of First Corinthians that made him uncomfortable. *The wife hath not power of her own body, but the husband: and likewise also the husband hath not power of his own body, but the wife. Defraud ye not one the other, except it be with consent for a time, that ye may give yourselves to fasting and prayer; and come together again, that Satan tempt you not for your incontinency.*

These words cut straight through him like a sword of truth. He had been defrauding his wife even while in his thoughts he lusted after her, but still he withheld his love. Their marriage could not be what it should be unless he gave her the opportunity to decide for herself whether she wanted to leave him and get the marriage annulled or come together as a husband and wife should with love.

Dear Lord, what am I to do? I can't find the words I need to make this right. Please help me be able to express this to Lorinda without hurting her, but also allowing her the freedom to choose to stay or to go. Every one of those words hurt as if it was a thrust of a blade into his heart.

Could his life be more complicated? He didn't see how.

CHAPTER 34

*W*hile Franklin and his cowhands drove the last of the cattle down from the high pastures to the paddocks close to the barn, frustration tied his guts into knots. He couldn't line up his feelings with the scripture he'd been meditating on. He was breaking the implied command in that scripture as surely as if he would break the law if he took his gun and robbed a bank. He couldn't see any way there could be a good outcome from this.

Yesterday, after Dave Jefferson left without the saddlebags full of money, Franklin took Lorinda into Breckenridge to meet with the banker. Of the five bankers in Breckenridge, Franklin trusted William Henry the most. He was the epitome of discretion. No one else in town would know about the fortune they deposited in Lorinda's private account.

Afterward, he took his wife to the Occidental House hotel for dinner. Mrs. Almeda Peabody owned and managed this most prestigious eating establishment in town. All through the meal, he and Lorinda kept a pleasant conversation going. At the time, he was trying to work out in his head how to bring up the subject of him giving her a choice about whether to stay married or have the marriage annulled.

How could he risk it? If she chose to leave him, some part of his heart would die. She could meet a man who would love her and have a normal marriage. A deep ache invaded his whole body just thinking about her going.

Franklin didn't have a problem with her past, even though from the few things she had told him some of it had to be bad. Nothing she had ever done could change his love for her. But even considering her marrying another man brought up pain that was much stronger than when Marvin convinced Miriam to leave him. He couldn't allow pictures of what she would look like in another man's arms to sneak into his mind. When they did, white-hot anger coursed through him. He would want to knock the man out and carry her off like some caveman. He could even feel the sensations he would experience with her sitting in front of him on Major's back. After all, the memories of the time she did were alive and well.

And he would spend the rest of his life in love with another man's wife. That couldn't be any better than continuing the relationship as it was. He hadn't found any way they both would be in a better situation if she left him. But if he gave her the choice, she might leave.

If he didn't make that offer, the reality was that he was keeping her in bondage as surely as if he locked her in a jail cell. Franklin tried to pray, but somehow, it felt as if the Lord had moved a long ways from him. No peace. No soft-spoken word in his heart. He was utterly alone in this dilemma...except for Lorinda. And they had made a binding agreement for a marriage without intimacy. But now he longed for that intimacy...and abiding love.

～

*W*hile he and the men stocked feeding stations around the pasture, Franklin's mind often wandered. His foreman had to ask questions more than once before they penetrated Franklin's thoughts. Thomas must think Franklin had lost all his marbles.

The freezing cold didn't help. Franklin no longer could feel his fingertips and toes. He and his men needed to get to shelter and warmth before they suffered frostbite or worse. Finally, they finished and headed toward the ranch house and bunkhouse.

Somehow, he had to come up with the right words to make her understand why he was giving her the choice. If she decided to leave, he'd give her as a going away gift the gold and sapphire eardrops he bought her. Maybe they would help her understand that he had no hard feelings against her. He loved Michael and wanted to see him occasionally. Losing him as well as Lorinda might make Franklin go completely crazy.

~

*L*orinda didn't feel comfortable with what happened yesterday. Mr. Jefferson brought the money for the gold he'd cheated Mike out of. Maybe, if he hadn't cheated her first husband, they would be snug in their cabin up on the mountain. But did she want that? Not really. Meeting Franklin was the best thing that ever happened to her, even though they were living in this sham marriage.

He'd surprised her when he wouldn't take any of the money. She thought husbands and wives shared their possessions, and he had told her they shared ownership in the ranch. She knew some men claimed everything their wives owned. Now she had an absolute fortune he didn't want any part of. *Why not?*

Of course, Franklin *was* a successful rancher, and maybe he didn't need her money. But now there were two sons to think about. He had tried to convince her that putting the money in her private account would help Michael later. But if Franklin wanted her son to be his heir, why would he need extra money? Wouldn't his inheritance be enough for him and his family? Even divided between the two boys, his ranch and everything else Franklin owned would be enough to sustain two families.

So what were his underlying reasons? A gnawing feeling in her belly told her something was very wrong. A sense of impending doom hovered over her like a dark cloud.

Franklin and his ranch hands had been out in the cold far too long. She hoped nothing bad had happened to them. She looked out the front windows at the clouds that were heavy laden...with snow, if the evidence from last winter held true this year. *Please, Lord, bring them back safely.*

With both of the babies napping, Lorinda paced a loop from the front of the house to the back while Mrs. Oleson prepared a hearty hot stew.

"Lorinda?" Mrs. Oleson called to her when she neared the doorway to the kitchen. "Are you all right?"

The enticing fragrance of cornbread met Lorinda as she stuck her head through the doorway. "I'm fine. Just waiting for Franklin to come to the house."

The delicious aromas caused her stomach to growl in a most unladylike manner. She patted her stomach.

"Would you like to go ahead and eat now?"

"No, I'll wait for him. I'm praying he'll get home soon."

After two more rounds from the front of the house to the back, Lorinda heard footsteps on the front porch. *He's home.* She rushed toward the door, arriving just as it opened.

Her husband stopped on the throw rug inside the front door and stomped his feet before pulling off his boots and setting them beside the hall tree. She still hadn't gotten used to seeing him without his boots. Somehow, seeing a man's feet, even if they were encased in thick woolen socks, had an intimate feeling to her. Although if there was one thing they weren't, it was intimate.

She went around him and quickly closed the door, shutting out the icy wind. "Are you okay?" She tried to keep the tremble out of her voice. "I was afraid you might get too cold. That's dangerous." Of course, he already knew that.

Franklin's coffee-colored eyes turned toward her. For a moment, she noticed something intense and troubled deep within. Had anything bad happened while he was gone? One of the men or maybe some of the cattle dying...or something like that. Then the look vanished like snow melting under a warm spring sun.

"Something smells delicious." He hung his heavy coat up beside his Stetson. "And I'm starved. Let's go eat." He glanced around as if trying to find or hear something. "Are both boys sleeping?"

Lorinda smiled. "For once, they are."

After a leisurely meal with Mrs. Oleson, Lorinda got up to wash the dishes.

As she started stacking the empty plates, Mrs. Oleson intervened. "I'll get these. You and Franklin go enjoy the fire in the parlor."

Before they reached the front room, two distinct cries started in the bedroom the boys shared. One, the mewling of a very young infant, and the other much lustier, from Michael.

"Looks like we'll have our hands full instead of a quiet visit." Nothing in Franklin's tone hinted that he was disappointed. "I'll clean up Michael while you take care of Andrew."

When her husband picked up her son, Michael stopped crying and started patting Franklin's cheeks. "Da, da, da."

Those sounds always brought a big smile to her husband's face. "Daddy's here, Michael."

Lorinda took clean clothes out of the chest of drawers for

each boy and laid them on the top. Then she wet two wash-cloths in the water from the pitcher and bowl on the washstand and handed one to Franklin. She picked up Andrew and started changing him from his wet gown and diaper and washed him before putting on a clean diaper and gown, then swaddled him with a warm flannel blanket.

Franklin finished cleaning up Michael. "Should I take him to the kitchen and feed him?"

She smiled at her husband. "I'm sure he'd love some of those potatoes and carrots from the leftover stew. I'll go ahead and feed this little one while you're doing that."

By the time she finished, Franklin and Michael were already in the parlor.

Her husband glanced up at her from the floor where he was playing with the baby when she entered the room. "Mrs. Oleson said to tell you goodnight."

Lorinda sat in the wingback chair closest to the fireplace. "I'm so thankful we have her. She's so much help now that we have two babies."

"And she enjoys them so much." Franklin picked up Michael and moved to the oval rag rug in front of the fire. "Every child needs at least one grandparent, and she makes a good one."

Lorinda smiled at her husband while she held Andrew on her shoulder patting his back. She usually had a much harder time getting him to burp than she had when Michael was so tiny.

"Let's trade." Franklin set Michael on her lap and gently slid the other baby from her arms.

She grabbed for Michael before he could slide off. He was always so busy, wiggling and kicking and exploring everything around him. She stood him on her legs, and he started trying to jump.

Lorinda liked watching Franklin with each of the babies. He

was a tall, muscular man who really had a way with them. Just then, Andrew emitted a substantial burp.

"Is he spitting anything on you?" She started to get up.

"Stay there. I'll grab another diaper in case he's not finished. So far, he's not gotten anything on my shirt, but if it was, I'd call it my badge of honor because I'm a dad."

Everything was normal tonight. A happy family enjoying each other's company. Why had she been worried before? Even this long after coming to this wonderful home, the horrible things that went on when she was with her father and uncle still affected her. She had to quit letting herself think something awful was coming in her future. Stop questioning in her mind everything Franklin did for her. He couldn't have any hidden, negative agenda.

Nothing bad is going to happen.

CHAPTER 35

*T*he next morning, dawn revealed a layer of white covering everything, and still the clouds hovered around the mountain peaks, pregnant with more snow. Franklin was thankful he and the hands had finished getting the remaining cattle ready for the winter. For the time being, the flakes had stopped falling. The stark whiteness covered every blemish in the landscape, reminding him of the scripture that says that the blood of Jesus can cover our sins and make them white as snow. With that thought, he realized he couldn't put off his talk with Lorinda any longer. As long as he continued to selfishly hold her in bondage to this marriage, his sins weren't covered. They were red like scarlet, and he felt every one deep in his heart and soul.

He needed a private time with his wife, but the regular events kept this from happening until early-afternoon when Mrs. Oleson went upstairs to rest and both babies were napping. He faced the confrontation with dread, knowing the meeting might not be pleasant...especially for him, if she chose to go.

The fire in the parlor made the room cozy, in spite of the cold winds whistling around the sides of the house. He waited near the doorway, watching for Lorinda to exit the bedroom the boys shared. When she came out and quietly closed the door, his heart leapt into his throat. A few blonde curls had escaped the bun that rested low on the back of her head. They hung along her face and neck, outlining her with a bright halo. As his gaze followed the path of the curls, the desire to drop kisses along its length almost took his breath away. Her beauty overwhelmed him, because he knew she was lovely both inside and out. A woman any man would be glad to share his life with. Have her as the mother of his children. What a fool he'd been to make decisions based solely on his own selfish needs...or what he'd thought he needed. How wrong he had been. What he really wanted was to be that man and spend the rest of his life loving her.

Oh, Lord, please help me get through this. And if it's possible, let me keep my wife...for real, this time.

"Lorinda." He kept his tone soft so he wouldn't startle her or awaken the boys.

She glanced at him, a bright smile spreading across her face. "Yes, Franklin?" His name spoken softly like that felt like a caress.

That smile made him desire her even more...in every way. "I'd like to talk to you, if you have time." *No, I wouldn't...not about this, but I have to.* The words soured on his stomach.

"Of course." She entered the parlor like a queen in her own castle. That's what this house should be...her castle. She belonged here just as much as he did.

The twinkle in her eyes told him she had no inkling of what was coming. He knew what he had to say would remove that spark. What else would it do to this dear woman? *Lord, give me the right words.* That whispered prayer didn't bring him any comfort. He felt as if it bounced off the ceiling and got no closer to heaven.

She glided like an angel floating on a cloud and settled into one of the wingback chairs close to the warm fire. He dropped into the matching chair across from her. *Now how should I start?* He didn't hear any words from heaven to help him. He was on his own, and he'd already made such a mess of things.

After an elongated period of silence, Lorinda leaned toward him. "What did you want to talk about, Franklin?"

With a loud harrumph, he cleared a boulder from his tight throat. "Just some things I need to say to you." *How awkward.*

She nodded, and her smile wobbled a little.

He leaned his forearms on his thighs and clasped his hands between his knees. That didn't help. He just needed to start somewhere and get it over with.

"I've been thinking a lot about us and our marriage." He glanced up at her face and caught a confused expression. This wasn't going to be easy. He didn't want to watch his words hurt her, and they might.

"What about our marriage?" Her voice had a tremble in it.

"I've come to believe I took advantage of you when I shouldn't have."

She scrunched her forehead. "How?" The word was barely above a whisper, but he heard it loud and clear.

"You were vulnerable...and you needed help...help I could give."

Her nod was slow. "So?"

"I was selfish. I took what I wanted without considering what you might want...or really need." His tongue tasted the bitterness of the words.

"You're talking in riddles. What are you trying to say, Franklin?" She clasped her hands so tight her knuckles blanched as white as the snow outside the window.

"I've been defrauding you with our sham marriage. I wanted just what I wanted and nothing more."

A frown puckered her lips. Lips he'd like to kiss again the way he did at the wedding. The thought that he might never again taste their sweetness almost unmanned him.

She sat up straighter in the chair, her back stiff as a board. "That's the agreement we made with each other." She bit out the words like bullets from a gun.

This isn't going well. And why should it? He gritted his teeth and tried again. "You really don't need my financial help now that you have the money from the gold mine you and Mike owned."

∽

*U*nderstanding dawned on Lorinda. That was why he hadn't taken any of her money. He planned to get rid of her. Tears sprang to her eyes, but she lifted her chin so they wouldn't leak down her cheeks. "So what are you saying? You don't want to be married to me anymore? Is that it?"

He whispered a word under his breath, but she heard it. One she'd never heard him use before. But she'd heard it from her father and uncle, and a myriad of bad memories sprang to the surface of her mind, escaping the dark place where she'd kept them shut away. She felt as if a sword had been thrust through her mid-section. She placed her arms protectively across that spot and began to rock to and fro.

"I'm doing a bad job of this." He huffed out an exasperated breath. "I want to give you the choice of whether you stay with me or not. If you don't want to, we can quietly get the marriage annulled, since it wasn't consummated."

Each word another wound. "So, now that you have someone else for an heir, you don't want me...or my son." Her tone rose with each word.

He turned startled eyes toward her. "How can you say that? I love Michael. He's my son as much as he is yours."

"No... He. Is. Not." Tears streamed down her cheeks, and she swiped at them with both hands. "If you don't want me, you don't want him."

"But I do." He raised his voice. "I'm trying to do right by you, and you're twisting my words."

"Oh, I know what you're trying to do. Get rid of me." She gave him as harsh of a glare as she could muster. "If I go, so does my son. And who will take care of Andrew if I'm not here to nurse him? Have you thought of that?" She stood and stomped toward the fire, turning her back to him. "Of course, he would be your heir then."

Franklin jerked as if she had hit him and almost knocked over the lamp on the table beside him. He grabbed it and set it back where it belonged.

Lorinda couldn't let herself look at his face. She'd fallen in love with this man and hoped he was falling for her. But she was so very wrong. She had known all along that the sham marriage was a lie. Why had she agreed to it? She clasped her hands on her upper arms, trying to shield herself from the hurt, but nothing really could.

As she awaited his reply, she heard his boots beat a staccato down the hallway to the front door. Before she could turn around and follow him, the door closed with a loud thud. When she looked, Franklin's warm coat and Stetson were no longer hanging on the hall tree.

She considered starting to pack, but she didn't have anywhere to go. This had become her home, and she didn't want to leave. Maybe everything would be all right if she just waited and let him think about what he'd said.

A sham marriage was better than loneliness, wasn't it?

～

*I*n the barn, Franklin saddled Major. He didn't know where he was going, but he knew if he stayed in the house any longer, all he would do was hurt her more. Maybe if they both had a chance to cool off, they could come to an agreement about this. He hoped she wouldn't be gone when he got back.

Each tear that rolled down her cheeks landed on his heart, burning a hole through it. This was not supposed to happen. They should have been able to just talk this out, sensibly like adults.

He wanted to hit something...hard. He gripped his right hand into a fist and smashed it against the barn door. The divider rolled partway open. Thank goodness it did. If it hadn't, he would be hurt worse. Right now, the sharp pain settled into all the bones in his hand. He shook it and spewed out expletives he hadn't used since he was a sixteen-year-old kid trying to make the other guys think he was grown up. What he'd just done was every bit as bone-headed as some of the things he did back then. He swung into the saddle and rode outside, controlling the horse with the reins in his left hand.

Why was it so hard to talk to Lorinda about important things? He didn't have any trouble talking to anyone else. Mrs. Oleson, the ranch hands, Brian Nelson, other ranchers, bankers, businessmen. None of them tied him in the knots Lorinda did. All he wanted to do was give her a choice, all the time hoping she would choose not to leave him.

Deep in his own thoughts, Franklin turned from the lane onto the road leading to town. He tried to shut out the cold weather completely. Before he paid attention, he was over halfway to town. Wishing his father were still alive, he couldn't think of anyone else he could trust as much. Of course, he had talked to Brian, but he didn't want to share this with him.

Mrs. Oleson wouldn't understand how a man feels. And she

didn't know about their marriage pact. So he surely couldn't talk to her about it. Of course, she might've heard a little of that last discussion. It got louder as it went along. He hoped she couldn't understand the words he and Lorinda exchanged.

He'd made a royal mess of things when all he wanted to do was give her a choice of whether to take the way out he offered her or choose to stay with him because she loved him.

Love. He hadn't even mentioned the word to her. He slapped his thigh with the end of the reins. Franklin had gotten angry before they reached the place where he could tell her how he really felt. He remembered his father often telling him that he had to learn to control his temper. He did almost all the time. Why not today?

An especially icy wind hit him full blast. A shiver ran through him. What was he doing out here riding in the cold weather when he should be home by the fire? At least his anger had also cooled down, which was the reason he left the house.

The ride back to the ranch would take longer than getting to Breckenridge. He chose to go to town first and warm up. He could stop by Belle Turnbull's café for a slice of her wonderful Sponge Gingerbread slathered with melting butter and a cup of strong black coffee. That should warm him enough to face the long ride home.

When he stepped into the café, the heat hit him so hard his fingertips tingled, and he felt his face turning red from the strength of it. Rand Morgan and two other ranchers sat at a table near the counter. They waved him over to join them.

Belle came to take his order, and soon he was sinking his teeth into the warm gingerbread that melted on his tongue, awakening his taste buds. Stopping here was just what he needed. Away time with other men, jawing about what was going on at their ranches. The meeting was like an oasis in his desert-dry day.

When he went home, he'd be better able to continue his

discussion with Lorinda. They were both adults, and they should be rid of their anger by the time he got there.

CHAPTER 36

orinda stood by the front window and stared at the lane leading to the ranch house. How long had it been since Franklin rode off? It felt like forever. She glanced at the clock. Only an hour.

The heated words they'd flung at each other scorched her soul. Did her words destroy any chance she had for happiness? She had tried to force him to listen, but she hadn't listened to everything he had to say. Had her words run him off for good? Surely not. This was his ranch. He wouldn't just leave her and plan not to come back. Her heart sank at the thought. She wanted him back. This time, they needed to have a calm discussion.

She rubbed her sleeves as a chill ran up her arms, raising goosebumps in its path. The temperature outside had to be sinking, because it was becoming harder to keep the rooms warm. She hoped Franklin wasn't still out in the cold. If so, by now, he could be nearing frostbite. *Lord, please protect him and bring him back to me.*

When he got here, she'd try to control her emotions and let him finish saying what he meant. Perhaps he hadn't wanted her to leave. He was just giving her the choice. That's what she'd always desired, wasn't it? For the man in her life to let her make her own decisions, instead of controlling her.

"There you are, Lorinda." Mrs. Oleson came into the parlor. "Where's Franklin? He didn't go back out in the cold, did he?"

Lorinda cringed at the thought that their argument had been heard. Maybe their housekeeper hadn't understood the loud discussion.

"He was in here talking to you when I went up to take a nap." The housekeeper sat in a wingback chair and picked up her knitting from the basket beside it.

"Yes, he was. He left." Lorinda didn't want to tell another lie, even to keep their secret. "We had a disagreement. He didn't tell me where he was going."

Mrs. Oleson studied her for a minute. "That's unlike him. I hope he gets home soon, so we won't have to worry."

Lorinda dropped into the chair across from her. "He's been gone an hour. I'm already concerned."

Loud banging sounded on the front door. Lorinda hurried into the hallway. It couldn't be Franklin. He wouldn't knock.

She opened the door, and one of the older boys, who often wandered around Breckenridge trying to find some kind of work to do because their fathers had been lost in a mine mishap, stood there. He shivered in his ragged clothes that couldn't possibly withstand the harsh winter that was already upon them. How did he get all the way out here without freezing?

"Can I help you?" She said through the screen.

"Gotta note fer Miz Vine." His teeth were chattering. "Ain't you her?"

She opened the screen and invited him in. They moved into the parlor. The boy headed toward the fireplace and hovered beside it, still shivering. He dug in the pocket of his ragged trousers and brought out a dirty, wrinkled piece of paper and handed it to Lorinda.

"Would you like a hot cup of coffee, young man?" Mrs. Oleson dropped the knitting back in the basket. "It'll help warm you up."

"Please, ma'am. I'm half froze."

She hurried to the kitchen.

Lorinda read the scratchy writing.

Franklin has been hurt. He's calling for you. Come quickly.

Lorinda turned toward the boy, just as Mrs. Oleson handed him the cup of coffee. "Young man, where did you get this note?"

"A man." He wrapped his fingers around the warm mug and took a gulp of the hot liquid. "Paid me t' bring it t' you."

"Where is my husband? Is he hurt bad?" Lorinda needed to know.

"I dunno. I never seen him. Just the man." Fear shone out of the boy's eyes.

Lorinda handed the message to Mrs. Oleson and began wringing her hands. Had their quarrel sent Franklin into danger? If so, she was responsible for what happened to him. She had to go to him right away.

Mrs. Oleson helped her gather what she might need to help Franklin. Lorinda got blankets, bandages, ointments, and warm clothes. She put on two layers of Franklin's union suits, then his trousers and a flannel shirt. She had to belt the trousers up tight to keep them from falling off, but she needed protection from the extreme cold.

Mrs. Oleson filled a gunny sack with food items and poured coffee in a Mason jar and wrapped in several towels to keep in the heat. "This will help keep you and Franklin warm."

By the time they were back in the parlor, the messenger had finished his coffee.

"How am I supposed to find him?" Lorinda hadn't seen any directions on the note.

"I'll take you." The boy pulled on his ragged gloves that didn't really cover his hands.

Lorinda went to get an extra pair of gloves from a drawer in Franklin's dresser, and she snagged an older coat. She thrust them at the boy. "Put these on over yours. They'll help some."

The boy nodded. "Thank ya kindly."

Lorinda turned toward Mrs. Oleson. "I'll be home as soon as I can."

"Just be careful. It's not really safe to be out there too long." Worry lined her forehead and darkened her eyes.

"I know." Lorinda gave the older woman a hug.

She picked up a lot of the things they had gathered, and the boy grabbed the rest. When they went out the door, she noticed a broken-down horse standing beside the gate. "That yours?"

"Yeah. He was my dad's."

The boy followed her into the barn. She saddled Golden Boy, who had completely recovered his strength. They loaded saddlebags evenly with most of the supplies she was taking, then rolled the blankets and tied them on behind the saddle. While she was doing this, she found an older horse blanket.

She glanced at the boy. "Here. Wrap this around you. It'll help keep you warmer."

His eyes rounded with surprise. "I ain't never had a blanket just for me." A smile broke out on his face. "Thanks, ma'am."

As they left the ranch, Lorinda glanced back at the house with all the windows blazing with light. She hated to leave the babies right now, but her husband needed her...and she needed him.

She followed the boy from the lane onto the road, then off the beaten track toward a tight grove of naked trees. Only a narrow trail made its crooked way between the thick trunks to a small clearing. Lorinda glanced around but didn't see her husband.

"How much farther?"

The boy glanced at her, then away. "Just a little ways." He led her between two trunks on the other side of the stark clearing.

A man stepped out from behind one of them. At first, Lorinda didn't recognize him, then it hit her. He was the drifter she'd run off her property soon after Mike had left her alone. Before she could do anything, he grabbed Golden Boy's bridle. The horse tried to shy away, but the man held fast.

"I see you brought my horse back to me." He sneered and jerked hard on the bridle to pull them off the path.

"He's not your horse. He's mine." Lorinda had to grab the pommel to stay on the horse.

"Oh, no, little lady. He's mine...again."

Lorinda didn't like the way he looked, the way he smelled, or anything else about him. He had to be Marvin. So that meant he killed Mike and did the other things Miriam told them about.

Without a word, he pulled her from the horse and tied her to a tree.

"What do you want?" Before she could get out any more words, he thrust a dirty bandana into her mouth and tied it tightly behind her head.

Marvin turned toward the boy. He pulled an envelope and a silver dollar from his pocket. "Wait for an hour, then take this note to the same ranch. Remember, I know where you live, and I know about your mother and sister. If you cross me, you'll never see them again."

The boy high-tailed it away as fast as the mangy horse could move...which wasn't very fast.

"Now, Miz Sullivan, oh that's right, you're Miz Vine now. I have you right where I want you. Don't try to get away. I'm going to untie you and put you on the horse. Don't try to fight me. You'll be sorry if you do."

Chills not associated with the weather scampered up and down her spine like a whole nest of spiders. She started to tremble.

Marvin threw her on Golden Boy. He tied her hands again, this time in front, so she could hold on to the pommel. He led her to a horse he'd hidden among the trees, mounted, and led her horse behind him.

They went a short ways to get out of the grove of trees, then he turned off on a trail that led up and over an outcropping of large rocks. She had to hold tight to the pommel to keep from falling from Golden Boy. She glanced down and saw that they weren't leaving hoofprints. How would anyone be able to find them if there was no trail to follow?

The farther up the mountain of rocks they went, the more talkative Marvin became. He poured out venomous words and thoughts about Franklin. Lorinda wished she could refute every word he said. He must not know her husband very well. Then he began to brag about all his horrible misdeeds.

Mike wasn't the only person he'd murdered, but he was particularly angry about her first husband.

"I spent time getting to know Mike, plying him with enough booze to loosen most tongues. He did tell me about the gold and that he was going to take it to Denver to be assayed. But he was a wily one. He told me he was going to take the gold, but he gave me a false date. That's why I killed him when he didn't have the gold or the money when I finally found him. Nobody crosses Marvin Pratt and lives to tell about it."

His last words chilled her even more. All the layers of clothing weren't doing her any good. Lorinda was tired of hearing his whiny voice. She wished he was the one with a dirty bandana stuffed into his mouth. She had never thought about really shooting anyone. She had just used the rifle at the cabin to scare intruders. But if she weren't tied up and had a gun, she wouldn't hesitate to shoot this man. Maybe not a kill shot, but maim him enough that she could get away.

"I'll bet those saddlebags are full of things I can use. Good food and all. Probably didn't bring any booze though, did you?"

How did the man expect her to answer with a gag in her mouth?

After what seemed like an eternity to her, they rode into the mouth of a cavern. She'd never been underground before. The dark dampness felt eerie, but at least they were out of the stinging wind.

Marvin dropped to the ground and picked up a lantern, then led both horses deeper into the cavern until they reached a large chamber. The farther they went, the more the temperature rose. When he stopped in the chamber, it was cool, but a long ways from the biting cold outside. Lorinda welcomed that. Even with her layers, she had almost frozen on the ride up the mountain.

"I'm going to untie you and let you down from the horse, but don't try anything. I'll shoot you dead if you do." His grating tone held a note of promise.

Lorinda believed the man meant every word. She decided to do what he told her to do but also watch for a chance to get away without him killing her. She needed to talk to Franklin again, and the babies needed to be nursed. Because she had been so cold, her milk hadn't come down when it was time to feed them. She wondered what was happening at the house. Had Franklin arrived at home? Was he even now out looking for her? She hoped so. That might be her only chance to get away from this crazy man.

Marvin struck a match and lit the lantern, setting it beside the cavern wall. The only other light came from the tunnel they had followed to get here, and it was very faint.

As she glanced around the large room, in the shadows she made out three other tunnels heading different directions from here. In her mind, she drew a picture of where they were in relation to the outside world. When she tried to get away, she didn't want to choose the wrong tunnel.

After he got her off the horse and untied her, he emptied the saddlebags. "Bandages, medicine, food. You really believed the message, didn't you?" His evil laugh bounced off the rock walls while he untied the extra blankets from the saddle. "And we'll be warm tonight."

He leered at her, sending another flock of chills up her spine. If that man touched her in any way, she knew where to kick him so it would hurt the worst. She'd had to do that one time with her uncle. He never touched her that way again.

Dear Lord, don't let this man touch me where he has no right to. She gritted her teeth to keep the tears from rushing to her eyes. She didn't want him to know how she feared him. It would probably just feed his ego and push him toward following through with his insinuations.

Sweet Jesus, please send someone to find me.

He pawed through the food she'd brought and gave her some to eat. She didn't want anything his hands had touched, but she knew she needed to keep up her strength. Even though every bite almost clogged her throat, she swallowed it down. When they were finished eating, Marvin tied her hands behind her and her feet together, then covered all but her head with a couple of the blankets. With the extra cover, her body felt cozy for the first time since she left the ranch house. But she worried about his motives. Why was he feeding her and keeping her warm? What nefarious plans did he have for her? The thoughts of what they could be chilled her clear to her bones.

He left his horse in the cave and took Golden Boy. She had no idea where he was going. She didn't know if she wanted him to come back or not. She just hoped Franklin or someone else could find her before it was too late.

CHAPTER 37

$\mathcal{F}$ ranklin didn't stay with the other ranchers any longer than it took him to warm up enough to get home. When he rode Major out of town, he gave the stallion his head. He knew the horse wanted to reach the barn as quickly as he wanted to see Lorinda. This time, he'd keep a tight rein on his anger and really listen to her.

As he rode down the lane leading to the ranch house, he noticed lights shining from every window. Something must have happened. Could something be wrong with Lorinda or one of the boys? Or even Mrs. Oleson? His pulse accelerated. *Please God, don't let anything be wrong with Lorinda. The last words I said to her were hurtful.*

When he stopped at the gate to the front yard, Rusty rushed out the front door. "Boss, what are you doing here?"

That wasn't the welcome he'd expected. What a crazy question.

"Where's Mrs. Vine?" Rusty's second question hit Franklin like a well-placed punch in the gut.

Franklin ran up onto the porch. "What are you talking about? Isn't Lorinda here?"

Rusty shook his head. "A boy from town brought a note saying you'd been hurt and needed her. She rode out to help you."

Franklin headed through the front door. "I'm freezing. Let's talk in here."

Mrs. Oleson must have heard his voice, because she came out of the parlor, holding a baby in each arm. Both of them were fussing. "Where have you been, Franklin? Are you hurt?" Her gaze swept past him as if searching behind him. "And where's Lorinda?"

Rusty had followed him in and shut the door.

"Okay." Franklin looked from one to the other. He didn't think he could live with losing Lorinda knowing he hadn't expressed his deep love for her. "Someone tell me what's going on."

Mrs. Oleson handed baby Michael to him, and his son rested his head on Franklin's cold shoulder. He slid the baby inside his coat and focused his attention on the housekeeper.

She pulled a wrinkled piece of paper from her apron pocket and handed it to him. He read the words that didn't make a lick of sense.

"Where did this come from?" He was trying to keep his anger under control, but it was getting hard. That's what brought all this on, him losing his temper.

"A boy from town. One of the raggedy ones who's always roaming the streets." She cuddled Andrew closer and patted his back.

"How long has Lorinda been gone?" He crushed the paper and dropped it on the table near the front door.

"Way over an hour, maybe even two." Mrs. Oleson looked flustered. "I've lost track of time, trying to appease these babies."

She did look harried, which was unusual for her.

"Rusty, what do you know about this?" Franklin wanted to get to the bottom of it as quickly as he could.

"A boy, maybe even the same one, brought this letter and gave it to me when I came out from checking on the horses." He handed the envelope to Franklin. "Golden Boy wasn't in the barn, and I came up to see if the women knew where he could have gone. That's when I found out where Mrs. Vine went."

Thoughts in Franklin's head swirled like a dust devil. "Where did she go?"

"Well, that's the thing." Rusty rubbed the back of his neck and studied the carpet. "We don't know."

Franklin tore the envelope open and released a single sheet of paper. *I have your wife, Franklin, and I'm going to keep her until you give me what I want. Mike Sullivan owed me some money and when you pay me $20,000, I'll give her back to you. If you don't do it in the next forty-eight hours, you'll never see her again. MP*

"MP? That's got to be Marvin Pratt." Franklin crumpled the sheet of paper and started to drop it beside the first one. Then he tried to get the wrinkles out before he laid it on the table. "He's kidnapped Lorinda, and we have to find her. According to Miriam, Marvin is a murderer, an arsonist, a cattle rustler, and who knows what else?"

Rusty grabbed his coat and hat. "What do you want me to do?"

"Ride to town as fast as you can. Ask the sheriff to form a posse and bring them out here." Franklin wasn't going to wait for them to get here to start looking for his wife. "Oh, and see if one of the nursing mothers in the church can come to help Mrs. Oleson with the babies."

"Sure thing, Boss." Rusty hurried out the door and headed toward the barn.

Franklin knew his ranch hand was glad to have something to do to help. *Now, what am I going to do?* He couldn't just go off half-cocked with no plan in mind. He knew he'd be looking until he found her. He gathered blankets, food, and a jar of hot coffee. When he went to gather more warm clothes, he found that some of his long underwear were missing as well as some of his outer clothing. *Thank goodness, Lorinda dressed warmly before she left.* And she did it to try to help him. Surely, she had some kind of feelings for him. He hoped that was a good sign. The sooner he found her, the better.

He found his warmest wool scarf and wrapped it around his neck and across the bottom of his face before putting on his heavy coat and gloves. He hefted the pillowcase of provisions over his shoulder and went to the barn. Rusty had put some oats in Major's feed trough, but he'd left the stallion saddled. His long-time ranch hand knew he would be leaving soon.

Franklin loaded the saddlebags evenly with the provisions and tied the blankets on behind his saddle. He assumed Lorinda did the same before she left. He had to believe that...and that she was somewhere safe and out of the deadly cold.

~

*L*orinda's kidnapper had been gone for at least an hour when she heard someone riding into the tunnel toward her. She was tired of being alone, but she didn't really want Marvin Pratt here with her. What terrible plans did he have for her now? She knew he was still mad at Mike for deceiving him, and she was pretty sure he didn't like Franklin either. Would he take out his wrath for her two husbands on her?

Would she ever see the babies again? Even though she tried to keep them corralled, tears streamed down her cheeks. She wanted to wipe them away before he saw them, but she couldn't with her hands tied up and wrapped in blankets.

He dismounted from his horse and led him to the other side of the large area. There he tied the reins to one of the rough stalagmites, down near the bottom, so the horse couldn't work it loose. Then he looked straight at her.

"Missed me, huh?" He stared at her face, his eyes following the trails of tears.

She dared not say anything to upset the man. No telling what he would do.

He came over and unwrapped the blankets from around her, then untied her hands. When he did, blood rushed into her fingers, making them prickle with pain. But soon they felt better.

"Don't get all excited. I only untied them so you can eat. I don't want you dying on me. Not yet, anyway."

His words sent another chill through her. He could kill her at any time. *Please God, protect me.*

He started toward where the supplies she'd brought with her were stacked against the wall. He picked up the jar wrapped in towels. "Well, looky here. Coffee." His cackle sounded demented.

However, he did pour some into two tin cups and give one to her. The liquid soothed her dry throat.

Next he dug out two large roast beef sandwiches. He unwrapped one and shoved it into one of her hands.

He bit into the other one and chewed with his mouth open.

She looked away to keep from gagging.

"I really like me some good roast beef. Must be some of Franklin's fine cattle. Miriam and I enjoyed one of the yearling I stole from him a while back."

Lorinda tried to ignore him and ate her sandwich in silence. She was very hungry, and she savored every bite.

Soon he came closer than she wanted him to. "You sittin' there hoping Franklin will rescue you? Ain't gonna happen. Jist gave him several false trails to follow b'fore I came back. And it started snowin', so even those'll be covered soon. He'll git you back when he pays me th' ransom, and not a bit sooner."

Her heart dropped to her stomach, making her want to

throw up every bite she'd taken. *God, I trust You, but I'm getting scared. Please help Franklin find me.*

~

*A*s Franklin rode out, snow began to fall. He knew the trail would soon be covered. He couldn't let it get him down, but he had to find his wife as soon as possible.

Thoughts jumbled in his brain. How could he have been so fooled by Marvin? They'd played together, gone to school together, gone to church together. He remembered vividly the day both he and Marvin walked that aisle during a revival and asked Jesus into their hearts. At least *he* invited Him in. Did Marvin just go down because he did? Was he just making a show?

How could the boy who'd been his best friend turn into a hardened criminal who robbed and murdered and deserted the woman who carried his child? Why didn't he respect her enough to marry her before he seduced her? Maybe he just wanted Miriam because Franklin had her. Marvin hadn't ever exhibited any tendencies toward sin and lawlessness before he enticed her to fall for him instead of Franklin. Or maybe there had been signs and Franklin didn't have enough sense to recognize them. He thought Marvin was the same kind of boy that he was. But he had been so wrong. Franklin had never seen him again after Marvin and Miriam left, so he didn't see the man change even more.

Miriam paid the price for Marvin's sins. Franklin realized he hadn't really loved her the way a man should love his wife, but he'd never wish the kind of life she'd lived on any woman.

He wondered if there was an event that turned Marvin away from the Lord. Had Marvin turned his back on God, or had his heart never let God inside in the first place? Franklin didn't figure he'd ever know the answer to this question.

But even more important, what was Marvin doing to Lorinda? The thought soured his stomach, and his heart bled for his wife. *Lord, I'd give my life in exchange for hers. Our sons need her.*

I need her.

CHAPTER 38

*a*s darkness fell, Franklin made his way toward the ranch house. With no moon tonight, he could ride close to where his wife was without seeing her. They would need to start searching early tomorrow. His tired horse could rest overnight and be fresh to ride then. Discouragement sat heavy on his shoulders. *Nothing.* He'd found nothing that would tell them where Marvin took his wife. How long would she be safe? Mrs. Oleson said that Lorinda took what she thought she might need to help him, so she had food, coffee, and blankets. And she wore some of his warmer clothes. But if she was out in the weather…

He hoped Marvin had taken shelter somewhere she could be safe. But nowhere would be safe with that murderer. That dirty, rotten scoundrel. Franklin wished he'd never known the man. If not, maybe Lorinda would be at home with him right now, and his heart wouldn't be breaking for her.

Franklin rode up to the gate in the picket fence where Rusty and the posse had gathered. Maybe they found her, but when he looked at their faces, he knew they hadn't. More disappointment. He dismounted and passed the reins off to Rusty, who led

Major toward the barn. The sheriff was on the porch steps talking to the milling crowd.

"Thank you, men. Since we didn't find anything today, we'll meet here at dawn to start again. We'd appreciate everyone who can come to help us."

The men started mounting their horses, preparing to ride home.

Franklin walked among them, thanking each one individually. He knew they dropped whatever they were doing to help. Hopefully, tomorrow they'd find Lorinda...and that rat, Marvin.

When he reached the front porch, he asked the sheriff to join him in the parlor to warm up before he headed to Breckenridge. Mrs. Oleson quickly headed toward the kitchen to retrieve mugs of coffee for him and the sheriff.

"Are the boys all right?" Franklin welcomed the hot drink from her.

"Yes, Molly Malone came soon after Rusty went to town. She brought her baby and plenty of clothes to stay a few days so she could nurse all three of the babies. The boys settled down pretty soon after their stomachs were full." Mrs. Oleson quickly left the two men alone.

Franklin leaned one arm on the mantel. "I'm sorry I wasn't here when you and the posse arrived. I just couldn't sit around and wait while my wife was out there somewhere."

The older man dropped into the chair closest to the fireplace. "Didn't expect you to be here. I know I wouldn't wait if my wife was missing. So where did you search?"

Franklin took another big gulp of the hot liquid before setting it down on a nearby table. "First I rode out to see if I could follow the tracks. There were two horses. They led to a fairly small copse of trees. I followed them into the woods and across a small meadow. On the other side, another horse joined them. Then one horse headed back toward town. The other two rode the opposite direction. At one point, there were several other horses, some going one way, some another, with their trails crisscrossing. They seemed to double back to that one place, until all the hoof prints were mixed up. No matter how hard I searched, I couldn't find a trail where the two horses branched off." He stared out the front window at the deepening twilight. "I sure hated to stop looking, knowing Lorinda was out there and I couldn't find her." He swiped his hand across his eyes where moisture had gathered.

The sheriff stood up and leaned on the other side of the mantel. "None of us wanted to stop. We had spread out like a wide net and searched every inch we had time to cover." He rubbed his hand across the back of his neck. "I'm sorry we didn't find her. Now I need you to tell me everything you know about this kidnapper."

By the time Franklin finished his tale, darkness had fallen like a cloak over the valley and mountains. No moon in sight and not enough light from the millions of stars above to help anyone find his wife.

Mrs. Oleson entered the parlor. "Sheriff, can you stay for a bowl of venison stew? It's hot, I made biscuits, and we have fresh-churned butter."

The lawman glanced at her. "I was planning on going back to town right away, but that sounds and smells mighty good. I'll eat with Franklin while we discuss what we'll do tomorrow. Then I'll have to get home and get some rest before we start out again."

Franklin was glad the man agreed to eat with him. He really didn't want to be alone with his thoughts before he had to. "We have plenty of room for you here. Why don't you stay? We'd get an earlier start tomorrow that way."

"Thanks for the offer." The sheriff followed him into the kitchen. "I'll take you up on it."

Even with his friend staying at the house, all kinds of bad

scenarios of what Marvin might be doing to Lorinda made his heart heavy.

⁓

*O*ff and on throughout the day, Marvin left Lorinda alone in the cavern. She didn't like it when he was near her. Fear and disgust filled every moment he was there. So did his terrible body odor.

When he was gone wasn't much better. Tied to a tall slag-mite, one horse still shared the space with her, and she couldn't get anything to drink or eat, wrapped up in two blankets with her hands and feet tied. At least he had untied and let her go deeper into the cavern to relieve herself when he was there. She didn't go too far when she did.

The quiet darkness of the cave filled her with fear. Evil lived here. A malevolent force bound her as strong as the ropes that bound her hands and feet. As if there was no one else in the world.

She was totally alone. This was worse than the months she had spent snowed in at her and Mike's cabin. Then at least she could move around and had plenty to eat and drink. Thinking of that made her mouth and throat dry up, crying out for suste-nance and water. She dropped her head against her knees that were drawn up inside the blankets.

Please, God, rescue me from this man's clutches. I'm sure there are many people out there searching for me. Guide them, Lord. Calm Franklin's heart and spirit. If I ever...when I see him again, I'll assure him I don't want to leave our happy home. I will finally express my love for him, no matter what he thinks about it. Amen, Lord Jesus.

Now she wished she'd memorized more Bible verses when she had a chance. Repeating the words would help calm her.

Once again, she heard a horse walking through the tunnel toward the cavern. *Please let it be Franklin.*

"Did you miss me?" The voice she hoped never to hear again grated against her nerves. She wished her hands were untied, so she could throw one of the rocks nearby at the hideous man.

His eerie laugh bounced off the rock walls. She wanted to cover her ears with her hands. Then he came into sight.

"Okay, we'll eat again. At least we still have some provisions." He dismounted and led the horse over beside the other one and hobbled him.

As he unwrapped the blankets from around her, she tried to hide her disgust when he brushed against her skin. After he untied her hands, he handed her a tin plate with cold beans and an even colder biscuit.

"This is getting close to the end of our grub." An evil grin split his face.

She shuddered while taking a few bites.

"You better hope that husband of yours takes my letter seriously." He shoveled a too-large bite into his mouth.

She dropped her chin against her chest and kept eating. What would happen when they ran out of food? Would this bad man go out to find something more for them to eat? She really couldn't see him doing that.

"He needs to bring the ransom to me by tomorrow. If not–" The outlaw took his knife and ran the tip across his own throat without breaking the skin. "–he'll never find you in time to save you."

A strong shudder ran through her whole body. At least, the man was too interested in feeding his face to notice.

Help me, Jesus...help me, Jesus...help me, Jesus. The words ran over and over through her mind, a way to cling to her sanity.

"I watched that posse of fools looking for us, but not one got a glimpse of me." His words were filled with an evil kind of glee.

Lorinda shut out his words, overcoming them with the words she kept repeating in her mind. Her only hope was in Jesus.

*ranklin slept fitfully that night, and when morning arrived, he felt spent. He grabbed a quick breakfast with the sheriff and met the other men outside the ranch house at dawn. They divided into teams of two and spread across the valley. They swept across the area, searching every canyon, draw, smaller mountain, and river or stream on the way. As the day progressed, Franklin became more and more desperate. *How long can Lorinda last in this cold?*

Late in the afternoon, all the teams met and encircled a large rock formation that lifted high above the valley floor. As they looked up toward the top of the formation, they saw a horse and rider. A cry went up and spread from team to team. They closed ranks and blocked any path of escape.

Franklin rode around the pile of boulders until he reached a place where he could see the man was indeed Marvin Pratt. By that time, the sheriff was riding beside Franklin.

"Marvin—" Franklin yelled up at him.

The outlaw stopped and stared down at him.

One of the members of the posse raised his rifle and aimed for Marvin's heart. "Want me to take the shot, Sheriff?"

"No!" Franklin rode to stop the man. "If we kill him, we won't know where my wife is."

"You bring my money, Franklin?" Marvin sounded very sure of himself.

Franklin seethed. The man was one ornery son-of-a-gun. He wished they could shoot the man, but not before he knew where Lorinda was.

The sheriff stood tall in his stirrups. "Marvin Pratt. We have you surrounded. Ride down with your hands up."

"Want to make a deal, Sheriff?" Marvin still looked as if he thought he was in control.

"What kind of deal?" The lawman frowned up at the criminal.

Franklin turned toward the sheriff. "You can't make a deal with this desperado. The man's a murderer, arsonist, cattle thief, and we don't know what else."

The sheriff held up his palm to stop Franklin's tirade.

"I don't have to have the money." Marvin shifted in his saddle, and his horse moved restlessly beneath him. "I'll trade the whereabouts of Mrs. Vine for my freedom."

Franklin started to speak, but the sheriff stopped him.

"Marvin, you know I can't let you loose. You've committed too many crimes—murder, arson, stealing cattle, stealing horses, and who knows what else? We can't have you riding around in this area. So come on down, and we'll see what the law can agree to if you help us find Mrs. Vine. That's the best I can do."

Franklin held his breath. Would Marvin give up? Would this soon be over? His heartbeat accelerated. *Please let it be over, Lord.*

"I ain't goin' back to prison. B'sides, most of my crimes are hangin' offenses. Last chance to let me go?" His hate-filled, beady eyes stared at Franklin. "You've had the love of two women. I couldn't beat you...until today."

"No deals." The sheriff shouted.

Quick as a flash, Marvin's gun was out of his holster and pointed against his own head.

"No!" Franklin's shout coincided with the crack of the gunshot.

Marvin dropped to the hard rocks below his horse's hooves.

Franklin jumped off Major and scrambled up the side of the huge mound of boulders. Maybe he could get there before Marvin died. If so, he'd make the man tell him where Lorinda was.

The sheriff climbed right behind him. They both knelt beside the body of Marvin Pratt. Franklin didn't have to check the man's pulse to know he was gone.

He hunkered on the rock, tears streaming down his face. "What are we going to do?"

The sheriff stood beside him. "We keep searching. We'll find her."

Franklin hated Marvin more than ever since he took his own life.

Hated that he'd argued with Lorinda.

Hated that he'd been too much of a coward to tell her how much he loved her.

CHAPTER 39

*W*hen they finished searching for the day, Franklin rode up to the ranch house, wearing dejection like a new suit of clothes that were a size too small, his gut tied in knots that felt as if they would never let go. There was nowhere they hadn't looked. The men needed to get back to their businesses and ranches. For all they knew, his wife was dead. But he still felt a connection to her. She had to be out there somewhere...alive.

The sheriff once again stood on the porch talking to the men who finished the day with them. "I know we're all discouraged. We don't know where else to look for Mrs. Vine. Go home. Pray. If anyone comes up with somewhere else to look, please come to town and get me."

Franklin's boots felt as if they were made of lead, instead of leather as he walked up the front steps. He turned toward those gathered. "I owe you a debt of gratitude. I'll never be able to repay for what you've done so far. I'll understand if you need to get back to your own business or ranch. I hope tomorrow brings a new goal for our search." He turned and trudged into the house.

Molly Malone opened the door to the room where the babies slept when Franklin walked down the hallway.

"Hello, Franklin?" Worry winkled her brow. "Any good news yet?"

Disappointed, he shook his head. "No." He glanced over her shoulder. "Are the boys awake?"

"They should wake up from their naps soon." She looked back at the three babies, one on a pallet on the floor, and the other two sharing the cradle.

"Good. I want to spend time with my sons after I clean up and get something to eat.

He had Mrs. Oleson heat water, hoping a hot bath would help him sleep. He was so tired he could hardly stay on his feet, but his mind wouldn't let go of the fact that he had to find Lorinda...and soon.

After the bath, he ate the rest of the venison stew from yesterday. He forced each bite down. How could he sit here eating, knowing Lorinda probably didn't have anything left of the food she'd taken with her? He wondered if Marvin had even shared the food with her? Pain lanced through his heart, and he couldn't keep tears from forming in his eyes. He wiped both eyes to remove the blur.

Rusty came in from the bunkhouse and sat beside him at the table. "What are we going to do, Boss?"

"Maybe Marvin took her back to the land she and Mike owned. There's a soddy there where they had stored food." Hope took root in Franklin's heart.

Rusty frowned. "Nah, we already looked there. It's as empty as it was after we moved her provisions down here to the ranch."

The flicker of hope died. Franklin hadn't believed he could feel any worse than before, but he did. He was close to wanting to give up, but he couldn't. He needed Lorinda more than the babies did.

"I don't know of any place we haven't searched, even the outlying ranches." Rusty straddled one of the kitchen chairs and laid his arms along the back. "It's not looking good, is it?"

His ranch hand stated the obvious, but Franklin wouldn't accept giving up. "I'll try to come up with other places for us to search. Of course, Marvin's mind was so devious and twisted, who could figure out what he was thinking?"

Rusty went back to the bunkhouse.

Franklin got up slowly from the kitchen chair. His discouragement made him move like an old man. Maybe time with the boys would help him feel better.

He asked Mrs. Oleson to help him with the boys. They went into the bedroom and each picked up one of them. They took the babies into the parlor.

He clutched Michael close. He wondered if the babies could sense all the tension. After a few minutes, he started to play with his son. At one point, he wanted to throw him up in the air, because the boy liked it so much. That would get him laughing. *Lorinda wouldn't like it.*

No, she wouldn't. Instead, he sat down and crossed one leg over the other. He settled Michael on his boot and played Ride a Little Horsey with him.

Soon he and Mrs. Oleson exchanged babies. Miriam's baby settled into Franklin's arms. He loved holding the younger infant. He'd like to have more babies … with Lorinda.

Molly Malone came to get the babies. She took the baby from Franklin's arms. "It's time to feed these two."

Mrs. Oleson followed her out of the room.

When they were gone, Franklin went to bed. He lay on one side, but couldn't get comfortable. So he turned on the other side. Same thing. He forced his eyes closed and tried to clear his mind of all thoughts, but Lorinda kept intruding. Why, oh why had he made all the missteps with their relationship? Now he might never be able to make things right. He gripped his hands into fists, wanting to lash out and hit something...hard.

After tossing and turning for a couple of hours, Franklin got up and put on his warmer clothes. He went out and paced across the drive between the house and the barn, praying. His heart and mind cried out to God, begging for his wife's safety. He stared up at the heavens and looked at the myriad stars created by God's hand. God knew where Lorinda was. He wished the Lord would write it in the stars, like a banner. *Lorinda is here.* Maybe form the stars into an arrow, pointing to the very place. *Yeah, like that's going to happen.*

Lord, I love you, and I trust you, but this is hard. Show me what to do.

As he swung around to pace the other direction, a flicker of light caught his attention. What was that? It was too close to the peak of the mountain southwest from the ranch for there to be a house, but still the light remained. He stared at it. Could it be a fire? It didn't flicker as a fire would. The longer he stared at it, the more the light expanded, then it stopped growing.

While he was a boy, he and Marvin had explored every mountain, canyon, and forest that connected with the ranch. But that light was above the timberline. Franklin followed the sawtooth ridge of peaks around the valley. Could that be where the cave they found was located? He tried to remember every detail of how they found the large cavern. It had been so long ago, he'd completely forgotten about the adventure.

He closed his eyes and let them get used to the total darkness. When he opened them, the bright light was still there, like a star fallen from heaven. *Lord, is this a message from you?*

Indescribable peace enveloped him, and he no longer felt the bitter cold.

He hurried into the house and awakened Mrs. Oleson.

"What do you need, Franklin?" Sleepiness clung to her. "How can I help you?"

"I know where Lorinda is." He had to be positive about this thought. Hope was back.

"Where?"

But he was out the door, headed toward the bunkhouse. He awakened Rusty, leaving the other ranch hands to their well-deserved rest.

"I want you to prepare Major and your horse for a long ride. I'm going into the house to get supplies to take with us. I know where Lorinda is. It'll take us a while to get to her."

Franklin went back into the house and told Mrs. Oleson to start plenty of water heating after breakfast, so Lorinda could have a hot bath when he brought her home.

In half an hour, he and Rusty set out across the valley in a different direction from the one Marvin took when he kidnapped Lorinda. Some places would be harder to traverse on this trail, but it should take much less time than it would to go up the way Marvin had. Still it would take the rest of the night and into the next day before they would return.

~

*L*orinda had been tied up in the same position so long, she didn't know if she could even stand up if...when... someone rescued her. Cramps in various muscles came and went with closer frequency. Is this the way it feels to starve to death? Stiffness was her present reality. She wanted to cry, but she didn't have enough moisture for tears. At least, her body functions had ceased. If only it had happened before she soiled herself.

How long had Marvin been gone? Much, much longer than any other time. Her mouth and throat were so dry, her tongue stuck to the roof of her mouth, and her teeth felt cottony. She felt dirtier than she'd ever been, even when she was a child living with her father and uncle, who didn't care if she was clean or not. Hunger clawed at her stomach like a living monster, and her head ached whether she held it up or leaned it against her knees.

She had no concept of how much time had passed since Marvin left. She did remember it had been daylight when he left, but had there been only one night or two since then? She wasn't sure. Her thoughts were muddled.

She missed holding baby Michael and baby Andrew. Her heart longed for the comforting presence of her husband. If someone didn't come to find her soon, they might only find her body.

Jesus, help me...Jesus, help me...Jesus, help...

~

*a*s Franklin and Rusty picked their way up the mountain trail, the glow of the light near the peak continued to shine bright. Franklin had brought a lantern in case they might need it, but so far the strange light had somehow lit the pathway even though there was no moon. Here they were near the end of November, with snow falling all around them, but the snowfall hadn't reached blizzard proportions. So it didn't block out their surroundings.

Franklin couldn't help thinking about the wise men who came from the East to find the Christ child. Having the star shining on their path to guide them. Maybe they felt a little like he did. He recognized that the light leading them had to come from God. Every one of his heartbeats sang out in thanksgiving to the Lord. Somehow, he knew this beacon would lead him to Lorinda. With God going to so much trouble, he had to find her alive. The family would really have something to celebrate on Thanksgiving Day.

Dawn was just barely peeking over the rim of the mountains when they reached the opening of the tunnel just where he remembered it. One streak of morning light shot a beam right at the opening, scattering the darkness inside.

When they were out of the wind, Franklin lit the lantern so they could see as they went deeper into the ground. "Lorinda!" His shout bounced from the rock walls of the tunnel and echoed back at him.

No answer came. *Please, Lord. Don't let us be at the wrong place.*

The next shout was answered by a whinny. *A whinny?* A horse was in the cavern. He rode closer and closer to the large room he and Marvin had discovered. When they turned the corner into the vast space, another whinny sounded much closer. He lifted the lantern high, and Rusty followed behind him.

Golden Boy stood near the far wall beside a large lump of something. His muzzle lay against the top, and he blew a whiffle of breath against the mound. Something moved under his head, and he stepped back.

When Franklin caught sight of the dirty, blonde curls, he knew he'd found her. And she moved. Relief shot through him.

He jumped from his horse and ran toward her. "Lorinda, are you all right?"

Major followed behind him.

Her eyes opened a little, but she didn't look as if she knew where she was. No recognition shown in her eyes.

Marvin has been dead for almost twenty-four hours, and who knew how long he'd left Lorinda alone here?

Franklin grabbed his canteen. "Rusty, bring me a couple of those blankets."

He sank beside her on the cool rock floor. His heart beat so strong, he had a hard time catching his breath at this high altitude.

Gently, he tipped her head higher. "Lorinda, sweetheart, open your mouth. I have some water for you."

After opening the container of drinking water, he tipped it

against her dry lips. When the first drops touched her, she opened them a little. He dribbled small amounts into her mouth and waited until she swallowed. It took several tries before the liquid started to revive her. When she opened her eyes again, a light shone in them.

"Fr...anklin...you...came...for me."

"I'm going to give you another drink, but not too much." Once again, he tipped the canteen only a little.

This time, she sucked in more fluid. "I knew you would." The words were so faint, he had to listen closely to hear them. "Jesus..."

Now that she was more alert, he unwrapped the two blankets surrounding her. His heart nearly broke when he saw she was tied up. While he worked the ropes loose, she whimpered. Oh, how she must hurt.

"How long have you been tied up?" He tried to keep anger out of his tone. If Marvin wasn't already dead, he'd want to hunt him down and beat him to a pulp. *I know, Lord. These thoughts aren't right, but... He. Hurt. My. Wife.*

"Don't know." This time her voice was a little stronger.

When the ropes were all gone, he reached toward her.

"No, Franklin. I'm so dirty." A glisten of tears appeared in her eyes, but none fell down her cheeks.

He lifted Lorinda to her feet. He started to let go, but her legs buckled. He grabbed her up in his arms before she could fall.

"Do your legs hurt?"

She nodded against his chest.

He held her close to his heart, cradling her with his love, until she was able to stand up. With one hand, he tilted her face toward his and settled his lips against hers. He didn't want to hurt them, but he wanted to pour his love into her. The kiss was gentle, but it lasted long minutes. She melted against him and raised her arms around his neck, pulling him closer and closer.

Just as the one at the wedding, this kiss took on a life of its own. He was as gentle with her as he could be, but he didn't want to break the connection.

When their lips finally parted, he leaned closer to her exquisite ear and whispered, "Lorinda, I love you with all my heart."

"I love you, too, Franklin."

Her words startled him. How long had she loved him? Had they been living the lie with both of them wanting more from their marriage? What an idiot he had been when he suggested such a thing. They had a lot to talk about. But not right here. Not right now.

When he turned around, he saw Rusty had unloaded food from the saddlebags. And even though they had ridden through the rest of the night, the coffee had been wrapped so well that a little bit of vapor rose from the cups. Two blankets were spread beside the food.

Rusty waved his hand toward the bounty. "Breakfast, anyone?"

CHAPTER 40

*T*he breakfast, even though it was cold, tasted like a banquet to Lorinda. She wanted to just shovel the food into her mouth and not stop until she was full.

"You need to eat slowly, since you haven't had anything for over twenty-four hours." Franklin must have read her mind. "We don't want you sick before we get you home."

She slowed down and enjoyed every bite, surprised by how little it took before she couldn't hold anything else. The coffee helped perk her up, but the cold water was most soothing to her dry throat and mouth.

When they all finished eating, Franklin helped her stand. She still didn't feel too steady, so she was glad he stayed close beside her.

"Rusty, there is a natural spring just a short way from the opening of this cave, to the west. Please take the horses so they can drink before we head back to the ranch." He reached for the extra canteen they hadn't opened yet. "I'll keep this one here for Lorinda, and you can fill the rest."

After Rusty left, Franklin grabbed a gunnysack that had been tied to one of the saddles. "I didn't know why before I left, but I stuffed some of my warmest clothes into this. I'm glad I did."

Lorinda wondered why Franklin needed to change. He was very clean compared to her. Every thread of clothing on her was soiled and she stunk so bad she could hardly keep from throwing up.

"Now that Rusty's gone, you can use this water to clean up the best you can, and then you put on these clothes. We'll take the ones you have on back to the ranch and burn them."

Lorinda's eyes widened, and she could feel a blush creep up her neck into her face. She loved Franklin, but she didn't want the first time he saw her naked to be in this sorry state. She shivered in apprehension.

He smiled at her. "I want you to come over by that wall that's near the tunnel opening to clean up and dress. I'll stay in the tunnel with my back to you unless you need help." He leaned down and kissed her forehead, the tip of her nose, and then a kiss as soft as a butterfly on her cracked lips.

She smiled as he strode away. *Thank you, Jesus, for bringing me such a wonderful husband.*

By the time Rusty returned, she was as clean as she could get from the small amount of water and fully dressed in warm, clean clothes.

"Thanks, Rusty." Franklin took Major's reins from his ranch hand. "I'm going to wrap Lorinda in two blankets and we're both riding Major. We're leaving right away. Please load anything salvageable onto your horse and Golden Boy and bring it home."

He quickly wrapped her in the blankets. Then he mounted his horse and had Rusty lift her into his lap. She was so thin, she fit comfortably between him and the saddle horn. This reminded her of the time he brought her down from the mountain after her log cabin burned. That time, she tried not to touch him any more than she had to. This time, she nestled against him, enjoying the comfort of his arms around her and his broad, muscular chest for her to rest on.

Although exhausted, Lorinda couldn't rest without telling Franklin everything she'd been feeling. She poured out her heart to him, and she reveled in the love he covered her with. Finally, this ranch was home where she wanted to be, and she knew now that he wanted her there with all his heart. The gentle swaying of Major's gait lulled her to sleep and she rested knowing her husband loved her and would protect her from harm.

Just before they reached the ranch headquarters, Franklin woke her gently with a kiss. She yawned and stretched as much as she could wrapped up in the blankets, surprised that the sun was now coming more from the west than overhead. *Must be after noon.*

When they rode up to the house, Franklin's foreman, Thomas Walker, ran out of the barn to meet them by the gate. "Welcome home, Franklin. So good to see you, Mrs. Vine."

He let out a yell that could be heard all around the ranch headquarters. The hands poured from the bunkhouse and surrounded them, all talking at once, expressing how happy they were seeing her home safe. Their enthusiasm warmed her almost as much as Franklin's love did.

Mrs. Oleson came out on the porch, wiping her hands on her apron. "I'm so glad you're home. We have a bath poured for you, Lorinda. And as soon as you finish, I have dinner ready for both of you."

Thomas helped Lorinda down from the horse. Franklin dismounted.

"I'll come out to take care of Major in just a few minutes, but you can have someone take him to the barn and unsaddle him."

Thomas motioned Charlie over to take the horse. "As soon as she can get ready, Jake, you can accompany Mrs. Malone into town, then go tell the sheriff Mrs. Vine has been found."

Franklin picked up Lorinda and carried her into the house, and she didn't mind at all, even though all the ranch hands were still milling around. He took her into her bedroom where the bathtub stood ready, surrounded by clean clothes, towels, and rose-scented soap.

When he left, Mrs. Oleson came in. "Is there any way I can help you, Lorinda?"

"I've been so cold I've wondered if I still will be able to nurse the boys." She stared down into the clean water.

"I believe you will. I've heard of women who haven't nursed for longer than the three days you've been gone who took it right up again. Let's see how you feel after you are clean and warm." The older woman gave Lorinda a big hug. "I'll stay close-by, in case you need me. Just call out. I'll be here."

Lorinda undressed and slid slowly into the heat of the water. For a while, she just sat there and soaked in the warmth. Her muscles began to relax and the soreness melted away. She was afraid she'd go to sleep and slip underwater, so she sat up and washed every part of her body, especially her hair that felt as if it had a ton of dirt and debris in it. She wished Franklin hadn't seen her so filthy, but it didn't keep him from telling her how much he loved her. If only they'd talked about their feelings long ago. They had lost so much time to that silly marriage agreement.

Never again.

When she finished, she noticed that the dress laid out for her was one she hadn't seen before. And it was made from thick wool. She wondered if someone made it for her while she was gone.

Franklin would be returning from the barn soon, and she had something to do before he got back. She hurried to dress, then went into the dressing room between the two bedrooms.

Lorinda picked up the fluffy pillow Franklin slept on and hugged it to her, breathing in his masculine, woodsy scent. Her warmer body reacted to the fragrance. Desire for her husband swept through her, almost drowning her. She pulled the sheets off the single bed and stuffed them into the corner. She'd take them to the wash room later. When she heard the front door open, she rushed into her bedroom and placed the pillow on the bed next to hers. He would be surprised to find his bed unmade. Tonight would be their first night of truly being married in every sense of the word.

Thank you, Jesus.

~

DECEMBER 24, 1894

Franklin, Lorinda, and Mrs. Oleson climbed into the back of their big sleigh with the babies, and Rusty took his place in the driver's seat. Two wagons full of food and gifts had headed toward Breckenridge an hour ago. All the ranch hands accompanied the wagons.

Life had been so good this last month. After a wonderful Thanksgiving together at the ranch celebrating the rescue of Lorinda, the family decided to host a Christmas party after the Children's Christmas Eve program tonight at church. They would set up the party in the school building, the same place where their wedding had been held.

The reason for the party was two-fold. One, as a form of thanks for all the people who had helped search for Lorinda and care for the babies while she was gone. Most all of them came from their church. Those who didn't attend were sent invitations for themselves and their families. Franklin had a good time ordering cases of oranges from California. He found a way to order the white candy canes from a German candy maker in Ohio. So every member of every family would receive an orange and a candy cane from the Vine family. He also bought small toys to give each child. He wanted everyone to have a good Christmas. He felt more blessed than ever before.

By the time they reached the schoolhouse, the ranch hands had all the tables set up for the food and a Christmas tree in one corner of the room. Lorinda and Mrs. Oleson set to work hanging all the candy canes on the tree while Franklin and Rusty tied the small toys to the limbs. That's all the decorations the tree needed.

He didn't want to use candles because of the large crowd with many children playing around, it would be fire hazard, and they'd had enough tragedies in this year to last a lifetime.

The oranges were put in bowls at the ends of the tables with a few scattered among the covered dishes. When the program was finished, they'd all come over here to the schoolhouse to enjoy the party.

Franklin had made arrangements with Pastor Nelson so Franklin could talk to the congregation at the party. After everyone was inside the building, the pastor called for attention. Then Franklin and Lorinda went to the front of the room and stood beside him.

Franklin was nervous, and he knew his wife was even more so. He held her close to his side with his arm around her waist. She was more beautiful than he'd ever seen her, even at their wedding. She had a glow about her that radiated deep happiness.

Franklin wanted to tell about their agreement and how he later came to believe it wasn't God's will. They needed to know to really pray about everything so they didn't get caught in a situation like he and Lorinda had.

He took a deep breath and spoke with all the strength he could muster. When he was finished, their pastor once again had them repeat the vows they had spoken at the wedding. This time both of them meant every word. Even Lorinda spoke loud enough for everyone in the room to hear.

When he was finished, Reverend Brian Nelson said, "You may kiss the bride."

Franklin hadn't been expecting this, so he glanced down at his wife. Her smile was so sweet he couldn't do anything but press his lips to hers. This kiss was a repeat of the one at the first wedding. This time it connected two hearts and two lives that pledged their marriage for a lifetime.

The party continued far into the night, with everyone enjoying the festivities. Many people approached Franklin and Lorinda, who continued to stand together, and expressed how much it meant to them to hear Franklin's confession and recommitment to his wife. Some admitted how it changed their thinking about something in their lives they were striving with. So other lives were changed that night as well, which was a great blessing to Franklin.

Mrs. Oleson and the ranch hands shooed him and Lorinda out the door when the party was over. Their gift to them was cleaning up after the party and giving them some time alone. Even the babies slept quietly in orange crates sitting under the Christmas tree when they left.

When they arrived at the house, he escorted Lorinda into the house, where he once again kissed her. He looked forward to many long years of sampling her luscious lips and expressing their love to each other. After he stirred up the coals in the fireplace in the parlor and added the needed wood so Lorinda would be warm, he went out to return the sleigh and horses to the barn. He hurried through taking care of the horses so he could join her.

He stopped off in his office at the front of the house before he went into the parlor. She glanced up at him from one of the wingback chairs in front of the fireplace. When he went to her, she arose, and he slipped his arms around her, pulling her close.

"I have a special Christmas gift for you." He reached into his pocket and produced a small box wrapped in blue paper with a golden ribbon around it.

She stepped back and took the present. When she opened it, sapphire and pearl eardrops, set in gold, nestled on a bed of white cotton.

Lorinda gasped. "They're beautiful. I'm glad Mrs. Oleson talked me into getting my ears pierced so I could wear your mother's pearl eardrops." She reached up and kissed him on the cheek. "Thank you so much."

He grinned. "I've had them for a while, since I decided to start courting you. Remember when I gave you the piano music box?"

"Yes, but I didn't know you planned to court me."

"I know. That didn't work out very well, did it?" He pulled her back into his arms. "The stones reminded me of the color of your eyes."

She looked deep in thought for a minute. "I have a special gift for you, but it's not something I bought for you."

"Really? What is it?"

"I'm almost certain I'm carrying our child."

The words startled and thrilled him. "So soon? How can you tell?"

"Changes in my body. Subtle things. My skin dried out overnight. The only time it's happened before, I didn't know it but I was carrying Michael."

Franklin let out a whoop that could curdle cream. "Tomorrow, I'll go to Breckenridge and get some of that French body lotion for you."

He grabbed her and swung her around with her feet off the floor. "I didn't think I could be any happier than I already was, but this is even more wonderful. Since we have two sons, I hope this one is a girl...that looks just like you."

He poured all his passion into the kiss they shared, thanking her for the heart gifts she had given him.

Did you enjoy this book? We hope so!
Would you take a quick minute to leave a review where you purchased the book?
It doesn't have to be long. Just a sentence or two telling what you liked about the story!

Receive a FREE ebook and get updates when new Wild Heart books release: https://wildheartbooks.org/newsletter

Don't miss *A Heart's Forgiveness*, book 2 in the Love's Road Home series!

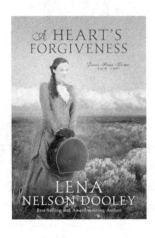

~

Chapter 1

EARLY SPRING, 1890
GOLDEN, NEW MEXICO

"*A*re you plumb crazy?" Jeremiah Dennison's loud retort bounced around the main room of the adobe house and returned to mock him. "Where did you get such a harebrained idea?"

Trying to control his anger, he shoved his clenched fists into his denim trousers' pockets, paced to the window, and stared out, paying scant attention to the piñon trees bending in the wind. He loved Philip Smith like a father, but the man could vex the weather. And this latest idea was the most farfetched yet.

Philip gave a snort. "Harebrained?" He put his rocking chair into motion that sent out a rhythmic squeaking. "Why'd ya say that? It's worked fer other men."

Jeremiah tried to calm down. He wanted to measure his words, season them with wisdom that would awaken his elderly friend to all the pitfalls he would face. "What would you do with a mail-order bride?"

The old miner stilled the chair and stared at Jeremiah, obsidian eyes piercing under his bushy white brows. "Somethin'"—he smothered a hacking cough with his fist, then swiped a clean handkerchief across his face—"has a deadly grip on me."

"I know you're sick. I take care of you, don't I?" Jeremiah resented the fact that what he'd done wasn't enough. Otherwise, Philip wouldn't even consider such a preposterous proposition.

His old friend reached up to scratch the scraggly beard he'd worn all the years he was a miner, but it no longer covered his clean-shaven chin. Old habits died hard. "Jerry, I don't wanna be a burden on ya."

"You'd rather be a burden to a woman you don't even know?" Jeremiah regretted his cynical tone the moment the words flew from his lips. He softened his tone. "I've never considered you a burden any more than you thought I was a burden when I came to the gold fields as a greenhorn."

Philip clutched the arms of the rocking chair and slowly rose. He took a moment to steady himself before he ambled toward Jeremiah. "I ain't come to this decision easy." He squinted up into Jeremiah's face. "I done studied on it fer a while."

Jeremiah straightened the fingers he'd gripped into fists and relaxed his stiff spine. "What do you mean, 'studied'?"

"Well, I figure a woman who'd answer them ads in the newspaper must be purty needy, maybe even desperate to get out of a particular bad situation." He gave a vigorous nod that riffled his snowy hair. "Made me a fortune when I sold my mine. More money than any man can spend in his lifetime. What good is a fortune to an old-timer like me? Won't never have a family of my own. Maybe I'll git me a woman with children. She can take care a me, and my money can take care a her." Another nod punctuated his last statement. "And her young'uns, if she has any."

How could Jeremiah deny his mentor's request? Philip never asked for much. If he didn't do this, the stubborn old man would look for help from someone else. A lesser friend might have a wagging tongue and spread the story all around Golden. Philip didn't need people gossiping about him sending for a bride. And other miners might try to nab her for themselves when she arrived. If Jeremiah had his way, it would be fine with him if they did, but his friend would be too disappointed. He didn't want to break Philip's heart, just talk him out of making this mistake.

"Jerry, ya ain't mad 'cause I'm plannin' to give my money to someone else, are ya?"

The words stabbed Jeremiah's heart. How could Philip believe that about him? "I don't need your money. I have more than enough of my own, thanks to selling my own mine and starting the ranch like you told me to."

The hoary head nodded. "That's what I figured."

"Where you going to send the ad?" Jeremiah couldn't believe he was considering being a part of this crazy scheme. But what else could he do?

Philip limped toward the sturdy pine dining table where a stack of newspapers was piled haphazardly beside blank paper, an inkwell, and a pen. "I read all these, and I think I'll send it to the *Boston Globe*." He picked up the top newspaper and shoved the rumpled pages toward Jeremiah.

Taking the newsprint, Jeremiah glanced at the headlines on the front page. An unusually hard winter had left many people out in the cold. "Why Boston?"

"Don't want jist anybody. Wanna help a *lady* in distress." Philip folded his scrawny arms across his bony chest. "Figure most a the women in Boston are ladies. My aunt Charlotte come from Boston, and she was a lady." He stopped and cleared his throat, then wheezed out a slow breath. "You do the writin', 'cause mine looks like hen scratchin'."

Judging from the stubborn tilt to the older man's chin, Jeremiah knew Philip's mind was made up. He dropped the newspaper back on the stack and pulled out the chair beside the stationery. "What do you want to say?"

He picked up the pen with the golden nib—another of the things the old miner had bought after he'd sold the mine. It had never been dipped into the inkwell until now.

Philip leaned both hands on the table, puffed out his chest, and wrinkled his forehead in concentration. "How about, *Wanted, a...* No. Makes it sound like she's an outlaw, or somethin'. Do it this way. *A Christian man in Golden, New Mexico, is seekin'* ..." He waited for Jeremiah to finish writing the phrase. "Sound all right so far?"

Wanting to laugh, Jeremiah kept his eyes trained on the words before him. Philip was so serious. "What are you seeking?"

The old miner scratched his head. "I want a lady. Done already told ya that."

"Maybe we could say, *a Christian lady.* That should cover it."

Jeremiah dipped the pen in the inkwell. When he held it poised over the paper, waiting for Philip to agree with his suggestion, a small drop fell and quickly spread into an unsightly blob. "I've messed up this sheet. Do you have a pencil? I could use it while we figure out the wording. Then I'll copy it in ink."

Philip made his way to the sideboard against the back wall of the large open room and pulled out a drawer. He shuffled through the contents before holding up the stub of a pencil. "Here's the onliest one I got."

"It'll do." Jeremiah reached for the pencil and continued, "*A*

Christian man in Golden, New Mexico, seeks a Christian lady... where do we go now?"

Once again, Philip was deep in thought. "...who needs a chance at a new life."

Jeremiah nodded and added the words. "I like it. Do you want to say anything else, or should I just put your name and address?"

"That's enough, but put General Delivery as my address." A smile crept across the older man's face, bringing a twinkle to his rheumy eyes.

He returned to his rocking chair while Jeremiah copied the words with ink, folded the message, inserted the paper in an envelope, and wrote the address for the *Boston Globe* on the front.

"I suppose you want me to take this to the post office." He knew Philip didn't get out much in the chilly spring air of the Ortiz Mountains, because it aggravated his breathing problem.

"If ya don't mind." Philip reached into the watch pocket of his trousers and pulled out a coin. "Here's the money."

"I don't need your money." Jeremiah headed toward the front door. "I just hope you aren't making a mistake."

Philip cleared his throat. "Jerry?" Huskiness colored his tone. "I'm thankful fer all ya do to help me." He paused until Jeremiah gave him a nod. "I've talked to the good Lord about this. I'm sure He agrees with what I'm doin'."

What could Jeremiah say to that? *Nothing.* He couldn't explain why, but when Philip Smith talked to his Lord, things happened. Jeremiah pushed his hair back before donning his Stetson and exiting through the front door, being careful it latched behind him. He didn't want Philip to have to get up and close it again if it should blow open after he was gone. Let him rest in his rocking chair. After all his long years of mining, he'd earned it.

Marching down the cobblestone street toward the post

office, Jeremiah hoped he wouldn't meet anyone who wanted to talk. The sooner he got this letter mailed, the sooner he could wash his hands of the whole situation. Maybe no one would answer the ad. Or maybe he could just tear the whole thing up and not tell Philip he didn't mail it.

If he wasn't honorable, he could get away with that. But he couldn't lie to the man who meant more to him than anyone in the world. Wouldn't be right. He'd make sure to look over any letters Philip received. He wouldn't let some floozy use his friend as her meal ticket and think coming here was her golden opportunity—in more ways than one. No sirree, he'd watch anyone who came with an eagle eye. She would have to pass his inspection before he'd introduce her to Philip. Even if his old friend did say he'd talked to God about it.

As Jeremiah walked into town, he fastened the top button on his long-sleeved shirt. The day would heat up later, but spring brought cool breezes in the early morning. When he passed the hotel, Caroline Oldman stepped through the door and started sweeping the boardwalk.

"Morning, Caroline." He tipped his hat to the proprietress, who was also the wife of the preacher. They'd been good friends to Jeremiah since they arrived in Golden. Their influence had calmed the rowdy town a lot.

He kept walking toward the post office. Would Philip hear from a woman before summer? Jeremiah hoped the old miner wouldn't receive a single answer to his ad.

Jeremiah thought back to when he came from Missouri to New Mexico searching for gold. Philip was the first miner he'd met. Thin and wiry, the old man's face was almost hidden behind his long beard and thin gray hair that reached to his shoulders, but he had a heart of gold. He'd befriended Jeremiah and helped him learn all about mining. He was even there when Jeremiah's partner was killed in a cave-in at the mine they owned together.

Philip had listened to all of Jeremiah's rantings and guided him toward becoming a cattleman. He knew Philip prayed for him all the time. But Jeremiah couldn't accept all that God nonsense himself. Where had God been when train robbers killed his mother and he was left in the clutches of his cruel uncle and father?

With a shudder, he shook his head to dislodge the images invading his thoughts. The less he thought about the past, the better. Too much pain and suffering there.

He was sure Philip had prayed about sending this letter, but Jeremiah wasn't convinced there was a God. And if there was, why would He care whether some greedy woman came to fleece the old miner?

No, Jeremiah would guarantee that didn't happen.

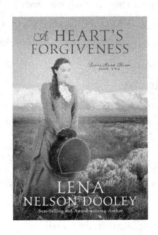

GET *A HEART'S FORGIVENESS* AT YOUR FAVORITE RETAILER.

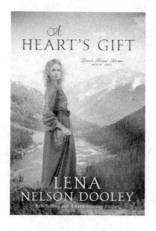

Book 1: A Heart's Gift

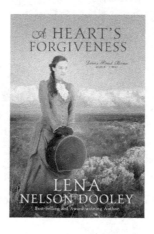

Book 2: A Heart's Forgiveness

Book 3: A Heart's Forever Home

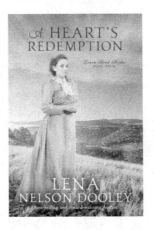

Book 4: A Heart's Redemption

ABOUT THE AUTHOR

Multi-published, award-winning author Lena Nelson Dooley has had more than 950,000 copies of her 50+ books sold. Her books have appeared on the CBA and ECPA bestseller lists, as well as Amazon bestseller lists. She is a member of American Christian Fiction Writers and the local chapter, ACFW - DFW. She's a member of Christian Authors' Network, and Gateway Church in Southlake, Texas.

Her 2010 release, *Love Finds You in Golden, New Mexico*, won the 2011 Will Rogers Medallion Award for excellence in publishing Western Fiction. Her next series, *McKenna's Daughters: Maggie's Journey* appeared on a reviewers' Top Ten Books of 2011 list. It also won the 2012 Selah award for Historical Novel. The second, *Mary's Blessing*, was a Selah Award finalist for Romance novel. *Catherine's Pursuit* released in 2013. It was the winner of the NTRWA Carolyn Reader's Choice contest, took second place in the CAN Golden Scroll Novel of the Year award, and won the Will Rogers Medallion bronze medallion. Her blog, A Christian Writer's World, received the Readers' Choice Blog of the Year Award from the Book Club Network. She also has won three Carol Award Silver pins. In 2015 and 2016, these novella collections—*A Texas Christmas, Love Is Patient,* and *Mountain Christmas Brides* have all appeared on the ECPA bestseller list, one of the top two bestseller lists for Christian books.

She has experience in screenwriting, acting, directing, and voice-overs. She is on the Board of Directors for Higher Ground Films and is one of the screenwriters for their upcoming film Abducted to Kill. She has been featured in articles in Christian Retailing, ACFW Journal, Charisma Magazine, and Christian Fiction Online Magazine. Her article in CFOM was the cover story.

In addition to her writing, Lena is a frequent speaker at women's groups, writers groups, and at both regional and national conferences. She has spoken in six states and internationally. The Lena Nelson Dooley Show is on the Along Came A Writer Blogtalk network.

Lena has an active web presence on Facebook, Twitter, Goodreads, Linkedin and with her internationally connected blog where she interviews other authors and promotes their books. Her blog has a reach of over 55,000.

- Website: https://lenanelsondooley.com
- Blog: http://lenanelsondooley.blogspot.com
- Blogtalk Radio:
  https://blogtalkradio.com/alongcameawriter/2

facebook.com/Lena-Nelson-Dooley-42960748768

instagram.com/lenanelsondooley

pinterest.com/lenandooley

goodreads.com/lenanelsondooley

twitter.com/lenandooley

amazon.com/author/lenadooley

linkedin.com/in/lenanelsondooley

ALSO BY LENA NELSON DOOLEY

The McKenna's Daughters Series:

Maggie's Journey: Near her eighteenth birthday, Margaret Lenora Caine finds a chest hidden in the attic containing proof that she's adopted. The spoiled daughter of wealthy merchants in Seattle, she feels betrayed by her real parents and by the ones who raised her. But mystery surrounds her new discovery, and when Maggie uncovers another family secret, she loses all sense of identity. Leaving her home in Seattle, Washington, Maggie strikes out to find her destiny. Will Charles Stanton, who's been in love with her for years, be able to help her discover who she really is?

Mary's Blessing: When her mother dies, Mary Lenora must grow up quickly to take care of her brothers and sisters. Can love help her to shoulder the burden? Mary Lenora Caine knows she is adopted. As she was growing up, her mother called her "God's blessing." But now that she's gone, Mary no longer feels like any kind of blessing. Her father, in his grief, has cut himself off from the family, leaving the running of the home entirely in Mary's hands. As she nears her eighteenth birthday, Mary can't see anything in her future but drudgery. Then her childhood friend Daniel begins to court her, promising her a life of riches and ease. But her fairy-tale dreams turn to dust when her family becomes too much for Daniel, and he abandons her in her time of deepest need. Will Daniel come to grips with God's plan for him? And if he does return, can Mary trust that this time he will really follow through?

Catherine's Pursuit: In book three of the McKenna's Daughters series, Catherine McKenna begins a journey to find her lost sisters that turns into a spiritual journey for the entire McKenna family.

Lena's work is also featured in the following recent collections: *8 Weddings and a Miracle Romance Collection, A Texas Christmas: Six*

Romances from the Historic Lone Star State Herald the Season of Love, Warm Mulled Kisses: A Collection of 10 Christian Christmas Novellas, and April Love: A Collection of 10 Christian April Fool's Novellas.

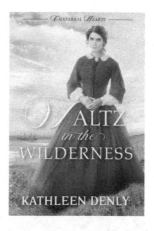

When disaster befalls them in the remote wilderness of the Southern California mountains, true feelings are revealed, and both must face heart-rending decisions. But how to decide when every choice before them leads to someone getting hurt?

~

Lone Star Ranger by Renae Brumbaugh Green

Elizabeth Covington will get her man.

And she has just a week to prove her brother isn't the murderer Texas Ranger Rett Smith accuses him of being. She'll show the good-looking lawman he's wrong, even if it means setting out on a risky race across Texas to catch the real killer.

Rett doesn't want to convict an innocent man. But he can't let the Boston beauty sway his senses to set a guilty man free. When Elizabeth follows him on a dangerous trek, the Ranger vows to keep her safe. But who will protect him from the woman whose conviction and courage leave him doubting everything—even his heart?

~

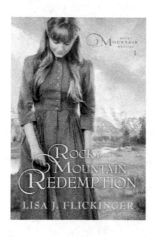

Rocky Mountain Redemption by Lisa J. Flickinger

A *Rocky Mountain* logging camp may be just the place to find herself.

To escape the devastation caused by the breaking of her wedding engagement, Isabelle Franklin joins her aunt in the Rocky Mountains to feed a camp of lumberjacks cutting on the slopes of Cougar Ridge. If only she could out run the lingering nightmares.

Charles Bailey, camp foreman and Stony Creek's itinerant pastor, develops a reputation to match his new nickname — Preach. However, an inner battle ensues when the details of his rough history threaten to overcome the beliefs of his young faith.

Amid the hazards of camp life, the unlikely friendship growing between the two surprises Isabelle. She's drawn to Preach's brute strength and gentle nature as he leads the ragtag crew toiling for Pollitt's Lumber. But when the ghosts from her past return to haunt her, the choices she will make change the course of her life forever— and that of the man she's come to love.